Flat Out

Anthologies & Shorts

System Apocalypse Short Story Anthology Volume 1

Valentines in an Apocalypse

A New Script

Daily Jobs, Coffee and an Awfully Big Adventure

Adventures in Clothing

Questing for Titles

Blue Screens of Death

My Grandmother's Tea Club

The Great Black Sea

A Game of Koopash (Newsletter exclusive)

Lana's story (Newsletter exclusive)

Debts and Dances (Newsletter exclusive)

Comic Series

The System Apocalypse Comics (7 Issues)

Stars Asunder
Book 9 of the System Apocalypse

By

Tao Wong

License Notes

Stars Asunder

Copyright © 2020 Tao Wong. All rights reserved.

Copyright © 2020 Sarah Anderson Cover Designer

A Starlit Publishing Book

Published by Starlit Publishing

PO Box 30035

High Park PO

Toronto, ON, Canada

M6P 3K0

www.starlitpublishing.com

Ebook ISBN: 9781989458747

Print ISBN: 9781989458754

Hardcover ISBN: 9781989458761

Books in the
System Apocalypse Universe

Main Storyline

Life in the North

Redeemer of the Dead

The Cost of Survival

Cities in Chains

Coast on Fire

World Unbound

Stars Awoken

Rebel Star

Stars Asunder

Broken Council

Forbidden Zone

System Finale

System Apocalypse – Relentless

A Fist Full of Credits

System Apocalypse – Australia

Town Under

Contents

What Has Gone Before

When the System arrived on Earth, it brought monsters, aliens, and glowing blue boxes that altered the reality of humanity. Gifted with Classes that must be Leveled and Skills that provide reality-altering powers, humanity struggled to survive when modern electronics failed under the flood of Mana. In a year, over ninety percent of humanity fell, leaving the remnants to pick up their lives.

John Lee is one such survivor, starting in the depths of the Yukon and traveling south to aid humanity in its struggle to stay free of their Galactic overlords. As a settlement owner in British Columbia, he joined forces with the remnant military forces of the United States on the West Coast and proceeded to wage a war to free the Canadian prairies and the US West Coast. Forced to take his Master Class Quest by the Erethran Honor Guard and the Erethran Champion, John returned from the Forbidden Zone planet he was teleported to with new powers, only to find a changed Earth in the four years he was gone.

Together, the newly Master-Classed John and his friends fought the Galactic interlopers, forging an alliance of human and aliens to form the first planetary government of a Dungeon World. Doing so cost, as it always did on the broken Earth.

To ensure the government continued to survive and take its place on the Galactic Council, John Lee and Mikito Sato along with the planetary representatives and other interested parties left Earth for Irvina, the System's capital planet. Their presence angered many, and forced John and his friends to lash out, fighting back against oppressors who targeted him and the planet directly.

Years passed, as John and his friends – Mikito and Harry – waged a guerilla war against those who would restrict Earth's expansion. Eventually, tired and worn, the group, with pirate captain Dornalor, stop at Spaks, an infamous pirate station. There, they are caught in an all out war between the pirates and the Galactic Council, whose objectives are deeper than they appear.

John meets the Corrupt Librarian Feh-ral, who gifts him the accumulated knowledge of the Corrupt System Questors. In the last clash of the war, John is forced to fight multiple Master Classers alone. In a last ditch attempt to stay alive, he opens a Portal and steps through, only to find his Portal leading him not to the station but to the Erethran Empire.

Now, John will have to complete his promise to the Empire, to fulfil his duties as a Paladin of Erethra. But in doing so, John Lee, the Redeemer of the Dead, might find himself angering forces even he should not contend with.

Chapter 1

Queen Karlelo is no demure, wilting flower of femininity. She's hot in the Xena, Warrior Princess way rather than the petite, demure Disney Princess manner. Even seated on her throne on the raised dais, the Queen dominates the room. She's at least seven feet tall, ripped and beautiful from generations of gene editing. Her presence is a palpable force, one that constantly sets off my Charisma and Aura Resistances. She rests on the throne on the Erethran capital planet of Pauhiri, her golden eyes boring into mine and glittering with amused curiosity.

Every inch of her is bedecked with enchanted Master, if not Heroic, Class items. There's a diadem around her forehead that screams defensive equipment. Her light blonde hair is cut short, and a metallic plate feeding information into her brain takes up one side of her hairline where diodes glitter and sparkle. The purple dress suit covers her body, with small etchings and glittering embroidery in a language I don't read offering offensive and defensive enchantments. The spear that rests on the throne is a Legacy Weapon, as is the bracelet around her right arm. I could go on, but suffice to say she's casually bedecked in more—and higher Tier—equipment than the entire planet of Earth.

"So. This is our latest Paladin," Queen Karlelo says.

I can't help but glance at her Status information again.

Empress Hasbata Karlelo of the Erethran Empire, (more) (??? Queen Level ???)

HP: N/A

MP: N/A

Conditions: N/A

"Yes, Your Majesty," I say. At least, that's what I think is the right term. I really don't know. It's not as if I've spent a lot of time interacting with royalty. If I'd considered it, I might have bought a System information pack, but who expects to get dragged to see royalty?

"Smaller. And weaker than I'd expected."

"True, Your Majesty. But he learns fast. Levels faster. And, occasionally, surprises us," Ayuri d'Malla speaks up.

I turn my head to eye the woman, my captor and Erethran Champion.

"*Rude. I'm right here,*" I grump mentally to Ali.

While I might be as rude as a bull in a china shop at times, throwing out words and actions as carelessly as cheap necklaces from a Madris Gras float, I've still got some sense. And not backtalking the Queen in her center of power is one bit of it.

"*I wouldn't, boy-o.*" Ali, my two-foot-tall floating friend sends back to me. Like myself, Ali's changed his clothes and mirrors me in my sky-blue Erethran military uniform, with its high collars, epaulets, knee-high boots, and green trimming. The only thing he has different is the design on the epaulets. His is a minor variation on mine, indicating his role as a Spirit Companion to me—a Paladin of Erethra.

My "special" Master Class technically gives me a rank within the militaristic Erethran Empire. In fact, I report directly and only to the Queen herself. Paladins are part of a separate branch in their society, playing the role of wandering judge, jury, and executioner. We're the troublemakers and problem solvers. At one point, there were as many as three dozen Paladins in the entire empire.

Now, there's just one.

Me.

Technically, I'm not the only one still alive. My master? Sponsor? Mentor? The person who approved my ascension into the Master Class still lives. But she's not coming back. Not anytime soon. Not ever, if she has anything to say about it. Which leaves me as the idiot holding the giant bag of shit that is the Erethran Empire.

"Wouldn't what? I'm being good. Not telling them how pretentious and dumb-looking this entire room is. How much I'm getting flashbacks of Germany," I reply to Ali.

The Spirit companion link is purely mental, run through the System. Over the years since the advent of the System and the destruction of Earth, I've gotten used to replying to him without showing it.

The throne room is less an ostentatious display of power and more of a functional bunker. It's a structure with guards, shield projectors, and full-on artillery emplaced within. No gilt, no gold, no imposing pictures of past rulers. Hells, other than a few holographic projections of banners taken from the corpses of beaten armies and kingdoms—and in one case, a dragon's head—it's the least impressive throne room I've seen. Says a lot about the culture when they showcase their battle glories rather than gold and riches.

"I would listen to your Spirit, Paladin." The Queen leans forward as she speaks, fixing me with a flat, disapproving gaze.

I feel the pressure she exerts, her Aura suddenly focused. For a second, my legs buckle, wanting to give way, wanting me to kneel and grovel for forgiveness. I can barely breathe, the pressure is so great.

Aura of the Empire partially resisted (90%)

I have to admit, I'm kind of impressed with myself. I wrap myself in the stubbornness, the muleheadedness that makes up who I am, and I refuse to kneel. It takes everything, even biting my own tongue till blood, coppery and salty, fills my mouth to focus and lock my knees. But I manage. The weight of an empire sits upon my shoulders, pressing on me in both a mental and physical sense.

And I resist.

Too bad I don't have enough strength to offer a quip.

The tension in the room continues unabated for long minutes as I fight against her disapproval and the Queen turns aside to chat with one of her advisors. Her casual dismissal sets my anger alight, and I push back harder, no longer needing the goad of pain to stand.

Eventually, she relents, and I feel the pressure disappear. I stagger as the sudden disappearance throws off my sense of balance. As I catch myself, the snarl that threatened to erupt comes out. By the time I manage to control myself again, return my demeanor to something resembling polite, the Queen has leaned back on her throne.

Her fingers trace the upraised buttons on her steel gray throne as she speaks to Ayuri. "Barely adequate. He will need more Levels."

"We know that. We did plan for him to conduct the training in the meantime."

"What training?" I snap as they talk over my head. I was willing to be patient, but after that little display, I'm just about done being nice.

Fine. Maybe I don't have a lot of sense.

"Of the other Paladins, of course." The Queen sniffs then looks at Ayuri. "Are you sure he has specced into Intelligence?" She doesn't wait for Ayuri to answer before continuing, already turning to another of her attendants. "Have it done."

The moment she finishes speaking, Ayuri's snaps off a left-handed salute, grabs me by the shoulder, and drags me out of the throne room. She doesn't even wait for me to offer my own salutations. I could resist her—I might even be strong enough these days to physically stop her from moving me. But I don't really want to stick around. So I follow.

"What other Paladins?" I hiss at Ayuri, only for the Champion to shush me as she hurries us out of the throne room. She's probably scared that I'll say or do something stupid. Again.

For my first introduction to royalty, I wasn't stabbed, shot, or condemned to death.

I figure it was pretty good.

***

Once we're striding down the hallway, open windows showcasing the distant and massive alien capital, the Queen and her aura a memory, Ayuri finally deigns to speak. "I told you to be polite. All you had to do was present yourself, wait for her to give you an order, and get out. How hard is that!"

"Well, she was the one who decided to listen in on my conversation."

"Of course she was listening. We all were. That was the throne room. Did you think we wouldn't have security measures to listen to potential threats? At the very least, it'd be a safety breach if we didn't." Ayuri threw her hands toward the ceiling. "Now, you just made it a lot harder than it had to be."

"Really? And how did I mess up these plans you haven't told me about?"

"I can't say."

"And more, neither of you have actually told me why you want me here. You kept on saying she'd tell me. But now, it sounds like even if I had kept my mouth shut, it wouldn't be enough." I cross my arms and plant my feet, waiting for her to come to a full stop. I still remember the Queen's quip about my Levels.

"She would have been fine if you hadn't insulted her. You only need three more Levels. We could have grinded the Levels together and called it done."

"For what?" I let exasperation leak into my voice, into the way I stand. I let her see my true feelings, while hiding the lie of my true Level. In truth, I'm only a single Level from reaching the next tier of my Class Skills, but I've taken to using the Ring of Deception to show my Level as a little lower than it really is. Keeping some information hidden is good for me, especially since I have a feeling they want me for more than my Skills.

Ayuri stops, looking me up and down, then looks around us. Next moment, I feel the Mana around us freeze as a silenced area pops up within ten feet of us. Nothing, no sound, no Mana, can be sensed outside of that bubble. The sudden change catches me out, making me wonder what Skill it is.

And, as has become more common lately, a piece of information unfolds within my mind. Knowledge, that I didn't gain naturally, making itself known.

Skill: Sphere of Gramus (Level 1)

The Sphere of the Gramus is a Skill that seals an individual away from reality. First pioneered by Gramus himself, the Sphere allowed him to contemplate the multiple variations of tastes that accompanied the consumption of his own body. Unfortunately, his continued eating of his own form, without sharing with the rest of his tribe, made him a heretic. Only the creation of this Skill allowed him to continue his private journey.

Effect: The Sphere of Gramus seals the user and an area off space (currently a radius of five (5) feet from user) from all external manipulation. No divination, Skills, and spells will enter or exit the sphere during periods of activation.

Mana cost: 500/minute

Ever since that godsforsaken Librarian stuck the entire Corrupted Questor library in my head, I've been getting little flashes of information. At first, it was pretty contained. Only when I decided to tap into the encrypted data would the squished-together information unspool. But whether it's because I've been poking at the information, or because the Librarian's Skill is degrading, I keep getting these little blips of information.

I now know more about Skills than I ever wanted or needed to. I guess that makes sense—knowing what Skills are being created by the System helps us understand it. It was just never an area I studied in great detail. Doesn't mean that someone didn't at some point in their search to answer the System Quest.

I blink away the information and focus on the Champion. I also do my very best not to think about that description. Or the other, rather disturbing, graphic imagery of Gramus, his people, and their entire race's eating habits that the library provided. The universe is a very big place.

And it just keeps getting weirder.

"The Queen needs to designate an heir. She cannot put it off any longer. And before you ask, her choice as Queen was a compromise that ensured the survival of the Empire at that time. Along with the compromise was her promise to not give birth," Ayuri finally spoke after she finished deploying her Skill. "There are three methods for us to choose a new Queen. Civil war. The Empire Trials. And the choice of the Paladins."

"Great. So just get the contenders to take part in these trials," I try to say lightly. Because the other options just do not sound fun.

But Ayuri isn't willing to kid around. She stares at me, waiting for me to acknowledge the truth. I don't want to. I don't think it's fair. But when she threw me through the Portal on Earth, she made me promise to come when they needed. At least once. So this is the once. This is what she needed me for.

"Seriously. Why not do the trials?" I ask.

"It is not that simple. The potential candidates are all powerful, pillars of our society. We don't choose our royalty, our leaders, from just anyone. We're a warrior society. A military-based one. If you aren't able to garner the respect of the military, you'll eventually fail."

I might be slow, but I get it. "What you're saying is, it's people like you who'd be contending. High Master class, Heroics, maybe even a Legendary?"

"No Legendaries." Ayuri shakes her head. "But it's not just that. The trials were created ages ago, when we were land-bound to our planet. They value physical strength, the ability of an individual to take on an entire army by themselves. But these days, we need more than that in our Empress. We need range, skills that can reach across stars, even abilities to command multiple armies and ships at the same time. The ones who contest for the throne know that. They've built their Skills, their abilities to lead armies."

"So the PR is a lie. You don't need the person who can kick ass best, you need the person who can help all of you kick ass best," Ali says, chiming in with a grumpy look. "And let me guess. These trials. There is only one survivor."

"Yes."

I exhale and shake my head. Obviously there's only one winner. Why would you want to keep competitors alive? Better to kill them all, salt the earth with their bones, and eat their flesh. Or something idiotic like that.

At least that explains why they won't use the trials. It'd almost be better to have a full-on civil war. At least then there would be multiple survivors from alliances and those who just give up halfway. Looking at it from that viewpoint, it'd be better to have your top men—your generals, admirals, marines, and whatever other forms of champions—not all die trying to contest for the position of Empress. Which…

Kind of leaves me screwed.

"You do know I don't really know your society all that well? You're asking me to choose your next Empress when I don't even know what would work best."

"Empress Apparent," Ayuri replies. "The main contenders will all bring their own advantages to our Empire. That is, after all, why they are the contenders. The choice itself will trigger the System to provide us those benefits, which we need."

"Need?" I frown. "Sounds like you're rather desperate."

"No, but the wars could be going better. This is the best choice from a series of really bad options." Ayuri shakes her head, eyeing the dark walls of the sphere. "Don't worry about it. By the time you're done, you'll understand us well enough to make a good choice."

"What makes you think I won't just sell it to the highest bidder?" I say peevishly.

I don't deal well with getting pressured to do things I don't like. And playing Praetorian Guard for an entire empire is kind of messed up. It's a hell of a lot of pressure. I ran away from Earth because I didn't want that kind of responsibility.

"Because you're a Paladin," Ayuri says.

If what I threatened to do bothers her at all, she's not showing it one bit. I'm torn between feeling chuffed that she thinks I'm that honorable and annoyed that I didn't manage to get a rise out of her.

"But you will be targeted. Especially by those who don't think they will win your approval. Not right away, perhaps. But you will eventually."

"Great." I don't bother trying to hide the sarcasm in my reply.

"How long does boy-o have? To learn an entire empire?"

"Some time. The choice cannot be made until the Queen makes the announcement and request. She won't do that until you Level," Ayuri replies.

As I said, I'm not exactly stupid. Between all the Intelligence points I've gained and some innate smarts, I put together the pieces pretty fast. "It's the Shackles. The last tier in my Skill tree. You guys need it to keep the contenders in line."

Ayuri nods but refuses to explain further.

I'm not exactly happy, but at least it gives me an idea of what's coming down the road. On the other hand... "I'm not going to use my Skill points on that."

Her eyes narrow. When I don't balk at her disapproval, she sighs. "We have the budget for the purchase. We'll need you to have multiple levels in that Skill anyway."

I grunt, making note of that. Might be worth finding out what the difference between the levels would be. In the meantime, I cudgel my brain for other things I need from them. "So about the training..."

Before I can continue speaking, Ayuri lifts her hand sideways and the world returns to normal. Her Skill disperses and noises return.

"You'll be training a half dozen of my best Honor Guards. They're all ready to ascend to the next tier, ready to become Paladins. You only have to train and test them, just as your mentor did you," Ayuri says. "This job is important, Redeemer. We do not want another incident like you."

I frown but kind of accept it. Can't be nice, having to ask a random human, one who isn't even part of your Empire, to judge the fate of your entire society. So they need to make sure that everyone I train can survive and keep growing to train the next generation after me.

On that note…

"You never did tell me. Whatever happened to the rest of the Paladins?"

"They fell."

Chapter 2

We walk through the corridors of the palace in silence. Like the throne room, the Erethran Royal Palace—the eleventh of thirteen scattered throughout the Empire—was built and furnished more like a military base than a sumptuous location to relax. Bare corridors, multiple blast doors, the occasional sharp turn, and nano-woven organic walls that will grow crenellations for people to hide and shoot from. We stride down the corridors, keeping pace with one another, and spot the occasional guard, scurrying servant, and cleaning drone moving about, interspersed with the slew of administrators required to keep an empire running. I wonder how that works. With 3D holograms that look and feel just as real as being there, is there a reason for people to be next to one another?

Idle musings as we walk and float to our destination, Ali darting through the occasional wall to poke his nose around before exiting. He occasionally bounces off the walls, coming out swearing as Skills and enchanted material stop his passage. I'm playing the waiting game, curious to see how long Ayuri will hold out on explaining her last statement. Curious to see what is about to happen. She's withholding information, refusing to add more details, and I'm not sure why.

So I'm not asking. Not because I'm being stubborn for shits and giggles, but because I want to see what she decides to tell me. And when. Sometimes, what people will tell you and when can tell you just as much as their words. The rest…

Well, there's a reason Ali's being rude, darting around like a crazed pixie on meth. And it's not just because he's Ali.

"You've learned patience," Ayuri finally says after we've walked for a half hour.

Yes. A half hour. That's how big the damn palace is and how much ground we've covered, especially when you consider how fast we can move with our higher base stats. We're out of the main building, walking through open courtyards and passing numerous buildings, strolling along as we watch members of the Honor Guard train.

I grunt in reply.

"Or subtlety," Ayuri says, eyes crinkling in humor. "Or you're just stubborn. As usual. In all cases, you should ask. If you want to know."

"Know why all the other Paladins are dead? Nah. I'm okay with certain doom hanging over my head," I drawl.

Ayuri gives an exasperated huff. "You would do well not to anger one of your only allies in the Empire, Redeemer."

I offer a smile, but she doesn't rise to the bait. Yeah, okay, maybe I am being a bit of an ass.

"Paladins have a very short lifespan in general," she says. "When they aren't working for the army directly, they are off 'questing,' completing Empire-generated Quests or their own idiosyncratic honor-bound requirements. Some worked alone, others in small teams. Their actions angered many of the powerful. Their questions and their Quests harmed numerous interests.

"One hundred and three years ago, our former King's family was targeted by a pair of Paladins during a routine System-generated Empire Quest. In their usual mode of operation, the Paladins purged two-thirds of the King's family, including his daughter." Ayuri hesitates then reluctantly adds, "The Quest authorized them to do so, but they went too far. In his rage and grief, the King enacted a purge of all remaining Paladins, commanding the armed forces to go to war. Not that there were many Paladins left at that time.

It's kind of like lawyers, doctors, and dentists on old Earth being some of the most easily exploitable groups for fraud. They're so confident in their own expertise that their arrogance gets them in trouble. And when they are taken, they often don't learn from it or tell others—too ashamed by their failure—so they just end up screwed again. Or let others of their kind get screwed.

"If that's the case, why the heck would the Queen want me to train up a new batch of potential problems for her?" I say.

Everything I hear makes Paladins sound more like troublemakers than a balancing force. Though I guess if you push a swing hard enough, it'll eventually come a stop. Even if it means you've wrapped the chain around the post to do it.

"Because the Paladins are necessary," Ayuri says heatedly. "Without them, we're tottering on the edge of a civil war. They keep the peace. They go where our armies cannot and deal with threats that escape the borders of our Empire. They are investigators and judges, searching down corruption within our own ranks."

Ayuri draws a breath and then lets it out slowly, forcing calm on herself. "And they're part of our System-enforced Empire contract. If not for your mentor, the System would already have generated multiple new members before your arrival." A slight pause before she continues. "We'd much prefer to have control of our membership."

"Ah. Right." I get it. They're sending me people to train and turn into Paladins who are already loyal to the Queen. They won't make a mistake of ending up in a civil war again. Which kind of makes sense, though I wonder how long that'd last. If they're looking for me to find the Queen's heir, then there are some deeper waters here. After all, there's no guarantee that the new Paladins will be just as loyal to the new ruler. "So. I assume there are also going to be a large number of people who aren't happy with me doing this?"

"Of course."

"Great." I say sarcastically. Not only do I have to worry about the real reason why she wants me here, even the cover is going to get me shot at.

Before I can say anything more, Ayuri leads me through another corridor into a courtyard. One filled with a half dozen aliens milling around, chatting or training.

The Champion waves her hand around. "We're here."

***

Here is a wide open courtyard edged with the cylindrical cones and the diagonal-sloped faces of shield projectors, all enclosed by the wings of a three-story building with large, reflective windows. Blast shutters hang over the windows, ready to deploy in the event of a problem. I wonder who, what, is looking out at us from the rooms, but I dismiss the silver buildings with their blue edging and numerous, semi-hidden field artillery. I've got more important things to focus upon, such as the threats before me.

A half dozen and one individuals stand before me in the Erethran Honor Guard uniform, looking like a special effects wet dream. They're dressed in the usual armored-pants-and-tunic ensemble, sporting the exclusive Erethran royal family's colors—purple and silver. Different from my own sky-blue uniform.

Of the seven, two of them are Erethrans, just like Ayuri, standing seven feet tall with their coral-like ears and slitted eyes whose giant yellow pupils seem particularly startling next to the almost non-existent nose and beak-like overhang of their face.

Another guard is a rock creature, all granite and brown rock, hands on his hips and laughing with a roach-like flying figure that hovers next to him, wings beating a low drone. There's a Movanna, all pale and thin and pretty, hands on the bladeless hilts of basket swords strung on his belt, sneering at everyone as he looks around. And lastly, rounding out the non-Erethran group is a short, snappy, and furred Pooskeen chatting with a just-as-short Grimsar-dwarf.

Even if the entire group looks pretty relaxed, they face us the moment we arrive, conversations dying like a roach on a fireball.

"Attention!" one of the Erethrans shouts, and the group falls in with precision.

They stand there staring at me, chins and chests jutted out, feet together, wings folded, arms by their sides. It isn't the kind of stare you give to people you like, but a challenging gaze, a weighing observation. They're here to see who I am, what I am. I glower back as the planet's giant sun beats down on us and wispy white-pink clouds drift past.

"Your initiates, Paladin," Ayuri says. There's a tone of quiet amusement in her voice, almost gloating as she looks over the group.

My lips twist, while Ali finally pops up the series of blue notification boxes about their Statuses. I ignore the group while I read.

Once I get past the third, I realize most of them are the same. Max Level or close to it. It's bloody annoying that there are so many of them, but then again, they've got an entire damn Empire with hundreds of billions of individuals to draw from. Finding seven people who are dumb enough to want to be a Paladin should be simple.

I let my gaze run over the group one last time, gauging their stiff backs, the jut of their chins. As I'm about to speak, the memory of a voice comes back.

It's languid. Lazy. Each word is drawled out, as if there's great effort in speaking. The voice hints at the pain, the weariness and burden of its speaker with every word. Or maybe that's just how I remember it after all the time I was on that planet, after all I remembered and learned. *"Everyone thinks they know what a Paladin does. But few are willing to pay the real price. Are you, child?"*

"Paladin?" Ayuri's voice rises, as if she's called my Title a couple of times. I blink, my senses returning fully.

"You might want to drop the creepy smile, boy-o," Ali sends to me urgently.

I realize I'm smiling, a toothy pull of the lips and cheeks as I stare at the group. It probably veers into crazy or savage, and I'm not particularly sure which one. One of the Erethran soldiers has dropped out of standing at attention, the woman going into a bladed stance with her backhand down by her side and front hand raised slightly. The others are all tense, but no one else has broken ranks, even if Roach flares its wings a little. When I wipe my smile, she relaxes slowly.

"All right, you bunch of loli-loving wannabes, let's get something clear here. Being a Paladin isn't a picnic, nor is it just another promotion. If that's what you're looking for, I suggest you become an Erethran Commander or General or whatever else Master Class you've got available." Rather than insult them or make them annoyed, I'm surprised to see the soldiers relax. Maybe all soldiers, alien or human, are masochists? "To become a Paladin, you have to do two things."

I let the silence stretch out, just 'cause I can. When Ayuri glares at me, I continue, letting my voice project. "You need to prove to me you have what it takes to become a Paladin. And then, you're going to have to fulfill the Class-change Quest."

Ayuri twitches at the blatant repetition of what has got to be obvious information.

For a moment, I consider warning them that they could lose their lives, that the Quest I have to give can't be made easier—or at least, not by much—because the System has its tenterhooks in it. Like all Class quests, like all System quests, there's only so much I'd be allowed to change.

***

Another memory, another slew of data. Of tests, of attempts to change the System. Class-change Quests, System Quests generated from a Settlement sphere, Guild Quests, Dungeon Quests, on and on. Every type, every kind. Questors, with their Skills, attempting to manipulate them from outside, pitting themselves and their will against the System. And failing, with the backlash tearing apart Skills, pulling away health and experience. And sometimes, lives.

Questors on the inside manipulating the Quest itself, using the same Skills, adjusting the ratios, the payouts, the risk and details of Quests as they offer them to others. Fighting the System to offer more than the System wants. More than it is programmed to do. And some, a few, succeeding. Data, recorded, noted, parsed down, and then, another experiment. And another. Till, they fall.

But the information, always kept. Always recorded. For another Questor, another researcher willing to pit themselves against the System.

All to get another percent in their System Quest.

I shudder, seeing my own completion rate tick up. I get the flood of experience as memory goes away, leaving me reeling internally. But I can't let them see it, so I don't.

And I focus. Into the silence, as the group stares at me, waiting to hear what else I have to say. These people standing before me, they're not likely to turn away because there's a small chance of death. At least, not if I know anything about the Erethrans and the Honor Guard.

"You're dismissed, for now. I'm sure Ayuri has a bunch of documentation to send me about you. After which, I'll speak with each of you." I pause. "Personally."

"In the meantime, while I read, I want you to keep an eye on them. Talk to them, make friends if you think they'll find you spying. I want your in-person judgment." I send the last to Ali.

And then, turning on the balls of my feet, I walk back out the way I came. It takes Ayuri a few moments to catch up and follow, letting me stride off down the corridor for a bit and nearly out of the building itself before she speaks.

"You do know we're going the wrong way to get to the offices, right?"

I grunt. A man has to make a good exit.

***

Luckily for my image and self-esteem, a simple Portal by Ayuri gets me to the right location. The office I take over consists of boring-ass pale blue walls, a single kidney-shaped table, and a pair of all-too-comfortable office chairs facing one another. A central door opens into the room, directly opposite the big window. Lighting in here is slightly off, just like the rest of the hallways— just a little too bright, just a little too hot.

Weird alien lighting schemes is an ongoing issue in the Galaxy. It's one reason why most people dump some points into Perception and Intelligence, even if they aren't going to use them for combat. The System helps us adjust across a broad range. The enhanced Perception offers us the ability to see and interpret light—and other senses—in a wider range than human—or alien—normal. The higher Intelligence points allow us to retranslate that back into our norms, or close enough that it doesn't frag our brains.

And trust me, I've seen the results of lopsided Status attributes. It's not that you need a lot of points—and for those who can't afford the attribute increases, there are tech solutions—but at the Master Class Level, very few keep their exclusive and super-specialized builds, just to head off potential problems.

Once we're in, Ayuri walks over to one corner and pulls a small circular cone from her Inventory, triggering the mobile hard light furniture creator. A moment later, a hard light lounging chair appears, onto which she flops. I mostly ignore her, for in the corner of my vision, a more interesting piece of information has appeared.

The full military records of our volunteers.

Taking a seat on the opposite side of the desk, I start reading. There's a lot of information to get through. Everything from their full Status Sheets as of the last week to their battle records, their commendations, previous commander notes, build recommendations, and even a full psych profile. It's kind of disturbing how detailed the information is, even though I know it's routine for the Honor Guard. Maybe it's disturbing because it's routine. Either way, I learn more about these people, their families, and relationship situations than I know about my own companions. Which is rather sad, if you think about it.

Maybe I should ask a few more questions of my friends…

Chapter 3

A couple of hours later, I'm finally ready to see people in that little office of mine. In the meantime, I've adjusted the lighting to the human visible wavelength, transformed the Erethran-sized chair and desk to human norms—which make it just a little shorter than what they're used to—and put up a nice outdoor vista on the walls. It's a Pacific Northwest rainforest, a scene taken from the archives of the System. Peaceful and normal—and not at all filled with hungry monsters and mutated trees that produce carbon monoxide or eat you when you fall asleep beneath them.

My first visitor is Freif, one of the two native Erethrans. Can you even call them natives, when they abandoned their homeworld thousands of years ago to the System? Something for the alien anthropologists out there to answer. When he marches in and stands at attention, I'm idly reviewing his file again.

Freif's build and personal weapon choice is clear. He's the guy who sits on the rooftop somewhere, watching out for bad guys, or is sent far away, deep into enemy territory, to deal with enemy commanders. Outside of the basic Erethran Soldier and Honor Guard build, he's got a few Class Skills that emphasize aimed and single shot damage. Of them all, Freif has the least number of "Slayer" titles, because outside of routine operations, he isn't meant to be mixing it up directly.

Once again, I flick my gaze over his Status screen, lips pursed.

Freif T'raoor, Slayer of Kobolds, Trolls, Goblins, (more), Marksman Champion IV, Krismat Pathfinder, Chaumi Desert Survivor, ... (Erethran Honor Guard Level 50)
HP: 2780/ 2780
MP: 2510/2510

Conditions: Life Suppression, Scentless, Not the Droids, Ten Steps Closer, Mana Drip, Anchored Return

But that's his Status screen, his sheet. That's not him. And as I stare at the man standing at parade rest before me, hands clasped behind his back, I can't help but wonder if he has what it takes. His psych profile reminds me he's a loner on duty, but a people person—a crowd pleaser and joker—when he's with his peers. On top of that...

"You've been through three separate physical cleanses, all because you've not been able to keep clean." I don't recognize the names of the drugs, but I don't need to. Their effects are clear enough from the report. "Can't handle the pressure?"

"The incidents were twenty years ago. Paladin Sir," Freif answers me with a tight tone.

"We'll see." When my pronouncement gets a flat-faced return stare, I go on. "Why do you want to be a Paladin?"

"I was ordered to show up for this recruitment process. Paladin Sir."

"Drop the Paladin Sir nonsense." I point a finger at him "I didn't ask why you were here. I asked why you wanted to be a Paladin."

"Because they are linchpins of the Empire. Paladin Sir." Freif barks out the answer, his gaze fixed on my face but not meeting my eyes. It's a trick I've used before, to seem respectful but not.

I snort and wave him out. It's not much of an answer, but it's an answer I'll take.

For now.

***

"Ropo Dhagmath. Master Brewer. Poison Master. Slayer." I flick the Status Screen to stay right above the bearded Grimsar. Unlike our fantasy Dwarfs, he's got a small beard, neatly trimmed to ensure it doesn't get in the way of putting on a battle suit. The beard is streaked with white and gray, mirrored in his braided hair that covers his head in tight bundles. He's the oldest in the bunch, nearly hitting a hundred eighty, and it shows in the hair and lines on his face. "Not your usual secondary build and occupation for an Honor Guard member."

Ropo Dhagmath, Silver Axe Thrower of the Sixth Deep Warren, Master Brewer, Poison Master, Slayer of Trolls, Goblins, Hakarta, (more), ... (Erethran Honor Guard Level 49 / Poison Specialist Level 38)

HP: 4180/4180

MP: 2340/2340

Conditions: Loved by Poisons, Venoms & Toxins, Necrotic Damage Resistant, Serve them Twice, Tip the Tender, Potions to Mana Siphon, Alchemist's Inventory, Stand my Ground

"Poisons and toxins are a major source of fatalities among our forces, Paladin." Ropo's deep voice rumbles as he speaks. "Some of our enemies and dungeons are toxin-filled. Training to gain resistances to join the Guard is required. Not all of us were able to skip such training."

My eyes narrow slightly while Ayuri's close-eyed grin widens. Of course, Ropo can't see her grinning since she's behind him, but she's obviously amused. I do wonder if this kind of backtalk is normal for the Guard. Then again, I'm not in their direct chain of command. Or am I?

For that matter, are they even using the correct forms for talking to a superior officer? They are talking in Erethran, which is distinct from Galactic itself. But the details sometimes get lost when you buy language packs from the Store. Blindspots you never knew you had until they hit you in the face like a falling tree.

"So you were the medic before you joined the Guard. And during. And, of course, having someone able to treat poison as an Honor Guard is a good idea. Which is why you're specialising in bodyguard Skills, like Sanctum." I watch Ropo nod at my words. "Comfy, stable job. So why do you want to be a Paladin?"

"A Grimsar has dreams."

I raise an eyebrow and dismiss the dwarf. That's an interesting choice of words. He's old, but stable. A family man, though all his kids are grown. Grandkids abound, and even some great-grandkids. That's an obvious weakness, compared to the other candidates. A leverage point. I wonder if he's willing and able to sacrifice them, if it came to it.

More to the point, he's a dreamer. Aren't they supposed to die early?

***

Next up is the rock man, whose very movements send miniscule shocks through the floor. I'm surprised, because the floor itself is reinforced. And even if I'm extremely sensitive to motion these days, it's still one heck of a feat. Unlike the usual full-sleeve-and-pants uniform rig of the others, the rockman's uniform is made up of short-sleeves and cargo shorts.

"How come Rocky's playing rock and roll with his feet?" I shoot the thought to Ali, while I study the Status Screen hanging above Rocky's head.

Kino Kaan, Last Survivor (II), Medallion of the Kozma, Bearer of the Yellow Flame, Sapper, Slayer of Goblins, Yerrick, the Deep Lovers, Wendigo, Enfields, ... (Erethran Honor Guard Level 50)

HP: 4500/4500

MP: 2140/2140

Conditions: Increased density, Juggernaut, Resistance to All, Stand My Ground, Geopositioned, Triple Health Regeneration Nanites, Memorised Form

"The Risen are all denser than they appear. Makes them the perfect tanks because they've naturally got a physical defense resistance over a hundred plus percent," Ali sends back. *"Increased density and weight is just one of the side-effects. Of course, most get a Light Foot Skill or two to off-set that."*

I grunt, recalling the Skill in Rocky's notations. That means he's either choosing to make a point by stomping in here or he's so dense, his Skills are still not enough. I'm not entirely sure which option I like more.

"So, Rocky, you're the tank. The perfect bodyguard who stands in front of the Queen until everyone else gets her out. Or the guy who lets the battleship fire upon him while his platoon preps the anti-ship artillery."

I'm not great at reading rock, but the slight shiver that sends rock dust floating to the floor shows I've scored a hit. I've been hit by that kind of fire. Even if you survive, it still hurts. Rocky's granite face makes him look like a less expressive Uncle Ben from the Fantastic Four, which isn't useful. I'd rather have Jessica Alba myself.

"So what makes you want to be a Paladin?"

"Because I can survive it."

"We'll see about that." I gesture Rocky away, watching as he tromps off.

Solid. Quiet. Your typical tank. Except the Risen are few in number, almost all of them joining the army at some point. Their family system is weird, with children born when a Risen decides it's time to split. They shatter themselves, creating a mini them that then hibernates for a century or two before rising. Weird, but it means every child is precious and taken care of by the entire race. And the loss of a single one is to be mourned.

No easy handles at least.

***

"Are you just calling them in to ask that single question?" Ayuri says while we wait for my next victim. Sending them down to the courtyard and back without teleporting means we've got time to wait. Not as much as you'd think, since the higher Dexterity in all their abilities means they're basically hot-footing their way back and forth.

"Pretty much."

"Why?"

I grin at Ayuri's question.

"Seriously, Redeemer. Why?"

"You've trained them too well," I say, gesturing to the window and the courtyard behind me. "Other questions won't get a proper response. So. One question. Then I'll figure out a way to tease out the truth."

"Oh? And how would you do that?"

I shrug, not having found an answer yet. Though I have hints.

Before we can speak further, the door chimes and slides open, leaving me to regard the horror-inducing appearance of my next speaker.

My next victim-volunteer arrives, wings flaring a little as he steps through the door. I lean back, eying the roach-flyer—a Che'dah from a Dungeon Planet just like me—as he regards me with its compound eyes. I shudder a little, an atavistic instinct making me want to squish the bug. Preferably with a ten-foot hammer.

And I know exactly where to find one.

"Redeemer."

I cock my head at the greeting. It's a breach of protocol in a way. But not really.

The usage of Titles is a social construct of System-created society. Titles that matter more to specific cultures are always used first, in front of other Titles. So the usage of Titles varies depending on social standing.

As an example, the Hakarta are more likely to use my Monster Bane Title over a general Slayer Title—if I ever get one. In turn, they'd discount my rank of Paladin entirely, since that's a Class and only Erethran. Redeemer of the Dead is the Title most commonly used, because it's a unique Title, even if it has no other direct benefits like Monster Slayer.

Other cultures might see social rank Titles—like Lord and Lady or Duke—as more important. It's a little bit of a mess, but the big thing is that rather than using the "correct" Title—in this case, my rank as a Paladin for their armed forces—the roach has decided to use my Redeemer Title. It says something about the society the Roach lives in, though what, I'm not sure yet.

Smo'kana Sa'l'a'la, Monster Slayer, Slayer of Goblins, Isooma, Yerrick, Nuckelavee, (more), 12891st Spawn Survivor, Multi-Classed,... (Erethran Honor Guard Level 47)

HP: 2940/2940

MP: 2840/2840

Conditions: Multi-Classed (Shadow Stalker), Fire Resistant, Ablative Impact Resistance, Fountain of Mana, Shadow Consort

"So, Smo, you're a fellow Dungeon World survivor. Don't meet many of you guys," I say. "How come?"

"Swarm perish. Mother Brood Die. Sixth Cycle of Rebirth of the Third Line." Smo's got a clicking, buzzing tone to his voice, as if he's a bad transistor radio that has never been tuned properly.

I dart a look at the lounging Ayuri for clarification.

Silence stretches out until she finally cracks an eye open and replies, "Sargent Sa'l'a'la's race is birthed from eggs, produced by queen Che'dah. Their race is one that was uplifted by the System integration, but during the process of integration, the majority of uplifted queens were lost. There are now three remaining queens on the planet, leaving them vastly undermanned." Ayuri pauses then adds, "It doesn't help that each birth swarm goes through a period of intense cannibalism. It does mean survivors have a headstart on Levels though."

"Oh." I eye his title, realizing it wasn't just a throwaway note. Then again, most Titles aren't. They're gained due to either Galactic Council or System intervention for notable achievements. Which is kind of disturbing when you consider how many siblings he probably ate that the System felt it worthy of a Title.

Ugh.

I suddenly decide I need a bath. "So why do you want to be a Paladin?"

"First in Line. Power. Consume. Rebirth."

I glare at Smo while Ayuri explains. "One of the powers of the queen's class is the consumption of their brood to pass on Skills to the next generation. Greatly weakened, of course, but it can allow the development of unique Classes. The queen is quite interested to see what the consumption of a high-Level Paladin would engender."

"Yeah, okay. That's just messed up." I shake my head and point at the door. "Out. And send in the next."

I get a click and buzz, the Che'dal's wings flaring as he turns and flies off. Cannibalism. Fun for all Galactics.

Not.

***

She's cute. That's my first thought now that I'm able to look closer at the female Erethran. Slim, muscular in the athletic and active way, the Erethran Honor Guard stands at rest with a wariness in her eyes. As I flick my gaze over her, I note the rather extensive list of buffs she has on. Unlike many of the others, she's nerfed her passive regeneration like Bolo in return for ongoing Skill effects, including a wide range of buffs.

Anayton Nichortin, the Everlasting Light, Winner of the 185th Cross-World Bollman Race, Mana Fount, Flesh Golem, Slayer of Goblins, Leoucroucta, Nuckelavee, (more), ... (Level 50 Honor Guard)

HP: 3140/3140

MP: 3230/3230

Conditions: Time Compression, Double the Gain, Double the Pain, Greater Regeneration, Save Point, Greater Mana Regeneration, Battle Flow, Strength of the One, Agility of the One, Mind of the One, When the End Comes, (more)

"By the way, I've been meaning to ask. What do you guys have against Goblins?" Every single Honor Guard I've met thus far has had that Title.

"They are a common pest and one that we need to deal with across all our planets, sir. Basic Units are sent to deal with growing nests as training. They are an easy source of Level Ups while fulfilling our ongoing peacekeeping efforts," Anayton replies.

"Oh. Huh," I say. "You guys send entire units to wipe out a Goblin nest?"

When she nods, I can't help but feel somewhat sympathetic for the poor Goblins. My team managed to take out a Goblin nest by ourselves—and we were all pretty much Basic Classers back then. For them to send a whole unit seems a tad overkill.

"Goblins are a pest. No matter how many you kill, they always return. Like ants, in your world. Or your *Common Cold*."

My eyes narrow again, curiosity pinging. She's the first to show any indication that they've done research on me. Not to say the others didn't, but she's blatant about it. "Fair enough. So tell me. Why do you want to be a Paladin?"

"Is answering your question an order?"

"Not yet," I say.

When she clamps her mouth shut and continues to not answer me, I gesture her out.

The moment the door closes, Ayuri drawls, "I know you're no military man, but allowing your subordinates to defy you is bad for discipline."

"Good thing I'm not in the military. Or training a military unit." I flash her a grin, then ignore her inquisitive glance as I focus on the next Status screen. Let her mull over that.

As for Anayton, I remember how she flowed into a combat stance. Her reports all indicate a level of minor insubordination coupled with extremely high marks for performance. Her background as a commoner from a

Restricted World. She's mouthy, without any real ties to those outside of the Guard. And few close ones within.

A loner.

***

"Don't see many of your kind in the Empire," I say, my gaze roaming over the Pooskeen. Long snout, short ears, short hair with traces of stripes that make me think of a hyena more than a real dog. Especially with the reddish-brown-clay fur that covers the creature. "And you're the first non-Honor Guard."

"I'm grateful for the chance," the Pooskeen yips, its voice high and grating. I kind of want to rub at my ears, the way it speaks.

"Not chance. You earned the spot, from what I can see. Ancillary support Shaman for the fire teams. You've been forced to work with them, but not be part of their actual command and payment structure. Hard living, not being paid your full rate and still facing the same—if not more—dangers. Though I'm a little puzzled by your Skills." My gaze rakes over his Status Screen again, picking out his buffs.

Gheisnan of the Two Palms, Minor Seer, Cassandra, Rebel Marked, Slayer of Goblins, Uyyi, Qawe, (more), … (Four Eyed Shaman Level 50)

HP: 2640/2640

MP: 2380/2380

Conditions: Eyes of the Future, Twisted Destiny, Scion of the Fates, Personal Timeline, Fate Siphon, Greater Mana Regeneration

"*Cassandra?*" I send to Ali. He's a distance away, but I can still talk to him, though I'm trying not to bother his spying. But this is a new one.

"*Greek mythology. I figured it'd be more fun than 'Forecaster of doom that no one listened to.*'"

"Prophecy and foretelling," Gheisnan says. "My people have much Skill at that."

"Your people…" I flick my hand sideways.

A notification floats in front of him, stolen and replicated to Ayuri's side by a twitch of her finger. It's a recording, a piece of data I've kept stored in my implant. Sent years ago by the team to inform me of what was happening in another part of my then domain. A small town where bones and other unmentionables lay gnawed upon and discarded as humans whimpered in the corner, staked to the ground in their own refuse. Pooskeen bodies lie, weapons drawn, facing out—slain by the team sent to liberate the town while we fought through Alberta.

"Tell me why I shouldn't kick you out right now," I say.

"Those are not my people," Gheisnan yips, his fur bristling, that short stubby tail flicking so agitatedly that I can spot it behind his body. "Fallen clans. A twisted kingdom."

"Pretty sure they're from your main planet."

"Twisted and fallen." Gheisnan snarls, fists clenching. A green, sickly light radiates from his body as he speaks, his entire body leaning forward from his hips as if he could shove the truth, along with his words, down my throat. "My people are the true heirs of the Pooskeen heritage. We are nothing like the twisted creatures the Oynaci Dynasty have created. They have destroyed our culture, our heritage. All to keep themselves on top." Gheisnan almost froths at the mouth as he speaks, having taken an inadvertent pair of steps closer. "Paladin or not, I will not let you declare us the same as those things."

"Touchy, are we?" I can't help but admire the fire though. If there's one thing a Paladin needs, it's fire. Passion. Because when the chips are down, when things are at the worst, you can't just back off. Not now, not ever. "I'm curious what makes you think you can become a Paladin. Pretty sure it was only open to me because I was an Honor Guard."

Ayuri speaks first, well before Gheisnan can say anything. "It's uncommon. But there have been cases of non-Honor Guards being elevated to the Class. It requires a Prestige Class at the minimum, which the adjunct has. The Quest itself grows significantly harder. And, of course, it requires the agreement of a Paladin. That is rare enough to get."

"I see." I fall silent, eyeing the short dog-like creature. My own Quest had been a simple one—if you could consider killing over-Leveled monsters in a Forbidden World simple. Still, the first step was having me agree to give them the quest. Which leads me to… "Why do you want to be a Paladin?"

"For the honor of my people. My real people." And when he finishes speaking, Gheisnan glares, daring me to challenge his words.

I decline and send him off.

***

Lastly, we have the pretty little duelist Movanna. All elf ears, long hair, and beauty. The annoying part is, I can tell he's not even put points into his Charisma on purpose. He's just that pretty naturally. Makes me want to gag at the unfairness of genetics.

As he saunters in, all cat-like grace and the arrogance to match, I can't help but check out his Status information again. Of them all, the Movanna has the longest and most in-depth documentation. I'm curious why he got the Title for Century Guard when Ropo didn't. System-centric racism?

Magine a Clarson, Century Guard, Monster Slayer, Loadah Champion Duelist (VIIX and VIX) & (more), Slayer of Goblins, Kraska, Wexlix, Frakin, (more), Dueling Addict,...(Erethran Honor Guard Level 50)

HP: 2740/2740

MP: 2540/2540

Conditions: Blitzed, Face Me, Aura of the Duelist, Burst Attack, Greater Resistance, Ablative Shield

"I didn't expect to see a Movanna in Erethra," I say, showing that I've yet to learn to not stereotype the races. Or I have, but I kind of want to see what he has to say.

"There's a small community." Magine shrugs. "Live a few hundred years, and you start wanting to travel a little. My parents found their way to Erethra before they were killed by pirates. But you know that." His gaze flicks upward to where my notification screens hang.

"I do. I also noted that your stated goal was to become a Champion. So why give that up now?"

"Because the option is no longer viable."

"Paladin's your second choice," I say.

I can understand that. The Champion sub-Class is a unique Class, one that can only be held by a single person at a time. Not to say there aren't other types of Champions, but the Champion of Erethra Class Ayuri has is unique.

It's part of why her Skills are so insanely powerful. Or not. That's the double-edged sword of being a "Champion." Many of the Skills scale according to the strength of whatever you're linked to. A failing Empire could nerf the Class significantly. Of course, there are also other restrictions on the Class—like being forced to be subservient to another. Which, I'm guessing, is why he's given up on the other Champion options.

"A distant, if respectable second. But the Champion has shown her mettle," Magine says, turning his head slightly to take in the lounging form of Ayuri. "She will stand for the Empire. In turn, I must find another form of service, and returning honor to the Class is a worthy task."

I wonder if that last line is a barb against me. Or how much of a barb. "Well, that's clear enough."

I dismiss Magine, leaving me to stare at the closed doors. I've got my answers, an idea of who these people are. And soon, I'll get an idea of what they are like when I'm not around, when Ali is watching them. Even so…

"Are you satisfied?" Ayuri says, sitting up from her chair. "Or do I have to find others for you?"

"You guys really want more Paladins, don't you?"

"They are a pillar of the Empire, and their lack shows." She gestures to the door. "They are the best we have, of what we believe should work. Others, at lower Levels, might be suitable but…"

"But you don't think I have enough time to Level them."

Ayuri inclines her head in acknowledgement.

"I don't know what you expected to happen, but I'm not about to wave my hands and just give them my assent to acquire the Class."

"Why not?" Ayuri raises a carefully plucked, graceful eyebrow. "Would it not simplify the matter? If you're worried if they are suitably loyal, that was our first criteria."

"Loyal to your Queen, perhaps." I shake my head. "But being a Paladin is more than loyalty to your Queen. Or, hell, loyalty to your Empire." I put a hand over my heart. "Case in point."

Ayuri's eyes narrow. "Are you saying you're a threat to us?"

"No." I shake my head. "At least, not in the way you think." I kick back, putting my feet on the desk. I stare at the ceiling, memories of my time in the Forbidden Zone coming back to me. "Did you ever wonder why Suhargur never came back? Why she's putting the lives of an entire planet over that of the Empire?"

"I have a feeling you're about to tell me."

"We're here to protect the Empire—its citizens and what your Empire is supposed to be. Not what you think it is," I say, looking at her through parted feet. Ayuri's lips thin through the V of my crossed legs, and I wonder if she's going to hit me. I'm giving her the best shot she'll get.

But taunt or not, she doesn't rise to the bait. "So. You're not going to rubber stamp our choices."

"Not without running a couple of tests," I say.

"And what would those be?"

"Well, funny thing you should ask..." My grin widens behind my feet. "I'm going to need to make a call. Or two."

Chapter 4

Ali finds me in my quarters a while later, the personnel files of my recruits spread all around me. I have my feet up in the air—literally as force wards cushion me as I lounge—while scanning through the documents and accompanying videos. I'm still waiting for my call to be put through, but I'm not worried. It's only been a few days since I was yanked all the way here, and my last message to my friends cautioned them that I'd be busy. They're probably doing their own things and not in any hurry to speak to me.

On the other side of the window—plain, reinforced glass windows backed with a nearly invisible force shield—the sun is setting. I haven't been around long enough to figure out their seasons, but in this world, days are long and nights short. With a pair of moons hanging overhead and light filtered to make the sky purple at this time of day, it's a strange and unsettlingly beautiful sight.

"So?" I ask the Spirit.

"The Poos found me," Ali says, floating over. The brown-skinned, goateed Spirit floats along in his favorite orange jumpsuit, flicking his gaze over my datasets before turning to me fully. "But I listened in for a bit. They're a pretty buttoned-up group."

No surprise, if they're the elites. Ali keeps talking, filling me in on his impressions. For the most part, it confirms much of what I gathered. The group is generally well-mannered, grouping into small clusters along the lines of previous engagements and missions fought together. They talked about past missions, old friends, and quietly measured each other up.

No one showcased any real notable Skills, but most considered Freif— the marksman—the most dangerous of the lot. Well, either him or Magine, from the way they interacted. Ali couldn't tell for sure, but those two were the snarling male lions of the pack. It's a subtle thing though, no giant posturing by either.

"Fun. I got another question for you," I say when Ali finishes by relaying a horrible story that he overheard about an Erethran pangolin, a stick of dynamite, and a latrine.

"Of course you do. What is it?"

"Why is Ayuri letting me scupper their plans?"

"Scupper?"

"Mess with. Destroy. They want Paladins. All I really have to do is give them my blessings and… whoosh. Off they go."

"Ah." Ali scratches his nose. "You still need me to answer the question?"

"Obviously."

"Surprised. But it might be a little too political and obvious," Ali says. "Good to know I'm not completely useless."

"Blah, blah, blah. I hear a lot of talking, not a lot of answers." I wave for him to hurry it along, then I have to reposition my windows when they follow my hand motions. Most of the time, the System is fine, but occasionally, it messes with me. Or it could be Ali doing the messing.

"You got to remember. You're a separate organization in their hierarchy. Ayuri can't exactly order you to do what she wants. Even the Queen has to be careful. Secondly, if you read your data pack, you'd remember that the picking of Paladins is a time-honored internal tradition. Messing with that—"

"Could mess with the first point." I say, catching on. Right. If you let people—and in this case, that includes the Queen—interfere with how Paladins get picked, you'd end up with not an independent organization but an extra arm in their armed forces. "Still, it's not as if I knew that. So if they pushed me…"

"That brings me to point two. Advanced Master Classes—prestige Classes—all have restrictions on their creation and their development. Mess with the requirements or details of Classes too much and the System can just as easily take away the Class," Ali says.

"It can do—"

Before I can finish my sentence, information blooms. Data. So much data. It rips through my mind, makes me tense and twist in my chair so much that I fall. The kiss of the floor is so distant, it might as well be a kitten's first nuzzle. I'm distracted as videos, articles, and voice recordings decrypt themselves in my mind.

"I will not!" The voice is panicked, loud. So close to breaking, so close to insanity.

A chainsaw grates, cutting into another tentacle. The speaker writhes, purple and white limbs thrashing. The attacker doesn't stop until the limbs are lopped off entirely. And the alien thrashes, health falling and falling. Until a glow encompasses the thrashing alien, healing and sealing off wounds. And then, they regrow.

"Sign. We can do this all year."

Such a cold voice. Clinical. I can't see the speaker, I can only sense them, through the recording. Sense them, and see, feel, the limbs, all the limbs that twist and twitch beneath his feet that tell a tale. A shortened, grotesque tale of how long they've done this. How often.

"I'll sign…" the alien sobs.

Memory breaks. The video speeds up or maybe my memory of the video blips.

*The alien is thrashing, its one tentacled-hand raised toward the notification. The one where it rescinds heritage rights to its own family. Breaking its own Advanced Class, that of the **Podkeeper Scrooge**. Destroying the tenents of its own Class.*

And the System acts.

Tearing it from its Class, stripping it of its additional attributes, throwing it all the way back to a Basic Class. The process is painful, dangerous, and at the end, the alien is dead. Too much leftover damage, too low a Constitution—or perhaps too much pain.

The creature lies dead while in a corner, the researcher's hands are outstretched, flicking and twisting as he manipulates the System information windows he's reading. I know that because in the corner of my mind, the same data is unscrolling. Mana levels, data streams, and System code-gibberish—all of it displayed and unencrypted. All of it being prodded, pulled, and compared against other research, other test subjects.

I shudder as another memory pushes this one aside. Another experiment. Less gruesome, with less lethal results. But this was because the previous experiment had found the final member of the Class and broken it; while here, they just broke the herm.

Data. So much data, most of it gruesome. For these tests, you could record the occasional historical instances, but for good, reliable data, you needed to run your own experiments.

And I'd once thought the Questors were relatively benign.

"Boy-o?" Ali's worried voice finally pierces my clouded mind.

I find myself on my knees, spitting out blood from a bitten lip, wiping a bleeding nose, and groaning. In the corner of my eyes, I absently note the damage counter, the amount resisted from mental debuffs and injuries. Twice in one day, the library assaults me.

If I was anyone else, if I had a weaker Class…

I spit and stagger upward, casting a simple flame spell to burn off the blood and a Cleanse to clean up. When I spot Ali, he's looking all too grim.

"The usual?" he asks.

"Yup."

We don't dare say why. What happened to me, the stuffing of the entire damn Corrupted Questor's library in my mind. It's dangerous. Quite potentially lethal. Better to stay silent on it until we know exactly how much danger I'm in. How much I've changed. Because I have changed, beyond knowing more than I should, seeing more than I should.

It's possible that it doesn't matter. It's possible that Feh'ral got away and replicated the library somewhere else. That I'm just a backup and they don't care about the data anyway. They went after him on Spaks because he neared Quest completion, because he reached the ninety percent mark. Not because of the library. Or so I hope.

System Quest Update!
+238,912 XP, +18,281 XP, +8 XP,...

System Quest Completion Rate: 84.7%

Or so I think.

But those experience gains have been increasing. My percentage is creeping up, no matter what I do. Not that I don't want it to go up—but a little more control would be nice. A little more clarity. I'm learning things about the System, but I don't have context. I don't understand.

What is the System?

And why is it important that the System can take away Classes? That it's limited by Mana density? And yet it breaks down in Forbidden Zones, where

Mana is more than abundant. Even when, in totality, there's more System Mana there than anywhere else. Why is the System-script both completely legible Galactic and completely illegible runic script? Runic script that no computer, no databank, no AI or Class has ever gotten even close to deciphering? The script defies understanding because it changes, morphs in meaning and context with every look, every attempt at reading. Why does the code change, even for the very same Skill and the same person?

Too many questions, too little answers.

But my Quest completion rates keep going up.

I shudder and push aside the thought and focus on what I can handle. What is right in front of me. Because anything else—well, that'll just scare me.

"So. Politics."

"Politics, boy-o. It's always politics with Galactics," Ali says as if he's seen it all. And I guess he has, in some ways. The Spirit is enigmatic, his history clouded, but I know he's thousands, if not tens of thousands, years old. I'm just the latest in a long, long line of companions for him. The Spirit floats off to the window, staring outside. "And knowing you, you're going to mess with their plans. So. What do you intend to do?"

"Nothing on purpose," I say, flopping back into my chair. "I'm not planning on making enemies."

"You never plan on it."

"But it happens," I finish for the Spirit. "I need to make sure they can survive. No point in giving them their Quest, then watching them die completing it. Or a month later, when they don't realize what it means to be a Paladin."

"And you do?" Ali says, turning around to look at me. "You're not exactly Erethran. Or, you know, part of their society. Nor have you done any of the Paladin's traditional job."

I grunt. "You have a point. But I know more than they do." At Ali's raised eyebrow, I shake my head. "They've not had one for too long. Or maybe they don't want them to survive."

"And what does it mean to be a Paladin?"

"Being the ass that everyone targets."

***

When the call finally comes through, I've been reading for hours. At this point, I'm mostly reading because the minor details I might be picking up subconsciously could be helpful in their training. A quick scan was more than enough to get me ninety percent of everything there was to know about each initiate, but at the levels we operate at, that last ten percent is where eighty percent of deaths occur. When fights happen in milliseconds, the tiniest edge can mean all the difference.

"Mikito. Good to see you. Are you guys okay? Anything I should know? When will you be here?" I greet the short-haired, severe-faced Japanese woman with a barrage of questions. It's been a while since I've spoken to them, days even.

Not that they're in that much danger, I think. Mikita is with Bolo, who I notice in the back of the transmission. The ram-horned giant of an alien is a Master Class at the same Level as me. And stronger. After all, he didn't skip the entire Basic Class. He's got a wider variety of Skills, a lot more experience, and Dragon Lords are geared toward one-on-one fights. They are, basically, a pure Combat Class.

A Paladin of Erethra isn't.

My only real concern is that, as of their last message, Dornalor doesn't have his ship yet. After all that fighting, the docks are extremely busy. It'll be a while before they replace the *Heartbreak*, even with the funds the station has released. He's still debating if he intends to wait for them to build him a new ship at a significant discount or just take the Credits and buy one somewhere else. There are advantages to both options.

About the only person who isn't happy about the end of the war is Harry. He's been running around finishing up the last of his missives, playing war journalist and sending out reports. Even so, his viewership and experience gain has taken quite a hit.

On the other hand, Harry's reputation has really climbed the news charts. From what I understand, he's doubled his fan base, and they're paying into his account just to watch his regular streams. Thankfully, our prior agreement means he doesn't do live streaming around us—at least not without warning us beforehand.

"Not much longer," Bolo answers quickly for Mikito, not letting the Samurai answer. I raise an eyebrow because that's not suspicious at all. "We have it handled. We're just waiting for the final payment to come through and then we'll be there."

"I thought everyone had to deposit the payments before the auction?"

"Normally, that's the way." Bolo shrugs, his enchanted emerald scalemail rippling and glinting as he does so. "But I struck us a side deal as well." When I raise my eyebrow, he grins confidently. "It's fine, it's fine. It'll all be done in the next six hours. Until then, the Gremlins will hold onto the Leviathan corpse."

"Mikito?"

After glancing at Bolo, Mikito says, "We can handle it. The deal is good."

"All right then. I might need you guys here sooner rather than later. You mind taking a Portal?"

"Of course not." Harry speaks up as he wanders into the shot. The British man of African origin flashes me a grin, those pearly white teeth of his still perfectly in place. "We going to Erethra?"

"She is." I watch the flick of hurt and uncertainty cross Harry's face before I relent. "Whether you're coming is up to you. Don't you have a lot more reporting to do?"

"Eh. I'm a war reporter. Reconstruction is important but rather boring. Anyway, my fans prefer following you around. New worlds, new alien races, more death and destruction. Whatever you're up to will be a lot more interesting."

I snort. "I wouldn't bet on that."

I doubt the Erethrans will allow him to record the training I'm going to put their people through. And dry politics is rarely riveting.

"I would." Having said his piece, Harry wanders out of the frame again.

"Anything we need to know?" Bolo speaks up, leaning over Mikito's shoulder. "The last message you sent, I was expecting to have to break you out of the Empire."

"Wait, we?" I frown. "You coming?"

"Mmmm… for a fight? Yes. Otherwise, no," Bolo says. "No offense, Redeemer…"

"None taken. You're welcome to sit it out," I say. "Mikito, when you arrive, make sure you're ready to fight."

***

The next morning, I meet the Paladin initiates in the same square. Privacy curtains are up, ensuring that the ongoings inside the courtyard will not be seen by even those staring out the windows. The Paladin initiates are all standing at attention, waiting for me to say something. I'm just waiting.

Ayuri finally turns up, flanked by her companions. This is the first time I've seen them, Unilo and Mayaya, since they yanked me out of my Portal and dumped me here. As usual, Mayaya looks bored with the entire proceedings, the master Portal-maker staring about with a blasé look on his face. Unilo is much more perky, flashing me a smile. I'm a little worried about what she's got to say to me, considering I owe her a personal debt as well. Somehow, I'm getting the feeling that whatever I bargained for previously has even more implications than I had considered.

That's part of the reason why Ali isn't here with me right now. I sent him off to go chat with the rest of the companions and AIs. One thing you have to say about the Galactics. While familiars, companions, and AIs aren't open to everyone, they are quite common. And that commonality has created a whole subculture that's hidden from us System-users.

More than once, we've used that subculture to our advantage. You'd be surprised how few people treat their companions well. With the wide variety of social classes and individuals involved, and the System-enforced loyalty—slavery in other words—it seems to make people think that they can do what they want.

"Champion," I greet Ayuri as she comes to a stop next to me.

"Paladin."

"That's Grand Champion," Unilo pipes up with a twinkle in her eyes.

"It's fine, the Redeemer is known for his lack of courtesy." Ayuri's lips widen in a smile. "In fact, a subsection of his historical predecessors were known for being extremely rude. So he could be said to be following tradition."

"Funny." I glance at the clock in the corner of my vision and sigh. I still have another five minutes to wait before it's time. We could potentially open up early but the...

You know what, I really don't want to do small talk.

"Can you open the Portal?" I ask Mayaya.

Of course, he looks at Ayuri for confirmation.

"Redeemer, you do realize there are numerous restrictions involved in using the Portal between worlds? Teleportation and other mass transit, mass movement spells and Skills are a strategic threat. Receiving the right to make such Portals through our defenses is an involved process and requires significant planning," Ayuri says.

"That a no?"

"Yes, you dungeon-born, uncivilized, System-deficient cretin. That's a no," Mayaya snaps at me, which makes me chuckle.

"You know, this is probably the first time I've ever seen you react. For anything. That includes the time we almost had those monsters eat your face."

This time, Mayaya doesn't rise to the provocation. In fact, his face slips back into that blasé look. I make note of it, how Portal-making and its attendant bureaucracy is his sticking point.

Unfortunately, that leaves me with another four minutes or so to wait. While doing so, I regard the waiting Paladin initiates. They're all standing silently, faces carefully tended to ensure that not a single inch of alien feeling shows through. Even the ones who have tails—or in the Roach's case, wings—are careful to keep them from moving. Which the Galactic body language download tells me is unusual. It's a level of control that's uncommon and speaks more of focused attention than it does of relaxation.

"All right. I guess I should tell you why I called you all here." I regard the group, waiting to see if there's any reaction to those words. Of course there's not. "Today, I'm going to show you exactly how far you all are from being viable Paladin initiates."

That triggers a reaction. Especially from Magine and Ropo. The others are less blatant about their surprise, and in Gheisnan's case, something tells me he expected me to do this. If so, maybe his Skill set isn't completely worthless.

After that, I let them stew in silence until time runs out. Mayaya doesn't bother to ask my permission, just glances over to confirm with Ayuri before he snaps open the Portal. It's a black void in space, a circular oval that consumes all light entering it. It's not very big, about ten feet tall and five feet wide. What it is is more than big enough for those who come through.

I can't help but grin. This should be fun.

Chapter 5

The first to come out, to my surprise, is Bolo. For all his protestations and the friendship we struck up, he has a life on Spaks. I'm not sure why he'd travel across the galaxy to join us. But it's not the time to question him.

The Dragon Lord is standing tall today, all of his nine feet stretched to the limit, his hammer held idly and blocking the majority of his torso as he strides out of the Portal. It makes little sense for a hammer to be that big in real life—except, of course, for System shenanigans.

Because of the System, Bolo has the strength to wield a ten-foot hammer and, I'll admit, the larger surface area makes it much harder to dodge. In any sensible, physics-laden universe, wielding a weapon as big and heavy as that would make no sense. Luckily, the ability to alter our Strength and the strength of the molecular bonds of our surroundings make swinging weapons like that viable, without boring physics causing problems.

His scalemail glints in the sunlight, its emerald-green shade darkening under the slightly pinkish hue of the sky. That the sky isn't the usual blue—or gray, if you live in Vancouver—is due to the different particulate matter on Erethra. The science behind it is out of my scope of learning, though it does mean that their animals and other flora and fauna are more vibrant in coloring. Also, Ali has pointed out that the native animals have a tendency to see in infrared as well.

Once Bolo has cleared the Portal, Harry strolls in, clad in Adventurer chic—an armored jumpsuit with strapping for weapons and equipment—with bright yellow markings instead of the duller colors favored by true Adventurers. As usual, upon entering a new location that might be of interest to his viewers, he has his hands spread out on either side, his fingers split apart in an L shape, holding up invisible camera lenses and recording. He swings his hands one way and another and freezes. A moment later, he curses.

"No recording in the training areas. Or palace grounds," Mayaya snaps at Harry. Mayaya continues a moment later. "Delete your current files. You also need to receive a full press review."

"Even if he isn't recording?" I ask.

"Yes. Many of these journalists, these news junkies, can extract memories to create recordings. None with any great fidelity as compared to an actual recording, but still salable." Mayaya shakes his head and spits. "We do not allow just anyone to walk around in our government locations. And we require them to all sign the necessary documentation and promises."

I frown, considering whether or not I should override Mayaya. I adjust my mental notes too, from stickler with Portal bureaucracy to just bureaucracy. Prodding him would be amusing, but it also could cause more trouble than it would be worth. My theoretical rank doesn't necessarily extend to my friends. It doesn't do Harry any good if I let him record and then have the Erethrans assassinate him later.

"It's fine, John. The Erethrans are more into military announcements and public distribution of information from qualified sources. I'm sure, once I get my clearance, I can produce work that Galactics will actually want to watch," Harry calls as he keeps walking to me, his hands down by his sides. He flashes the trio of Erethrans a grin as he slides in his own dig.

Behind the journalist comes Mikito. The samurai has her polearm at the ready, the heritage weapon masquerading as a soulbound tool. She's armed and armored in a space-age battle suit, a transforming mecha with compressed layers of metal and built-in weaponry. It's an upgrade to her old mecha, a new addition to her wardrobe. Even as it covers her form, it's not too bulky, barely a few inches more across her entire form. On top of the mechasuit, she can throw up her ghost armor Skill, giving her full protection when needed. That's down for now though.

The Portal stays open for a second longer before Mayaya, seeing no one else entering, speaks to Mikito.

"I was told to expect four."

"Dornalor is staying behind. He wants his ship built to his specifications. We left him grumbling about dockworkers and cost-cutting," Mikito says.

In reply, Mayaya snaps shut the Portal.

While my friends make their way over, I note how the Paladin initiates stare at them, some with open curiosity, some with rising dread as they puzzle out what I'm planning. Some—like Magine—just look unimpressed.

"I'm glad you're here," I say to my friends, returning handshakes and fist bumps. "So who wants to be first?"

Bolo doesn't even hesitate, pointing. "I'll just take that corner, shall I?"

"All right, ladies and gentlemen. As you probably guessed, today's a beatdown day. We'll start it easy. Two of you can play with Bolo over there. I recommend you pick the two best you have. And don't worry, I told Bolo not to kill you."

The words make them bristle for the most part—all but the Pooskeen, who shrinks backward. He's obviously not interested in having a big, strong Dragon Lord pound him into the dirt. Quite literally.

The first to volunteer is Magine, the dueling maniac. Freif joins him after glancing at the group. It's not a bad team-up, considering Freif will need to hide behind and set up if he wants to take out Bolo. Unfortunately, the flat arena won't do him any real good. That's no way to hide, to back off and open fire on the Dragon Lord. It's not the ideal environment for the marksman and I'm sure he'll complain about it later.

The pair set up as I expect them to. Magine stands before Bolo, weapons held down and to the side, a short dueling sword in each hand. These aren't big honking pieces of steel or even the curved elegance of a katana. No, these are dueling swords, tiny weapons about four feet long with a blade that's maybe a millimeter in diameter. The blade itself appears from a hiltless basket guard, formed of Mana and a thin extrusion of metal. Instead of a single flat edge, they're an irregular triangle of blade edges, with diamond-tipped edges to increase cutting area. On top of that, low-level energy projections erupt from the blade edges, giving the weapon a monofilament edge.

That Magine wields two at once, and with the lightness of the weapons, means he'll be attacking faster than Bolo. Theoretically.

Freif stands behind Magine, at the far edges of the courtyard. This leaves Freif little space to retreat, but Magine is ready to intercept Bolo. Unlike his melee-wielding partner, Freif is hauling around a sniper rifle that's nearly as big as he is. System physics means that he can carry it without a problem, though he has additional braces emerging from his armored body, along with force-projected stabilizers, that help anchor the sniper rifle to himself and the ground.

All the while, as they set up, Bolo stands there, leaning on the shaft of his hammer, waiting with a smirk. "*You want me to beat them, correct? With flair?*"

I glance at the party chat that Bolo sends his notice to us from and keep my face still as I reply. "*No deaths. Feel free to cripple. Heck, that'd be preferable.*"

"*Not very nice of you,*" Harry sends.

"*Good training.*" That's from Mikito, the samurai eyeing not the fighters who are stepping out to deal with Bolo but the rest of the group who hasn't. She'll be taking her turn soon after. And unlike Bolo, she'll take this seriously.

"*Whatever. I've been itching to hit someone,*" Bolo sends his reply.

"You intend to signal the start?" Ayuri says, gesturing out to where the opponents wait.

"Nope. When they're ready, they can start," I reply idly.

As if he was waiting for me to say that, Magine launches himself at Bolo. He crosses the twenty feet between them in a flicker of blurred cloth and steel, Haste already turned on. He's fast. Faster than me, I'd say. Agility focused, but with significantly less Health.

Rather than pick up his hammer, Bolo reacts by punching. He's moving so fast, everyone is moving so fast, that I'm not even sure the Paladin initiates spot the slight deviation Bolo makes while punching. A deviation necessary to take in account Magine's dodge. One moment, Magine is a blur approaching Bolo. The next, he's being punched in the face, that fraction of a second when his momentum is canceled like a photograph in our minds. His face, crumpled, a blade sunk into Bolo's arm half a foot deep. And then, of course, momentum takes over and Magine is flying backward nearly as far as he was charging, tumbling head over heels.

A crack, the noise from the projectile thrown down field as it crushes the sound barrier, informs us that Freif is joining the battle. Freif reacted as fast as Magine, but they're all moving so fast, the crack only arrives a fraction of a second before the noise of Magine's own breach of the sound barrier.

The projectile lands on Bolo's chest, just slightly off center and at an angle, shattering on the scalemail and showering the ground with shards. Bolo's enchanted armor doesn't even scar.

Neither of the initiates take their failures lying down. Magine is already bouncing to his feet and charging into the fray, blood streaming from a broken nose, swelling already forming on his face. He circles sideways, making sure to give Freif a clear line of vision. He's learned his lesson, circling rather than doing a straight, face-first challenge. Freif is reloading, taking his time as he pumps Mana into his next Skill attack. No hasty shots here.

And Bolo? He's grinning.

What happens in the next few minutes is a massacre. Bolo never even bothers to pick up his hammer. Instead, he alternately punches, kicks, and in the end—while holding Magine's hands apart—head butts his opponent into submission.

As for Freif, even after conjuring weaponry all around the arena to increase his damage and slow down Bolo, he fails to do much to the Dragon Lord. After the first shot, Bolo dodges. His movements are almost languid, but he shrugs off, disperses, and dodges the vast majority of Freif's major attacks. The rest of the drones and automated weaponry, Bolo ignores.

When the Dragon Lord is finally done with Magine, he slowly stalks over to Freif, dismissing or plowing through the mines, chaos grenades, smoke particles, and illusions to grab hold of his opponent. Then he throws the Erethran sniper to the ground and stomps on him. Even from where I am, I hear the snap, crackle, and pop as pelvis, hips, and fingers are destroyed.

"I think that's enough."

Bolo grins, looking up, and kicks Freif over to the edge of the arena. The duelist staggers back to his feet, battle recovery and stubbornness getting him up, but he's swaying, his reconjured swords in hand.

"I think we'll do three next," I say to the Honor Guards, some of whom are quite, quite angry.

Not scared though. Not worried. Not even surprised. Just angry. They don't show it much in their faces, but I've been observing them for hours, watching their combat videos, their training logs, and eyeballing them during our interviews. I've begun to put together a picture in my head, build a baseline.

They're angry, but not scared or worried. I think that says something about the kind of training they've received. And, I have to admit, I wonder if what I'm doing will even drive home the point I intend. Who knows, maybe getting their asses kicked by a higher Class opponent is a common thing in their training. Memory returns, informing me that that's true; but sometimes, lessons have to be relearned.

***

Bolo trashes the next three with as much ease as the first group. It doesn't help that their best fighters grouped up to begin with. When I make it four, Magine and Freif join up again. I almost want to comment about them being masochists, but I restrain myself.

Guns fire, spells flash, and for the first time, I get to see what Gheisnan brings to the table. Freif stays close, laying out mines and drones to protect the Pooskeen. Magine and Kino confront Bolo directly. Together, the pair of Honor Guards are strong enough that they make Bolo pick up his hammer and wield it, battering the pair around even through their blocks.

That's what the Shaman brings. He ties in everyone, what the others are seeing, hearing, and sensing. He layers in his own understanding, his own predictions of what Bolo will do, and so, he coordinates the offense. It puts Bolo on the defensive for a few minutes, wears down his Mana and health while the Dragon Lord gets his footing in the new battlescape. It's a good showing.

It's not enough.

No matter how good you are at seeing the future, at predicting your opponent, it's useless if you can't stop them. My own proof of that is my last fight with a Master Class speedster. In Bolo's case, when he gets serious, he smashes apart the defenses of the Honor Guards. Perfect blocks divert some of the energy, but not enough. Soul Shields absorb, flash, and shatter in single swings. Kino falls first, then Magine. After that, it's just mop up.

When the fight is over, I gather them all again.

"Well, that went about as well as I expected. What did you all think?" I speak casually, in contrast to the orders that they're probably used to.

"Permission to speak freely, sir," says Ropo.

I eye the dwarf, remembering how he ate one of Bolo's strikes, the way it sank him all the way to his chin before he threw himself out of the ground. Stubborn, good fighter. His Poisoning Skills helped to add a damage over time attack to his own efforts and his friends'. Even if he mostly concentrated on defense in this fight, he was useful. Too bad Bolo's base recovery levels and resistances overrode his efforts.

I nod. "We might as well make this clear. You all have the right to speak freely to me at any time, any place you want. If I don't like what you say, I'll let you know. In a very direct manner." I flash them a wide grin at that.

"Then you're a poison-swilling fool. There's no way an Advanced Classer, capped or not, can beat a high level Master Classer. Add the fact that the Dragon Lord is a prestige Master Class, geared for fighting alone, and this was a waste of time. We know we can't beat Master Classers, and if you thought this was a new thing, we might as well drink a Thrice-Croaked potion," Ropo says with tension high in his voice, his jaw jutting out.

"And why is that?" I say.

"Because, you towering, infected donkey's penis, we are Honor Guard. We're trained to fight Master Classers, either alone or in teams, the moment we were recruited. There's no point to this. We know how to fight and survive. But there's never a winning scenario, not against him." Another jerk of his bearded chin takes in Bolo.

"And is that what you all think?" When my question to the group meets sullen silence, I get my answer. I turn to Mikito next. "How many do you want?"

The samurai glances over the group, taps her lips, then calls out, "One on one." Then she walks over to the corner that Bolo had started all his fights from.

"All right. You heard the lady. Line up and get your asses kicked."

While Ropo grumbles and moves to face off against Mikito, Ayuri sniffs and turns on her heels. She stops, calling out to me when she's halfway to the exit. "Paladin. I want a word with you."

I note the glances the initiates shoot at me. They're probably speculating that I'm going to be told off by Mommy. As I join the Champion, I toss behind me a drone so that I can continue watching. I'm not worried about my conversation with her, for I have a plan.

I just don't know if it's a good one yet.

***

"What are you doing?" Ayuri says, once we're away from the playground and out of earshot.

"Making a point." I flick a glance back to where Mikito is getting them sorted out. I split my concentration between the drone I left behind and Ayuri.

"And what kind of point is that?"

"Well, that depends on who we're talking about. Freif is a great sniper, but even with all the points he's put into his Skills, he can't really hit a Master Class like Bolo. And when Mikito has him alone, she'll still beat him like the redheaded stepchild he is."

"He's not a redhead. He is a stepchild, but that has no legal standing," Unilo says, looking a little confused.

"Earth culture. You should read the books," I say. "Real mainstay of Canadian culture."

Ayuri ignores my nonsensical remarks while Unilo mouths the word Canadian. "He knows that. He's a sniper. His job was never to be in the front lines, fighting directly. You're not teaching him anything he doesn't know."

"Maybe he knows it, but you guys obviously don't. What is he going to do when you make him a Paladin? When his enemies come for him in the middle the night, when he's all alone and injured, when things are bleak and he hasn't had time to set himself up for that perfect shot? He's not a Paladin," I say.

I wince as I watch Mikito boot Ropo in the nuts. The fact that the dwarf continues coming says a lot about his stubbornness and his innate resistances. The fact that he's tried to use a bunch of poison gasses and weapons is an interesting new addition to his fighting technique. Not that it helps.

"Freif's just a target waiting to be ended."

"He's not you, Redeemer. We will provide security and teams for all of our Paladins," Ayuri says.

"And that's where your next mistake comes. We don't work for you, or your military, or even the Queen. Whatever teams you put together, the Paladins will have to trust them with their lives and more. They have to trust the team to be loyal. To let them, as a Paladin, do whatever the heck they think is right," I say. "If they decided to kill your Queen, would the groups you create follow them?"

I snort when Mayaya stirs and Unilo frowns. Ayuri's the only one who doesn't react to my almost treacherous words.

"Any group you create for them will be a compromise," I say. "That won't work."

Ayuri shakes her head, dismissing my words. "We're not looking to create another group of insurrectionists. We don't intend to have a repeat of the War of the Seven Systems."

"Then you've got the wrong people. And I won't give them my approval."

And finally, finally, Ayuri reacts. She steps close, looms over my shorter form, and stares me down. Her aura turns on, and I don't know if it's conscious or not. The pressure she exerts is much, much stronger than nearly any aura I've ever felt. Only the Queen and the Librarian were stronger. It's as though the weight of an entire star system is behind it, the regard of the population of an entire empire and their favor bearing down on me.

I stay upright and keep my face impassive under the building pressure. But as is my way, as she crushes me with her aura, I reach for that kernel of anger within me, that raging ocean that never seems to end. Pain, never resolved, turned into anger and passion. I use it the same way I always use it, and it reinforces my backbone.

Eyes narrowed a little, I snap back. "Drop it. You wanted a Paladin. You have one. You can't intimidate me, Champion."

"Maybe we'll just try again. With someone a little more agreeable," Ayuri snaps, fists clenched at her sides.

I note that the other two members of her group have moved to flank me. Mayaya is probably ready to open a Portal and shut it with me halfway through. Unilo—well, I'm not sure of her plans. Probably something involving that spear she wields.

"You mean like the two dozen guards you sent before me?" I watch Ayuri's eyes widen, watch as she realizes I'm not as oblivious as I've played.

I know more than she thinks about what that planet once was. Of the layers of pain it contains. "I know about them. I know about all the failures, everyone you sent to the Forbidden Planet in search of Suhargur. Every single failure. All the rejected ones. I am literally your best option. Now get out of my way and let me do my job. Let me let you get a Paladin."

Ayuri continues to stare at me, never releasing the aura that makes the space around us warp. In the corner of my eyes, I spot the way the hallway itself twists, buckles. I meet her gaze even as notifications of the aura being resisted ping off a corner of my vision. She stares and stares, her gaze turning inquisitive after a while, searching my own eyes for something. And then...

She laughs.

The aura disappears as quickly as it arrived, allowing me to roll my shoulders as the metaphorical weight vanishes. All the while, Ayuri laughs and laughs. She claps me on the side of my shoulder, the impact making me stagger. I'm sure I'm going to get a bruise from it.

"Good. Don't let anyone, anything intimidate you, Paladin."

"So. Was that all a test?" I'm getting a bit whiplashed from the way that she's been treating me. Telling me that the Paladins are our own players, then trying to make me do things her way.

"Weren't you testing me as well?" Ayuri says, a smile still on her face.

I shrug. Still chuckling, Ayuri slaps me on the shoulder again and walks off with her friends. I watch her back as she goes, then finally turn around and head for the training grounds.

I'm still not sure who came out that interaction better off. But my head is still on my shoulders, so I'll take it as a win.

***

Mikito's fights afterward are a letdown. After the bone-crushing, shattering, explosive sonic attacks of Bolo, hers are just boring. She restrains her Skills and attributes, fighting at the same level as the Advanced Classers. Matching them, as best as one can, in terms of skill and strength.

She still wins.

Compared to the triumphant thrashing of the guards before, Mikito's restrained victories seem to have a deeper effect on the morale of the group. Even if she is a Master Class, the fact that she's not using her higher-level Skills is telling. It's a lot harder for them to discount her ability when she's not triggering and using Skills that give her an insane advantage.

The fight with the Roach is a great example. Smo'kana has the height advantage, able to swoop down, attack, and retreat as his wings deploy. They allow him to hold in place or swoop away with equal ease. The roach wields a pair of blaster pistols in his first set of hands and a pair of cutlasses in the second.

Mikito doesn't hold still though, constantly shifting her position as she picks her attacks with her weapon. The ghostly armor deflects the occasional beam blasts that S'mo'kana releases against her, but for the most part, the roach darts in to do battle with his swords. It's no surprise, since even with Skills, beam weaponry doesn't transfer the attribute bonuses of Strength and Skills as well.

Not unless you specialize. And the Roach is a generalist.

Under her Haste Skill, Mikito darts back and forth, lashing out with her naginata whenever he comes close. At first, the fight looks to be at stalemate, with Mikito never doing enough damage nor the Roach able to hit her. But on the tenth swoop, Mikito jerks her hand toward herself and hidden gravity mines trigger.

They yank Smo'kana down, forcing him to the ground as he suddenly weighs much more than his wings can handle. Even if he could adjust his weight, the strength of his wings, and his attributes to make it viable to fly again, he never gets a chance. A series of quick strikes rips off portions of his wings, takes a hand, and ends up with the naginata placed against the center of his torso. As quickly as that, even as the dust from his constant flying around is still settling, the fight is over.

Mikito swings the naginata to the side, discarding the brownish blood with a flick before she steps back to her original starting point. She settles in, ready for the next fighter. Gheisnan glowers and growls, the next in line, but he still approaches. Knowing that the beating he'll receive isn't something he can avoid.

As the Roach crawls out of the way, the other recruits take care of him, casting healing and regenerative spells, fixing broken bits. The Erethran Honor Guard Skill means that his limbs will reappear in time, but the additional magic helps speed up the entire process. Otherwise, he'd be down and out for next day while he rebuilds his limbs. Too long.

When it's all done, when Mikito has torn through the entire group, when she's bruised and bloodied and content, I walk back out and regain their attention.

"Well. That was enlightening." I let my gaze run over the group, idly noting how some of their clothing has already patched itself up. Nanowoven protection combined with organic growing threads, all of it stitched together with high density metals and other Artisan Skills. I've even heard of clothing that will regenerate from a fist-sized piece. "Anyone care to tell me what they learned?"

"She's a sadistic little oxygen-breather. And he's a battle-crazed Hakarta," Anayton says.

"Not true and true." I swing my finger around and around, gesturing for them to keep going. When she doesn't answer my body language, I use my words. "Go on."

Anayton crosses her arms. "And you have no idea what you're doing."

"Very true. Anyone else have anything else to add?"

"You want us to beat them. One on one. And if we don't, you're not going to give us your approval," Magine says while fixing his gaze on Mikito.

Magine was the last one to fight, and the closest to come to winning against her. He's fast, focusing more on speed and precision than strength. He doesn't have a legacy weapon, but he uses his soulbound weapons in the same appearing and disappearing technique that the Honor Guard is known for. That he combines the style with both hands filled with soulbound blades and the multiple additional blades of Thousand Blades creates a blizzard of floating weaponry.

He's better at the Honor Guard's blade dance than I am, but Mikito has been training with me for years now, and the style is no longer new and interesting. He might do the Erethran sword style better, but better isn't enough of an edge. Not when he doesn't know her style, her way of fighting. And really, her weapon's a lot better than his.

Not that we're going to tell them that.

"Wrong." I look around, waiting for someone else to speak.

"You wanted to see if all those recordings were true." Kino, the big rock creature, rumbles. His fight with Mikito was quite one-sided. He's too slow to land any attacks on her, but he's also highly defensive. If not for Mikito cheating with her weapon, it probably would have been a draw. As it was, the added damage from Hitoshi was enough to level the playing field and allow her to down the tough tank.

"Correct. Next?"

"You've already made up your mind, so why are you dragging this out?" Gheisnan calls, the little kobold glaring at me. I wonder if he thinks that he's on the chopping block.

He is, just not today.

"Fair. Smo. Pack up your things. You're done."

I watch the Roach buzz, wings flaring and folding, insect-like hands twitching in agitation. He takes a step and another away as commanded before he spins around and looks at me. When he speaks, that harsh, painful-to-the-ears buzz of his voice catches me. "Why? Failed Brood. Why?"

"Because you're looking to be eaten. I'm not looking for Paladins who are looking to die. That's not our job. As an old Earther once said, your job isn't to die for your Empire but to make the enemy die for his." I look around at the group, meeting the defiant gazes of the initiates. "I don't need heroics from all of you. I just need you all to survive. Your Empire needs you all to survive. You want to know the lesson? It's simple. Get back up. And keep going. No matter what." I let that stupid, idiotic, passe sentence die its ignominious death in the dirt of the courtyard. "Or else in about another ten years, I'll be back here, doing this all over again with a whole new batch of idiots."

Smo twitches and buzzes, moving back and forth on its legs agitatedly, its wings flaring so much so that it hovers in place. In the end, it flies away down the corridor. Hopefully he knows where to report in. But I don't really care. I dismiss him and his future from my mind, focusing on the others.

"Homework for all of you. Go over your Skills, your build. Figure out what you're missing. Figure out what you need to do to fix it. Then come to me with a plan. You're not fighting in teams anymore. You're not one of many. You're single fighters. Single survivors. Figure out how to make it work." I pause, then gesture at them to disperse. "I'll see you tomorrow."

As they walk away, leaving at my command, I watch them through the security cameras and drones scattered through the building. Watch to see how they took the news.

Ropo, Gheisnan, and Kino look unperturbed. Magine smirks, as if he expected no more from someone like Smo'kana. Freif is still casting glances at Mikito and her weapon, as if she's more important than anything that has to do with the selection process. As if he might suspect something. As for Anayton, the female Erethran looks concerned.

And just like that, my first day with the initiates is over.

Chapter 6

Of course, that's not the end of my day. I drag my team along, heading to my temporary residence. It's a bit of a trek, since they don't allow us to Portal around wherever we want. The entire planet is secured by spatial locks, Portals and quick spatial movement accessible only to a select membership. Most of them in the Honor Guard. It says something about my status that I'm not automatically approved to jump about wherever I want. I could probably push it and get myself approved, but I've got bigger fish to fry. Still, it's on the to-do list.

I'm lodging off-site, not near the palace residence but still on state grounds. Just not palace grounds, if that makes sense. In fact, rather than being set up in the barracks rooms or anything like that, I've been given a small mansion to call my own.

I designate rooms for my friends within, making the echoing and empty building a little livelier. When I first arrived, the mansion had been colored in salmon pink with purple edging and a noveau gothic design with weird Erethran gargoyles covering the entirety. I changed that to a calming sky blue and cream edging for the walls but left the gargoyles. Partly because some of them were mechanical golems. The walls adjust with the barest of mental nudges, all controlled by the building's System interface.

Of course, appearances aren't the only thing I'm given access to. The entire building's defense grid, the alarm systems, even the room configurations are all available at the touch of a finger. Included as well are the expansive grounds, which I can landscape to my heart's content—or adjust the emplacement of the various anti-aircraft artillery. I ignore most of it, beyond verifying the multiple escape routes built into the residence and double-checking the defense grid settings.

Once we're in the office, a minimalistic room with liquid-metal furnishings, we grab seats and I send the robots to get us snacks.

For the next few hours, we catch up. The team informs me of the deal they made, gloss over the problems they caused and the need for Bolo's appearance. What little I glean indicates that Bolo's side deal ended up causing more trouble than he expected. They did let slip that they'd managed to annoy one of the Station Masters in the first ring. Staying in Spaks was no longer an option for the Dragon Lord, not after that.

"So why join us?" I ask. After all, just because he had to leave doesn't mean he had to choose us.

"We worked well together. It is rare for three Master Classers to still work together at this stage of their development," Bolo says, crossing his arms. "Most bounty hunters will stay away from such a team."

Not entirely sure he's correct about that, since I recall quite a few Master Class teams. But there might be a matter of selection bias in my recollections. I only meet Master Class teams because I run in a team. Statistically, Bolo might be right—and my memories from the library seem to agree—but this is one of those cases where statistics gets beaten by lived experience. Often at the edge of a very pointed bat.

"You know, being your shield is getting really tiring," I grumble.

"Don't act as if you're not getting something out of it. Like an example of what a real Master Classer can do for your initiates," Bolo says.

I grin guiltily, having been caught out. Bolo really was the best example for them to fight. But more importantly… "I want your thoughts on them. What do they need to fix?"

"Assuming they're fighting alone?" Bolo says, then at my confirmation, runs a hand along one arm, humming in thought. "There're a few things that come to mind…"

I lean forward, listening. Mikito eventually interjects, adding her own analysis. The conversation runs through the strengths of each Honor Guard. Truth be told, many of them are similar, so the adjustments are a matter of personality and attribute fit. Eventually, we sit back, waving at the detailed notes I've taken.

"Why ask us though? I'd think an Empire like this has their own Class specialists," Bolo says.

"They do. I've requested reviews for them all." I flick my fingers and new documentation windows appear, floating in front of the pair. Harry's still off, doing his thing. This kind of conversation isn't his thing, for obvious reasons. "They've even taken into account my own notes from yesterday, for their analysis."

The pair falls silent as they read over the recommendations. I'd let the Class specialists run wild, make the most optimal builds.

"And you think they'll let the initiates buy all that? That's quite a bit of spending," Bolo says, not without a little envy.

"They're an Empire," I say with a sniff. "I doubt it's more than a drop in the bucket. The trick will be training them to use the new Skills properly."

"That sounds reasonable. It certainly won't hurt, even if they reject your budget," Mikito says, turning the teacup that she's extracted from her inventory round and round in hand.

I look closer at the gently graded teacup, smiling slightly at the description.

Fujiwara Ever Warm Teacup

The latest work by the famous potter, this teacup is guaranteed to keep tea warmed to the perfect temperature without affecting its taste. Both a work of art and a practical piece, the teacup is one of the first vaguely acceptable creations by the master potter to be sold.

Dismissing the message, I pick at the sandwiches that the robots have delivered, asking further questions. Catching up on trivial things, on stories about my friends. Harry eventually joins us, freed from the bureaucracy required to get his press pass. But soon enough, I see the restlessness, the exhaustion that creeps up on my friends. Whatever it was that happened in the last day, it's wiped them. Not physically, but psychologically. There's a point where healing, the System's fixing of us, is insufficient. When we just need to stop.

It's strange really. You can let the System fix your body, fix your mind. You can have it rip out the wounds, the damage you have acquired. You can replenish your health and your Mana. And still feel worn down.

It's as though the mental and physical are separate from the spiritual.

Sometimes, just sometimes, all you need to do is stop.

Breathe.

And move on.

"Go. Rest. We'll talk tomorrow. We're going to have to push them tomorrow. Can't have you guys falling down and messing with the good impression you made," I say.

"I am fine," Bolo says, straightening himself. Glaring at the implication that he's less than the perfect soldier.

"I'm sure. But I want to think about this a little more," I say, gesturing at the notification windows that show their recommendations and the Class specialists' that I make reappear. "And you guys are rather noisy."

Bolo's lips curl up, but I wave him off. Harry is already half out the door, muttering goodbyes. On the other hand, I'm pretty sure he'll just go back to his room and work. Even the little glimpse of Erethra he's achieved is more than most humans would have, and I know he's got a lot of human fans. Even if that same information is available in the Shop, it's not from a human point of view, not as seen by one of us. And that makes a difference.

I watch the pair walk off, watch Bolo disappear around the corner of the doorway. But Mikito lingers, carefully packing her teacup in its container before storing it in her Inventory. Carefully cleaning her hands and the table, even though the robot has done it once.

"What's wrong?" I say.

"My question. Not yours," Mikito replies, dark eyes narrowing.

I draw a deep breath, looking around the office. I frown, sick of the blue, and shift it to green and increase the lighting, adding a little more UV to the output. Mikito says nothing, waiting with studied patience for me to stop fluffing around.

"I have no idea what I'm doing," I finally admit.

"What's new?"

I chuckle. Too true. But... "This is more than me. More than us. It feels like I'm playing a game of blocks, pulling them out with my eyes closed. Do it too fast, tug on the wrong thing, and everything will come down. But there are innocents standing on the blocks. An entire Empire." I stare at Mikito, showing her a little of the fear I'm trying to keep hidden. "I don't know what I'm doing."

"Good."

"Pardon?" I blurt out.

"Good." Mikito shrugs. "Then they won't know what you intend to do." She gestures around us. "If you don't know, they won't either."

"That's a good thing?" I say, a little incredulous.

"Can't be worse than where they're headed, can it?" Mikito says.

I grunt. Well, thus far… what was it that concerned them? Civil war? If that's the case, it's not so bad. Still… "And if I make a mistake?"

"You will." Mikito shrugs. "You're human."

"People will die."

"They'll die anyway," Mikito replies. "But maybe you'll do good too. Shake things up. Make these Paladins work."

"You mean restore them to working order?"

Mikito offers a thin-lipped smile, flicking her gaze upward. I remember where we are then reevaluate her words before I sigh.

"I'm going to rest now. You…" She glances at where the notification windows continue to hover before me, then shrugs. "You continue studying."

I feel a little betrayed at being left alone. Even if I did ask her to do that. Especially after that talk. As she walks out, I return my gaze to the windows. And I can't help but question the world I've been thrown into.

I can almost feel the Empire shifting beneath my feet as I pull up reports. Information I've purchased. Recordings from the Erethran news network, the closest thing to their media. I read about the constant wars on the borders, the skirmishes. The protests, the dropping recruitment rates. I read about the loss of more worlds to the Forbidden Zone.

I read. I listen. I learn.

And I remember, what is, is.

***

Ali shows up hours later. One second, he's gone. The next, he blips into reality next to me, almost making me jump. For the last few hours, I've been watching multiple data feeds, official channels and unofficial notes. Things that I only gain access to because of my rank. Dominating one corner of my notifications is the Erethran equivalent of entertainment—the latest, greatest cut of their most recent border skirmish.

More and more, I'm disliking the *300*-like world view I'm getting of this society. It's one thing to read about them, another to be immersed in their culture. Or lack of it. Theoretically, there are multiple news streams— journalists, bloggers, and more—but all of them are heavily censored. Most don't even need that much censoring, so immersed in the party line that they sing the same praises. Those who don't drink the Kool-Aid have heavy safeguards in place to keep them from being too critical.

What little criticism there is is carefully contained. To specific programs like waste and "dishonorable" actions. To people who aren't doing their job to the utmost. So corruption and other mishandling is heavily rooted out by journalists, even if the effects of those reports are often swept under the rug.

Questions about another way of life, of cultural touchstones that might not involve a never-ending expansion, a never-ending empire of Leveling up? Those are pushed aside or only carefully, ever so carefully hinted at.

You'd think it'd be impossible within a world where the Shop exists. But while all information is available for purchase, information can be hidden, suppressed. Skills and just a flood of data hiding the truth. It's the people with the biggest wallets who win out in such a game. The only way to avoid being caught saying something bad, never being considered a threat, is never to draw attention at all. To watch every purchase, every word you say. To self-censor everywhere but in your own mind.

Even Skills that block out purchases can be overridden with enough money. Add that to the use of Public Relations Consultants, Media Influencers, and Culture Shapers and you get a society that's not so much evolving as it is shaped. One whose goal is the strengthening and expansion of the Empire.

One that eats its young in a never-ending grind for Levels.

And yet… and yet, I can see why.

Even if the information I'm seeing now is shaped by the movies, by the very Skills I'm whining about, I can't help but understand it. Six hundred years ago, the slowly growing Erethran Kingdom was attacked. Not by another kingdom, not by a powerful Guild. But by a single man, a high-Level Heroic. Using hit-and-run tactics, he destroyed multiple fleets, wiped out army bases, and the personnel within. And when the kingdom refused to become part of his personal empire, he started going after cities.

For four years, the kingdom was besieged. A once-burgeoning kingdom fell back on itself, people mass transported and put under contract, drawn into major cities for safety or spread out to reduce targets. In that time, their kingdom was reforged. The people grew stronger, tougher. They dedicated themselves to Leveling, to Combat Classes.

The Heroic—whose name is nearly impossible to say but roughly translates to The Heavenly Sky above All Peons—made one mistake. Rather than kill everyone he fought with at each fight, he left a few survivors. Those survivors kept Leveling, kept fighting and growing. New Classes were created—the Champions and the Paladins—as these survivors continued to fight the Heroic and, when they could, Level in hidden dungeons. Finally, finally, they beat him.

Not without deep, heart-rending cost.

That final battle is probably the most recorded / re-recorded / remixed event in the Empire. Like Earth's D-Day. Over two thousand plays and countless radio shows, movies, experiential downloads, and more. Their third largest city—renamed Sky's Demise—was destroyed. But they survived.

And grew obsessed. With never letting it ever happen again. And that meant Leveling. Growing stronger, growing their own Heroics.

"But there's a problem, isn't there?" I say to Ali as I gesture to the screens.

"Problem?" the Spirit asks as he floats, staring at the movie. "I mean, sure, I can see the bad rendering, but it's not that bad."

"In their struggle for Levels. Because we still die. All of us," I say. "Doesn't matter if your Queen or Emperor becomes a Heroic. Sooner or later, they die. The one thing the System can't do is bring back the dead. And age takes us all."

Oh, higher Constitutions increase lifespans. But it's not to the extent of eternal life. Even someone who specs entirely for lifespan increases is held back by their initial biology. At most, a maximum increase of ten times seems to be the limit before age catches up. After that, whatever it is the System does breaks down. Obviously certain creatures—certain species—get the better end of the deal, but there seems to be a balancing act in play. Like a drop in fertility, a higher incidence of violence, and increased difficulty in acquiring higher Classes or experience.

"What's new?" Ali says. "Pretty much every major group does that. Whether it's a bigger or smaller variation, entire Classes, social structures, and groups push for better Classes, higher tiers. Some are just less..." Ali pauses, searching for the word. "Obvious."

"Yeah. The tyranny of Levels." I shake my head. I can see how it affected Earth and me too. All of us surging upward to get as many Levels, as many Classes as possible. Because anything else was a failure, anything else left us vulnerable. "The failure of the System."

And I don't need my own memories to tell me that this is all too common. Dungeon World, rim world, or core world, it's the same. Levels are all.

"Or success," Ali says, gesturing around. "All of this, these technological advances, the way people can progress, that's the System too. You just need the chance to fight—and the Erethrans give it to all—and you can progress. Hell, if you don't want to fight, you can be an Artisan. And they provide for those too."

I grunt. That too is true. For Erethrans, schooling is paid for, including training and dungeon entries. The best, the most gifted, the most driven are allowed to take additional classes, acquire additional material, enter higher Leveled dungeons or the same more often. All to improve, to push for more, better Classes. Of course, the Artisans are "requested" to focus on Combat support Classes. Leaving out those who just want to be artists, just want to entertain or live a quiet life.

"Still messed up."

"But that's not what we're here for, right?" Ali says.

"No. We're here because they want us to…" I shut up when Ali points upward. I grunt. Of course we're being watched. Not much more I can say. Even the stuff I have on me—the Skills active, the new and better enchantments—can be beaten. "Get them new Paladins. So tell me about them. Tell me about the Empire they're going to have to fix."

Ali grins and floats down. "All right. As you guessed, there are more than a few who will be upset with you. Let's start with Brerdain Ramanner, Chief of the General Staff." When I frown, Ali adds, "That's second-in-command of the regular armed forces—the army basically. Above him is the Minister of Defense, whose serves at the Queen's pleasure."

A twitch of his fingers makes Brerdain's information pop up. Brerdain's in full silhouette, both his known attributes and Skills as well as his Status information displayed in the hovering notification window. I'm amused to see he's a little portly around the middle—just a little pudge, not a lot—and there's some flaking around the horns that can be spotted even in the picture. He's old. Not as old as the Queen, but maybe a couple of decades younger as far as I can tell. Other than his age and dad bod, he could be any other high-ranking, uniformed thug, so boring is his face.

Brerdain Ramanner, Chief of the General Staff of Erethra, Commander of the Eight Fleet, Victor of the Prasat Battle, Umnak Clash,…; Slayer of Goblins, Hakarta, Movanna, Truinnar, Lurkers,…, more… (Erethran General Level 50)

HP: 2140/2140

MP: 4280/4280

Conditions: Aura of Command, Command Experience, Strength from Above, Greater Attitude Adjustment, National Security Interest

"What Skills do the Generals get anyway?" I ask, eying the Conditions section. Most of those Skills are new to me, beyond the Aura of Command. I feel pressure from the library insisting on giving me the information, but I push it back. I'm too tired to deal with the flood of information.

"Mass buffs. Generally extends to those within the ranks. Much like many Queens, Kings, Lords, and the like. Whenever there's a person in power, those kinds of Skills show up," Ali says. "On the personal side of the equation, they generally lean toward either early attribute gains at the Basic Level or at the Master Level, defense and escape Skills."

"Really? How come I've never run into them?" I say.

"Mostly? Because you suck at being part of groups," Ali says. "Heck, you even declined to join that Guild full-time, remember? Guilds generally provide such buffs too, just at a lower level. Or more widespread. Also, you never dig into your stats. Here."

A flicker of light and a new screen appears, one that I haven't seen before.

Current Experience Modifiers

Grouped Experience Modifier -16% (Variable)

Erethran Empire Citizen Modifier (+0.000004%)

Erethran Armed Forces Modifier (+0.00000023%)

"Huh. Why the negative on the group?" I say. "That's not normal, is it?"

"Nah, that's 'cause you're being power-Leveled by Bolo and Mikito."

I frown before I get it. The same reason my Monster Slayer Title gives me extra damage even against same-Level monsters is why I'm getting negative modifiers. As far as the System is concerned, I'm still on my second tier—Advanced—even if I have a Master Class. But since I've got both Bolo and Mikito in my team now, I'm getting negative modifiers. I bet Harry does too—if he gets any real experience from combat. His War Reporter Class is weird.

"Seems like a tiny amount for these experience increases. And only two?" I say.

"Small individually. But the Queen's works on every single citizen, no matter their Class. And the military modifier is because you're too high up to be affected by anything other than the Queen and the Minister of Defense." Ali gestures and a new screen shows up—one for Ropo. There's a much, much larger list of modifiers involved there. Every single commanding officer of his has a Skill that gives him an experience boost, and on top of that, I note a couple of Clan-based Skills adding to his experience. "That's what they got before they transferred over."

"So about four to five percent total." I eyeball the numbers. "Still not a lot."

"For every fight and every time they increase their XP? Over the entire year and across the entire army or Empire?" Ali points out. "It adds up."

"I guess." A buff is a buff. And I can see how having a large army would add to the strength of these Skills. Makes me wonder though. "But this is more a quantity over quality thing, isn't it?"

"That's the Erethrans for you. Bolo's people do the opposite. They've got dedicated Skills to buff up individuals. Mentor-mentee relationships are much more important there and give higher individual boosts. Mentors also get a boost, both in status and on their sheet. Obviously, it can't be used for as many," Ali says. "They've even got Skills that give more experience back to themselves the higher Level their mentees get."

"Is that why..." I gesture out the door.

"Why Bolo's persona non grata with his people? Yeah. Exile is nasty, for both the mentor and mentee," Ali replies.

"Huh." I fall silent, wondering once again about Bolo's background. I could find out so easily, but... there are some things you don't do, not to friends. Or allies.

I can't help but wonder how Earth intends to build its relationships, how it intends to grow. Knowing us, we'll probably end up with a mixture of options, depending on the various cultures and groups. I'm sure if I dug into it, I'd find specialist's groups—even more specialized than the Erethran Honor Guards—who might do the same as the Dragon Knights. It's not as if Erethra's a monoculture. Those don't really exist, outside of lazy scifi writing and a few hive minds. "I think we got a little side-tracked."

"You did."

I bite my lip and gesture at Brerdain's information. "Why him? And what's with his Level?"

"Well, if you'd let me finish without interrupting, I could explain." When I glare at Ali, the Spirit chuckles. "Brerdain's the leading contender among the regular armed forces to be the next in line. He's got the backing of quite a few of the Generals—as much as that matters, which is a lot—but the Queen doesn't like him, if rumors are true. He's more of a hard-line hawk, wanting to get the Empire mixed up in even more fights. His age is a major negative as well." A flicker of light and the notification highlights his Level. "He's stayed stuck at Level 50 for the last few years, waiting for the Queen to die. That's gotten him quite a bit of goodwill, since he's 'banking' all that accumulated experience. It'll make him Leveling the King Class much faster than any of his opponents, and that's made quite a few people happy."

I grunt. "What's his problem with us?"

"Well, beyond the obvious fact that you're adding a whole slew of people to the Paladin ranks when he's grown up his entire career without them?" Ali shrugs. "Nothing at all right now. Word is, he's waiting to see what happens. But if he opposes you, or the Paladins, it'll be a mess."

Left unsaid is the fact that if he's got the army's backing, he's probably quite high on the contender list for taking over in a civil war. Potentially the leading applicant. Which means he's got the most to lose.

"Why not the Minister of Defense?" I ask. "To be the leading candidate."

"Way too old. He's even older than the Queen. Also, he's a career military man. The way he built his Skills, he's better off where he is than as the King. If he took over, his effectiveness would drop by a good quarter. No one wants that," Ali says.

"Why would he…" I shake my head, chiding myself. "Never mind. Not everyone wants to be king, right?"

"Exactly, boy-o." Ali smirks. "Next, we've got her."

The new image that shows up is a striking female. Tall, even for the Erethrans and they're normally seven feet tall. Androgynous in her midnight-blue-and-yellow-trimmed uniform. If I remember correctly, that's the uniform of the Admiralty—the space fleets. More striking than her height though is the long, angular nose that dominates her face. It's hard to see anything but the beak.

Julierudi K'nillam, Viscountess of the Purple Sky March, Victor of the Blade of Kalruz, Bane of Leviathans, Slayer of Goblins, Spacejelly, Ismaki,... (Erethran Space Lord Level 23) (H)

HP: 1470/1470

MP: 3420/3420

Conditions: Aura of Space Domination, Command Experience, Dominion of the Stars, Better Training, Empire Security Protocols

"Dominion of the Stars?" I ask.

"Oh, that's an interesting Skill," Ali says, pulling it out for me.

Dominion of the Stars (Level 1)

For the Space Lord, the stars are home. Everything within their domain is theirs to use, whether in enemy territory or without. They control all that they survey and all those within. Friend or foe, all must bow to the supremacy of the Space Lord in their dominion.

Effect 1: All allied ships, fleets, and individuals gain the following increases while within the domain of the Space Lord:

+0.01% Experience Gain within domain

+10% increase in speed and other forms of movement or cost of teleportation Skills

-0.1% decrease in calculated size of domain

+0.1% increase in effect of all Skills

-0.1% decrease in effectiveness of all Skills used by enemy combatants

-10% decrease in speed and other forms of movement or cost of teleportation Skills

-0.1% decrease in effects of all Skills

-0.01% Experience Gain within domain

Effect 2: Above domain effects occur within the presence of the Space Lord.

Effect 1 Range: Variable (dependent on domain and control)

Effect 2 Range: All allied ships within 210.854 billion kilometers radius of the Admiral are under effects of the Skill

"So it's basically a combined buff Skill," I say. It's good if you consider it affects the entirety of the Empire. She basically buffs every allied spaceship and debuffs every enemy ship wandering in. In particular, that movement speed and domain size portion would allow them to reposition faster than would be expected. "Heroic Skills are evil."

"Well, you'll get one some day."

"About that—"

Ali cuts me off. "Nope. Staying on track for this discussion. Viscountess K'nillam is the first in line to inherit the planet Covintah. She's also the leading candidate among the noble legion and the second Space Lord. She'd be first, but politics and age have kept her from taking the Space Lord's place."

"Heroic."

"That she is. It's one of the reasons why the military isn't as enamored. For her to Level as Queen, it'd take a while. In the meantime…"

"The Empire takes a big hit. So why's she got any support?" I say, frowning.

I'm trying to remember the social structure lessons I've consumed, the data about how their society works between the military and the noble classes. If my memory is right, the Erethran nobles are like knights of old, given their place due to service. Unlike Earth history though, their titles can be stripped for lack of service. Along with that, the lands, the planets, and even the industries they're in charge of are only theirs so long as they provide for the Empire. There are minimum targets they must meet, and those who don't—or who step too far out of line—can lose it all. They're not so much nobles in the traditional human sense as contracted merchants and knights.

"They'd rather have one of their own in charge than anyone else," Ali says. "Brerdain's a military man through-and-through. He doesn't come from any of the noble houses, so they'd expect him to oppose their usual grifting and other no-bid contracts. And, if you're wondering, they don't want more Paladins because historically, Paladins have targeted the noble houses for audits and other verifications. After a hundred years…"

"There's going to be a heck of a lot of graft," I say. Of course. Which might be why Brerdain is willing to keep an eye on me rather than act. "Can we expect overt action?"

"Unlikely." Ali shakes his head. "The Queen's made her wishes known. And some of the staunch traditionalists actually want you guys back. Of course, some of them might try to slip in their own kind of Paladin…"

I grunt. Yay. So no guns in the night. Just corruption. At least until I make waves. That doesn't make me feel any better. I gesture with my hand for Ali to keep moving though. Not much I can do about it but keep an eye out.

"Third major party to worry about. Spuryan Chaiwan. Leader of the Reluctant Survivors Church. Or cult, depending on how you look at it," Ali says.

Spuryan Chaiwan, Reluctant Survivors Prophet, the Golden Tongue, Master of the Golden Bell, Master Craftsmen,… (Level 33 Prophet) (M)

HP: 2390/2390

MP: 3480/3480

Conditions: Aura of the Survivors, Aura of the Prophet, Social Vortex, A Little Reasonable Request, Passive Passion

Looking at Spuryan, the way he doesn't dress like a military man, and along with Ali's words, I can't help but confirm, "Not part of the military."

"Not at all."

I eye the shorter-than-normal Erethran as he floats in my notification window. Spuryan is- five feet ten inches, almost a midget by their standards. Maybe it's because of his height, but of the three, he seems the most perfectly coiffed. His horns are embellished, shined, and filled with jewelry. His skin is smooth and well taken care of, his cheeks a bright, blushed red. There's a light, comforting smile on his face, even as the resplendent robed cult leader stands with his arms crossed before him in the image.

"Why's a cult leader upset with me?"

"Oh, not you in particular. The establishment." I make an enquiring hmmm, which gets Ali talking further. "He, and his people, believe that Erethran society has gone too far. That a change is required to one that doesn't expand externally, but instead focuses internally."

"So no more wars?"

"No more wars. More culture. More economic development between solar systems and planets within. And a focus on the Forbidden Zone and taking back planets that have been lost," Ali explains.

I sigh. Tired of sitting, I minimize the images and head over to stand before the window. I stare outside, seeing not the green grass of the flat lawn but a blasted, torn red landscape, a world devoid of everyday life. Until it isn't, and the teeth and fangs of the Forbidden Planet monsters emerge, seeking my throat.

"That's impossible."

"So long as Mana increases," Ali says, shaking his head. "But continually picking up and moving planets isn't exactly healthy either."

Too true. So many planets, so many lives lost because they couldn't afford to leave the solar systems that have fallen into the Forbidden Zone. It's not sustainable, not really. Especially when the new, life-bearing planet numbers keep dropping. When you have to rebuild a new society every few hundred years.

"He and his group are the most likely external threats you will face," Ali says. "They aren't likely to do anything too overt or aggressive, but…"

"But?"

Ali shrugs. "If he or his people can influence you, they will. If they can make the Paladins support their cause, that'd be a win in their views."

I turn away from the window and look back at the Spirit. "That it?"

"Nope. I still got a dozen more. Lesser importance, but we've got others who might want, or think they deserve, a shot, or who might have issues with the initiates. Or you. Including some external organizations, like the Blacklist Asteroid pirates," Ali says.

I sigh, flopping back in my chair and conjuring a big box of chocolate. "Fine. I guess we're doing this then."

Ali grins and I roll my eyes, but I get to listening. And while I do so, I keep an ear out for what he doesn't say. For the threats to my other task, for the real danger that lurks beneath it all. I keep an eye on the information he feeds me, the data downloads, as my mind that's been pushed and expanded by the library tackles the problem head-on.

And I wonder, a small part of me, how far away from human I've come. And how much further I'll go before this is over.

Chapter 7

The next evening, it has taken me an hour or so to track down the Champion. I'd spent the morning and most of the afternoon with the initiates, working through their requests. Funny to think that I found her in the city itself, a good teleport circle away. Those things were keyed to only push authorized people back and forth, hard-line coded so that you couldn't use them to pop out—or in—anywhere but the circles. Good safety procedures, but annoying after spending so long blipping around wherever I wanted.

I wait, leaning against the wall opposite the building the Champion is in. I attract the attention of more than a few passersby. There's even a security guard standing inside the grounds, watching me. I guess the sight of a human lurking before a school building in the middle of a city is all kinds of suspicious. Especially when said alien has his Class hidden.

Still, it's probably better than me wandering into the center of the school and demanding to speak to the Champion while she's busy doing a classroom visit. I mean, I'm an ass, but messing up the kids' treat goes from an ass to just rude.

Even as I ponder the fine line and browse the information streams, a floating car pulls up. Anti-gravity propellers on the bottom allow the vehicle to hover just off the ground as it glides almost soundlessly up to me. From inside the gray-and-black vehicle step two Erethrans, dressed in the same colors, sheathed swords and guns on their hips. A large glinting bracer sits on their off-hands, ready to pop up a moving shield generator when it's needed. Small, circular manacles sit on their belts, distortion equipment to lock me down if necessary.

"Excuse me, sir. We'd like a few words with you," the Erethran closest to me says once he stops a few feet away. Just outside of my reach, but easily within his.

His friend is farther back, flanking him with his hand on his gun while eying Ali, who floats beside me.

Erethran Peace Officer (Level 34) (B)

HP: 690/690

MP: 690/690

Conditions: Aura of Orderly Peace & Stability

As his Aura pings off my resistances, I pull out the notification on the Aura itself.

Aura of Orderly Peace & Stability (B)

A mainstay Skill among Peace Officers the Galaxy over, this Aura is less threatening and increases individuals' suggestibility to commands. It encourages a calm and peaceful interaction, muting anger and other passionate responses.

Effects: +10% increase in chance for command obedience

-10% decrease in hormonal and emotional responses within field

Range: 10m diameter

Cute. Probably a useful thing, considering the amount of stressed and grumpy individuals they deal with. It's a lot less harsh and in your face than a military officer's Aura of Command, and generally makes working in crowd control or just walking down the street easier and more peaceful.

I tilt my head, eying the other officer.

Erethran Peace Speaker (Level 39)

HP: 450/450

MP: 810/810

Conditions: Eye of Truth, Aura of Volubility

His Aura is a good complement to his Skill. The Aura makes you want to talk, while the Eye of Truth verifies if you're telling the truth. Obviously there's the usual issue with "truth"-telling spells, ranging from how they verify truth to what kind of truth it verifies, but I'm going to ignore all that. Add the Aura of Orderly Peace & Stability to the mix, and you end up answering questions without even meaning to. That is, if you can't resist them.

"Sir?" the first officer calls again.

"Sorry, Officer. Boy-o gets distracted," Ali replies for me, floating over and adjusting his angle to be at eye-level. "What can we do for you?"

I eye the street, noticing how the Erethran public is backing off, disappearing. There are notable exceptions. A pair of teenagers glare at me, hands by their sides. As if they're ready to jump in. And an older man, seated down farther from me, sipping on his drink. He pings off as more of a danger—not just his Class and Levels but because of how calm he is. He's a vet or an Adventurer, someone who's seen shit.

"Just a routine check, sir. We've had reports of a suspicious individual lurking before the school," the first officer continues speaking. He has his legs apart, backed off just enough that I have to crank my head up a little to meet those brown eyes of his. There's a polite smile on his lips, but his eyes are cold and passionless.

"Lurking would require me to be using a Skill to hide, no?" I say, then frown. "Unless there's a translation or cultural error." I tap my lips before chopping down sideways. "Doesn't matter. I'm not lurking. I'm standing in full view."

"For what reason?"

"I'm waiting." When my statement is met with frigid silence, I sigh. "For the Champion."

There's a puzzled pause then. They're not concerned I'm going to attack her. That'd be dumb. She's their Champion. The very idea of me being able to beat her is inconceivable to them.

"Are you a uniform chaser?" the Speaker finally asks, his voice doubtful as he eyes me.

"A what?"

"Uniform chaser."

"Repeating doesn't explain anything," I snap.

"Uniform chaser. Someone who's a fan of those in uniform. Sort of like your groupies or puck bunnies," Ali explains.

"Wait. You think I'm here to sleep with Ayuri?" I say, my jaw dropping.

"Sleep with? *No*! How dare you. The Champion would never—" the Officer starts up, getting agitated and angry.

"Carmaz. Stop." A pulse of power originating from the Speaker shuts up his colleague. "Now, what are you doing here?"

"I'm waiting to speak with the Champion. Not sleep with her. Or get her autograph." I pause. "Do you guys do autographs? Or is there something else? A System e-mail? Notification that's specially added? A tattoo? Branding?"

I'm getting weird looks now. Well, weirder. The Officer has calmed himself, but he's also stepped back another half-step as his eyes narrow just above my head. Mana swirls around him as he triggers a Skill, then another one. Then he gestures with one hand while buffing himself. The Speaker's eyes are flicking side-to-side. If I had to guess, she's calling in more help.

"It is a crime to conceal one's Class from a Peace Officer," the Officer says, his voice dropping a notch cooler. He's calmer now that they think I might be a problem. Calmer than some veterans of the apocalypse I've met. I'm impressed.

"Sorry. Didn't realize that. One sec." I touch the ring on my left hand.

As I turn it off, my Status information flickers on again. Ever since I've begun using Daghtree's Legendary Ring of Deception, I've been amused to learn that it has a lower-Level effect that can be triggered without using a charge. It's part of its own ability to conceal its effects, making it look like a simple Ring of Deception. Once willed, the information hiding my Status disappears, leaving it open for anyone to read. Of course, I keep on the secondary effect that hides my true Level.

"Rings of Deception are restricted materials. I will need to see a permit," the Officer says, his eyes locked on my hands, both of which are still clasped in front of me.

"Don't have one, sorry," I say. "Ali, can you make a note on that?"

"What am I? Your secretary?" Ali throws up his hands.

"We're going to need to confiscate the ring then." The Officer isn't even trying to hide his wariness, having pulled his pistol.

I idly eye the weapon, noting it's a Tier II. It'd hurt if I got shot, but it wouldn't do more than annoy me.

"Carmaz," the Speaker says, his voice urgent. Rather than drawing his weapon, his eyes are locked above my head and my newly revealed Status.

"Hand over the ring. Slowly."

"Not happening." I shake my head.

The pistol rises. "I won't ask you again."

The Speaker's voice grows more frenetic. "Carmaz!"

I eye the surroundings idly, noting how the two teens disappeared the moment my Status became visible. On the other hand, the vet has made a giant beam rifle appear. It's sitting across his knees, but I do note that the barrel is pointed in my direction.

"What?" the Officer snaps at his partner.

"Look at his Status!"

Carmaz visibly yanks his gaze upward, resting above my head. His eyes widen then narrow. He looks at me—at my face, at me resting against the wall still—and takes a large step back. The beam pistol doesn't move from my chest though.

"I am arresting you. Failure to reveal Status. Use of class 7 restricted items. Impersonation of government officials," Carmaz recites the words by rote.

"I'm not impersonating anyone. That's my name. And my Class." I tilt my head at the Speaker. "Ask your partner."

"He speaks truth. But that's not possible."

"Put up your hands. I want to see them. We're waiting until prisoner transportation arrives."

I groan, moving my hand up to my face. Ali's trying to say something to calm the man, to deal with the misunderstanding. I even hear Carmaz bark at me to stop rubbing at my face, but I ignore him. Mostly. I do toss up a Soul Shield, not wanting to actually get shot.

"That Skill…"

"I'm adding use of restricted Class Skills to the charges!"

"Look, boy-o really is telling the truth. Just check with your bosses—"

"There are no reports of a new Paladin!"

"Oh, shit. Yeah, maybe Ayuri hasn't let it be known…"

"Put your hands up! You are under arrest."

I'm kind of grateful that they're well trained and not shooting me. Since I'm not doing anything aggressive, they aren't risking getting physical or escalating things. Not without reinforcements. Smart. Because you never know.

Another Skill washes over me, one that attempts to shut down access to my Skills. And I frown. Because that's normally the start of something more...

The pistol that hasn't shifted glows, the finger slips over the trigger. The Peace Officer keeps barking orders about me giving up and lowering my defenses to let them cuff me.

And then, Unilo and Mayaya pop into existence right beside us.

The beam from the pistol hits my Soul Shield, flaring once then dying. Another, more serious attack comes from the vet. It almost drills right through the Shield. I'm impressed. Very much so.

Having fired at me, the Officer is turning, readying himself to deal with the new threats while the Speaker claps his hands together, stilling Mana. Sirens blare above us as the newly arrived prisoner transport with its artillery-sized weaponry deploys out its sides, laser targeting sights locking onto my body. My still-leaning-against-the-wall body.

"Oh, hey, guys!" I greet the Honor Guards with the hand that was rubbing at my face. I don't change my stance or let my body language change, even with the attacks. I do refresh my Soul Shield though, just in case. "About time you arrived."

∗∗∗

"You couldn't have done this a little more discreetly?" Ayuri snaps at me two hours later, the moment she strides back into her office on the palace grounds.

After Mayaya and Unilo settled the police—and added my information to the public database so that this wouldn't happen again—they'd dragged me out of public sight. Even if their society didn't have reporters or paparazzi per se, it didn't mean the gossip network and other word-of-mouth systems of information didn't exist.

"I tried," I protest, throwing up my hands and nearly spilling the drink in my hand. It's a bright, glowing pink and tastes a little like a good mead. Sweet, dry, and with one heck of a kick. It's from Ayuri's personal stock, hidden behind a false wall but not locked.

"Give me that!" She snatches the bottle from my other hand, leaving me with my glass as she pours herself a drink. "And how was announcing your presence on the planet by creating a public incident discreet?"

"I didn't come into the school because I was trying," I grumbled. "I was just waiting around. How was I supposed to know you hadn't told them I was around?"

"You've been watching our broadcasts! Did you see us announce the return of our Paladins?"

"No..."

"Exactly!" Ayuri spits out.

"Oh, come on, you yourself told me that anyone who's anyone knows I'm about. How was I supposed to know that didn't include the police?" I say.

"I meant the powers that be! The Generals, the Space Lord, the Minister of Defense, and the noble houses." Ayuri drains her cup, pours herself another, and growls. "Not the general public. We didn't want them to know."

"Why not?"

"Oh, now you want to be the public face? You want to take on the role of the Paladins properly?" The Champion's lips curl up. "Well. Now that's good to know."

"I didn't..." I flick my gaze over to where Ali is. I can't see the Spirit of course—he's on the other side of the wall, hovering and chatting with the other guards. But I can sense him, talk to him. "*What are the usual things Paladins do?*"

"*What do any unbending, intrepid dreamers do?*" Ali sends back to me, amusement dancing in his voice. "*They go on crusades. Corruption among the nobles, in the military. Fixing injustices in the civilian population. Hunting down criminals who are too entrenched and others refuse to pursue. Righting the wrongs of the world, of course.*"

My lips rise while I reply, "Doesn't sound bad."

"Great. I have a dozen school visits that I need done," Ayuri says, already flicking her fingers at me.

"Uhh..." I shut down the notification without looking at it.

"*Oh, you mean what they do for the populace? PR. Kissing babies. Teaching inspirational speeches. You know. What the Champion was doing.*"

"That isn't going to happen. I might take on a few corrupt noble houses though."

"I might hold you to that," Ayuri says. "But, really. What do you want? You didn't cause a scene like that to say hi. Or steal my kevia."

"Is that what it's called?" I raise the glass, sip on it, and make a mental note to add it to my shopping list. "I need a budget."

"Budget?"

I flick my hand sideways, giving her access to the information the initiates provided me this morning. There'd been some aggressive negotiating, and I'll go over it all once more. But in the end, I'm going to let them choose what they want. Because part of being an adult is making your own choices.

And if there's anything more adult than choosing to pursue a job that no one with any sense wants to do, I can't think of it.

"The initiates aren't going to survive, not as they are now. They need new Skills, new equipment. And that requires a budget," I say. "So. Show me the money."

Of course, Ayuri doesn't react to that. It's not as if it's an Erethran thing. Funnily enough, with so many entertainment options spread across the Galaxy, the idea of memes, of a shared entertainment culture is rather fragmented. Outside of the occasional smash hit, it's Classers—Legendaries and Heroics—who are well known and have a tendency to cross cultural lines.

"A budget…" Ayuri grins and slams back the kevia, emptying her cup. I feel a chill run through me at her smile. "I know just where to send you."

"Uhhhh…"

***

Ayuri is banging on the residential door, one hand holding the bottle and a glass of kevia. It took her less than a minute to get here, abusing her ability to Portal around the planet to end up in this dreary, carpeted hallway. That the light brown floor moves and twitches on its own is a little disturbing, though the low light it gives off is a beautiful thing to behold. Down the hallway with its projected outdoor forest wallpaper is the sole window, showing the twinkling lights of the streets outside.

From what I can tell in my minimap, we're in the middle of a suburban residential neighborhood. A rich neighborhood, with the way the grounds are spaced out. No apartments here, stacking people, one signal on top of another.

"Open up, Saimon. I know you're in there," Ayuri calls.

"You do know this is late at night, right?" I say.

Not that late—the alien planet equivalent of nine in the evening. But late enough. Especially if the two dots being placed right on top of one another when we arrived is anything to go by.

"Go away, Ayuri!" The voice that calls out is rather short of breath. And a little muffled. It's somewhat high-pitched, but not feminine necessarily. Or at least, not what I'd consider feminine for the Erethrans.

"No. Come out, Saimon."

"He's busy, Champion." Another voice, quite deep and not at all amused.

"Oh, you're there too, Lord Braxton?" Ayuri's grin widens. "Perfect. Now, come out or I'll come in. Ten seconds."

"You wouldn't dare!" Saimon shouts. But I hear scrambling from within.

"She would. You know she would," Lord Braxton mutters. If not for my enhanced Perception, there'd be no way for me to hear him. Then again, he probably knows that. "Ever since you broke up with her, she's been on the warpath."

I raise an eyebrow at Ayuri, who crosses her arms.

"It's not like that," she says.

"Uh huh."

"Ten!" Ayuri counts down, even if the count is only, like, four or five. She slaps her hand on the access panel, not that she needs to activate it. But I get the feeling she's doing it because she wants to. "Here I come."

The first sight to greet me is a tall, slim figure. I catch sight of small breasts on a muscular torso being covered by the closing touch-zip of a jumpsuit. As my eyes track upward, they meet pursed, full lips and green eyes. Shoulder-length hair frames delicate cheekbones, but there's a masculine jut to the jaw and in the sweep of coral ears. I blink, thrown off by the conflicting information.

Saimon Calicus, Seeker of Truth, Ten Thousand Audits, Golden Reviewer, Slayer of Goblins (Forensic Accountant Level 41) (M)

HP: 980/980

MP: 2780/2780

Conditions: Forensic View, Auditors Authority, Eyes of the Scales

"Why are you bothering me, Yuri?" Saimon snaps, smoothing out the lay of his jumpsuit, his voice the more feminine one.

"Oh, I'm sorry. Did I interrupt you? Maybe sleeping with another husband?" Ayuri retorts. "And don't call me that. You don't get to anymore."

Lord Braxton is lounging, one slim, toned, hairless leg thrown outside of the cream blankets. The other leg—and other important bits—is covered by the silk sheet. His chest is bare—hairless, as well, but toned in the way an office worker who hits the gym once in a while might look. Not a pure fighter then, at least not by his physique. His Status confirms it too.

Lord Leral Braxton, Baron of Unsqe, Houndmaster, Royal Aide,...
(Galactic Steward Level 38) (M)

HP: 860/860

MP: 1520/1520

Conditions: Bestial Instincts, Strength of the Pack, Distributed Pain, Enhanced Senses, On the Hunt, Engorged

"My partners are more than aware of Saimon," Lord Braxton says with a low drawl. "In fact, we're discussing adding him to our triad."

"Well, isn't that nice of you. Doing it the right way." Ayuri's voice drips venom as she glares at Saimon.

I listen at first, then try to trigger a Blink Step. It fails, of course, but the swirl of Mana around me is enough to draw the attention of all three. Even the pain of the failed Blink Step is less than that of listening to the lovers' tiff.

"Don't you dare move, Paladin," Ayuri snaps. "You're the reason I'm here."

"I'm pretty sure it's your hurt feelings that brought us here, dear," Ali offers helpfully. He's floated into the room, idly eying the occupants and the furnishings. More the half-dressed Braxton than the furnishings. "But don't worry, we aren't holding it against you. Not that boy-o here knows how to handle his relationships any better."

"You wanted finances. And Saimon here is the Minister of Finance." Ayuri waves at the man/woman/herm/another alien or System combination that might make my head hurt. "If you need a budget, Paladin, you'll need to talk to him. And since Lord Braxton is here, he can take over dealing with you."

"I'd prefer—" I begin.

"I don't care. I'm the Champion of the Erethran Empire, not your personal servant. If you have questions, you can talk to these two. I've got better things to do."

"Like visiting schools and bothering your ex?" Ali says.

Ayuri punches out with a fist, dismissing the Spirit with a push of power. It's such a smooth execution of energy that Ali goes pop without me even being able to do anything. Then, before I can bitch about it, she disappears, Blink Stepping away.

"Uhh…" I scratch my head, looking at the empty spot then at the pair of bemused lovers. "So. That happened."

***

"Thank you." I sip on the Galactic equivalent of coffee, rotating the drink in my hand. Unfortunately, unlike real coffee, this drink is more sour and bitter than dark and smooth.

Still, production of coffee in the strength required to affect Adventurers is lagging behind. Earth has more important things to do, and even the few producers there are have only managed to get their beans to affect those in the low hundreds of Constitution. That doesn't even include my own Resistance to poisons. Basically, it'll be years, if not decades, before I can actually enjoy coffee for its effects again. Though I still keep a couple of bags around for the taste.

"So. You and the Champion." I raise a single eyebrow, doing my best not to smirk. "You're a lot braver than I am."

"We were cadets together, many years ago. We've been on and off since then," Saimon says before he shrugs. "I wanted something a little more permanent. She didn't. But when I started seeing others, she objected. Said I was betraying her."

Society's Web tells me there's more to this discussion. More to the twisted thread between it and Ayuri, glistening brown and red. There's another thread, this one golden and red, that leads between him and Lord Braxton. And Braxton himself has more of those golden-red threads—two others. I know what those mean, love and passion, twisted with expectation. But

Braxton has others, brown-gray, knotted with ties that lead to him, dozens of them. Duties, obligations, loyalty—almost all one-sided. A touch of my mind, and I know they're for his hounds. It doesn't take much more than a question to Ali to clarify what they are. Not actual animals – not anymore – but spies, saboteurs and assassins.

I debate asking more but decide I really don't need to know the interpersonal drama among the individuals in the Erethran government. I'm here for another reason entirely.

"Credits," I say. "Was she lying?"

"No. In fact, I'm probably the best person to discuss this with. As you know, the Paladins have been a foundational pillar of the Empire for many years. Because of that, they've had a large budget assigned to the institution and upkeep of their services." Saimon pauses, visibly thinking about what he wants to say next.

Lord Braxton leans forward, his own cup kept warm in his hands. Behind him, the bedroom that we haven't left is displayed, hints of their dalliance still visible and fragrant. I'd have preferred to have moved to someplace less intimate, but they haven't suggested a move. I'm not sure if it's an Erethran thing or just a damn the Champion thing.

"What Saimon is trying, and failing, to say is that your budget is currently being used by others," Lord Braxton says.

"Others?" I'm getting a dreadful feeling here, one that says that Ayuri's sudden actions might have more to do with these "others" than wanting to get back at her ex-lover.

"You must understand, even if the budget set aside for aiding the Paladins was not significant compared to the military budget, it was still a massive amount in totality. After a decade, it was decided that we could do better things with the funds than letting them collect untouched." Saimon's fingers run around the cup as it thinks. "In the end, a directive was passed and the budget was allocated to a variety of other individuals."

"And now? Now that I'm back? Now that the Paladins are returning?"

"Many will not be happy. There are corporations and planets that rely on the additional budget to stay afloat," Lord Braxton says. "The trading to determine where the budget goes every year is a major mainstay of the current political climate."

"Great." I shake my head, discarding the idea that I really want to get involved in that. Instead… "Look. I really don't care. I just want you guys to find me enough funds to pay for the initiates' Skills and equipment."

I send them the documentation, the long list of Skills and the Credits that we require. I might have tacked on a few more Credits for myself, just because. But not a lot.

Their reaction is quite interesting, for they skim through everything, looking not so much at the individual Skill information or equipment requests, but instead the Credit amount at the end.

"Is that it?" Saimon says.

"For now. I'd prefer to have access to a lot more than that, especially as I expect we'll be fine-tuning some of these requests as we go along," I say.

I know asking for tens of millions of credits is a bit much. But they're also asking me to raise a bunch of Paladin initiates. Without the right Skill sets, without the right training, they'll probably just die. I expect they'd rather we get this right than waste my time and their lives.

"Oh, it's not that," Saimon says. He glances at Lord Braxton, who chuckles as well. They gesture at the final amount. "This is actually significantly less than we expected. I could free up that much from the Queen's petty cash easily. Returning the funds to there would be a little more difficult, but not impossible. In fact, we should still have the majority of this amount in the revolving discretionary account."

I blink at the pair of administrators. And then I realize, once again, how big the difference is between a single individual like me and the Empire. Even if I'd thought I'd adjusted my idea of what was considered a "high" amount, I obviously hadn't adjusted it enough. They might not have the strength of an individual Legendary, but when you have millions and millions of people contributing to your tax base, tens of millions of Credits is nothing.

"Well, once you release the discretionary funds, start working on getting back the rest of the budget. In the meantime, make sure my people get trained. That means real trainers with the right Skills." I grimace as a thought strikes. "Once they start buying Master Class Skills, I expect that the expenses will increase again."

"Of course, of course." Lord Braxton waves his hands sideways. "In the meantime, if you're looking for specific equipment that you need to purchase, I ask that you send the requests to me beforehand. I already see a number of requests in here that I can replace with similar and cheaper, or similar and better, equipment. Through our mercantile contacts, that is."

"Fair enough."

We'd gotten the quotes from the Shop itself, knowing that that would likely be the most expensive manner of getting what we need. If they can find ways of cutting corners without cutting quality, I have no objections. We'll need our budget in as best a state that it can be, for once they do become real Paladins, the System will allow them to purchase Master Class Skills. Still...

"Why do the Paladins need so many funds?"

"For much of the time during their presence, many of the Credits used by the Paladins were for bribes, restitution, and replacement costs for things destroyed. Unfortunately, our Paladins were well known for their disregard for property and individuals in the pursuit of justice," Saimon says, his lips turning down slightly. "In addition, the bureaucracy required to deal with the fallout was significant. Especially when some of our Paladins journeyed to other empires and kingdoms."

I grunted. It's one thing for me to play Bounty Hunter and kill bad people on other planets or kingdoms. Anyone I annoyed could track me down, but they didn't really have a lot they could do other than killing me or placing a secondary bounty on my head. On the other hand, when you're representing an entire Empire, the Empire can't really run away from responsibility as much. I'm kind of glad that a bureaucracy has grown up to deal with the fallout, leaving the Paladins to do what I do best.

"Good to know. Who do I talk to about beginning to staff the Paladin's bureacracy again?"

"Do you expect to need such help soon?" Lord Braxton looks a bit worried.

"Not yet. I'm planning for the future. No point getting my initiates trained up as Paladins and leaving them without backup. I expect it'll take a while to find the right people. Best to get started soon."

Lord Braxton and Saimon share a relieved look before Braxton adds, "Well, it's nice to work with someone who's thinking ahead. We'll need at least a few months."

"And the funds?"

"I will get her Majesty's approval tomorrow and you should have access soon after. The rest of it…" Saimon hesitates then shrugs. "That might take longer."

"Just get it done." I down the last of their drink and stand, nodding to them both. "I look forward to hearing from you."

"One thing," Lord Braxton speaks up, his gaze focused on me. Even seated, they aren't much shorter than I am. Almost reminds me of the decades I spent being the short guy in Canada. "Will you be open to meeting those who might be affected?" When I frown, he hastily adds, "You are asking for a change to a System that has worked for decades. Surely you can spare a few minutes to talk to those affected."

Suspicion gnaws at my instincts and my eyes narrow. "And who might those be?"

"Members of the noble houses. A few Guild leaders. Corporate tycoons." When I continue to frown, he adds, "Viscountess Purple March."

"Ahhh…" I breathe the word and almost decide to turn him down. But then I remember my real job. The choice I'll have to make. And I realize at some point, I'll have to meet her. "Fine. Set it up."

I get a relieved smile from Lord Braxton, but the primal, sensuous image I had has crumbled, disappeared under the cold dash of reality. No one, not at this level, is just one thing. They're all political animals of some stripe. And it seems I've found where one of the alliances lie.

After that, it's just a few more kind words before the pair shows me out. And then, the very long wait for an automated vehicle to bring me back to the palace. Annoying, but it does give me time to think. I'm not sure if Ayuri really meant to drop me off with them to annoy her ex-lover or if she's playing a deeper game. I get the feeling there's little bit of both in there. A way for her to introduce me to the players without being too upfront. But setting up the Paladins is slowly looking more and more complex.

At least I should be able to pick up a few new toys though.

Chapter 8

The floating aircar I rest within is both more and less wondrous than I could ever imagine. It floats soundlessly, cutting through the atmosphere at hundreds of kilometers a second, the G forces entirely canceled out by anti-gravity tech. At the same time, the insides are no different than any car I've been in. Indulgent, soft-as-a-cloud seats, arm, and leg rests add to the luxury, but it's still a car interior. There's no steering wheel and even fewer controls for the vehicle itself. Most of the vehicle's operation is done by the AI traffic control system and the backup, semi-sentient AI within the car itself.

I sit in silence for a time, watching the ground pass by. Twinkling lights for buildings and individuals, the occasional flare of magic and beam weaponry opening fire on the monsters that press against the edges of civilization. Not many individual flying armor suits at this time of night, all the good citizens of the Empire tucked away in bed. Even so, the push against the monsters is ongoing.

The planet of Pauhiri might not be a Dungeon World, but it lies quite a distance away from the Galactic edge, relatively close to the Forbidden Zone. And because of that, the overflow of Mana has seen the increased birth of monsters. They pop into existence constantly outside the Safe Zones, at the edges of the cities and emplaced positions, ready to attack, to kill and Level. And they're just as quickly dealt with by the citizens of the Empire, ensuring the civilians of Pauhiri are safe.

Except...

It's a bad idea. A bad plan. As history, as false memory tells me all too easily.

... has shown that the creation of natural dungeons are an important Mana-cleansing method of the System. The birth of dungeons and the monsters within them allow a

higher flow-through of ambient Mana, such that the System is able to catalogue, cleanse, and divert the Mana to low ambient Mana environments.

Based upon these findings, it is recommended that monsters—in particular, Alpha monsters—be allowed to be birthed in non-Dungeon Worlds and, furthermore, be cultivated to higher Levels before their deaths. Their development will lower the environmental Mana amounts in the region (see charts 128.3, 128.4 and statistic tables in appendix 128 for further detail), increasing System-planet viability timelines.

It is further hypothesized that the abandonment of planets near the Forbidden Zone at the earliest period will see a decrease in viability period of neighboring planets. (See the Ofelia and Ums Cases by Hed & Zaritskaya). Initial indications are that the outflow from the Forbidden Zone has seen a decreased timeline for System planet viability.

I shudder, shoving aside the memory of the academic study. It's not the only one, not the only document, video, and memory recording that tries to take over my mind. Graphs, tables of recorded data, speaking heads in pale blue labs. All of it flowing through my mind in a blip and leaving me reeling.

And, as always, another tick upward in my System Quest experience. Another hole filled in. But still, I grasp at the edges. Even as some things, some questions are answered.

I push aside the thoughts and finally, finally call forth the only person I can talk to. At least, to some extent. It requires some Mana, an effort of will against reality's barrier. And then, the olive-skinned Spirit reappears.

"Ali."

"About time. What took you so long?" the Spirit grumps at me.

I shrug. There is really no reason. Other than a desire to be alone. And that's hard enough to get sometimes.

"Whatever. Where are we going?" Ali says, when I offer him no explanation.

"Home." Or the closest thing to home right now. Better to say the place I'm putting my head down, but semantics. "Why?"

"Because we're not." Ali waves and a map appears. Much bigger, taking in all the city. A flicker in the top right highlights the palace. Another blinking dot on the bottom left shows my location, and a dotted line shows our flight path. Away from the Palace.

"Crap." I wasn't paying attention. Not thinking I was in danger. Not thinking anyone would take action on the capital planet. But here I am, flying to an unknown location. I buff myself while I consider my options.

Destroy the aircar? Possible, but it'd throw me out into the middle of nowhere. Which might be what they're looking for. I don't know what the repercussions of destroying an aircar in the capital city might be. And while I have some protection as a Paladin, it's all theoretical.

"Call for help." Probably blocked but worth a try.

"On it," Ali says, his eyes going blank.

I could stay here and wait. But tough as I am, whoever is taking action probably knows all about me and what I can do. Walking into an ambush is a bad idea, no matter what I tell the initiates.

"I'm blocked," Ali says moments later.

That's it. I raise my foot, ready to stomp down, and am halted by a new voice.

"Paladin. Our apologies for the interruption. There is no need for violence." The voice blaring out of the aircar's speakers is rough, as if they've been smoking a couple of packs a day for the last couple of decades.

"Pretty sure there is." But I put my foot down. I can still break the car with a thought, but I'm willing to wait. *"Keep an eye out for threats, will you?"*

"Teach a Goblin how to populate a planet, why don't you?"

"The Prophet just wants to speak with you," the voice comes again, just a touch of pleading in it. "We promise you, we offer you no harm."

"Then open up communication channels. Three seconds, or else I make my way out of this vehicle." I'm curious, especially when they mention the Prophet, but I want more than a verbal assurance.

"Done."

"Let Mikito and Bolo know. Keep them updated on our location," I send to Ali. At the same time, I reach within and pop out Hod's Armor, placing my hand over the box and letting it begin the process of armoring me. I hear a slight squeak from the voice, but I never promised to come unarmed.

"Well... you'll be here in a few minutes. Please, remember we are just here to speak with you," the voice says a little breathlessly.

I smile grimly, leaving the helmet unformed. Activating it, covering myself would take only a second. Might be too long, but I figure that between Sanctum and my Soul Shield, I should be fine. And if not, I'm sure Mikito will bring fire and flame down on them in revenge. Never mind Ayuri.

Killing me now that my friends know what's going on seems much less likely.

"They've confirmed receipt. Bolo's cursing up a storm about getting woken up. And Harry wants to know if he can ride along in the armor's recording features."

"Go for it. He might see something I don't."

"I want to know if we're telling the Champion."

I consider then shake my head slightly. Even if she would be good backup, running to her for every little problem is getting old. Her sending me to Saimon and Lord Braxton was a pretty clear indication that she expects me to take care of things myself to some extent. And while political maneuvering in a place I don't know might be a little much, violence is something I do know.

Very, very well.

"Understood." I glance at Ali, at our projected course, then flick my hands at him. *"Go ahead. Get me the lay of the land, will you?"*

Ali nods and disappears from normal visual view, floating through the car and zooming ahead. As he does so, I feel him reaching into my inventory, pulling out drones, and dropping them behind in our flight path. Setting up fallback positions for when things go wrong.

Paranoid?

Me?

Not at all.

***

The aircar drops to the ground, floating to a stop in the middle of a courtyard complex. Multi-story-high buildings float around us, each decorated with gold effigies and sculptures of the various alien races that make up the Empire. I say float, because the ground floor is bare, the entire complex held aloft by anti-gravity mods. Walkways, glowing with power and contained by force shields, lead between the building complexes in an intricate cat's cradle, leaving me to eye the numerous sniping points distrustfully as I step out of the vehicle. The aircar drops the rest of the way with a slight thump, turning itself off and stranding me.

More important than the lack of transportation are the individuals awaiting my arrival. A half dozen robed and dressed Erethrans, all of them flanking a rather recognizable figure. Spuryan Chaiwan, the Prophet of the cult or religion. Or philosophical party. I'm not sure which is more appropriate. Or, truthfully, what the difference is at times.

Spuryan looks similar to the image I've seen. Coral ears embellished, shiny and filled with jewelry. Smooth skin, robes that gleam yellow and gold, enchantments twisting the Mana around him. After all this time, I've learned to read the way enchantments affect the Mana flow around them, the way they twist and shift depending on their guided uses. These are defensive enchantments, movement boosters, and a few shields for the most part. Just ways of letting him escape potential sticky situations.

Does it make me a bad person that I'm already charting out the Skill uses I need to stop him? When he's offered no violence?

"Paladin," Spuryan says, walking forward to greet me.

A trio of his people follow, each of them sternly daring me with their gazes to try something. Worse than their baleful regard is that they're Combat Classers. One's got a civilian offshoot of the Erethran Honor Guard bodyguard build. The other two are pure smash-and-grabbers. Further back, even more attendants hang by and watch, the attendants a wide range of races though, as always, the Erethrans dominate.

"Thank you for being willing to speak with me," he adds.

"Didn't really get a chance to say no, did I?" They keep coming, closing the distance, and I hold up my hand when they're about five feet away. "That's close enough."

I see a flash of irritation on Spuryan's face, even as my resistances ping. I grunt, feeling his Auras press down on me. It's not that powerful, not like the Queen's. But it's noticeable. And unique, in the ability to wrap two Auras around one another.

"Certainly. We wouldn't want you to be uncomfortable. We are here just to speak," Spuryan says, then tilts his head from side to side. "I do wonder— where is your Companion? The redoubtable Spirit."

"Ali's out scouting," I say, telling him the truth. It's not as if they couldn't figure out that one themselves. Not with the ever-increasing amount of automated drones and linked firepower showing up.

"Such precautions aren't necessary."

"Well, tough. If you didn't want me to do that, you should have tried calling and asking first."

"We would, but we're not exactly..." Spuryan seems to search for the word. "In favor. There were concerns that our requests would be blocked."

I can see how that'd happen, but it's a lie too. Because they could have sent it via the Shop and broken through any blocks with enough Credits or Mana. No, they wanted to have this conversation out here, in their place of power. To throw me off just a little. Or maybe just to get in the first word before the others have a chance to pitch themselves. I wonder how much analysis they've done of how I'd react.

My silence seems to embolden them, for Spuryan continues. "We wanted you to see a part of us, the reality of the Reluctant Survivors and not the lies that they tell you."

I almost want to point out that I've yet to hear of them from others but decide against it. Better to stay silent and keep him speaking. To see where the lies lie.

"We are no cult, no subversive organization. What we want is the best for our society, for our people. Unmitigated expansion, the wars that we fight, those only bring blood and tears. The loss of our people. Unending war with other sapients is not the only way to Level." The words flow with well-rehearsed cadence, the phrases resounding with passionate conviction.

He sounds like a television evangelist or an auctioneer, so rehearsed with his words that he can brush past your initial objections and assault your better senses before you know it.

Each word, each sentence comes with a flash of a notification, the thrill and a jolt of pleasure as his Skill cuts through my defenses partially, dropping serotonin direct into my body.

"I'm not going to argue with the idea that war is bad, but it seems to me saying it and changing an entire Empire are two different things. Sort of like teaching people to eat less," I say.

My last sentence gets a bunch of puzzled looks. System-enabled worlds have much less of an issue with obesity, since most high-Level individuals burn more calories than they can hope to intake. Without Mana boosting their bodies, they'd wither and die. It's why Technocrats who leave System-enhanced space are often extremely low-Leveled, or have attributes dedicated to non-physical stats.

"There is much to do, for certain. Changing an entire culture is not simple. But we can do it if we all work together," Spuryan says, waving his arms to encompass the buildings. "Look. Look at your map. See how many have already chosen another life, another way of living that does not require blood to be spilt endlessly. And these are but a small portion of those who believe in us, in our cause. We need only a chance, an opportunity to allow those who dare not speak up to do so. To enforce the change that we need."

"Interesting choice of words." I look up, eying the hundreds of dots that make up the compound. I wonder how many of them have guns pointed at me. How many of them are here by choice. "But that's a pretty good pitch. Does leave the question, how do you expect to Level up otherwise?"

"Internal development. Increased investment for city dungeons, exploration of the Forbidden Zones. Additional exploitation of the Dungeon

Worlds. And the development of new Dungeon Worlds—uninhabited of course," Spuryan details his plans with ease.

"I thought you couldn't do Dungeon Worlds without inhabitants?"

"Incorrect. It is more difficult, since the System needs a sufficient number of sentient personnel to provide the linchpin for its start. It is possible however, with the right seed population inserted beforehand," Spuryan says.

"Seed pop—"

I don't get any further. Tests. So many tests. I see the way they've tried to do it beforehand, the various methods the Galactics have tried. Tests by the Questors, by the Galactic Council, by kingdoms and other groups on the down-low. All trying to find ways to make more Dungeon Worlds, to gain access to the resources a Dungeon World creates and slow down the progress of the Forbidden Zone. Ways to skirt around the System, around the Galactic Council, around the notice of their enemies.

Tests. Not a dozen, not a hundred, but thousands. Spread over the course of the entire life of the System, from when it first began to now.

Tests. And deaths, failures, the way the System reacts—badly—to manipulation.

I watch worlds burn, intelligent beings warp. I read the reports of how once-sapient creatures become twisted, distorted nightmare versions of themselves. Lycanthropes, shifters, chimera... even more unspeakable monsters, like the Galactic equivalent of the wendigo.

"Paladin?" Spuryan says, as races scream and the System strips scientists of their Classes, offering them new ones in my mind's eye.

I've seen myself a couple of times when the information comes crashing in. Having a friend like Ali means that I get to see recordings of my most humiliating moments all too often. On occasion, when he thinks I'm getting too big for myself, he'll pop up a window of his "Boy-o highlights."

When the data unfolds, when my mind is taken over, my face twitches, my eyes flicker and go dark, and during the worse times, I might even get a nosebleed. Once, my eyes themselves bled. Even if the entire download, the data unfolding takes only a few seconds, the process of analysis, of understanding might last longer. And it is disconcerting to come back to myself, to the physical world of aliens and pain, after leaving a mental one of pain and twisted studies.

"And you think you know the right numbers?" I say, ignoring the puzzled looks, the question to ask my own.

"We are not certain, not yet. But there are a large number of volunteers within my apostate who would be willing to go. For the greater good. We will learn the correct numbers."

He's given the wrong answer, acting as if I wouldn't know the truth of it all. No surprise. I don't think there's anyone in this world—other than maybe a few top-level Questors—who understands what he's really suggesting.

After all, there have been successful attempts. Two, to be exact.

The first lasted all of four thousand years before the Mana Density grew too great and the planet was lost. The other lasted for a year before the System stopped flooding the world with Mana. Now the planet lies vacant, a perverted and rotten parody of a Dungeon World. Too much Mana within it to be a normal, residential planet. Too few resources and too much unsynchronized, uninitiated Mana to be a Dungeon World.

In the end, Mana is all around us. It's what makes the System work. But it's also what makes the System break down. Because there are two types of Mana, in a way. The unmarked, unaspected, uninitiated Mana that has never gone through the System. And the Mana that has passed through it, whether through sapient creatures or monsters. Mana that is marked, encoded, and thus useful to the System.

Understanding that little bit, understanding the differences in Mana gave me a huge jump in my System Quest. The realization that the Mana available in the city, that can be used to make a city a Safe Zone, the controls put in place all come from the sapient members of a city and the monsters slain is important. Everything the System does, it can only do because of this marked Mana. Unfortunately, this marked Mana slowly degrades, becoming unaspected and unSystemized after a period of time. Worse, monsters only mark Mana after a while, as they Level, and it only releases when they die. So there's a balance to be struck between murdering them and letting them grow. And, like the Forbidden Worlds, there's always more unmarked Mana arriving.

That's why we have Forbidden Worlds. Because at a certain point, we aren't able to handle the flow of Mana anymore. Even the System's last-minute controls, the explosion of monsters that precede the start of the loss of a world isn't enough.

In the end, the System is a means of control for Mana. That, I am certain of now. But who made it, how they made it, why they made it? And, perhaps just as important, where all this Mana is coming from and what it is? Those are still unknown.

"*Boy-o! Stop drifting off,*" Ali calls.

Unfortunately, ever since Feh'ral dumped the library in my head, this has been happening more and more. I don't know if it's my mind compensating for the information or the fact that I feel—I *know*—that I'm so close to the answer.

"My apologies. Just thinking about your answer. If you want me to believe you, then I have a request." I offer Spuryan a smile, curious to see if he bites. I let my gaze track upward, checking out the glowing walkways that hang above me, the lit-up buildings around us. Looking for attackers.

"Of course, anything you want." Spuryan glances backward to where his bodyguards stand and pauses. "At least, if my bodyguards allow it. You understand, of course."

"I doubt they'll worry about this. You can leave." I smile wider, flicking my gaze to the three guards. "Because the person I want to speak with isn't you. As you said, you've got hundreds of people here. Let me speak with them."

"About?" Spuryan looks puzzled but not worried. I wouldn't be either. I'm assuming the people here are the most committed of his cult.

"About you. About your beliefs and what you intend for us all. Let me talk to them, let me see how it works in reality."

"It will be poor example, when we are forced to live as we are, forced to adjust our vision to the society that hates us." Spuryan says, already making excuses. "But if you wish it."

"I do."

Spuryan nods, gesturing not behind him, not at his bodyguards, but at a couple of others in attendance. They walk forward, crossing the grounds to stop a short distance away from me, closer even than Spuryan himself. I let them come, figuring they'll be my guides. The pair are a male and female, one an Erethran, the other a female Yerrick of shorter stature.

"I could come with you, if you wish. You are a somewhat intimidating presence," Spuryan says.

"Don't bother. You can go. I'll even make my own way home." I flash the cult leader a grin, gesturing at the pair of attendants. "They will more than do."

When Spuryan opens his mouth to speak, I dismiss him by turning on my heels and walking toward the nearest floating entry chute to the buildings that surround us. I watch through Ali's eyes as Spuryan's face twitches in annoyance before he gestures for the attendants to follow me.

Yeah, turning my back on the cult leader was a bad idea. But if there's one thing I've learned, it's when passions are high, when people are angry, that's when you find out who they really are. Not the face they show you, the mask we all wear to get by in our daily lives, but who we really are. The lines that we draw, the things that anger us, they tell more about who and what we believe in than any kind words or mealy-mouthed social talk could ever do.

What we will fight for is the truest guide of the inner self there is.

***

One of the first things I noticed about this residence / manufacturing hub / Artisan Center and religious building is that it's just as decorated on the inside as the outside. Pictures, moving video wallpapers, and statues abound, even in the hallways that lead to the individual rooms. They all depict Spuryan's utopian society where races—Erethrans, Yerrick, Grimsar, and more—Combat Classers, and Artisans work together in blissful, brightly colored harmony. Happy, content, beaming faces stare back from the glowing paint and holographic images. All strangely content—even the ones battling the monsters on the outskirts of the sprawling, green-and-purple cities.

Getting the floor plans for the building from my attendants is simple enough. Comparing it to the floor plan that Ali has managed to acquire shows that they aren't hiding anything. No hidden floors or secret rooms where they build plagues or bombs. At least not in the first couple of floors we check out.

The bottom floors are all social locations. Living rooms, social loungers, large kitchens in cafeterias dominate the layout, with the addition of a few land-based garages for vehicles that run on the ground. There are even some training rooms, for those violently inclined. Above the social floors are workshops, individualized and equipped for various professions. Surprisingly, many of those workshops aren't empty, even at this time of night.

"And you've been working for them for how long?" I asked the elderly Erethran Artisan whose workshop we've invaded.

The workshop is barebones, all nanoformed steel tables and workbenches and covered cupboards. They're all protected, built to withstand the occasional catastrophic failure. Each workshop is roughly ten by ten—good enough for a single worker, but not much more. It's also relatively neat, since storing movable equipment in one's inventory ensures it doesn't get destroyed.

The Artisan was working on a drone, putting it together from the ground up. Using materials crafted in other nearby workshops, melding them together with blueprints. There's a degree of specialization involved, but not as much as you'd think. If a person can make a computer chip, they can just as easily make it for large drone vehicles or planetary destroyers. The Skills transfer over, especially when you can download the knowledge and blueprints from the System with enough Credits.

"Eleven passages of the planet nights now, your justice." The artisan refuses to meet my eyes, mumbling his answers. He's not the first I've spoken to, all of them happy enough to talk, but offering little divergent information.

"You like working here?"

"I build drones, your justice." He gestures to the drone he was building. "Civilian market, delivery drones. It's good work."

That too is normal. Nearly all the Artisan work goes to the civilian market, with a small number going directly to the Reluctant Survivors' own monster hunting team. They try to extract themselves from the military industrial complex as much as possible. Or at least, that's what they're telling me.

"Ali, do we have stats to show they're telling the truth?"

"How the hell would I know? I can look it up later…"

"Do so."

"That's great," I say. "You find it rewarding?" I get a nod for that. I try again. "You have family? Someone you care about in the complex?"

"Yes, your justice. Two wives and six spawn." For the first time, a trace of pride.

"And how do they like living here?"

"Well enough. We have food, shelter, safety from the monsters. My spawn enjoy playing with the other children. It's a good community, though there's not enough purple."

I frown at the last, trying to figure out if it means anything. A flicker in my mind as data downloaded comes to the rescue. Cultural saying, mostly to deal with the color of the greenery. As our version of green, their desire for more forests and open areas. I keep trying to get him to relax and just chat but give up after a few minutes and move on as the Artisan grows increasingly uncomfortable.

My high Charisma stat might be useful for intimidating and scaring people, for forcing my Aura on others. But it's not as useful for being the sociable huckster. That just isn't me, and the System seems to agree, having grown my attribute in other ways. In the end, I give up and move on.

It doesn't matter where I go, how deep I head into the residence, knocking on doors and chatting with people. I get deference, smiles, and polite invitations in to chat, even from those who wake up grumpy. Fear, hidden within courtesy. Uncertainty, the same kind you get when speaking to a police officer back on Earth. I get nowhere, not talking to them at least.

Not directly.

But I persist.

For I have other Skills. Eye of Insight is always on, alerting me when someone is actively using Skills to lie to me. Purchased knowledge about body language and my higher Perception allow me to pick out mundane cues for when people are lying or just shading the truth on a mundane level. Most aren't lying. No more than normal people do. Mostly around questions like, are you happy?, do you like it here?, and the like. For most people, there's always a level of uncertainty, of concern and doubt when asked a question like that. Most people have that niggling sense of doubt that comes from living an unfulfilled life. Of believing that it could be better.

Sapient creatures just aren't very good at being happy.

More useful is Society's Web. I watch the lines radiating from people, how they twist and thrum as they speak. How they connect and interconnect between individuals within the building. At first, I follow lines, verifying the information I get. Following up with questions on different groups that lie throughout the entire complex. Then I start veering away, finding different clusters, different social groups. All to corroborate the picture I'm developing.

Have to admit, I'm rather impressed. When the attendants shoot me a questioning looks, I realize I've spoken that out loud. I give them a smile and don't elaborate.

It's been nearly four hours of walking back and forth, bothering people in the middle of the night. Eventually, I walk out the complex, waving goodbye to the attendants and dismissing them. Not that they leave, watching my departing back as I walk toward the city. I start composing a note to Saimon to get my Portal pass approved. All the while, I'm waiting for the public aircar I've called to arrive.

I stay silent, keeping my thoughts to myself until I'm picked up. I even stay silent when Ali returns from picking up all our toys. We stay silent, floating through the air, until we make it back to our residence. That's where Mikito and Bolo are waiting, no longer at the ready for potential trouble, but too high-strung to go back to sleep. Instead, they're training against one another, playing at violence.

I watch for a few minutes, marveling at how Mikito pushes aside Bolo's huge hammer, deflecting rather than blocking, using her greater speed and precision. She's gotten better, much better, even in the few weeks that we've known him. If my Intelligence increases have been to handle Mana and create vector pathways, to deal with information flow better and to handle the insanity of war, hers seems to have been focused on her skills. She improves her martial skills at a rate that is staggering.

I sometimes wonder if it's a conscious choice.

Studies from the library indicate that there is a little bit of conscious variation in our development of attributes. But just as much, there's an unknown factor, the System's influence, that even multiple and exhaustive tests have yet to uncover. Oh, there are hypotheses—but none of them have been definitive. There's no rhyme or reason why an accountant can suddenly play musical instruments, find perfect pitch in a song while increasing his attributes. Or why a Combat Classer can do high-level mathematical formulas, complex equations involving six-dimensional math without touching a calculator. There are hypotheses that in those cases, the System isn't building the capacity for us, but for itself.

Though why it needs the capacity, why a sapient can pick out the addition of a flake of salt from a spoonful of soup is a question no one has an answer to.

The pair notice my presence soon enough, pausing in their play. And it is play, for they aren't using their Skills. At least, not any active ones. Breathing just a little hard, they stroll over to me, weapons over their shoulders, almost mimicking one another. It makes me smile. Harry, seated inside the building, comes out as well, obviously not interested in watching them. I'm sure he's got more than enough footage of them.

"How'd it go?" Bolo says. "We need to lay down the hurt?"

"Aren't you some kind of Lord, noblesse oblige and all that?" I reply.

The Dragon Lord looks puzzled until his face clears up as the information download on our culture clarifies it for him. Sometimes, the data isn't fully integrated. It's decent most of the time, but English and its random borrowing of other words from other languages can trip it up.

"Not that kind of Lord. Anyway, I was never very good at diplomacy," Bolo replies. There's a flash, a quick change in his face, the memory of something darker crosses it. But then it's gone, like the passing of the cloud, and he's focused. "So? What was it like?"

Mikito makes a noise in agreement while Harry raises his hand, beginning to film. I wave my hands at him, indicating for Harry to stop. I know he's recorded most of my interactions, tapping into my neural link and Hod, using it for his feeds. I don't mind, because I'm going to make him look for my own information. But what I have to say now, it's not for public consumption. Not yet.

I take a few moments to turn the house's privacy screens to maximum. Another second and I turn on my own Skills. Bolo and Mikito replicate my actions, layering their Skills on top of mine. It's not as effective as the Champion's power, but it's better than nothing.

"What did you think, Harry?" I ask. He's the most used to watching, interviewing others. Whether in this world or the previous one, he has experience to draw upon.

"The people you talked to, they were telling the truth. They are, mostly, happy. Some doubts, some concerns, but nothing out of the ordinary. In fact, it's a little too ordinary, a little too happy. There's some nervousness when talking to you, but that's not uncommon when speaking to *Your Justice*." Harry says all this while his gaze focuses slightly off, as if he's looking at notification screens we can't see.

"Anything else?"

"Not exactly my area of expertise, but a lot of the answers were a little too rote. Whenever you touched on their leadership, they were a little too enthusiastic. Not because they're being forced to say it. I'd say they're all true believers." There's a little hesitation in Harry's voice, probably because he's straying into speculation.

"Cult?" Mikito jumps right to the point.

"Close enough. Are social movements cults?" I shrug. I'm sure a sociologist could tell the difference between people really believing in something and a mind-washed, brainless mass. But that line is way too fine for me to cut. "That entire location was a setup. A lot of them don't really live there. There are too many ties, too many strings attaching them to other locations. Spuryan dragged all of them over to make a perfect little location for me to visit."

Bolo frowns at my revelation.

"I don't know if he really thought I was that dumb," I say. "Spuryan must know of my Skill, must know that I probably would have guessed he was putting on an act. So I don't know what the point was. Either that or he really underestimates me."

"Not the first person, boy-o," Ali points out. "Your history is rather rife with 'Beacon first, ask questions never' episodes."

Mikito and Harry cannot help but smile, making me even more annoyed. I'm not that much of a barbarian.

"Any idea what his goal was in the end?" I ask the group.

"Lie or not, that was still a few thousand people who truly believe in his cause. And by all indications, even if he doesn't have billions of true believers, it's still a substantial number. The siren call of not being at war is powerful, even in a militaristic society like this," Harry offers. "Maybe he was just trying to make you see it. Maybe he's hoping you agree with him."

"Foolish," Bolo says. "Even at home, we fight. Monsters mostly, but we do leave to find other sapients. Adventurers, Guilds, and corporations come to our domain, thinking they can exploit us, exploit our land, our dragons. Levels are needed, and fighting others provide the best kind of experience."

I consider Bolo for a time. What I know of his world, I'd almost have thought he'd lean toward Spuryan's belief. After all, his people spend their days and nights fighting dragons and taming them. There just aren't that many civilizations around their world anymore. Not with it located in the Forbidden Zone.

"You do what you must, especially if Legendarys are targeting you," Bolo explains.

I can't help but nod. Over the years, the negative of the Erethrans' constant need to go to war, to expand is that they've made a number of enemies. Including individuals who started out as nothing more than an

Advanced Class and grew their Levels over the years. Or just ran away to Level and came back with a vengeance.

Now, they've got a couple of high-Level people gunning for them, though none of them are Legendaries.

Yet.

It's a constant spiral as the Erethrans rush ahead, trying to up their own Levels, to find their enemies and end them before they become too strong. Of course, when that fails, they help their enemies gain Levels and hurt themselves. Or they create even more enemies by hurting others. And so, it keeps circling. They've become their own Heavenly Sky.

Problem is, the other option is… well. Bad.

Because the histories are full of groups who haven't chosen to Level, who have chosen to try to be nice and look internally, and most of those end up destroyed. By those who want power, by the System failing on them.

"So you think this was just the initial pitch?" The group offer tentative nods, and I sigh and run a hand through my hair. "That means we can expect the others too."

"Very soon. They won't like the fact that they've been pushed behind," Ali adds.

I can't help but sigh again. Just another thing to look forward to. Never mind that we still have to train some idiots. Suddenly, I feel exhausted by what's coming. I stare at the ceiling and shake my head.

Time for bed. The problem of picking a new Empress and training a bunch of idiots is a future John problem.

Chapter 9

"Are you joking?" Magine's incredulous tone is reward enough for me. Not that he's the only one looking a bit thrown by my latest pronouncement.

"Nope. We have the budget, so all of your requests have been approved." Yeah, I might be smirking a little. "Put together a training plan for how you can integrate the new equipment and new Skills. I don't believe it would be a good idea for you to grab them all at once, so prioritize those that make the most sense and have the longest integration period. Any questions?" I don't even let them answer before waving them off. "Get me the training information by noon today. I expect you all to be buying your Skills by the end of day. Or equipment. Though I understand there might be some recommendations coming down on those. I might hold off on that, just a little."

The group hangs around, not moving, confused by my abrupt pronouncements.

I clap my hands together, dragging their attention back. "Well, come on. Get moving."

Some of them leave immediately, but Gheisnan hesitates before he speaks. "What if we have additional suggestions or changes we might want to make? To our requests."

"And why would you have those?" I ask almost teasingly.

Gheisnan wilts beneath my gaze, ears flattening against his skull as he refuses to answer me.

On the other hand, Anayton speaks up, hands on her hips. "Because none of us actually thought you'd get us the Skills. We thought this was just another test. So we hedged things, putting everything that we thought you thought we needed."

Almost, I consider telling them that they should have trusted me. That it's a little too bad if they didn't. But that would be petty. And self-destructive. One of the things I'm trying to build are Paladins who can make their own decisions. Which means choosing their own builds. With some assistance.

"Send us your revisions by the end of the day," Mikito says while I ruminate being naughty.

Gheisnan shoots her a grateful smile while Anayton sniffs disparagingly in my direction. Even the others who had started leaving have turned around, hesitating over our confrontation, listening in. I can't help but chuckle in dire amusement.

As they walk away, I look at Ali. *"Make sure to mark every change. We'll have to go over it, make sure they aren't buying any nukes or the System equivalent. Just because I'm giving them a blank check doesn't mean I have to do it the stupid way."*

Ali opens his mouth to comment then shuts it. It's probably a little too easy, even for him.

"So what now?" Bolo asks me when the group disperses. "More training?"

"Nope." I grin. "We do the same."

"Even me?" Bolo looks surprised.

"It seems that real Paladins had support staff. And those support staff could draw from the budget too."

Every word I say makes Bolo's and Mikito's grins grow even wider, then they make sure again that I'm not joking. When they get my confirmation, they dash off, headed to the Shop or library to figure out what other Skills to purchase. I expect Bolo will cost me the most.

On that note…

"Where's the nearest Shop?"

***

The entrance to the yellow-themed Shop is via the spherical System-orb located a short distance away. It's not the main settlement Shop orb, but a secondary linked one, but it makes little difference. Before I leave, I make sure to let Harry know I'm in need of his services to search out information on the contenders. As good as Ali has gotten at this kind of work, Harry's got his own skillset.

I'm teleported into the Shop only to be met by Foxy. The humanoid fox creature is dressed in a dapper set of robes, reminiscent of African colored robes, thrown over both shoulders rather than the Roman toga style. He sways over to me, bushy tail waggling, and I find myself smiling in greeting. Foxy's one of my oldest friends in a way, even though, in some ways, he's not really a friend so much as a good... hairdresser? Huh. I'm reaching for an equivalent designation.

"Foxy. Good to see you," I say. "I've got a challenge for you."

"Oh?"

"A near unlimited budget and a rather difficult task." I watch Foxy's eyes glitter with avarice at the first part, then dim with caution at the second. "Skills and equipment upgrades. For me."

That makes Foxy frown. He turns his head side to side before he eventually says, "You must understand, to do that, we will require—"

"Bullshit. You guys already know." I smirk. "Most of what I've bought has come right from here. And my current Status Screen is something you can see already, no?"

The fox grows still as he processes my accusation. I see the gears spin in his head before he finally inclines his head, acknowledging my guess. "Yes. Your equipment is powerful, but in here—"

"You have the advantage. So. Put together a buy list."

"We do need to ask a few questions…"

"About what kind of build?" I nod. "Limit reductions on regeneration. I expect in the future, I'll be in more slugfests against Master Classers and higher. So survivability and ability to win are paramount. That might mean burst attacks."

"Obviously."

"Some Skills or equipment—preferably equipment—to increase my stealth capabilities. And more versatility would be good," I say. "Upgrades and abilities to alter my equipment or keep them in working order in the field would be useful."

"Ah. I might have to caution you on that one—" Foxy says, raising his hand.

"The Skill-Mental ratio limit? I know it. Aim for the median resistance," I say.

"If you wish, we do have access to Class Skill Testers who might be able to verify your limits with better accuracy," Foxy says.

"Really? Hmm…" I consider, trawling through my mind for data on Skill Testers.

They're a weird off-shoot of general Class Advisors, individuals who focused on testing aptitude for various Classes. Mostly, they were used before an individual met the age of majority, but they also had a side-line set of Skills for those hitting the higher edge of Classes in the Advanced and Master Class stage. There, they tested for the Skill-Mental ratio limit.

There's no direct correlation in the Skill-Mental ratio—like, you can have ten Skills outside of your Class for every hundred points of Intelligence and Willpower. It's more that one's mental attributes form a pool of potential Class limit points. But each non-Class Skill uses a number of those limit points and adding too many such Skills eats into that limit.

Of course, that limit isn't a hard limit. And the number of points is unknown—again, because Intelligence and Willpower grow in different directions depending on the individual. On top of that, Classes by themselves limit or expand those limit points. Even when you "expand" all the points and overburden yourself with the Skills, there's almost no perceptible difference to the Skills themselves when they're activated. Instead, what happens is a lag in the non-Class Skills activation rate.

I kind of imagine it like a computer. There's core programming—the Class Skills—that are saved to a solid state hard drive (SSHD). Super fast access, guaranteed to work without a problem. And non-Class Skills end up being stored on the same SSHD for the most part. However, at a certain point, those additional non-Class Skills get to be too much for your SSHD and you off-load them to a cloud computing server. For the most part, it doesn't mater—but occasionally you get a lag.

Obviously, that's a problem when you're in the middle of a fight.

Less of an issue if you're an Artisan. All that being said, it's why Legendarys don't bother purchasing multiple Legendary Class Skills. Or Heroics, other Heroic Skills. A single non-Class Skill of that kind can force all your other purchased Class Skills into remote use. And since most Legendarys or Heroics specialize in their Class for a reason, it makes more sense to stay with what you know and can use.

That's the other part of the equation. While you get the Skill via the Shop—along with the understanding of how to use the Skill—you don't get the side benefits of a Class Skill like automatic integration and understanding. Not to say you don't still have to train your Class Skills, but it's much easier to do so and doesn't require as many uses. If you have to test, say, the ability to create a blackhole, the lack of automatic integration can be quite troublesome.

The obvious workaround is to only buy Artisan and passive Combat Skills, forcing the System to keep the passive Skills "loaded" at all times. Unfortunately, that brings its own problems—outside of the obvious decrease in Mana Regeneration—as the Corrupt Questors have found out.

"Sounds good. Set the meeting up with the Testers. I don't want to overload," I say.

Foxy flashes me a grin and chivies me over to a private room while he arranges for a Skill Tester to port in. In the meantime, I get to window browse, idly wondering what kind of Skills I should be purchasing. The room I'm in is quite bare except for a lounging chair and a meal dispenser. Both of which I make full use of.

"What do you think, Ali? What should I get?" I ask, staring at the numerous windows I've pulled up. Some list my own Class Skill Trees, others show a list of Skills from other Classes, and another a searchable feature by type of Skills.

"Well, added damage, added ability to survive, and escape options come to mind," Ali ticks off on his fingers. "Socially, you're actually pretty set. It's not as if you're the kind to lead armies or anything, so there's no need for equipment or Skill alterations to your build. You can tell when someone's lying. Maybe something to help you lie better?" Ali shrugs. "Then again, anything you can buy at the Advanced Level won't be that useful in the world we deal with."

I grunt. That's the biggest issue for my build. Due to the way I skipped the Basic Class, as far as the System cares, I'm still only Advanced Class—so I can only buy that high up in the Shop. It significantly limits what I can purchase, especially since it makes little sense to pick up things that would harm my Mana Regeneration in passives at the Advanced Level. After all, it just won't be as good as what my enemies might have. If I'm purchasing a Skill that increases my damage by 50% because it's an Advanced Skill, it still isn't as useful as a Master Class Skill of the same kind that increases shield health by 100%. And since, Mana for Mana, my Advanced Skill would cost more, I'd be running a negative.

At least on the numbers side. But that's where buying the equivalent of a burst damage Skill makes more sense. If I can increase the damage done by a single attack, and use it selectively and surprise my opponents, I might be able to bypass or overpower their defenses. Point for point, burst damage Skills are more powerful than their passive counterparts.

Which is why added damage spells are my best bet. Increased resistance Skills might be useful, but then I'd have to either buy a general Skill that wasn't as powerful or multiple Skills that targeted a single element resistance. Which, in itself, is a problem. Fine if you knew what you were fighting, but difficult in a surprise attack, which is what I'd be expecting. So. Generic resistance Skills, since more and more of my opponents have resistance cutting Skills.

Then, running away Skills—

"John?"

"Sorry. Just thinking of escape Skills," I say.

"And forgetting I was still talking?" Ali says, leaning forward. "You're doing this too much."

"I know. Too much data unspooling…" I shudder. "Shit. Tell Foxy to cancel the request."

Ali takes a fraction of a second to realize the problem. He's on it the next second, sending out the messages while I wince internally at the mistake I just made. Letting someone do a deep scan of my "partition space" might be a really bad idea. After what was downloaded and off-loaded into me, I'd guess my own Skill limit might be really, really tight.

Or not.

But I can't risk it. Can't risk people knowing. Which means…

"Damn. I can't buy anything, can I?" I say. Because the build I have now, while not great, is at least better than nothing. Having it shifted off-site might cause more problems.

"Equipment," Ali corrects, flicking his fingers. "We can buy better equipment."

I grin at the Spirit. True enough. "Tell Foxy. And let's see what we can figure out."

And even that much is a danger. But… there's only so much we can do. Before people start putting things together.

***

We leave the Shop grumpier than when we entered. One of the negatives of buying equipment at my Level is that Master Class equipment doesn't just hang off the rack. You special order equipment, you put in requests and look out for auctions. And then you hope something shows up in a reasonable timeframe. It's why things like soulbound weaponry and Legacy weapons are so popular. One grows with you; the other grows all the time and keeps growing. They're both rarish, though soulbound weapons aren't impossible to acquire with the right Skill purchase. In fact, most Combat Classers will eventually soulbind a weapon.

The argument of doing so early or late is varied. Early soulbound weapons will grow with their users. But due to the limitations on the individual's Level to bind weapons, you're limited in the strength of the weapon you bind. On the other hand, binding a powerful weapon at the Master Class stage means you might be able to acquire a soulbound weapon with special Skills, over and on top of the usual strengthening the weapon would undergo. The negative, of course, is that said powerful weapons are hard to acquire and will disappear upon death.

In the end, I walk out of the Shop with nothing more than a slew of one-use items that will be useful for the short-term. Or at least, I hope they will.

F'Merc Ghostlight Mana Dispersal Grenades (Tier I)

The F'Merc Ghostlight Mana Dispersal Grenades not only disperse Mana in the battlefield, the Ghostlight Dispersal Grenades degrade all Mana Skills and spells within their field of effectiveness. Used by Krolash the Destroyer, the Erethran Champion Isma (prior version), and Anblanca Special Forces. Five times Winner of the Most Annoying Utility Item on the Battlefield.

Effect: Reduces Mana Regeneration rates, Skill, and spell formation use in affected area by 67% (higher effects in enclosed areas)

Radius: 15m³

Evernight Darkness Orbs

When the world goes light, the Evernight Darkness Orbs will bring back blessed darkness. If you need darkness, you need Evernight!

Effect: Removes all visible light and mutes infrared and ultraviolet wavelengths by 30%

Radius: 50m³

Seven Heavenly Spire Wards

Quick to set up, the Seven Heavenly Spire Wards were crafted by the Thrice-Loved Bachelor's Temple of the Sinking Domain as their main export. Using the total prayer and faith of the temple, they produce a set of wards every month to ensure annoying pests and ex-girlfriends are kept out.

Effect: Creates a 30' by 30' defensive ward; protects against both magical and technological attacks and entry

Simple enchanted protection wards that can be thrown up nearly anywhere I want. Matched with my usual array of force shields, they can make for a temporary redoubt when needed. Not that I expect to need them, but you never know. The nice thing about the wards is that they'll protect against a number of magical methods of ingress—something the force shields often don't. Heck, even semi-technological methods of ingress and escape—like Lightwalk and Shadowform—get blocked by the Wards.

Fumikara Mobile Teleport Circles

These one-off use mobile teleport circles allow connection to existing and open teleport networks.

Effect: Connect to open teleport networks within a 5,000 km radius of the teleport circles. Allows teleportation of individuals to the networked teleport centers

On top of that, other than the single-use items, I bought a slew of Mana potions and Healing potions conditioned for reuse. I also put in an order for specialized potions, ones geared for me and my Status. They'll reduce the potion effectiveness disintegration level, making sure I can use more potions.

I wanted a replacement for my Mana Storage Bracelet, but they had nothing better on-hand. Anything else has to be special ordered, so that's on the pile of things to get fixed. Ditto with a replacement for my emergency Force Shield ring.

And of course, the prize of my shopping trip.

PoenJoe Goleminised-Mana Generator Mark 18

The latest Mana Generator by the infamous PoenJoe, the Mark 18 is guaranteed* to not blow up on you in optimal conditions. This partially sentient Mana Generator can extract up to 98% of a Mana Crystal's saved energy in 0.003 seconds. Currently loaded with an Adult Kirin Mana Core.

Effect: It's a Power Generator. Guaranteed to provide up to 98×10^{99} Standard Galactic Mana Units

*Not actually guaranteed. In fact, we're 100% certain that containment failure will occur.

It's actually a settlement Mana Generator, meant to be used to power an entire settlement about the size of Vancouver. Pre-Apocalypse that is. A million households using Mana for all their needs would easily be fed by the Mana Generator. The ability to increase the draw on the Mana Core is—theoretically—meant to allow the Shield Generator to withstand even fleet-level bombardment. Or the attack of another Heroic Level Combat Classer.

I say theoretically, because its creator—PoenJoe—is just a little insane. The child of a Legendary and Heroic Classer pair, he's infamous for his desire to create machinery that can withstand his parents' loving touch. Even in their old age, their abilities are so high that his work constantly crumbles.

And rather than take the time to build things right, he cobbles these things together, ever intent on drawing more power, more Mana.

With explosive results.

Luckily, System Inventory puts the entire thing into stasis. So I can carry it around, half-turned on, without it causing any issues. His Mana Generators are a lot cheaper than an actual System-enabled tactical nuke—or the System-damage equivalent—and less restricted. Undestroyed examples of PoenJoe's work are so uncommon, not everyone knows of him and thus his work isn't restricted. Yet. It's only Foxy's knowledge that got me access to this.

Lastly, I glance down. Hidden beneath my trousers, wrapped around my ankle is the last thing I picked up. It's an enchanted band with a most interesting Skill.

Payload (Level 2)

Sometimes, you need to get your Skills inside a location. Payload allows you to imbue an individual or item with a Skill at a reduced strength.

Effect: 71% effectiveness of Skill imbued.

Secondary Effect: Skill may be now triggered on a timed basis (max 2:07 minutes)

Uses: 22

Recharge: 10.7 charges per day in SGE

After all our discussion, after browsing through it all, I have to admit, I haven't bought anything in terms of Skills. Most of what I want, I've replaced with equipment, giving me access to the Skills without the concurrent disadvantages. There's some concern about over-emphasis on enchanted items and their Mana clash, but we were careful to ensure that they won't cause too much trouble. And, of course, equipment isn't as fast to trigger or use, or as powerful as an innate Skill. But I'm also about ten Levels away from reaching my next Tier. When that happens, I'll gain access to Master Class Skills.

Till then, I can hold tight on the major non-Class Skill purchases. Instead, I've purchased a couple of new Spells and upgraded a couple of my most lacking Skills. They should, theoretically, not cause issues with the System. At least, as far as I know.

For now, until I gain a few more Levels, maybe even get close to reaching my Heroic Class, I intend to keep the Ring running and hiding my true Level. Changing only that single line is easy—for variations of easy—though recharging the ring in the Shop was expensive. Still, I like the idea of having a little surprise in store, if things go bad.

Drawing a deep breath, I pull up my real Status Screen, reviewing the changes.

Status Screen			
Name	John Lee	Class	Erethran Paladin
Race	Human (Male)	Level	40
Titles			
Monster's Bane, Redeemer of the Dead, Duelist, Explorer, Apprentice Questor, Galactic Silver Bounty Hunter, Corrupt Questor, (Living Repository)			
Health	4620	Stamina	4620
Mana	4240	Mana Regeneration	359 (+5) / minute
Attributes			
Strength	312	Agility	402

Constitution	462	Perception	242
Intelligence	424	Willpower	459
Charisma	180	Luck	94

Class Skills			
Mana Imbue	5*	Blade Strike*	5
Thousand Steps	1	Altered Space	2
Two are One	1	The Body's Resolve	3
Greater Detection	1	A Thousand Blades	4*
Soul Shield	4	Blink Step	2
Portal*	5	Army of One	4
Sanctum	2	Penetration	9e
Aura of Chivalry	1	Eyes of Insight	2
Beacon of the Angels	2	Eye of the Storm	1
Vanguard of the Apocalypse	2	Society's Web	1

External Class Skills			
Instantaneous Inventory	1	Frenzy	1
Cleave	2	Tech Link	2
Elemental Strike	1 (Ice)	Shrunken Footsteps	1
Analyze	2	Harden	2
Quantum Lock	3	Elastic Skin	3

Disengage Safeties	2	Temporary Forced Link	1
Hyperspace Nitro Boost	1	On the Edge	1
Fates Thread	2	Peasant's Fury	1

Combat Spells	
Improved Minor Healing (IV)	Greater Regeneration (II)
Greater Healing (II)	Mana Drip (II)
Improved Mana Missile (IV)	Enhanced Lightning Strike (III)
Firestorm	Polar Zone
Freezing Blade	Improved Inferno Strike (II)
Elemental Walls (Fire, Ice, Earth, etc.)	Ice Blast
Icestorm	Improved Invisibility
Improved Mana Cage	Improved Flight
Haste	Enhanced Particle Ray
Variable Gravitic Sphere	Zone of Denial

Mana Imbue adds damage to my Basic Attacks, which means both my big finishing move—Army of One—and my more normal attacks are more dangerous. I didn't upgrade it too much due to the effect on my Mana Regeneration, but it was about time to throw some Credits at it. It's one of those linked Skills that make sense to increase.

The other one I increased was Thousand Blades. Again, it makes Army of One even more powerful due to the way they're linked, but just as useful, it adds another floating blade for me to play with. The only reason I've not added more to it earlier is the difficulty of coordinating their use. Even with my increased Intelligence, the training required to integrate it properly in my fighting style is onerous. However, since I'm about to be training these children, I might as well get some training in myself. One of the biggest advantages of being on Pauhiri is access to the Paladin's entire subset of training videos and journals, meaning that I should be able to up my fighting game faster.

As for the spells, I've mostly purchased them for the future. Gravitic Sphere is perfect in space to slow down attacks or just annoy people. Unlike most spells, it increases in strength the more Mana you throw in; so used properly, I can divert a missile in space or lock down a bunch of annoying initiates.

Zone of Denial, on the other hand, is a damage-over-time spell. Cast on a location, it targets everyone within that location and does damage to them so long as they stay within it. It's straight Mana damage too, which means it ignores most resistances. It's not a lot of damage, even if the zone is variable by Mana use. But when taken into a crowded situation, it can be highly useful.

They both cover areas I'm missing—a damage-over-time spell and an area control spell. I considered getting some specialized damage-over-time spells but figured something more generic would be more useful.

Now, I just wonder what those two crazy munchkins are going to come back with. Thanks to the time dilation on my Shop, I've got a bit of time to wait. Rather than waste it, I take over a training hall and leave Ali to keep an eye out for Mikito and Bolo while I work on integrating my new blade.

Chapter 10

Mikito finds me first, Bolo taking his time in his Shop. I was a little bit surprised to find that the Dragon Lord doesn't have a time-compressed Shop of his own, but when questioned during one of the lulls in the battle on Spaks, he muttered something about loyalty and enjoying the broader suite of services. When he started waggling his eyebrows when pressed, I decided to not push the matter. We weren't that close. Especially back then.

Mikito saunters over and I let my gaze wander over the Samurai. The short Japanese lady has improved her looks in subtle ways as her Charisma stat gets little boosts. Surprisingly, even if she has received the gene therapy upgrade, she had it done such that she stayed much the same. Including her height—or lack of it. I'm not entirely sure why, though I have a feeling it has to do with her pride in her heritage or her dead husband. Some things, you just don't ask.

As she arrives, I gesture and let the hard light projections disappear. The moving blue figurines I've been practicing against fade, leaving the room bare of anything but us. Even the walls are completely smooth, a pale gray that hides the increased durability of the setting.

Mikito stops in front of me and I offer her a smile, glancing upward to check her Status. I've found as she leveled her Feudal Bond Skill that my access to her Status Screen increased. These days, I have full access to her Status and limited details about her Skills. No more than general descriptions, but enough so that I know her attributes and Skill set.

I mentioned it to her the last time I realized this happened and the woman just shrugged. I know I'd be weirded out if someone had that much access to my Status. Well, someone who wasn't a three-foot-tall, pain-in-the-ass creature of pure Mana.

On that note, I take a longer look at my friend.

Mikito Sato, Spear of Humanity, Blood Warden, Junior Arena Champion of Irvina, Arena Champion—Orion IV, Xumis,...; True Bound Honor (Upper Samurai Level 23) (M)

HP: 3641/3641*

MP: 2625/2625*

Conditions: Isoide, Jin, Rei, Meiyo, Ishiki, Ryoyo, Feudal Bond, Blitzed, Future Projections

Galactic Reputation: 21

Galactic Fame: 14,327

I almost look deeper into her data but push aside the whim and instead, use my words like a big boy. "So, find anything you liked?"

Mikito's eyes narrow, her lips sliding into the tiniest hint of a smile. "Just a few."

She frowns in concentration, then the data slides across to me.

Blitzed (Level 3) (M)

A Messenger can be slowed, they can be delayed, they can be diverted. But they can't be stopped. And Blitzed makes sure that even those minor inconveniences are over in a flash. Speeding up the existence of the Messenger, Blitzed ensures you'll never live life in the slow lane. Mana regeneration reduced by 15 permanently.

Effect: Blitzed increases all physical and mental reactions by 120%

Caution: Blitzed increases physical existence speed, making subjective view of passing time significantly higher. A high Willpower and meditation skill is recommended to reduce chance of psychosis.

Future Projections (Level 3) (A)

You never know what might be coming up, without Future Projections. When active, Future Projections allows user to absorb and project potential actions into the future. Perfect for dodging oblivious pedestrians, blind teleports, and the occasional monster spawn.

Effects: Allow future projection of actions 1.2 seconds into the future.

Cost: 60 Mana per minute.

"That's just wrong," I mutter.

"He gave you enough trouble. And that Skill…" Mikito shakes her head. "It's better than anything else I've seen."

"Well, considering speed is his entire build, I'm not surprised," I say. "Do you have activation problems?"

Mikito raises an eyebrow at me and I realize I never told her. I proceed to explain the issue, eliciting a deep frown from the Samurai. She proceeds to test her Skill and then—just for fun, I assume—her basic Haste Skill on top of it. She literally vibrates when she's standing still, then flickers to the end of the rectangular room. Thanks to my higher Perception, I can just barely follow her movements—which is still an improvement compared to my experience with the Speedster Master Class. Then again, I wonder if it's a matter of attributes or her lower total speed.

"How is it?" I ask.

"Still instantaneous activation. But there's a greater than expected clash between my Skills. I'm not getting the boost I expected. It isn't as high as I was led to believe," Mikito says with a deep frown. "Mana cost is as expected though."

"So your need for speed was a failure?"

I hear her sniff, then she blurs and I don't manage to duck the light smack on my shoulder. After that, she just keeps blurring, activating movement Skill after movement Skill. She's got quite a few, from the basic Haste Skill and Flash Step, to her more specialized ones that give her smoothness of movement. After a few minutes of movement, she finally comes to a stop, her Mana nearly drained. She continues to look unhappy, reading information I can't see before she finally turns to regard me.

"You were training?" As she speaks, she draws Hitoshi, her naginata, and places it over her shoulder.

"Yeah," I say. "Added another sword."

"And more Mana to them all."

"You're angling for a fight, aren't you?"

In answer, Mikito flashes me a grin and I groan. Getting my ass kicked is going to suck. But she has a point. Due to the way I—and she—grew in the System, many of our attribute increases seem to really take effect when we're in battle. Even mock battle is enough. But plain training doesn't seem to work as well at triggering whatever expanded learning our higher attributes provide us. Which means…

"Just go easy on me," I say.

"I always do."

"No, you really don't."

All I get in answer to that is a slight smile as she backs off. Not that we're going to start until her Mana's full, but the point is taken. I sigh and conjure my own sword, ready to do some forms while I wait. Good training never hurts.

***

I hack out the blood pooling in my lungs, watching it dribble from my lips and out my nose. I clear it off with a swipe of my hands before I stagger to my feet. We've been at this for the last couple of hours, hammering away at each other, but this is the first time she's managed to land that particular attack properly. I glare at the Samurai, who retreated after putting the butt of her polearm into my chest, allowing me to recuperate.

"What was that?" I say hoarsely. I spit again, watching blood dribble out. The attack bypassed most of my defenses, slipping in and damaging my lungs, bursting blood vessels and filling my chest with blood rather than shattering the ribs that protect them. "New Skill?"

"No. A skill." I can somehow hear the lack of cap on the word, though it doesn't remove my confusion. "It's a striking technique that projects the force within. Hard to pull off."

I grunt and pull up the System logs, skimming through it to find the details of the attack. She's right—it bypassed nearly half of my resistances, but the actual damage it dealt was lower than her usual total. Of course, because she bypassed my resistances, the net damage was higher.

"Weird," I say. "Never knew you could do that."

"There are Skills that work the same. In fact, some Skills are just skills packaged up by the System," Mikito says. "Sort of like spells and Skills."

"I guess. That kind of makes sense," I say.

I don't really purchase many attack-based Skills, rather relying on more magical or passive Skills. But considering how Cleave seems to be a focus of both Mana and body and Harden is basically an infusion of Mana and a toughening of the body, I can see how they'd be something a dedicated individual could learn.

A part of my mind wants to give me the data, the information, but I manage to wall it off.

If that's the case…

"Should I be paying more attention to my skills?" I frown.

A long time ago, we dismissed the screen keeping track of that data. Occasionally I poke at it, ending up amused by things like my lip reading or alien body language skills getting an upgrade, but for the most part, I ignore it. As Ali pointed out, the skills are more a reflection of reality than something I can upgrade like my Skills. The screen tracks my progress or regress of skills. It's not a game where each "level" gives me another 5% attack damage or whatever.

"Aren't you?" Mikito gestures around us, taking in the combat room. Even as we stand in the barren land, nanobots slowly reweave the scarred and thrashed floor and walls, fixing incidental damage. While neither one of us pulled out the big guns—by mutual agreement—our normal attacks are enough to trash the place.

"Yeah but…" I wave at her. "You're, you know…"

"Better?" Mikito says. "I have decades of experience and the lessons from my grandfather to draw on. And my other teachers, people I learnt from when you were gone." She puts the butt of her polearm on the floor. "You can get better. You have the talent. But is it what you want?"

"Doesn't matter what I want, does it?" I grumble. "I always seem to end up in the middle of things."

"But is it what you want?"

I fall silent as I consider her words. What do I want? Really? Not violence, that's not really a "want." It's just a factor in my life. It's not helping people, though I do that because that's what you do. I'm not a bleeding heart like Lana, who has to help people because that's what she's built to do. I just can't look away. Not helping others is a bigger burden than a benefit for me. I don't even like people thanking me for it.

Which is weird, if you prod at the thought at all.

But it's not as if I help people because I care about the people. Nor is it because I have a burning desire for justice, for making the world a better place or righting wrongs. The need to "fix" a society or an event. That, I know, drives other Paladins. My mentor for one. Others in their histories. And even some of my initiates. Their need to make sure that the world they live in, their society works. Is fair and balanced for all.

That's not me. I'm too Chinese, grew up knowing too much history, knowing that corruption and racism and all that crap always happens. It's a feature, not a bug.

"I'm not sure. An answer, I guess," I say. Because that's what it comes down to. The question of the System. Everything else—bounty hunting, saving cities, beating up assholes—are things I do in between reading and learning. Trying to find an answer to the why of it all. "What about you?"

Mikito points her polearm at me instead of answering, indicating she's ready for the next round. I glare but settle into a fighting stance. She's been known to attack me even when I refused to play the game.

"Not so easy. I want an answer."

"Then beat me," Mikito challenges.

The next moment, she flashes forward. Mikito leads the first pass with a lunge with her naginata. She's triggered all her Skills, all the ones that allow her to move. And she cheats, using *Gi* to allow her attack to bypass my hasty block. It floats right over my hovering swords, dodging them by millimeters as I twist my body aside. But *Gi* is an uninterrupted, unfailing attack.

The curved, elongated blade of the polearm slides through space, popping my Soul Shield like an overextended bubble, and plunges into my chest. It cuts through Hardened skin and reinforced bones, piercing my chest and cooking it as Hitoshi's body lights up in flame.

I groan, finishing my cut upward, tearing the blade from my body in a splay of blood and a chest-sucking, slurping sound. Burnt flesh and the iron-tang of blood fill the air even as she takes the momentum of my block to spin the polearm around for another cut at my head.

Down. Down low I drop, sliding beneath my own floating weapons, snatching one from the air and cutting sideways at her with it, before dismissing my blade to snatch another. I push forward, stepping close as I begin the blade spin of the Honor Guard.

Five blades, free floating in space, move along the trajectory of the previous motion of the original soulbound blade. Their trajectories alter as I make the original blade appear and disappear, switching hands, switching positions. I fight, throwing cuts, blocking attacks, and launching my own Blade Strikes. The blades cut through the air, sometimes disappearing as I will them gone, sometimes reappearing as I bring them back, darting alongside my body as I attack Mikito.

The Samurai blocks and deflects each attack, her naginata spinning in an intricate dance, moving at such speed that the crack of the sound barrier being broken time and time again resounds through the room. A swirl of air erupts, forced aside by our movements, changing air pressure and creating a mini vortex.

The rush of wind mixes with the ring of metal blades blocked, the spark of ozone as blades clash. The smell of burnt flesh, of healing wounds, of freshly spilled blood swirl past my face, remembrances of our past fight. And the current battle, as cuts and surface wounds accumulate.

I trigger Cleave, swinging down with all my might, almost cutting into her collarbone. She blocks and sags to the floor under the strength of my blow. Her ghostly traditional Samurai armor cracks, shattering around the glowing edge of my blade. Mikito twists her hips and angles her hand, shedding the remnant energy to the side, then uses the same motion to block another swinging blade with the haft of her polearm. A Flash Step pushes her backward, moving her without her using her feet. The blade points at me and *Makoto* triggers, a beam of power lancing for my torso.

I hop over the attack, dancing across my own blade to continue to close the distance. Never wanting to give her space, a gap in time to recover. Her Stamina is one of her weak points. I pressure her as damage accumulates on both sides, as attacks that I fail to block get through. As Blade Strikes cut across her own blocks or tear away at her translucent defense.

We dance across the room, neither side willing to give up.

In the end, skill and Class win out. She has the advantage over me in terms of total Levels, in terms of a Class geared for solo combat. In terms of skill. I miss a block, get cut, and don't even see the grapple she set up with the attack, her polearm tangling my arms which she turns into a throw. I land on the floor and the blade sinks into my collarbone, pinning me.

Pain. I struggle not to scream as my flesh burns.

Brown eyes, filled with life and a dark joy, stare down at me. There's a crazed light there, a need. For a second, I wonder if she's going to end it, if she'll trigger a Skill to pile on the damage. She pants over me, hair falling to cover her face, leaving me only to stare into the slitted gaze of her smoky helmet, the flared edges of the curved bell rippling.

Then the blade is yanked out, leaving me curling around my side. It takes a lot to stop from screaming as flesh reknits. I stagger back to my feet, taking a cut from my own still-spinning blades before I dismiss them. And stare at my friend, who has retreated a distance away.

Silence dominates the room as we recover our senses and come down from the fight. And then, two words.

"I win."

***

We're seated, resting as I get my Health and Mana back. Nearly ten minutes have passed and I'm back—statistically at least—but there's a difference between stats and reality. Mentally at least, I'm not in the mood to duel again.

So I sit quietly, doing a light meditation of breathing in and out, letting tension and pain flow out. Finding an equilibrium and grateful that the System seems to ameliorate some of the pain, some of the terror. Not all of it—not even a lot in some cases—but a little. It makes it possible to consider another training session.

In the future.

"Sorry," Mikito says softly, breaking my reverie.

"Hmmmm?"

"I went too far." She gives herself a quick shake of the head, her lips pursed in anger and self-recrimination.

"Just a little." I'm used to my friend being dangerous. Just not necessarily a danger to myself. Especially with her Skills being tied so tightly to me. "What happened?"

Mikito falls silent, not answering me for a long time. Then she slowly speaks. "When it started, I was angry. Upset. I didn't want to live. I couldn't die."

A fist clenches around the polearm, around Hitoshi. The weapon her husband gave up his Classes, his boons for. All to give her a better chance to live. And I understand. The burden of that sacrifice, survivor's guilt—it can break people. Has broken many.

"Then time passed. And we did good. Killed the aliens. Saved the world." She shoots me a quelling look when I shift at the last sentence, forcing me to still rather than interrupt her mistake. "The pain lessened. But the anger didn't. And I was lost. I helped out when you were gone. Fought the monsters. The aliens. They called me the Spear of Humanity, because I was fighting. Always fighting. But... I couldn't stop..."

"You didn't know what else to do," I say. I know that feeling. The insanity that creeps up on you, the restlessness, the thoughts of anger and loss. "You can't stop, can't stop moving. Can't let go. Can't look back. So you keep moving, keep fighting."

"Yes." Mikito's assent is quiet. "You understand."

"I'm sure others do too." I remember Therapists, Psychiatrists, and Mind Healers, all offered to us. All available to help people heal, to get better. I even paid for some of those programs. They only work as well as you let them though.

"They did. And didn't." Mikito purses her lips, glancing at me sideways. "They don't... I can't... letting it go..."

I nod. She doesn't need to say it. Doesn't need to finish the sentence. And I realize why she's with me. Because unlike the others, unlike her friends, the other Champions, I won't push her to get better. To find healing or to make a life for herself in this new world.

I don't, because I refuse to get better myself.

I can't let the pain go.

I won't leave the quest alone.

Some people get over things.

Some of us, we nurse those grudges like fine whisky. Because if we let it go, if we accept it and move on, there might not be anything to move on to.

***

"What?" Bolo walks in on us twenty minutes later, silent and brooding over our losses. His eyes flick over our still forms, narrowing.

"Nothing," I say, shaking away the darkness. It takes a bit of effort, but I manage. After a while, pain like this isn't an all-encompassing thing. It's just the ache in your back, the hitch in your steps—metaphorically speaking. You get used to it, and only once in a while does it slow you down. "What'd you buy?"

Bolo shifts his stance a little and looks awkward. "So. You know. About that…"

"Yeah?" I prompt him.

"We never discussed me being here. Or you, you know…" He gestures between himself and us. "I mean, Harry didn't get anything."

"He did actually," I say. At least, I sent him the option, but the reporter was in the city when I did. I'm sure he'll decide on his buy later, when he's done filming his "first days in Erethra" episode. Having him wander around getting information and playing reporter is more important. For now.

"Right. But he's, you know, human."

"And I'm racist?" I frown. "Speciest? Alienist? The offer's open to Dornalor when he gets here too. Whenever that happens. In fact, I probably could upgrade his ship…" I trail off, my mind flashing with the implications.

"No!" Bolo snaps. "I meant, he's your group. You guys…"

"Dornalor's a merc. Well, mostly. I pay him very well and he does what we want," I say. "One day, I expect he'll probably leave. Once he's earned enough. And Leveled."

"I'm not a mercenary." Bolo crosses his arm in a huff. Then he freezes, eyes narrowing. "You drake-swapped egg. You're doing this on purpose."

I finally crack, breaking into gales of laughter and slapping my leg. I'm too busy chuckling to dodge the compressed air attack that throws me back into the wall. I still don't stop laughing as I peel myself off the wall and floor.

"Chill. You want in? You're in." I gesture to the smiling, cross-legged Mikito then out the door. "This isn't the Paladins. This isn't a…" I frown, looking for the word. "Cult. I don't even own these Credits. So if you want to use it, go ahead." I shrug. "No skin off my nose. Though I'd like it if you let me know if you're choosing to leave. I'd have to work out what to do without you."

"Without me for what?" Bolo says, frowning. "I understand giving the soldiers new Skills. They'll need some training to integrate them, but that's not really my Skill set."

"As if I'd trust you with training. You'd probably squash them like a pancake. That's not what I need you for. I want to see them in action." I pause, considering, and add, "And I want to see the kind of world I'm going to be putting them through."

Mikito frowns, while Bolo grins.

"What?" I eye the grinning Dragon Lord.

"This is going to create chaos, isn't it?"

I shrug. Bolo laughs, slapping his thigh a couple of times, before turning around and walking out.

"Hey! Where are you going?"

"To buy Skills!" Bolo continues to laugh until his voice is cut off by the closing doors, leaving Mikito and me alone.

The Samurai stands, shaking her head, and levels her polearm at me.

"Nope. I'm out," I say. A thought has me Blink Stepping over to the door. "Have fun!"

Mikito snorts but lets me run away. Even as I leave, hard light projections of her opponents appear.

Chuckling to myself, I saunter off to do some thinking. Reading. Despooling. Whatever you call dealing with an entire library in your head.

The first steps are taken.

Now, I just have to wait.

Chapter 11

I have to admit, one of the few things I've kept with me over the years—through apocalypse and international travel—is my love for food. Good chocolate for certain, but just food in general. And now that I'm in a new alien city—one that doesn't require me to hide out while finding my prey—I take full advantage of it.

B'oolyn is the equivalent of a three-star Michelin restaurant. The reservation list to get in is about a year and a half long, and that's if you can get on the list. They've got a limited number of tables open for those without the requisite connections. And a few tables set aside for those with the status to ignore things like reservations.

Which is how I end up eating here with the team. Harry's having the time of his life, tiny drones flying around and taking videos of the building. It's all carefully arranged and agreed upon by the owner of the establishment, ensuring that his guests—who all have their own privacy clauses active—are either not bothered or featured as contracted.

The pale cream walls and the marble-like columns that dribble down like melted candles, making the entire place look like the inside of a sculpted ice cave, show well, as do the lingering hints of past meals. A Galactic array of spices combine with the smells of perfectly blackened meat, glazed vegetables, and other foodstuff best not considered too carefully. Even so, Skills and extractors ensure that none of the smells are overpowering, the lighting set perfectly to ensure that an amiable atmosphere is available for all.

As for the patrons themselves, they're a wide array of celebrities, socialites, noblemen, and military personnel. In Erethra, the last mixes with the first three in strange ways, with the concept of the celebrity soldier dominating their culture. Entire units are created—or kept together—because of specific individuals. Individuals who might have been given unique Classes for their actions or because of their natural Charisma. There's even a subtle powerplay between various Generals as they promote their own armies, with Celebrity Soldier an actual Class. Of course, part of the requirements for them to be popular includes a series of death-defying stunts, so the lifespan of such soldiers is often limited.

When you add in the fact that the Erethran Empire spans literal solar systems and dozens of races make up their population, the array of patrons within B'oolyn is staggering. The need to draw support from a wide range of sapient races makes the breakdown of celebrities on species lines a little more equal than you'd think. The only reason there isn't a wider range is due to natural population and recruitment numbers among member races. After all, certain races—like the living rabbit-looking fuzzball Bignief—are just too cute not to use for publicity purposes.

All of which is a long way to say that even in a racially diverse cast of patrons, our particular table still gets a lot of eyeballs as we eat.

"You seem to be taking to the looks well," I say to Bolo, who chows down on his food.

The Dragon Lord is a big contrast compared to Mikito. She's hunkered down, glaring at everyone who even looks halfway at her. If she had Hitoshi out, I'd be a little more worried, but she's chosen to store it in her Inventory. Ali's floating above us, out of sight, in a portion of the establishment reserved for companions. They've got their own servings, their own set up which keeps them out of our hair. Though the occasional complaint from Ali tells me it's a lot less nice than the main room.

"We were much the same in Xylargh," says Bolo. "Attention, when earned justly, is not to be shirked."

"Good to know." I lean back, grinning at the occasional glances.

The restaurant maître d' appears by my side. It's a bit magical, the way he manages to glide through the room, making himself known but yet not disturbing his guests' enjoyment of their meals. He makes his presence known subtly, so no one gets twitchy when he does want your attention, yet he never impinges on our conscious consideration. It leaves people like Mikito able to handle his presence without stabbing.

"Is the meal to your liking, Paladin?" the maître d' asks, bowing low. He's a full Erethran, dressed in a variation of a pale-yellow-and-blue-trimmed serving uniform, almost looming over me as I sit. Almost, because he's standing far enough back that he doesn't tower. Nor do his luminescent yellow locks distract from the professionalism of his outfit and demeanor.

"Definitely," I say, gesturing to the empty plate before me. "That last dish was amazing. What was it called again?"

"Leontophone haunch, braised with walmer nuts and a touch of the opin herb mix, caramelized afterward," the maître d' replies. "We can bring a second serving, if the Paladin desires."

"No, not yet. Let's finish the suggested course," I say, shaking my head. No need to mess with their suggested menu. At an establishment like this, their menu is certain to build upon itself.

"Of course. Also, there's a gentleman who would like to join you," the maître d' says hesitantly. His eyes flicker to the side and I get a new notification.

So. And so.

Just about time then. I smile to set the maître d' at ease. "I'd be happy to speak with him. And his friend."

No sooner have I finished speaking than waiters appear, moving our utensils and adding a pair of chairs to the table that grows to fit another pair of diners with ease. I don't even have to scoot my chair back as it moves by itself. That gets a little yelp from Mikito and a glare that the waiters all studiously ignore. I don't ignore the small blade that Mikito disappears back into her Inventory with a twitch of her hand.

"Who's joining us?" Harry asks.

Before I can reply, our guests arrive.

Brerdain Ramanner, the General, leads the way. He saunters over, his Charisma washing over us all even though he's not projecting his Aura. Per usual social conventions, people keep their aura retracted around others unless they're looking to make a point. Even portly and older like he is, there's a Charisma to him and his presence that the vid did not showcase.

Beside him is an Erethran female, decades younger. She's clad in a twinkly, tight sleeveless dress that shows off the muscles in her arms and legs—thanks to the long slit up her leg—while the tasteful makeup on her face and coral ears accentuate her features. Interestingly enough, she's a little on the short side for an Erethran, at just about six feet six. As she smiles at me, I can't help but notice the way the light around her brightens a little, angling to deepen the cleavage, shadow her cheeks, highlight parts of the shimmering rainbow of her long hair.

"Paladin. Thank you for letting us join you," Brerdain greets us with a polite smile. He holds the seat next to me out for his date, letting her slide in. "This is Catrin Dufoff."

I flick my gaze up to Catrin's Status, curious about the light-bending companion as she sits down next to me, offering me a smile.

Catrin Dufoff, Empire Top Companion, Class 2 Human Resource, Slayer of Goblins, Wexlix, Crilik, (more)... (Administrative Companion Level 38) (A)
HP: 1210/1210

MP: 3480/3480

*Conditions: Always in Place, Never too Late, Perfect Lighting, Pheromones, A Good
Impression*

Companion it is. I'm debating if there are perks—or what kind of perks—
to her Class before doing a mental shrug. None of my business. From what
little I recall about Erethran society, they have no specific hang-ups about
paid companionship. No more than they do with any job that isn't directly
in the military, that is.

Society's Web, already running, let me verify the thread between them.
Thin, almost insubstantial, and green-gray, the color of Credits and duty.
There are more, many more, of those radiating from Catrin. She's as
connected to those in this room as any who have walked in, some of those
threads heavy with scarlet and burgundy, passion and lust. Others are
threaded with black and gray, heavy motes of duty and obligation. And there
are the common ones leading to the Queen, a brown-gray thread leading off
into the palace, a trio of purple-yellows headed straight up into the
atmosphere.

Brerdain's even more interesting, his threads numerous. Lots of steel-gray
for his soldiers. For those beneath him. I have to sort those out, cleanse
them. Then I cleanse his companions, his casual dalliances. And still there
are threads, so many to review. Even as I sort, I idly flick away a failed Charm
notification.

Brerdain takes his seat while returning introductions with the rest of my
team. My attention is pulled back to Catrin as she places a hand on my arm.
The heat of her touch and the chemicals in her skin set off another Charm
notification.

"Do you prefer to be called Paladin, Paladin Lee, Redeemer, or another of your many, many Titles?" Catrin's voice is low and husky at the same time, like thick maple syrup coating the waffles of my ears.

"John. I prefer John," I reply. Brerdain's ploy is rather obvious, the use of her almost laughable. I do a quick search through the System, tapping into local news sources and blazing through the data with the neural link and confirm my guess. "And you, Administrator? What would you prefer to be called?"

"Catrin." She smiles, inclining her head slightly. I absently note that her chair has reconfigured slightly, lowering her a little and allowing me to meet her gaze more easily. It also, I idly note, gives me a better view. I find myself smiling, drawing in a slight breath, catching hints of nutmeg and other, unidentifiable Galactic scents in her perfume. "Are you enjoying the meal?"

"I am." I flick my gaze down to her hand that rests on my arm, but I don't comment. Instead, I turn to Brerdain, offering him a smile. "So, General. Or is it Chief of Staff?" I cock an eyebrow.

"Well, if we are being informal, it would be Brerdain." He gives me a congenial smile, nodding thanks to the waiter who deposits their servings in front of them. "Thank you for letting us join you. Many of us are quite curious about the first Paladin to return in many years."

"I'm sure. But a bit obvious, no?" I nod to the young lady and the hand. She retracts it gently, picking up her utensil and not looking at all flustered. "She's not your usual companion."

Brerdain laughs, shaking his head. "I'm sure I don't know what you're talking about. I enjoy the company of young women."

I grunt. That's true enough. More than enough recordings and news articles to prove that. He and his wife have an open relationship, especially since his wife continues to serve on-board ship as a Marine Sargent. Sexual relationships are rather more open in their society, acknowledging the need for flexibility when partners might be literal light years apart for years, if not decades. Add in the extended lifespan—theoretically—of soldiers with high Constitutions, and their society has grown to accommodate a wide variety of relationship norms. Because of that, Brerdain's known for indulging his preference for pretty young female things.

Which, I guess, is why he brought her and not a man. Harder to pass off a new male companion to throw at me as a subtle bribe when you aren't known for them. But his most recent indulgence only started a week ago, and on average, he takes about a month to bore of his new friends. This is definitely a change in routine, even if the thin thread between them wasn't clear enough.

"Catrin is a friend of a friend. She's been wanting to indulge in the food here and I could help," Brerdain says. "I like doing favors for my friends."

Bolo lets out a loud snort while Harry picks at his food, head down.

"Just so you know, all recording has now been blocked. Everything I've got running is being blacked out. Overridden under a 'Need to Know,' National Interest order," Harry sends over party chat.

"A bit heavy-handed, no?" I return while sliding the latest delicacy into my mouth. Some green-and-yellow squirming thing that tastes sweet at first before going bitter. Just not too bitter.

"Not really. His Skill is always active. Makes it harder to sort out what's important, when everything is blocked."

Mikito flicks a gaze between the young lady and Brerdain then waves down a waiter and doubles her order of the dish before us. After that, she returns to ignoring the entire interplay. I wish I could do the same.

"I'm sure," I say. "So what do you want to know?"

Brerdain stares at me for a second, that congenial smile widening. "It seems you really are as blunt as the recordings."

I shrug while I note how Catrin seems to pull back, almost fading into the woodwork. I note the swirl of Mana around her, the way she triggers a Skill to help make her innocuous.

"But in truth," Brerdain say, "I have no great agenda here. I wish to learn about you. Your personality. Your history. Your plans."

"The first two are easily purchasable in the Shop," I say, pointing toward where the palace should be. "I'm really not that hard to understand. As for the last, I have a bunch of Paladin initiates to train. I'll get them up to speed, then let them loose."

"Let them loose…" Brerdain says, drawing out the last word. "And what would that mean?"

"You'd have to ask them," I say, opening my hands and the utensils I carry in them, letting them balance on the edges of my hand. I'd morphed the weird spork and knife combo into a simple human knife and fork combination, having decided that I wasn't interested in working with alien cutlery. Cultural assimilation is all well and good until you drop your two thousand Credit steak on your lap in a three-star restaurant with hovering paparazzi drones everywhere. "I'm just their trainer. Not their boss."

"No, you Paladins don't have that kind of hierarchy, do you?" Brerdain says, sounding almost satisfied.

I make note of his satisfaction, of the way he says it. And I remember that the Guards, for all their indication of being outside the hierarchy, are all still soldiers.

Silence falls over the table as the next course arrives. Another small portion of food shaped like spheres, glowing and individually colored like planets. Each fried, squished, or flash-frozen ball tastes different, even though I can tell that the material itself is the same.

Weird.

My comment elicits a more congenial conversation about the material used and the cooking methods for Mana-sourced monster meat, and that leads us to a friendly conversation about food across the Galaxy and the Empire that lasts nearly an hour. Catrin rejoins the conversation, but surprisingly does not stop her subtle flirting with me. She's toned down the expulsion of scent pheromones and other direct Charm attacks, but the obvious interest is not gone.

When the last dish—a dessert that towers nearly as tall as I am seated and made, of all things, human chocolate and ice cream—arrives, Brerdain turns the conversation back to business.

"This training you intend to offer the Paladin initiates. What are your intentions?" Brerdain asks. "I know that there have been requests for trainers…"

"Yes. Quite a few," I say. "Through the right channels, or so I'm led to believe. But of course, live fire exercises will be needed."

"No better training." Brerdain smiles. "If you want—"

"I'd be open to hearing about any problem areas that you need fixing," I offer easily. "Preferably something that a single individual or a small group can manage. Multiple problem areas in the same locale would be preferable."

"Threat level?" Brerdain says.

"High. I'd almost say deadly." I grin.

Catrin freezes for a second in the process of spooning her chocolate, before she continues. Harry gives me the side-eye but doesn't comment. Bolo, as usual, is grinning wide at the thought of more violence. That man has a problem.

"Complexity?" Brerdain asks.

"For this? None at all." I shake my head. "No need to make it hard for them. Yet."

Brerdain leans back and laughs, eyes twinkling. The lines along his eyes crinkle, his ears catching the glint of light. "I think I like you, Paladin." He flicks a glance at Catrin, who offers him a smile, and he gestures at the meal before him. "Though I must admit, I'm not a fan of this... chocolate of your Earth. Your ale, on the other hand, is a respectable addition to Galactic cuisine."

I pause and consider how much of an incident it'd be if I kill him. I am a Paladin...

"*No, boy-o. Down!*" Ali sends the thought to me, almost making me laugh.

"Well, we're all allowed our own tastes," I say with a smile. If there's a little more teeth than there needs to be, that's okay.

Having said his portion, Brerdain makes his excuses and takes the young lady along with him. She, at least, has the grace to look disappointed at not being allowed to finish her dessert. I can't be too sad about her departure. After all, I'm willing to sacrifice myself for the sake of Galactic hunger and waste.

As the pair stroll off, arm in arm, Bolo sighs. "That two?"

"Yup. One more to go."

Bolo shakes his head and turns back to the consumption of dessert. Somehow, he's sneaked the General's portion over to his side of the table. My eyes narrow before I dig into mine. As for the rest of the politicking, that can wait. More important things are at hand.

"Touch her dish, and I'll stab you."

***

I'm not surprised when, later that night, I receive a visitor. She arrives about half an hour after we finally make our way home. The others are taking the break to meditate, train, or just relax in their portion of the building. Leaving me to stare at the notification window of our visitor standing outside the gates.

"John?" Catrin stares at the small hovering drone, her eyes wide and alluring. The shift she wears is artfully draped off-shoulder, accentuating her charms as she looks up.

"Catrin. I'm surprised to see you here," I say. And that's the truth. I was expecting a much higher Level visitor.

"Well, your rather blunt refusal didn't make Brerdain happy. But he's a fair employer," she says with a smile. "Better than most in fact."

I grunt. "Doesn't really answer why you're here."

"Well, I'm no longer employed…" She bends her neck, letting hair fall over her eyes and hiding the cat-like-slit pupils for a second. "But I did find you intriguing. I've never met a Paladin before. Are your attribute gains as high as they are rumored to be?"

The way she arches that eyebrow makes me cough. She's rather blunt about her intentions here. A quick query sent to Ali at least assures me this isn't unusual. Between being a militaristic society used to clear commands and their more open policy about sex, Erethrans don't waste time on subtle flirting when they really want something.

"So, boy-o? You going for it?"

On the other hand, just because she says she's done with the employment doesn't mean that's true. Even Society's Web offers no help here. The thread tying her to Brerdain still exists, but it doesn't say why it exists.

Her presence, no matter what she says, comes with strings, of that I'm sure. Though strings based off female companionship seem rather a weak one to pull upon in a society that doesn't frown on such dalliances. Then again, maybe there's more to this that I'm not seeing. That I'm not—.

"If this is too complicated, I can leave. But it'd be a pity," Catrin says, shifting on her feet and making her body wiggle in a rather distracting way. I look for the notification but don't see it. So this is all skill, not Skill. "I understand it's been a while since your last visit with Lord Roxley."

Huh. The room is getting rather warm. Something definitely needs to be done about the heating…

In either case, Catrin's reminder makes me think. But Roxley doesn't care, and Lana was a long time ago. And, truth be told, it's been a long time since… well. Since.

And what can I say? There's a certain level of curiosity involved. Aliens are… alien. A hand pauses, and I find myself asking Ali for his thoughts. The query causes the Spirit to send back a rather risqué image.

I laugh and will the gates open, giving the Erethran Administrator access through the security systems. Sometimes, caution is all well and good. But as I told the initiates, sometimes, you just have to risk being shot at.

I watch Catrin sweep in. And if there's a self-satisfied smile on her face, I'm not sure I can blame her.

Chapter 12

"Are you certain this is a good idea?" Harry asks as we float high above the ground on the anti-gravity platform.

Around us, low-hanging gray clouds filled with soot and other, worse pollutants float, obscuring the ground from normal vision. Thankfully, multiple screens float alongside us, showing the feeds from the military drones. High above, I know the sun shines brightly, the large red dwarf of this planet's star offering scant heat in comparison to its size.

Alongside myself and Harry are the rest of the team—all but three of the initiates. Everyone has their own portion of the float to themselves, watching what plays out below and keeping an eye out for threats. And there are threats. Some of them are dangerous enough that the automated drones I've dispersed around us won't be enough of a defense. Among them are swarms of razor-beaked, insect-like creatures and larger, floating gas bag monsters with too many tendrils.

On the torn and shattered land below, three Paladin initiates make their way through the desolate landscape of the planet Seepgra in a separated V formation. Around them float a wide array of drones, feeding back telemetry data. Rather than green earth, the soil is black with charred carbon and foul pollutants, only broken up by the occasional lurid, mutated plant.

A drone floats too close to one of those plants and its orange leaves shoot outward, grabbing and twisting metal. We can't hear the drone's demise, but my mind adds the scream of metallic pain as the floating eye comes apart, its defenses insufficient. A second later, the component pieces are swept toward the heart of the plant. Roots burst from the ground, grabbing at other pieces and dragging them deep below the earth before the plant stills.

"It's good TV, isn't it?" I say, waving at the screens. "Not often we get to see a border planet like this."

"There's a reason for that," Harry says, eyes narrowing as he eyes the Zone Status information once more.

Warning! You Have Enterred a Restricted Zone!

Due to lack of Management by its owner, the planet Seepgra is facing significant Mana flow disruptions. Currently Zones are facing a ±87 Level differential in designations.

We're technically supposed to be in a Level 100 zone, but it could easily be much more. Or less. Though from our experience, it's much higher.

Kino releases another drone from his inventory to replace the gap in his net, while Freif takes a moment to fire upon the plant. His attack arches up high then slams straight down onto the plant, burrowing deep before exploding and showering the ground with plant matter and dirt. The last of their group, Ropo, just flicks his gaze over before returning his attention to his quadrant. I hear him murmuring orders as they close in on their target.

"Well, this way people will know why," I say to Harry, gesturing down. "And Brerdain was kind enough to find us these problem spots. It'd be rude to turn down his generosity."

Bolo snorts while I idly eye the way the initiates shift uncomfortably at what I say. Not to say Brerdain's disliked, but most think I've been compromised by my current, two-week-plus dalliance with Catrin. Even if she's indicated she's not in his employ, few believe her. Of course, she's not been my only visitor in the last few weeks, though most weren't as personal.

Even Julierudi's managed to make an appearance, having made arrangements to transport us here. That meeting was less than spectacular, with conversation stilted and formal over the Captain's meals. I get the feeling her position isn't as secure as Ali's initial analysis showed, with competing factions arguing over the reintroduction of the Paladins.

"But a Restricted Planet?" Harry says, shaking his head. "There's not much point for us to do... whatever it is you're having them do."

"Destroy dungeons," I say, clarifying the trio's orders below. "They're there to destroy three dungeons at least—more, if possible—in the next three hours."

Harry's lips thin. I know what he's thinking, and the number of dungeons as well as timeframe does seem a little arbitrary. Especially when Levels, and thus the threat rating they're facing, can alter so easily. But that too is part of the test.

"What's the point? Anyone with any sense has left the planet. Outside of a few highly fortified Guild and military bases, no one lives here. Not really," Harry persists.

I hum in thought then raise my voice, calling, "Magine. Explain to the reporter why we're here."

Harry, not one to lose an interview opportunity, spins around to face the pretty elf. Magine keeps his face neutral, though I can tell from the flicker in the strings that tie him to me that he's annoyed. All this time, training and goading the group has allowed me to read them—and their threads—much, much better.

"Restricted planets are not Forbidden Planets. Travel to and from Restricted Planets is not forbidden but is tightly regulated. This is due to the need to lower casualty numbers and, in some cases, to help the rehabilitation of those planets. In some cases, such as the planet Seepgra, it's introduction as a Restricted Planet is due to sapient disruption of Mana."

"English. Try English," I call to Magine. When he frowns at me, I grin. "Dumb it down. Harry's audience is a bunch of neo-barbs."

Magine's hand by his side twitches, and for a second, I can see him regulating his temper. Then he turns his attention back to Harry.

"Seepgra was the epicenter of four different battles between ourselves and the Mo'thma Kingdom. Multiple spells and Skills, as well as certain near-forbidden technology, was put into play. In the last war, two different Heroic Classes clashed. All of this induced significant Mana flow effects, damaging the System's hold on the planet as well as the System orbs that regulate Mana flow." When I narrow my eyes at Magine, he sighs and dumbs it down even further. "The Mana here is messed up. But it can be fixed, because we messed it up. It's not an overflow issue like other Restricted Planets near the Forbidden Zone."

"Good man," I say, clapping my hands together. "I knew you could do it." I turn to Harry, who focuses on me. "It's possible to pull back, even keep, Restricted Planets as residential planets, at least for a time. It requires a significant expansion of personnel, as you have to kill monsters, clear dungeons, reset them to the right locations, plant and build out settlements, and the like. But it is doable, as history has shown. We're just tackling an easier example below."

Below us, the trio pause for a fraction of a second as they cross the invisible boundary of the dungeon they're here to clear. This is an open area dungeon, meaning that Mana density is vastly increased within the dungeon itself, making dungeon monsters spawn more frequently. In fact, looking at it from the air, you can see the boundary—the way the earth changes, the increase in Mana-suffused vegetation. We can even see the sudden change in motion as monsters that lay dormant wake and approach the group.

"But why dungeons?" Harry asks.

"Dungeons are Mana sinks. Sometimes, that's a good thing," I say. "City dungeons allow cities to broaden the Safe Zone by adjusting Mana flows and sending overflows to the dungeon. Wild dungeons though, those created by chance, can create… whirlpools in locations. Areas where Mana keeps flooding in, making the dungeons bigger. Stronger.

"Rather than let that happen in zones where they're not meant to be, we destroy them. Help the System regulate." I run my mind over options before continuing. "Think of it as selective burns. The planet is an overgrown forest with too many trees and underbrush. Easy to set off. Rather than let it get worse, we do selective burns."

Harry frowns, then asks the obvious question. "So what's the fire?"

"Uhh… the monsters?" I pause, rubbing my chin.

Not exactly. Monsters are a by-product of the System attempting to shunt Mana into something it can control, but they're not exactly the fire. Or are they? After all, the production of powerful monsters, including over-Leveled Alphas or worse, do drop the surrounding Mana density. Not by a lot, but by a little. In fact… I look at Bolo.

The Dragon Lord meets my gaze placidly. "You are correct in your thoughts, Paladin. This is how Dragons were first created. A shunting of excess Mana. Though they then took the Mana and made it their own." Bolo grins. "Magnificent creatures."

"Uh huh," I say.

But his words trigger another avalanche of memory, of data. Streams of recordings about dragons, about their care and upkeep. Of how they end up in other worlds, helping to regulate the Mana flows, and how captive breeding of them has been attempted. A million tests, as many as there are worlds, all of it streaming along.

And at the same time, another data packet unveils itself. My head hurts as I struggle to grasp the information. Tests. More tests. This time, the experiments are to create another dragon, another creature that is as in tune with Mana.

The Kirin. Or the Galactic equivalent of it. A successful experiment, though their significantly decreased reproduction cycle was considered a failure.

But more often than not, failures as experiments go horribly wrong. Hydras, one of the failures, later taken by the System for use as monsters. The Ymir, the Namyz, more. So many more failures, creatures that were born and died, forced to evolve under a variety of Mana over-saturated environments. Sudden and gradual, over generations or a single instance. In and out of the System, right on the borders. And in Forbidden Zones.

My mind whirls as pain and data flows, giving me information that I never asked for. And when I come back, the boys are two-thirds of the way through the nest, fighting swarms of creatures. The monsters are warped messes, twisted versions of what they should be. The dungeon is meant to help them reproduce faster, to form and swarm and allow Adventurers to use their bodies, their Mana for the System economy. But with Mana overrun, with the System breaking down…

The creatures are macabre parodies of what they should be. Some have too many limbs, others too few. Hunched and twisted, fur, carapace, skin, and organs hang off them. They swarm and fight, unleashing claws, gouts of poison, and plasma in unequal portions.

Bolo and the initiates watch without moving a muscle, having seen all this before. On the other hand, Mikito has her face twisted up in disgust. And Harry… well, Harry is hocking his lunch over the side of the platform. Ali, being true to himself, is eating popcorn, watching a baking show on another screen at the same time.

"How, how can you stand staring at those things?" Harry says. "They're monsters. Demons."

"Eh, less disgusting than the ones I fought in the Forbidden Zone. You don't want to deal with warped slimes," I say.

I note the increased pulse in interest from the initiates when I mention my time away. They all know the history, the story of how I got my Class. This is their history, their heritage. If they pass. Not surprising that they're interested.

But I ignore their interest, turning my regard instead to the people below. They reach the dungeon heart and are met by the Alpha. The Hmefa Alpha. Cancerous growths sprout from its body, making it slow and sluggish. But as they land attacks, its body heals. As they fight, I take note of their styles, their flow.

Kino stands in front of the Alpha, literally brawling with it. For a Soulbound weapon, the Risen doesn't have a sword or polearm or anything traditional. No, instead both of its arms are covered in metallic gauntlets, gleaming dark red and brown as he blocks and attacks, keeping the creature's attention on him. His build is almost purely defensive, so he doesn't bother manifesting his equivalent of the Thousand Blades Skill. Instead, the other Skill he purchased is in play, a dark brown glow infusing his body with each blocked strike, each point of damage taken.

Retribution Delayed (Level 3) (A)

Passive effect that allows the Grudge Holder to collect damage done to it and release it in a single, retributive attack. Reduces Mana Regeneration by 15 permanently.

Effect: 6% of Damage Taken is stored in a Mana Cloud. When triggered, the next attack will deal 6% of stored Damage.

At first glance, the Skill might not be that useful. 6% of 6% is just 0.36% of damage taken. But there's literally no limit to how long Kino can store this damage. Which means in a dungeon crawl like this, he's been storing all the damage he's taken as he journeys in. All the damage, even damage he's healed, is just waiting for him to release.

That he isn't using it right now is a bit surprising, but I wonder if he considers the Alpha too weak for him to bother. After all, the longer he holds off, the more damage he can do. It's the kind of Skill that I considered, but even if I do play tank, I rarely get a chance to wait around for a single person. Still, I've mentally bookmarked the option for when I can find a Master Class equivalent.

Freif, the sniper, on the other hand, is showcasing the difference in his Skills. While his initial build mostly focused on stacking Mana Imbue with a small increase in Blade (Gun) Strike to increase range and penetration and a single point in Thousand Guns, his amendment has been to purchase up Thousand Guns. Now, rather than a single weapon, he has multiple rifles floating around him. Each of those are linked passively with other Skills, allowing him to independently control and fire them. They're almost automated, using his other Skills to increase damage and accuracy.

What it really means is that unlike his initial build of being a single-shot, high-damage sniper—with an alpha strike option of Army of One—he can now hold off the swarming minions on one side by himself. His floating guns fire and retarget constantly, drawing upon the base Mana density to make him a one-man army without triggering the Skill.

Of course, there's a negative to that—part of the reason he's so effective is the huge disparity in Mana density here. Otherwise, the guns he's using would run out of Mana much faster. On top of that, the damage is lower than his main weapon—unlike melee weapon variations of the Skill—which means he often needs multiple shots to kill a monster. Still, with his base Skills, he's able to cripple them with the first shots.

"New tactics," Mikito says. "They listened."

One of the aspects of our briefing was instructing them to mix it up, to change how they were going to do things. Normally, it'd be Freif who ends the fight while Kino holds off the monster. While Kino is still the tank, Ropo is the finisher this time.

I watch as the Grimsar sneaks around the back, using his smaller stature and enchanted equipment to make him easily ignorable. He lines himself up, his traditional axe by his side, and waits. Unlike the others, Ropo's used a generalist build in his attributes for the Honor Guard. He's a little like me, with a ton of different Skills all over the map, though he's put a greater emphasis on Sanctum. Sadly, he was a little unlucky and missed an Evoution for the Skill. That left him with the problem of lacking a finishing move. Even his secondary Classes don't help, since the poison and toxin Skills he has just don't add up enough.

Now, he's using a new Skill he purchased. It's not what I would have picked, but that's his call. And in this case, it makes sense.

The Waiting Doom (Level 10) (A)

A base Skill for the Assassins of Hansen, the Waiting Doom allows the assassins to prepare a finishing strike on their target. Feared for its ability to increase base damage of a single type of attack while hiding the point of origin, the Assassins of Hansen are barred from 2,985 solar systems at this time. Luckily, their need to be flamboyant and have a specific calling card makes them slightly less of a Galactic threat.

Effect: Total calculated damage of designated primary attack increases by 55% per minute while user is still and unmoving. Charged attacks can be interrupted. Upon use of attack, assassin gains a 0.55 second time displacement on light, sound, and other incidental effects of attack.

Cost: 100 Mana per minute

Duration: Channelled

It's not base damage, so this includes buffs and other damage increases. Combined with his Skills as a Poison Specialist, it allows him to stack damage in his attacks. On the other hand, the disadvantage of the Skill is that your primary attack has to be chosen, decreasing your attack options. If you're sneaking and hiding, waiting for the time to launch your attack, it's less of a concern.

In Ropo's case, he's able to combine the ability to sneak and Skills like Soul Shield and Stand my Ground from the Basic Class to ensure he can charge up the attack, even in a crowded battlefield.

Kino snarls, punching outward and catching a swinging claw as it arcs toward him. His punch shatters the claw, leaving it limp—much like the monster's other appendages, mutated tentacles. A few formerly mangled limbs twitch and rise as regeneration brings them back into play, but Kino charges in, grappling the monster via its arms, while a remaining sting-like appendage beats on his back. Freif looks back at the group, the reinforcements having died off. Literally.

Ropo is finally ready, the Alpha held still. He throws himself forward with a single, glowing swing, his attack launched from behind. Waiting Doom lights up his axe, highlighting the Mana imbued into the weapon and leaving a trail of golden and sickly green light. It's the least assassin-like attack I can think of, but there's a slight delay in what I see and his actual motion. The statistical number of the effect is tiny, but the actual effect in a fast-paced fight is huge.

By the time we—and the Alpha—see Ropo move, the dwarf has already cut through his opponent, leaving a six-foot-long gash across the creature's body. The wound pulses gold and green, the green rot spreading at speed as the poison modifiers within the attack stack up.

Damage notifications flare all over, but even with Ropo's charged attack, it's not enough to kill the creature. Not immediately. As it turns to flee, Freif fires a single shot from his rifle, burning through the stinger arm and tearing it off before it injects itself into Kino. Freed of the distraction, Kino roars and twists, tearing at the torso and the flesh that holds the monster together. The injured portions part, blood and viscera spilling out like a wet, noisy fart.

Probably smells just as bad too.

The Alpha dies, and with it, the Mana storm that makes up the dungeon dies almost immediately. The cleansing of so many monsters by itself was sufficient to start the process, but now, without the anchor of the Alpha, the System has more control.

The trio pant, staring at one another for a few seconds. Freif absently kills straggling dungeon monsters. And then, in unison, they run.

For this is only the first of the three dungeons they must clear.

***

Three hours later, the second team of Magine, Gheisnan, and Anayton are cleansing the fourth dungeon of the day. Deep within the remnant and twisted town, the group clear buildings—or in some cases, just tears them down. They're making good time, having taken over from the original trio, and are busy decimating the remaining monsters.

The monsters here are a weird semi-sentient amalgamation of golem and matter, so the group has to switch attacks constantly to deal the most effective damage. However, Gheisnan is making his usefulness known by calling out resistances well beforehand, allowing the damage dealers to really go at it.

Unlike the first trio, all of the combatants are clad in full powered suits, using their tech advantage in a different way. They still use a few drones, but those are tasked with dealing with smaller menaces—the usual array of Leveled insects, prey, and scrap eaters that make up the fauna of a world.

I'm only paying partial attention to the fight below. Instead, I'm facing the original trio. They're looking worse for the wear, though damage is quickly healing on Kino's side, leaving his rocky skin pristine. As for Freif, his scout power armor has been stored away, having taken quite the beating in the second dungeon. And Ropo is clad in his traditional enchanted outfit, axe casually held in one hand.

"Report," I say.

"Three dungeons destroyed as ordered. Thirty percent of forces in fourth dungeon were eradicated, but Alpha was not located for completion. We used seventy-eight percent of all allocated consumables, with no loss of life on allied part," Ropo barks.

"And how do you think you did?" I say.

"We completed the objectives as requested," Ropo replies without missing a beat. When I meet the Grimsar's gaze, it has no give in it. Nor any hint of his other thoughts.

So I turn from him. "Kino. Your thoughts."

"We comple—"

"Thoughts," I snap. "I want you tell me what you think, not repeat what Ropo said."

Kino freezes in place, the gentle crumbling of rock that makes up even the smallest of his motions stopping. Then he speaks, looking directly at me. "We could have completed the fourth. If we were allowed to use normal tactics. If we went with a trash-and-burn plan for the fourth dungeon when we realized the terrain."

I note Ropo shift, and I gesture for him to speak.

"We are Honor Guards. And Paladins-to-be. Our job is not to destroy planets, but to save them," Ropo says. "This town only fell two years ago. There are significant salvage options available, as well as numerous remains of our citizens. Destroying it to expedite a useless—" Ropo clamps his mouth shut.

"A useless training exercise?" I finish for the Grimsar.

The old Honor Guard refuses to finish his sentence, so I ignore it. Knowing him, he'd probably add a lot more inventive cursing to it. The only reason he's not right now is because we're on the battlefield. Even then, I'm curious how long discipline will hold.

Dismissing that thought, I turn to Freif. "And you?"

"The new Skills give me more flexibility in small group tactics," Freif acknowledges. "It decreases my Mana regeneration, which is inefficient in long-term engagements. It decreased my effectiveness by the third dungeon."

"And you were already heavily invested in Intelligence with low Wisdom," I conclude for him. "I'd look at fixing that on your next Level ups."

Freif inclines his head.

"Anything else before Bolo has his say?" I ask, flicking my gaze over the group. Challenging them to challenge me. To voice their opinion.

"I am considering purchasing another Skill to increase regeneration," Kino says. "It is more efficient for me to take damage and heal with my new Skill than to block damage. It might be even viable to respec entirely."

I frown, tilting my head. There's a little truth to what he says but getting a respec done is a painful and expensive process. There are also negatives in terms of experience gain in most cases. Resets of just Skills are even harder, requiring specialized individuals.

"I wouldn't go that far. Efficiency is one thing, but putting yourself out there to constantly get hurt gets old fast too. Training and will will only take you so far," I say. "I'd also hold off on any major changes until we get to phase two."

"Phase two?" Ropo frowns.

I wave Bolo forward. I have no reason to explain my plans to them, not till everyone is here. Instead, I let Bolo dress them down, explain where they failed in their tactics in working together, with the occasional interjection by Mikito on their individual failings. I keep half an ear out, mostly because I can learn a lot from the Dragon Lord on these aspects.

In truth, I kind of feel bad trying to bitch them out about their team tactics. Even with their new Skills and their new formations, they're smoother and cleaner, more professional than myself and my team. I've been learning a lot from watching them, seeing how the pros do it for real compared to the way myself and my team have done.

We've been learning and putting it into practice late at night, when the teams are done for the day or with their own trainers. Because at the end of the day, I'm just a talented amateur.

Luckily, Bolo isn't. And he's more than happy to advise and critique. I've not seen the Dragon Lord this enthused about anything before, almost as if he's missed working with groups, missed training others. Even if the Dragon Knights aren't as team-oriented as the Honor Guard, they still train and work together. They have to.

And so, half-listening, half-learning, I watch the group below take on the new dungeon.

***

Hours later, we're on dungeon number five for the second trio and time's running out. They're pushing faster and harder than the previous team—so much so that I'm a little concerned. I eyeball their Health and Mana bars, gauging their needs, and frown further. They've used all their potions, popped them into full regeneration and instant increases. Thrice. Additional uses will see significantly lower gains, to the point that it's not really worth it.

They're cutting it close with the way they're pushing. Taking risks, being aggressive. Trying to impress me? Or are they just competitive?

Magine is in the front of the group, dancing past the swarm of monsters coming at him. They got lucky in the previous dungeon, finding a low-level swarm spawn, creatures that looked like mobile tadpoles. Low-level, large numbers. They pulled out their grenades and high explosives, using area effect attacks to clear their way through. Easy.

Now, Magine is facing larger, canine-like monsters with stinger-like tails and eyebeam eyes. Their attacks dig up the ground, tear at his Soul Shield as he swings his swords and rips apart skin and fur, lops off limbs. He's in the middle of the pack, forcing them to choose to shoot and hit their own friends or face him in melee.

But these are monsters. And self-preservation and care for their own kind is low on their list of concerns. They attack their own friends, Magine, and the rest of the team with abandon, filling the air with the bright flare of their eyebeam attacks.

Anayton forges in behind, dancing around the group with her own weapon. She wields a chain and blade weapon combination, sending the burning, Mana Infused chain to wrap around, punch through, and rend apart monsters, all the while blocking attacks with the blade portion. Unlike Magine, she stays close, playing bodyguard to Gheisnan, buffing him with Two are One and intercepting attackers.

Gheisnan's the one guiding the group, the reason they're on number five. He's found the way to the nearest dungeons quickly. Worked out the weaknesses and routes to the monsters with his Skills and coordinated the pair. He's an amazing addition to any team, but in return, he's a liability.

A damage counter floats next to each head, showing the percentage of damage taken. And Gheisnan's hogging nearly sixty percent of damage of that statistic. Soul Shields, Two are One, resistances, all of it deployed to keep him alive. Small, mobile force screen drones hover around him, blocking attacks. And still, he is bleeding, injured, his regeneration barely able to keep up. His Mana hovering at the last fifth.

"Think they'll make it?" I ask Mikito and Harry.

Harry shrugs, content to not guess. Mikito holds up a hand, waggling it side to side.

"Yeah, me too," I acknowledge her hesitation. There's too much variability. Too much chance. It depends on the Alpha, on what they face. But… "Magine's doing well."

"He's leaving his friends behind," Mikito says disapprovingly. "Not working as a team."

"Only this dungeon."

"Only needs to be once," Mikito says.

"Once what?" Ali asks.

"To die, baka."

Ali crosses his arms, glaring at Mikito from where he twirls around. "Rude. John's the baka."

"You both are." She points at Magine's image on the screen. "Just like him."

I grunt and fish out a piece of chocolate to ease the pain of truth. It's from a chocolatery that restarted in Nepal of all places. However, it's really, really good and my current go-to chocolatier. Something the Yeti craftsmen do make it all the better. "Why do you think he's doing it?"

"Pride," Bolo chimes in. "I know his type. If we can temper it, he'll be a good Paladin."

"And if we can't?"

"Then he'll be a good target."

I snort but watch the fight below. Time continues to run out, with Anayton finally making the executive decision to pull back. She triggers a series of explosions in the nearby drones, clearing space for herself and Gheisnan to retreat. Leaving Magine as he continues his journey toward the Alpha, disobeying orders, even as time ticks down.

A minute and a half before Magine's out of time, the dungeon boss makes its presence known. The canine-creature is the size of a rhinoceros, its skin thick and plated with a reinforced dermis, dotted with multiple eyes. The good news is that those eyebeams only fire five at a time. The bad news is that there doesn't seem to be a rhyme or reason for their activation other than need.

Magine rushes forward, only to be targeted by three of the beams and thrown backward. His Soul Shield shatters, his health plunges. And I twist my hand sideways, creating the Portal so that he flies through it and onto our hovering platform. He lands and rolls, coming up to his knees, body smoking, blood dripping and making a mess. He rushes toward the Portal, intent on entering it, only to face the broad back of Bolo. The Dragon Lord is slow too, for Mikito's already through the Portal. I snap the Portal shut behind the Dragon Lord the moment he's through.

"No! That was my kill," Magine says.

"No chance," I say, shaking my head. "You don't have the Mana to pull off an Army of One," I say. "And you don't have the time to wear it down, even if you could."

And the last part is important, because I watch as Mikito eats fire from the eyebeams of the creature as she attempts to weave her way in. Of course, when Bolo makes his first big attack, the boss fully turns its attention to him. That big hammer of Bolo's, and its high damage output, is a clear indicator of who is the greater threat.

"Why are you letting them fight?" Freif asks, frowning.

"Might as well finish the dungeon," I say with a shrug. "And while we debrief, they can pick up a few hundred thousand more experience."

A large explosion trickles up from below the platform, echoed in the monitors of the ground below. I frown, anger trickling in. A gesture makes the monitors go dark and another makes a second Portal open, allowing the remainder of his team to stagger in.

"So what was that?" I ask.

"Four dungeons and a nearly complete fifth. We would have completed the fifth. If someone had backed me up." Magine's lips curl in disgust as he turns around and glares at Anayton and Gheisnan. "I told you not to retreat."

"And you were not in operational command," Anayton says. "Gheisnan was. You didn't listen to orders."

"As the Paladin has pointed out, we're not training to be good little soldiers anymore," Magine sneers. "We're Paladins. And running from a little danger is ill-befitting a Cha—Paladin." I frown as Magine corrects himself.

"I expected cowardice from the Pooskeen, but from you? I'm disappointed. With your standing—"

"My standing has nothing to do with what was a reasonable and logical choice," Anayton says. "There was no advantage to us pushing ahead. Receiving significant damage—or losing one of us—for a project that could be done with more safety and care made no sense."

"You're thinking of gains and losses like a guard. Like this was an army mission," Magine says. "But the Paladin is here to train us. We're here to show what we, as Paladins, can do." He spins and stares directly at me. "Isn't that right?"

I don't answer him, instead locking my gaze on the quiet third of the group. The one who has been key to their success. And yet has kept silent thus far. "And you? What do you think?"

"This one has naught to say," Gheisnan says, bowing his head to me. "We train at your pleasure."

I don't miss the slight mocking tone or structure of his reply. But my own reply is waylaid by the party chat request from below. I open my hands and twist, pulling open the Portal to retrieve my friends from below. They tramp out, covered in blood and guts and smoking a little. I don't bother waiting, reopening a new Portal moments after I shut the previous one, dumping them in front of the next dungeon. Harry hurries after them, preferring to join the pair and earn a little experience that way rather than stay up here and watch the drama unfold.

Once my friends are gone and our platform begins its slower journey over, I reply at last to the impatient trio. I raise my voice to include the others. "These training exercises are for me to understand who you are. So, yes. Do what you think is right, like Magine. Or Anayton. Or bitch me out like Ropo and still do your job. Because the gods know, you'll not have a chance again after you're a Paladin." I shake my head. "But you're also showing me who you are."

"*Think you said that already, boy-o.*"

"*Shut up.*"

At Magine's frown, I continue. "If you're so intent on leaving your friends behind, I'm not entirely sure I'd trust you as a Paladin. Maybe, sometimes, that's necessary. To sacrifice everything for the mission. But you do that when it's necessary. Not for a stupid test by a guy who you barely know."

I point at Magine. "Fail."

Anayton. "Pass."

"Fail." Gheisnan doesn't seem surprised.

Ropo is next. "Fail." That makes the dwarf frown.

Kino straightens when my finger passes in front of him. "Pass. Barely."

Freif looks stressed as I point at him last. I let the silence linger, watching the sniper twitch before I speak. "Fail."

There's a long silence when everyone takes in my words, then they all talk at the same time.

I snort and wave them down. "I'm not done."

The group silences pretty fast at that point.

"You have a month. Group together. Work alone. I don't care. You're going to clear this planet." I rub my nose. "*We're* going to clear the planet." I twitch my hand sideways, making a series of drones float over to the group. "These are the drones I'm gifting you. If they get destroyed, buy another. I recommend you buy a lot. I'll watch what you do. How you do it. Now, you're dismissed."

I don't wait for them to reply, instead jumping backward. A Portal opens up behind me, depositing me in front of the dungeon I've picked. From the group, I hear more than a few curses, but I can't help but smile.

Time to see what they do.

Chapter 13

The specter tears at me, its razor-sharp fingers filled with ice bearing down on my armor. Hod's Triple-Fused Armor is amazing for most things, and it peels portions of the Mana-generated cold away, but it does nothing to stop the insubstantial hands from passing through and scoring my skin. It and the dozens of others that float around me.

-14 Damage (90% resisted)

-17 Damage (90% resisted)

-3 Damage (90% resisted)

-16 Damage (90% resisted)

-9 Damage (90% resisted)

The damage notifications flicker up again, reminding me of how much my resistances help. I ignore them, absorbing the pain even as the Specters continue to tear into me. Because the biggest problem for the specters as they float around me is that they have to get close.

And my own swords have formed their bladed barricades around me. They spin and twist, lopping off ectoplasmic limbs and torso, tearing gaping holes that trail misty whiteness. Damage accumulates fast for these creatures before they die. But killing them isn't the problem.

It's keeping them dead.

If they weren't mostly insubstantial and translucent, if I didn't have as high as a Perception attribute and the ability to see across multiple wavelengths, I might not be able to see down the choked hallway. Even then, it's like staring down a road on a foggy winter morning, on those occasions when the temperature dropped below -40C and the water vapor from the river kept rising, cloaking the grounds of Whitehorse. When it gets that cold, the world itself blurs.

And it is cold. The walls are frozen, the ground is slick with ice, and the creatures themselves are shards of angry frost. I plow through them, refreshing my Soul Shield once in a while when I get tired of eating damage, when I need a little relief from the pain.

I plow through them, one after the other, while Ali strolls along, full size for once, hands behind his back. The specters try to attack him, try to tear him apart. They should be able to do so—but the damn Spirit has pulled out another trick. And so their attacks pass through his body.

"*You could help!*" I snap at the Spirit as I throw my knives, letting them tear through the specters. I'd noticed my lack of use of them, of using their ability to return to me, in my previous altercations. And, I admit, watching the other Erethrans fight gave me inspiration. The last few weeks have seen me doing my best to integrate the throwing knives into my new fighting style, especially since I've got a new sword to deal with.

"*And give away my actual position?*" Ali snorts. "*Unlike someone, I don't like getting torn into bits. Also, most of my skills aren't particularly useful against them.*"

I know that for the lie it is, but I'm a little too busy to call him out on it. I catch one of my swords, switch its position as it cuts down, deflect another of my own swords with my forearm and send it on another trajectory while making a third sword disappear before it lops off my toe. In the meantime, one floats above my head, ending its trajectory by decapitating a specter. Another finishes dismembering another specter, and the last just floats at my back, fending off potential attacks.

"*And I am helping.*" Ali floats on as another portion of the wall highlights itself.

I cut upward, watching my swords shift direction again, and I duck low, releasing my soulbound sword and snatching a knife from its sheath. An underhand toss and it tumbles through a specter, cutting through the wall. Behind, the totem shatters and a half-dozen specters howl and disappear.

Experience rolls in, discounted as the monsters aren't true monsters but dungeon creations. Specters, half-formed immaterial golems, are held and replicated by totems laid throughout the building. I've been grinding through this dungeon, the sixth largest in the damn planet, for the last three days. Plunging deeper and deeper each day, and all the while, a portion of my mind gets updates.

Data streams in from drones, verbal communications, and the party chat. Even the occasional report. All of it flowing through the neural link, all of it mixing with the slew of knowledge that keeps bursting into my mind from the library. Tests on golems, System creations that the Questors try to make sapient, AIs driven mad by the prods of Questors and System-manipulation, destroyed in fire and flame. Long-winded diatribes.

And more updates. On how my friends are faring. How the initiates are managing.

Magine fighting in a team this week. Chopping apart a half-dozen flying monsters, literally hopping from one monster to the next before bouncing off the mountain walls to ascend higher. Freif, hiding in the distance, providing covering fire and picking off monsters. Even as Ropo continues to climb stealthily to the top. Where a giant egg resides, the prize and ending for their dungeon.

Kino is fighting by himself, plowing through a marshy dungeon. Water-logged, dragged down, and pounded into the ground, the Risen struggles to his feet time and again to tear at the wet, seaweed-like tentacles that attack him. He punches his way through, the Thousand Blades option on his gauntlet making them larger, allowing him to hit harder. Blade Strike becomes a power punch projection from his gauntlets, shooting Mana-infused attacks into the water and showering him with seaweed and gore. Always pushing ahead, never concerned about being drowned. Or being alone.

Gheisnan is by himself too. He's been alone for the last half of the month, even as the other Paladins join together and split apart, tackling challenges in makeshift teams as necessary. Except for him. Where the Shaman used to rely on others, buff others, he's in the midst of the fight now. Teeth bared, small daggers plunging in and out of the creatures he fights like a sewing needle. He's savage, using teeth, claws on his feet, and his knives as he clears dungeon after dungeon. Trying to prove himself to me.

But I've noticed he never takes on one that's over-leveled. He always knows when to pull back. When to retreat and recuperate. And come back later with even more savagery and determination.

As for Anayton, she's working through the remnants of the fourteenth-strongest dungeon. She's been there for the last week, even when the other members of her initial team split off, deciding to clear other areas first. She's stubborn and persistent, constantly hunting the myriad monsters that have made the dungeon their home.

For the fourteenth-strongest dungeon is also the physically largest. Monsters of all kinds live in the remnants of the alien, skyscraper city. Forcing Anayton to travel up multiple floors, across creaking, worn floors and skywalks, to battle among crumbling remnants of civilization. Buildings fall, thunder rumbles, and monsters hunt her in a never-ending swarm. And still, she refuses to leave. Refuses to stop as she hunts for the boss. As she thins their numbers, all in preparation for the rest of us to help her.

Or end it herself.

There's a staggering arrogance involved. I would have dropped a couple of nukes—or Beacons of the Angels—and called it a day. But she's in no such luxury. Her Army of One Skill would drain her too much, take away her other options. She needs to grind them down. Step by step, kill by kill. And she does.

It's impressive.

It's idiotic.

It's perfect.

***

"WHO DARES DISTURB MY REST!?!"

The voice rocks my world, thrumming through my flesh and blood, vibrating within my very bones. It's dark and ominous, eerie in its pronunciation, more felt than heard. It cuts through Hod's Armor with ease, throwing up damage notifications with each syllable.

Fear Effect Resisted

Aura of the Final Passage Resisted (94%)

Even through my mental resistances, the pressure of the creature's aura, the terror it invokes with its words batters my mind, clutches at my soul. Reminds me of how mortal I am, that it is only a small step from life to death. When that eternal embrace will hold me, bringing me to my final end... just a small step, a closing of eyes, a blade in the gut.

"Yeah... creepy voice. Check." I eyeball the creature floating before me. The boss monster is nearly a hundred feet tall, having emerged from the ground itself when it finally deigned to make itself known. "Faceless void for a face. Check."

Black chains erupt from its body, crisscrossing the space between us. I jump and spin, dancing across the rattling chains, stepping on them, the air, and my own blades as I cross the distance to it.

"And of course, big flowing, spectral robes. Check."

A chain glances off my armor, throwing off sparks. More damage notifications flash up, reminding me of the danger I'm in.

"Chuunibyou confirmed."

Blade Strikes erupt from my sword, cutting at the monster. Spectral chains block the cuts, wrapping themselves together into an impromptu shield. I don't stop, cutting apart spiked chains as they reach for me, throwing out a few more Blade Strikes while dropping a couple of grenades. From the corner of my eyes, I'm watching, waiting. A trio of knives fly out, criss-crossing the space between us as I near the monster. But the closer I get, the denser the chains become.

Eventually, I slip up and get smashed backward. I land, flipping around and rolling, as I note damage reports. Soul Shield, even in its upgraded form, barely stops the blow. My own attacks have done almost nothing, with only a few edges of my Blade Strikes catching it. A quick cast places a Zone of Denial right on top of the monster, stacking area effect damage and degrading his chains. But I watch as its passive regeneration ignores it. I snort, absently debating using one of my Mana grenades on it, then dismiss the waste of equipment.

I have enough information now. Enough to gauge damage numbers, to understand resistances.

"I WILL SUP ON YOUR SOUL!"

The monster has been muttering things like that the entire time. It's rather embarrassing really. You'd think a faceless boss monster would have better lines than a twelve-year-old's first writing attempt. Thinking that, I can't help but repeat the thought out loud.

"YOUR CORPSE WILL BE REANIMATED, YOUR SOUL RETURNED TO ITS MANGLED REMAINS, ONLY FOR ME TO CRUSH IT ONCE AGAIN!"

"Okay, that was better," I say, cutting aside a trio of chains that manage to reach me. "Maybe if we keep this up, you might even get a decent repertoire."

"John, it's nearly time. No more playing around," Ali tells me. He's well back from the fight. Even his ability to adjust his position by bending light and displacing himself with his Elemental Affinity can't help him when there are so many chains flying around.

"YOUR FLESH WILL BE FLAYED FROM YOUR BONES AND EATEN BEFORE YOU. YOUR—"

"I get it," I say.

I've got enough information, so I start with the simplest of my Skills. Above the creature, a ritual circle appears, energy building. The boss notices—it's impossible not to notice—and additional chains erupt from its body. But for the first time, I see a limit, as it retracts some that it used to protect itself in order to build its defense.

Beacon of the Angels calls down a column of white light, a cylinder of burning energy that tears at the monster, melting the chains that protect it. One after the other shatters, dissolving into motes of Mana and steel. A single Beacon isn't enough though, and I trigger another and another, layering them on the monster and keeping it busy. Damage notifications flash, but I'm not done.

Next, I grab one of my knives and mentally trigger the Skill I bought. Payload activates, and I reach out to imbue the knife with Army of One. I then Blink forward, bouncing right past most of the chains and catching dummkopf by surprise.

Partly because I'm entering the attack range of my own spell. But not all plans are perfect. And in this case, in the midst of my Blink Stepping in and out, twice in rapid succession and adding Blade Strikes and the glare of my attack, the knife flies. Hidden.

To aid the spell, a simple area denial via Gravitic Sphere is formed, low to the monster's body. It drags chains down even as I channel more and more energy into it. Making its defense, above and below, difficult.

The knife goes right through the creature's remaining defenses, such a small thing that the boss specter never sees it. Never sees it before it lodges in its body, glowing. And then, in one second, all the strength of the attack, of Army of One, is unleashed.

Point blank range.

There's no replication of multiple blades, no showy special effects. No, it's just a bolt of pure energy that explodes through the boss, carving it apart and blowing a giant hole in it. And since the knife was still rotating a little when it impacted and twists, because gravity has a say, it continues firing and bisecting the monster. Body torn, defenses compromised, the remaining Beacon cuts through.

The scream it unleashes hurts, making my bones vibrate even as I Blink Step the heck out of there. I trigger Blink Step three times in quick succession, dodging the dying end of my spinning blade of doom, before the specter finally dies in an explosion of dark energy, its body parting in mists and shadows, Mana dispersing into the world and returning to the System.

I watch it die, bat aside the experience notification, and watch as Ali loots the glowing remnants. I idly kill off a few more specters that appear next to me, still intent on finishing the job. But without their alpha, their strength has diminished greatly. So much so that a few dozen drones keeps them busy while other hunter-killer drones get to work. In the meantime, I ponder something much more interesting.

Level Up!
You have reached Level 41 as an Erethran Paladin. Stat Points automatically distributed. You have 21 Free Attributes and 2 Class Skill Points to distribute.

Finally. It's taken ages to crawl up to Level 41, and that's after my big fight at the end of the station battle. Technically, this is the Level the Queen's been waiting for. The one that would give me access to the third tier. I'm not going to tell her though, because I want a few more Levels first. In addition, I can't afford to take a Class Skill—just in case the new Skill shows up on their reviews. Which leaves both my Free Attributes and Class Skill points unused.

Just as interesting, as I browse through my notifications, is the lack of dungeon completion notice. No dungeon completion notification. No title. No increased experience. In fact, the entire experience is quite different. And I realize once again why Dungeon Worlds are so important.

Back on Earth, this dungeon might not disperse at all. It'd stick around, allowing people to grind their way through multiple times. Depending on the System and the local settlement owners. But just as importantly, it'd give completion bonuses, experience boosts.

Here, nothing. I just get a notice that the dungeon is dispersing and I'm left to make my way out.

I'd ask why the difference, but I know. It's in the underlying structure of Dungeon Worlds and "normal worlds." The way they're first introduced to the System, the way the connections are built. They're quite different, and so, some aspects, some robustness of a Dungeon World's underlying systems are in place that just aren't on other worlds.

It's why Dungeon Worlds can take more Mana, why they can handle more monsters. And why they're so lethal for sapient species.

As I leave, abandoning Ali to do the looting and sorting of the drones, I can't help but wonder if there's an alternate reality where Earth never became a Dungeon World. Where our envoy was never killed, where Galactic politics hadn't interfered.

Where my family still lived. Where seven billion people integrated…

My eyes tear up a little and I swipe at them. Stupid headache. High Constitution or not, grinding and not sleeping for multiple days has consequences.

"*John? We're all waiting for you.*" Mikito's voice comes across the party chat, interrupting my thoughts.

"Sorry. Just cleaning up. I'll be there in a second." I draw a deep breath, wipe my face, and cast a Cleanse. Best look presentable. There's still work to be done.

I can rest later, when I'm done.

***

"Welcome back," I greet the initiates after stepping through the Portal.

The group is looking fine, if a little weary and frayed around the edges. Most are slumping ever so slightly, the shine of their new training worn off. Most have changed into their everyday uniforms, their equipment damaged and worn after a month of continuous fighting. Even Kino, the rockman, is looking crushed, left arm cradled tight to his granite body.

We're standing in the middle of the same floating barge, hovering over the remnants of the city Anayton was fighting in. To complete that dungeon, the vast majority of the city had to be destroyed under the combined assault of the initiates. Even then, they'd have failed if not for a last-minute assist from Bolo. Surprisingly—or not—our information had been wrong. The city had not been a single dungeon but a pair, with a much smaller, much higher Level dungeon hidden deep within the city itself—in its sewers. Its boss had risen upon provocation, nearly costing a few lives as it soared into the sky.

I've got partial recordings of the fight, since the incidental damage was sufficient to wipe out most of my drones. Enough to make me wonder how powerful Bolo really is. He'd taken the damn monster on by himself for the most part, going toe-to-toe, hammer and claw.

The boss had been a multi-story creature of darkness and dripping poison, lurid purple-and-green liquid flowing from its body, leaking from wide open pores. Bat wings, four of them, sprouted from its back, a horned half-head with a single, baleful eye that stared back. It screeched constantly, its wings twitching and guiding the half-blind monstrosity as it fought. Its very presence warped the air, poisoning it, decaying stone and steel in equal measure.

I remember the last few seconds of their fight, caught on one of the remaining drones.

A claw smashes into the ground, kicking up dirt and rubble. A nearby building, already teetering on its last legs, falls to the ground, throwing up more debris. The monster pulls its claw back, swinging its other arm as it does so. Poison drips down its body, coating the ground and making it sizzle, with each movement.

A small figure, almost too small to see at first in comparison to what he fights, appears from the smoke as the claw retracts from the dust cloud. It runs up the claw, flame wreathing his entire body, originating from the hammer head. It grows with each second, burning away the poison that tries to infect the Dragon Lord.

And then Bolo jumps—as the boss notices him. As it launches globs of living, twisting poison blood cells. Bolo blasts one away with a gesture, using a spell to cast it aside. To let him close the distance. Air parts and burns around the blow, the concussive force and speed pushing the poison away even before the hammer lands.

When it does, it crushes and tears through the monster's reinforced skin, muscle and skin warping beneath the blow. Flesh crisps and burns, kinetic energy pushing all the way through the creature's chest, delivering pain and damage. Energy, contained and released. The force travels through the monster, held inward for a second, before it bursts apart like a grape swung at by a golf club. Its body collapses backward, wings unable to hold it aloft as it crashes into the ground. A crater forms as even more debris is blasted apart. A crater painted with its insides.

Organs, spine, and nerves spin through the air, blasted miles away. Covering rubble and torn apart streets with gore.

And the boss dies.

"So you all survived," I say, flicking my glance over the others then shaking my head. "Even if some of you are worse for wear."

I take in the information about the state of the world. We failed, of course. One month for nine people to clear out a whole world of its Mana oversaturation problem was just a little much.

"You failed. Do you have anything to say for yourselves?"

Silence greets my question as the initiates regard me. I wonder if I'm doing it right. If there's a right in all this. I understand a little about Erethran military culture, and a little of our own, pre-System. I wonder what it's like now, after the System. How armies and other groups work together.

I know, theoretically, that elite teams were a little more relaxed in the way they interacted with one another. The way they talked back and forth, argued. Because everyone was an expert, how everyone had to know the whole plan to ensure they could carry it out. The Erethrans are the same way, because everyone who is in the Advanced Level are elites.

But I'm trying to train them to become Paladins. And that's different too. Because we are lone wolves who have to work in teams. We have to step outside of the boundaries of social custom to enforce justice. Or what we view as justice.

And really, the truth is, I'm making all this up as I go along. So…

"Come on, speak up." I gesture. "This is your chance to complain about how unfair it was. That this wasn't a viable mission to begin with."

"Why would we want to tell you what you already know?" Magine says, lips curling. "You never expected us to finish this. You just wanted to see us expend Mana."

"Mana and Health," I reply languidly. "I was curious how you'd react to pressure. And if you'd succeed. Because this was no impossible task." I turn to Bolo. "What did you say were their chances of finishing?"

"Twelve percent. If they took into account and planned for the formation of new dungeons in inappropriate locations as they continued their assault," Bolo replies.

"Exactly. And, it seems, none of you did," I say. "Any other mistakes you saw?"

"Not using us," Mikito pipes up, her arms crossed. "We never received a single direction from them."

"Would you have listened?" Ropo growls, arms crossed beneath his barrel chest. His beard floats and ripples in the high altitude winds, showcasing the white roots beneath.

"You'll never know now, will you?" I reply.

"Their coordination with local forces was decent. But they failed to call in additional help," Bolo says, shaking his head. "Some of the initiates"—Bolo stares at Magine and Kino, one after the other—"took too long in their mop-up. They should have left local forces to finish the minor spawns after they dealt with the boss."

There's a slight stirring at those words, but Kino nods slowly.

"And, of course, some felt the need to prove themselves more than finishing the job." This time, Bolo's words are directed at Gheisnan and Anayton. Their faces flush—or at least, Anayton's does. I have a hard time telling what's going on under all that fur with the Pooskeen.

"So. Final score?" I ask.

Bolo shrugs, not wanting to answer. I look at Harry, only to find the reporter slumped in the corner, sleeping. I snort, amused to see the reporter down. Unlike the rest of us, he's not specced for Constitution, but he's had the most work to do, recording, editing, and finally, broadcasting our results. It's only the debriefing that he has no hand in.

"Not for us to say," Mikito voices her thoughts softly.

"Nor mine. Ali?" I say, gesturing for the Spirit to do his thing. I'd already passed the message to him mentally, so this is just theatrics.

A moment later, a much larger viewscreen blooms, one that's visible for everyone to see as the light projectors form the face. It's a familiar face, at least for the initiates.

World Leader Hanna of Seepgra stares at us, coral ears scuffed and unpolished, bags under her eyes and lines across her face. But when she speaks, it's respectful. "Paladin. You called?"

"How is the cleansing going?" I say.

"Slowly. We don't have enough settlement cores or the personnel to guard the ones we do have. Reinforcements are still a week away, but we've been able to lock down at least seventy percent of the locations freed," World Ruler Hanna says. She runs a hand along her coral ears, then when she realizes she's doing that, she snatches her hand away. "Our Elites are dealing with some of the smaller, newer Alphas that are popping up. Your people did good work, cleaning out so many dungeons. Especially those in the top ten."

I nod, flicking my gaze sideways as a notification pops up. I grimace at the information it offers. "The Guilds?"

"Whining," Hanna replies flatly. "But they didn't get the job done. And we'll have more dungeons they can raid soon."

"Then, World Ruler, your final opinion?" I say.

"Passable," Hanna says. "In another year, we should be able to regain control of the planet. If we're able to hit my immigration goals."

Something in her voice at the end made my eyes narrow. But it's not something I want to tackle right this second. Another call then, later. "Thank you, World Ruler."

"You're welcome," Hanna says. And then she flicks her hand, killing the feed before me.

Her abruptness makes me smile slightly. I guess even the rank of Paladin doesn't hold much sway when things are as busy as it seems.

"Well then, boys and girls, you heard the lady," I say, turning to the initiates. "You passed." There's a stir from the group, surprise and happiness

217

that quickly gets masked by concern as I continue speaking. "Good thing too, because if you'd failed, I'd have to kick a few of you out."

I offer them all a smile then wave a hand. A Portal opens, one that leads back to the main settlement base of Seepgra. "You have three days. Rest, reequip, train. Stage two will get a lot worse."

As the group trundles off, I lipread Kino as he rumbles to his friends, "That wasn't stage two?"

I can't help but grin, especially when Mikito meets my gaze.

Yeah, stage two is going to be fun.

Chapter 14

It is the night of our return to the capital planet Pauhiri. Instead of having a nice, relaxing break, I'm here. Striding up the hallway, being stared at by many, many jealous figures, while I hang off the arm of my more beautiful and graceful companion. Multiple cloth banners—reproductions of military unit standards—hang from the walls, telling their own tale of victory. Scattered throughout the hallway are small pedestals holding captured trophies, military equipment, and the occasional Legacy weapon. And that's just the entrance walkway from the teleportation chamber.

We're in the Viscountess of the Purple Sky March's abode, invited to one of her semi-annual soirees. The invitation had been waiting for me when I got back, Catrin's call not far behind. She had been so excited, so thrilled by the idea of going, that I couldn't say no. I have to admit, it was smart of the Viscountess to send an invitation to Catrin as well—dependent on me coming, of course.

I still would have declined, mind you, if I didn't have my own objectives tonight. After my private talk with World Ruler Hanna, it was quite clear that certain steps need to be taken if all our hard work is not to be wasted.

"*Are you sure about this, boy-o?*" Ali floats alongside us, visible to everyone even if he wasn't directly on the invitation. After all, Companions are considered part of one's retinue, and a single addition like him is nothing compared to the dozens some of these nobles have.

In fact, as I walk, I spot a young lady—the Countess of Jade—with floating butterflies all about her head. Strange form for a companion, but then again, Ali is really a floating ball of spiritual energy and Mana. The only reason he looks like an overweight Middle Eastern man is because I somehow, somewhere in my brain, felt that was the ideal form for a spirit.

"Got to get going on stage two." I turn my head from side to side, searching for my target.

Problem is, even after gene therapy, I'm six feet two and everyone else, even the women, is at least seven feet tall. That means I'm at a major height disadvantage. Mostly, I see a lot of chins and necks, suited bodies and gowned women. And others, who float in between. Erethran biology is kind of fascinating...

"John?" Catrin leans in and murmurs into my ear, waking me from my reverie.

"Right. Keep moving. You lead, I'll follow." I offer her a wan smile. It's a bit annoying how fast she's picked up on my inability to stay focused.

"Find him for me, will you?" I send to Ali.

I get a mental assent from Ali before he buzzes up to the ceiling. He joins a bunch of other flying companions—some of them sapient and verbal, others just glowing balls of power. There are even a few flying AIs running drones up there. In either case, I'm sure he'll let me know when he finds who we're here for.

In the meantime, Catrin's tugging me along, dragging me over to meet our host.

Julierudi K'nillam, Viscountess of the Purple Sky March, is a striking figure clad in a purple outfit that swirls and shimmers with every motion. Stars appear, flare, and die on her clothing while projections of spaceships swoop in graceful arcs around the curve of her hips and down the slits, caressing her long legs. The entire dress is a masterpiece of military valor and glory, underscored by the subtle background of capital ships in muted colorings.

Unlike her military photograph, the Viscountess is significantly more striking in person. Makeup does a good job of masking the size of her nose, decreasing the visible projection of the extremity to make her beautiful. The mutation makes what is normally a tiny knob of a nose a dominating feature of her face, drawing eyes to it and her lush lips below. Of course, that's based off human tastes. As I understand it, she's considered incredibly ugly among Erethrans. It explains, among other things, her lack of companionship and relationships outside of the Admiralty.

It also says something about her personality that in a world where buying a new nose probably wouldn't cost more than a few thousand Credits, she refuses to do so. Not entirely certain what it says, but it says something.

"My dear Paladin, such a pleasure to see you." Julierudi steps forward, doing the entire air kissing next to my face thing. We get a couple looks, and I lipread people muttering about strange human customs.

I'm a little too amused to tell them that that's a European thing, not a North American greeting. And definitely not a greeting you'd give a physically repressed Chinese Canadian. Of course, having blood and guts spilled all over me and being in close contact, grappling and training, with all kinds of creatures has ridden me of my issue with physical contact.

Mostly.

"Viscountess. Pleasure to see you too. Thank you for the invitation. I'm sure you know Catrin," I say, stepping back and detaching myself from the Viscountess. At the same time, I offer up Catrin.

The two women offer their own greetings. This one is more restrained, a smile, a sweep across the tops of their chests where medals might have hung if they were in uniform. All it does is drag my attention to certain areas of the body. But it's a more traditional Erethran greeting. So who am I to say anything?

While I'm busy admiring the women, the two ladies have passed on their verbal greetings. But just as quickly, Catrin is discarded, relegated to a footnote as Julierudi focuses her attention on me.

"I heard you just returned from Seepgra?" she says. "I trust it was a good training period."

"It was good enough."

"Is the planet stabilized?"

"Not yet. It will be, once more immigrants arrive," I say those words with the same tone, same inflection as I would use to talk about dinner. Maybe a sports game. I'd be much more excited about dinner.

"Ah." Julierudi smiles at me, head tilting ever so slightly. "It's like that, is it?"

"I'm sure I have no idea what you're talking about."

Julierudi goes silent, her eyes going distant before she focuses again on me. "Well, I won't keep you. Do try the food and enjoy the dancing. Perhaps in the north hall?" When I nod, taking her hand and kissing over it, Julierudi smiles. "Do make sure to see me before the end of the evening. I would hate to not speak with you again." The Admiral then gestures to the side, and a young man bows slightly. "If you can't find me, please ask for my nephew. He's quite well-versed in most of my affairs and can help you with anything you need. Tonight, or in the future."

I incline my head in thanks, for both the directions, the invitation, and the introduction.

Seconds later, she's off, greeting another important noble, another player. Some corporate industrialist, from what I recall. It's only when she's gone and I've beaten off a couple more wannabe social rank climbers that we manage to begin our journey to the north hall.

Catrin leans into my ear and murmurs, "What is this about?"

"You'll see." I offer her smile, content to let her wait.

It's not a big secret. Not big enough that it really would change things in the next few minutes if I told her. But some aspects of their military culture have started catching on. Like operational security. She doesn't need to know. So I won't say.

We enter the north hall, sweeping past open doors with a smile and nod. Unlike the main greeting hall, the northern hall is decorated with a more tropical theme. Floating fish—chirping five-limbed, lightly furred creatures—swing from what I'd call tropical rainforests. If our trees moved and tried to eat its inhabitants. A significant amount of solid light projections are involved in the display, but as my fingers brush against one of the plants and come away slightly sticky; I realize there's just as much real vegetation scattered about. It gives the entire display a surreal and physical sense that hard light projections miss, for the plants bring with them the smell of turned earth, fresh oxygen, and bleeding sap.

"I found him." Ali's flashing waypoint on my minimap directs my feet as we edge around the hall.

Ali's floating high above, along with some of the more active guests. They're swooping through hanging branches and vines, dancing and playing. There's a game of laser tag—with real lasers—going on above, shield drones taking care to soak up errant blasts. A cyan buzzer goes off and one of the Erethrans grumbles, floating down to the floor as he's knocked out of the game. For now.

The sight catches my attention, and another piece of data unfolds. I shake it off, pushing aside the information. I have no idea how the rules and intricacies of a social sport has anything to do with the System Quest, and right now is not the time to explore.

Catrin shoots me a worried glance, leaning in close. "Are you okay?"

I can only offer her a half-smile, placating her. Telling her would be a bad idea. For millions of reasons. But I reassuringly pat her arm. It's nice to have someone show they care. Even if it is fake.

As we near my target, I turn on Society's Web. The Mana drain isn't the problem with the Skill—it's the strings that float everywhere. Even with training and practice, I still have to focus to make some strings disappear, make others come to the fore. After all, Society's Web shows all the obligations, all the duties and feelings we create with one another. And even for an introvert, it's a significant number. To help me focus, I turn to stare at Catrin, taking her in.

My date's in a shimmering dress, all tight curves, off-shoulder beauty, and plunging neckline. But I'm more focused on the threads that erupt from her body, that cover her form and attach themselves to the individuals around us and fly deeper into the city and the palace. A deep, dark purple, thick but shimmering in the way that denotes a shared obligation. That string is similar to the ones every single individual in this room has, all leading to the Queen.

Another, this one dark red with flashes of pink and mauve, twists and beckons. For an ex-flame I've never met, but for whom she still holds a little feeling. It isn't the only red and pink string. In fact, there are more of those than I care to count. Or should. A lady has her secrets and a gentleman doesn't pry.

Idly, I confirm that Brerdain's string with hers is the same. There's still some minor connection, but the color and thickness hasn't changed. I'd assume she's being paid a little for some information. Or it could very well be the simple acquaintanceship he mentioned.

There are numerous such connections, threads of those she's been with, obligations and favors owed as she continues her social journey. A dark brown-gray thread leads into the city. Another, lighter purple-white, that I know is for her hairdresser. She's arm candy and companion, friend and confidant. And more. And all that means she has one of the most fascinating webs I've ever seen, more layered and complex than the majority. Her relationships are never simple, all of them complex. Even the one she has with me...

"You're staring, my dear," Catrin says as she breathes into my ear.

I blink, tearing my gaze away from her, realizing we've stopped. Like the social chameleon she is, Catrin's hanging off my arm just enough to make it seem as though we're having a discreet conversation, and not that I've wandered off again into the maze of my mind.

"Can you blame me? When you dress like that? I love the necklace," I say, covering up my mistake. I push with my mind, shedding the majority of the strings, and look around, letting my subconscious work the angles, the data. It's harder than it seems, especially because so much of my processing power is taken up by the damn library.

"Well, we could leave and you could take it off me. Or we could find some place quiet..." Catrin teases, her voice low and husky.

I feel a stir down below but ignore it. She's good, but Roxley was better and I spent years learning to ignore that damn elf. I feel a flash of guilt but push it aside. We never promised anything to one another, beyond the barest of connections. It was never a viable relationship, not when he's a Truinnar and I'm... me. And if I know I'm lying to myself, that's between me and my conscience.

"Down, girl," I say. "There's work still to be done."

"For you." She smirks at me.

"And you. I'm sure there are few connections you want to make." I flash her a grin and she shrugs unashamedly.

"If you're willing. It's not as if you're going to be my sugar daddy forever."

I scratch my temple, wondering if it was a translation error in my brain or if she really used that term. It's not as if it's an organic learning of languages, this Shop download of Erethran. I don't exactly have a dictionary in my brain to check against. Occasionally, terms we hear are just close approximations.

"After I'm done," I say. "Though we'll have to see who wants to talk to us afterward."

She laughs, squeezing my bicep in support. "It's okay. If necessary, I can leave you to fend for yourself. I'm sure you'll find more than enough company either way."

She traces her gaze to a number of women, and a few men, who are eyeing us. Not in the political "what can they do for me" way, but in a more carnal manner. At first, I'd dismissed their gazes as being focused on her. But among other things, Society's Web ensures I'm not mistaken where their regard leads to.

I really could have used this in my twenties, in the club scene. Or maybe not. I'm not sure my ego could have handled it back then. Young, male, and unsure? I might have retreated into my code further.

Either way, it's a new thing. Being a person to be lusted after. And I know part of it is because of my Charisma, my aura, my status. It's still kind of nice. Not that I intend to take advantage of it, not anymore.

All of those thoughts fade away as I finally spot my target. Like most others in here, he's filled with lines, threads that lead between him and others. Except unlike most others, most of those obligations are toward him.

The Lord of the Infinite Keeps is from an old and prestigious house, having provided soldiers for the imperium since their very beginning. For their loyal service, they've been given great lands, entire solar systems. And of course, they've garnered the arrogance that comes with such prestige.

Kremnock Ucald, Duke of the Infinite Keeps, Cretigrad of the Spears, Malefactor Imperium, Slayer of Goblins, Slimes, Grishnak,… (more) (Level 34 Erethran Vice Marshal) (M)

HP: 3480/3480

MP: 2480/2480

Conditions: Aura of Marshal's Command, Under my Rule, Only Death and Taxes, Personal Force, Confidential Business

"*Vice Marshal?*" I send up to Ali.

That's a new one. Most go direct to General or in a few cases Admiral. I've not seen Vice Marshal, though I'm assuming it's an air force designation. Then again, from what I understood, the Air Force has been subsumed into the general army, since so many of the army can fly or are abusing things like hoverboots and mecha. In fact, outside of a small branch of dedicated transport specialists, the Erethran Army is mostly divided into the general army and the space navy.

Of course, there are units within those designations with individual Generals deciding on how they like to split things up, but the uniformity of the units and general training means they can also work together with only the slightest hiccup. It's still a little complicated, especially for someone like me. And, truthfully, I don't really need to know.

I seem to be saying that a lot.

"*Vice Marshal. It's a general rank for those without a unit directly under their command, but who still want some of the perks of being a ranking officer. Quite common about a hundred years ago but fallen out of favor recently among the Erethran nobles.*

Splits skills between personal bonuses, unit bonuses, and domain bonuses. Most put emphasis on the unit in their domain," Ali provides the details as usual, having anticipated my question.

But as he was detailing skills, we've already reached the man. He's noted my approach and hasn't made a move away from me. Which is a good thing. I'd hate to have to chase him down in public.

"Ah, Paladin. It's good to see you," Kremnock says when I approach. He even offers me a formal greeting, that weird salute from the chest. "I was just telling my friends that we've sorely missed having Paladins overlook our activities."

Even if I didn't have a finely tuned sarcasm detector, I could pick it out here. So instead of returning the greeting, I look him over. He's not wrong about the friends part though, as threads around him vibrate to his words. Multiple lines of obligation vibrate and twitch as his hangers-on and audience laugh as he wishes. More surprisingly, he's got a thick, brilliant red, burgundy, and pink thread leading to his wife who swoops and ducks above. The thread speaks of love. True love, if you believe in things like that.

Otherwise, when I filter for business and military contacts, the strings he has to pull on are numerous. They don't just include the nobles clustered around him, but more—much more. Prestigious, old, and connected.

When I notice that Catrin, in her usual social mode, moves to pacify him in my silence, I pull gently on her arm hooked onto mine. She's smart enough to stop, shifting from the beginnings of an apology to a demure smile.

"Paladin? It is common to reply to others, in Erethran society," says Krenmock.

"Oh, I was going reply. I just trying to decide if it was with a punch or not," I say.

My casual threat isn't taken lightly, with a few of his hangers-on putting their hands on weapons.

"But it would be poor taste to spill blood outside of a formal challenge," I say. "And that isn't the kind of party that the Vicountess has chosen to host."

"How have I generated the ire of our illustrious Paladin? After all, I do not believe we've met," Krenmock says. "Did I, perhaps, tread upon an Earth custom?"

"The planet Seepgra. Your men have been interdicting transports in," I say.

"It's for their safety. Seepgra is a restricted planet. There are too many dangers for the unprepared. We do not need to be feeding the monsters, increasing their Levels," Krenmock replies. It's smooth and almost plausible.

"Yet somehow, Guilds who have paid you off, who have close contact with you, get through without a problem. And on top of that, any native Erethran who is looking to Level is able to reach the planet." As we speak, I note the increasing number of stares and scrying orbs. We're good entertainment in a place that is always looking for gossip. "It's only non-Erethran groups, Guilds that are out of favor, and competing companies that get stopped."

"I don't deal with the details."

Krenmock's very careful, making sure that he never tells an actual lie, only partial truths. He doesn't deny knowledge. He doesn't deny stopping or giving those orders. Just that he doesn't do it himself. Its one way of escaping truth-telling Skills. Not that I have one. My Eye of Insight only stops Skills from working on me. They don't tell the truth.

I think the old Paladins were cynics like me. Society's Web tells the tale of actions taken, obligations and duties and emotional resonance. But only when those things are acted upon. At the end of the day, it's the truth of what we do that it shows, rather than the platitudes of what we say. Or try to say.

"I really don't care."

My words send a ripple of shock racing through the hall, and a few of his minions hem us in, trying to intimidate by presence alone. They are stilled by a look. Not mine, but the Viscountess, who has made an appearance, though she takes no other overt action.

I say, "Your obstructions stop now. In fact, you're going to make sure that every single immigrant ship arrives safely."

"That's an extremely wide-ranging order. I cannot stop bandits and pirates and lousy maintenance," Krenmock exclaims, playing to the crowds. "Surely you don't expect me to provide those immigrants with new ships if theirs break down."

"Again. I don't really care." I give the man a grin filled with teeth. "Get it done, or I'll find someone else who will."

The Duke's gaze sharpens. But before he can ask for clarity, if he's going to ask for clarity, I walk off with Catrin on my arm. I said what I wanted to say, and maybe it's the crowds, the way he acted, but he reminded me of Minion, of the mayor. Of the way they tried to shade what they did in the guise of a better world. And it sparked an old hurt. Made me be blunter, cruder than I needed to be.

Whatever.

What will come, will come.

For now, what is, is. And what is is that I've got a beautiful lady on my arm who wants to meet a lot of people.

Chapter 15

Julierudi finds me late that night, when things are dying out and I'm seated by myself in a corner. After my last pronouncement, the number of individuals wanting to get to know us had died down a little. A little. I still had to gladhand a bunch, talk to them about their problems, learn a little about what they wanted me to do for them and who they wanted to point me at. I listened, recorded everything, and promised to look into it. And then sent them on their way.

Toward the end of the night, Catrin parted with me, intent on making her own connections. That worked for me, allowing me to find a place to settle down, conjure chocolate, and steal passing food while watching the threads dance. I've got a minor headache from keeping the Skill up and running for so long, a mental exhaustion I'd be loathe to carry if I expected violence. But for all my warnings to the kids, this is one of the few areas I'm pretty sure I'm safe.

And the reason, arriving before me in her tall, elegant gown, offers a mocking smile. "Paladin. That was... interestingly done."

"Sometimes being blunt is the easiest."

"And sometimes it makes things harder. But you're not one to shy from the hard work either, are you?" Julieurdi says as she takes a seat across from me.

"Don't have the time," I say, gesturing around the group. "If I was here longer, I might have favors to call in, ways to get him to do what I want that aren't as blunt. But"—I shrug—"I don't. So I use what I have."

"The threat of violence," Julierudi says.

"Yes."

"And when that fails?" The Viscountess asks.

"We'll have to find out, won't we?"

Julierudi's eyes narrow, then she laughs. "You certainly are a breath of fresh air. I'll be interested to see how Krenmock deals with you." And how I deal with Krenmock. It could turn out badly for me, solving their problem of more Paladins. Which, I assume, is why she's supported me this much. "Tell me, are the initiates you're training going to be similar to you?"

I shrug. "That's up to them. I'm sure a few might be more diplomatic. Some might even support your abuses." I lean back in the chair, enjoying the plush comfiness, feeling how I sink into its cream-and-yellow embrace. I dismiss Society's Web, saving myself from the headache and beginning the recovery process.

"You say abuses, we say efficient distribution of work. Or do you think we should set out bidding processes for every contract? We should try for equality when it's quite clear who will get the job when we have the Levels and the Classes?" Julierudi says. "Equality is a nice ideal, but it pales under the light of the System.

"Classes and Levels are fixed and clear. There are Classes that are better than others, Levels which are higher. Put together into a corporation or Guild, it is easy to quantify and note who is superior. Why should we waste time taking part in pageantry and sacrifice efficiency? Why should those who have better Levels, who have strived for those Levels, sacrifice for those who are too lazy to improve themselves?"

"And what does Brerdain say of that?"

"Perhaps you should ask him. I wouldn't want to put words in his mouth," she says.

I flash her a tight smile. "But I'm asking you."

She hesitates before indulging my question. "He, and his people, would say that we are too dependent on a few groups. That in doing so, we leave ourselves vulnerable to shocks in the system. That our enemies could exploit that. By hogging Leveling chances, by keeping our services constrained, we harm the growth of our Empire."

"And?" I raise an eyebrow, curious to hear her rebuttal.

"His way sees the creation of a large number of low-Level Master Classers at best. Focusing our attention on a few, we can push a select number of Artisans to Heroic Levels."

"Not Legendary?" I say, lips curled up slightly.

Julierudi sniffs. "You should know the answer to that by now."

I nod in acknowledgement of her point. The gap between Heroic and Legendary is vast. Even for someone like me, my growth has slowed significantly. For "normal" individuals, the climb to Legendary could be considered impossible. At that point, even Artisans need to venture into the Forbidden Zone, need to achieve a number of truly lucky opportunities and take part in some extremely large battles, just to scrape together the experience needed.

No. The jump between Heroic and Legendary isn't something an Empire, even one as powerful as the Erethran Empire, can achieve just by desiring it. Not with the way experience is gifted, not the way it gets discounted when too much danger, too much help is blocked. I know this better than most.

For I have seen the statistics, watched as specialists, statisticians, and researchers run the numbers. As I think about it, the data floods back. The research tables, the videos, the memo notes. As Questors draw information from across the System Galaxy, across thousands of years. Data, compiled and tested, scenarios modeled. The simple answer is that the System wants individuals, needs individuals, to achieve Legendary Status alone. As if... as if it doesn't trust an empire with the power to make Legendaries.

This time around, as the information floods past me, I spot something else. Another piece of information, a discussion I'd missed last time. A series of research papers that had been redacted in the normal archive. Of changes in experience gains by the Council, jumps in Levels by those sponsored by the empires and the sudden shift, of new rules and Titles, of deaths. And the sudden cessation of their growth.

A battle played out between the Galactic Council and the System itself, as one and the other tries to push their own goals. It reinforces my knowledge, my understanding, that the System is self-correcting. The question is—is it a sub-routine or a deliberate choice? The problem with a good, self-learning program is that Turing's Test can easily be fooled. Even so, there are answers here in the way it discounts Titles or alters experience gains from Perks or—in one case—elevated an entire neighboring race to wipe out a hive-mind, single-organism race. The answer it hints at is a guiding intelligence, one that is more than just a sophisticated program.

"Well, it has been a while," Julierudi says, drawing my attention once again.

I blink, staring at her, and realize I did it again. Faded out as information passed through me. And in the corner of my eye, I notice the System Quest update blink and flash away as experience is provided to me. "A while?"

"Since I have been so thoroughly ignored," the Viscountess says. There's a slight smirk on her face, and a bit of a glare.

I'd flush in embarrassment, but I lost that particular concern a long time ago. "Just thinking."

"Of course," Julierudi says. "About what?"

"Your support. And those of the others." I look to the side, watching a few stragglers as they linger.

There's a group of them clustered around Catrin, chatting with her, vying for her attention. In another corner, a gentleman holds court over his own ensemble of men and women. Ali feeds me details, but I dismiss them.

Handsome boy's a socialite but a non-player. Sprawled across a divan, an older Erethran man, portly with a metal foot, lies, insensate off a concoction of toxins and boosters.

Robots move around, picking up and cleaning the area, putting it all back together. Ali's flying high above, floating on clouds—literally—as he chats with other Companions.

For all that, I'm also recording Julierudi's reaction as I speak. "I was led to believe I'd be facing more headwinds in the reestablishment of the Paladins."

"Oh, many aren't happy. They remember the purges, the audits. But you've done nothing thus far." She gestures toward the north. "Until tonight, that is. This, and how you and your initiates act, will see your Mana levels rise or fall." She sniffs. "We understand the need for your Paladins. And better a group that we know than..." She shrugs. "Well, let's just say the majority are waiting to see what we get. We do recall times when Paladins came from our ranks too."

"You mean when you found people who would help you nobles get your way," I say.

"We're not parasites, no matter what others might tell you. Unlike your politicians, we serve the Empire. Much like those nobles of yours once did," Julierudi says. "Noblesse oblige, was it? The improvement of our Classes, of our families and guilds, are for the betterment of the Empire. We have been the lance that pierces our enemies' hearts from the very start."

"And what many enemies you have. How many active wars are you fighting now? Ernak, Giel, KuzlaMana..." I trail off, trying to remember.

"Uswain, the Spiral Arms of Trenn," Ali says, floating down finally. "And those are the ones that are hot right now. There's another half dozen in abeyance, though not at peace. Never mind the other half dozen minor kingdoms which are working with your current opponents to strengthen them. Because they know they're next."

"The problem with constant expansion is that everyone knows sooner or later, they're going to be next. Which means everyone has a good reason to join together to fight you guys. If not for your espionage teams, you'd be facing a much bigger problem."

"I think you're mixing my stance with Brerdain's," Julierudi says. "While I intend for us to win our current battles, I do not believe further expansion is in our interest at this time. Our population is somewhat more stretched than I would prefer." She shakes her head. "We need to expand our population, consolidate our latest gains. Including our base on Earth."

I flash her a half-grin. That too is true. Having that space to develop has ensured the Erethrans can train a large number of their people in a Dungeon World environment. One of the other negatives of a Restricted Zone is the negative experience modifier we all face. It's due to the System breaking down, just like in a Forbidden Zone. And just like a Forbidden Zone, the experience is banked, but to a lesser degree.

"Not exactly true. You actually have a higher population density than ever," Ali says. "At least on the fringe worlds."

"Those undesirables?" Julierudi sniffs. "They aren't the right kind."

"You mean native Erethrans," I say as Ali shoots me the data he's picked out. It takes only a glance to tell the truth. For a galaxy-spanning empire, it's still the native Erethrans who hold the majority of the positions at the top. Well. Except for the initiates being trained by me. Which... is interesting.

Huh.

Sometimes I can be a bit oblivious.

"I meant those with the right Classes, the right heritage and training," Julierudi says. "Those you speak of have little to contribute. Most never make it past Basic Class."

I grunt, deciding to stop arguing. For one thing, I don't know enough to say if it's a structural problem or an actual societal one. Classes matter. A bad Class mix, especially in a militaristic society like this, might be a real problem. If a race trends toward artists and entertainers, they wouldn't do well in Erethra. Then again...

I shake my head. "Seems simplistic."

"The numbers are there. If you care to look," Julierudi says. "The military is open to everyone. Whether they take the offer or not, that is up to them. And once they've served their time, they are welcome to move to other planets, to find opportunity elsewhere."

I offer her a nod, acknowledging her point. I'm sure it's more complicated than that, but at least I have her stance. And I know what to expect, in part at least. She won't come after me or the initiates. Not yet. Not until I've shown myself to be her enemy. Or a problem.

While I'm contemplating the future, Julierudi stands, smoothing her dress down. "I should continue circulating. There are a few others I'd love to speak with. I'll trust you and your men to do what is best for the Empire. You might not agree with our society, with what we've built, but it has lasted thousands of years. Which is more than most can say."

As I watch her leave, I can't help but reflect on her words. As much as I'd like to discount her words, she's right. For all the flaws in their system, all the problems that I can see, they've survived. Where other empires, other kingdoms, other dynasties have fallen.

She glides off, already turning on the charm as she meets another of her wayward guests. And I contemplate the arrogance of wanting to change an entire Empire as an outsider.

***

Morning light peeks out from the horizon, slowly working its way up. I know the dawn will be on us quickly now that the sun has begun its rise. Daylight comes fast on this planet, at least this time of year. The planet's second moon hangs overhead, glittering with sunlight. After the ball, we'd used a public Portal to hop back to Pauhiri just so that we could rest in peace. Even if the residence they've given me isn't mine, we've taken steps to fortify its security.

Turning from the windows—which are already darkening at my behest—I stare at my companion. Her eyes are closed, her breathing deep and even. There's a smell coming from her body—flowery and light with that hint of nutmeg that I've realized is all hers. I know it's a tech upgrade, nanites working deep within to ensure her olfactory residue is pleasant for her companion. Have to admit, it works. But her hair is disarrayed, coral ears twisted, sheets carelessly discarded with a single foot out. So different from my other companions.

Roxley would be out of bed already, on his neural link and notification screens, working hard as he stretched out muscles. Every moment, every second packed with work and Leveling. Of course, he'd stop the moment he realized I was awake, to join me for breakfast or a meal. But he'd always have that hint of impatience as he longed to get back to work. Impatient to get back to Leveling, to rebuilding his prestige, his people that he'd once failed.

Lana was a morning person too, but she loved lounging in bed. She'd work because she felt it was necessary, because people counted on us. But she'd do it in bed, hair disarrayed, that bountiful, curly red mop of hers splayed around the pillows. If we had any. The gods know, we spent more of our time moving from city to city, fighting monsters, than staying in a single bed. Our times together were rushed, intense… and often heart-breaking in their tenderness.

As for Catrin, it's lovely. She's athletic, skilled, and willing to give time and patience. Willing to let me set the tone of our relationship, while insisting on lazing around, sleeping in late. For all that, there's a distance between us. One I'm not sure either of us really wants to bridge. Our time together is lovely, it's professional, but it's not real. What we have, it lies between a one-night stand and a relationship. And if I was the kind of person who brooded about relationships, I'd be concerned about it.

But…

Yeah, fine. I do, but only mildly. Too much of my mind, too much of my life is caught up in other pressures. Like the nosebleed I woke up to as my mind continued to process the library. I had to discard the pillow, store it away to hide the evidence.

"Morning." Catrin greets me with a smile and a quick kiss. It's minty and fresh, unlike my own. Nanites again. But she doesn't complain about my breath. "Admiring, or do you intend to do something about it?"

I briefly consider but discard the idea. I have something else to ask her. "What did you think?"

"Of?"

"Last night. Brerdain and Julierudi. The nobles." I gesture around. "All this."

"This being the initiates?" When I nod, Catrin smiles. "Are you really looking for my opinion?"

"I have a feeling your opinion will be quite illuminating." I open my Skill again, staring at the threads that dance across her form. Stare at the ones that reach into the palace and back into the city, the myriad numbers that fly into space. I let them fade a little from my notice so that I can more easily see the changes as she speaks.

Catrin regards me for a moment before she sits up, pulling the blanket along with her to cover her chest. With her other hand, she nudges displaced hair back into place. "Krenmock is going to ignore you. In fact, he was working on a coalition to block your actions. I'd be surprised if he hasn't requested additional bodyguards from the Guilds."

A quick mental query to Ali sets the Spirit to searching.

"If you really are going to kill him, you also need to deal with his family."

Her words surprise me, and I have to ask for clarification.

"A wife who loves him, a husband who hates him, and his four children. Of those, you can expect to have to kill the wife and the husband and two of his children. The youngest is probably too low Level for you to worry about." Catrin flicks her fingers, and notification windows bloom, providing me biographical information on those she speaks about. I glance through them quickly, realizing that most are in the low Master or Advanced Class stages. Only the two youngers are really low Leveled. The first hasn't even reached the age of System majority; the other is struggling up the mid-ranks of his Basic Class.

"Are you certain I'll have to kill them?"

"Most likely. His partners are fully complicit in his actions and are unlikely to change their minds, even after his disposal. Unless you intend to remove him from power and give it to someone else, they'll still be in charge," Catrin says. "Even if you did hand over ownership, the new nobles would have to deal with the loyal retainers."

"Yeah, I wasn't exactly thinking of rebuilding the entire noble sector for them." It would probably be a more elegant solution, but I have other things to deal with. Never mind the fact that I have absolutely no idea who to give his peerage to. "But what makes you think his family wouldn't stop after I kill Kremnock?"

"Pride. You don't become and stay a noble for as long as they have and just give in to the first threat."

"And the kids?"

"They might change, but they'd still have to confront you. You could never be safe with them out there," Catrin says this blithely, as if murdering people just because they're an inconvenience in the future is acceptable.

And I guess it is. For them. I'd object about how callous this is, but I've realized that for the Galactics, life is cheap. Any life but their own.

"The Viscountess won't take action until you do. But if you do kill him, she'll be forced to act."

"Because he's part of her standing?" I ask.

"Yes. Whether or not she likes them, whether or not she agrees with his actions, she can't let you chip away at her faction and do nothing."

I sigh. Nothing she says is particularly new or surprising. And maybe I shouldn't have threatened his life. Any action I take after this that doesn't involve me taking his head will make me look weak. Realistically, what I want to do is deal with the blockade. Not him.

I do wonder if Catrin's viewpoint is slightly wrong. After all, to stop me after I kill Brerdain, Julierudi would have to kill me. Kill the initiates maybe. And if that happens, they'll have no other choice but take part in the civil war that will come since there was no other option for the inheritance. Is losing one member of her faction worth that?

Then again, it's only a risk if she thinks I won't pick her. And if I destroy her base, she might take it as a sign that I'm not looking favorably upon her candidacy. I rub my temples, feeling a headache coming along.

Catrin make a little sound in her throat and shifts to lay a kiss upon my lips. Dawn light continues to filter in, slowly brightening the room as the windows note our increased wakefulness. It's a gradual process, just like I prefer.

"And Brerdain?" I asked her while reaching for the sheets and pulling them over her body to keep her warm. And to lower the distractions.

"I can't see how he'd object to your actions." She shrugs, shifting the sheets and threatening her decorum again with each motion. "He's never liked the nobles. All his objections surround the recruits and what they might do."

I finally give in to her distractions. I've gotten what I wanted as I watch the threads across her body pulse. I release my Skill and roll over, pinning her down before I begin my assault on her lips and skin.

***

"So?" Ali floats beside me as I walk out of my residence to my designated Portal zone.

Having been cleared to jump around—on a limited basis—has made my life so much easier. As I take in the weirdly colored vegetation of the planet, I mentally locate the image of my destination.

"About what we thought," I say. My conversation with Catrin confirmed some suspicions and musings, which means phase two is a go. But to get there, I have to have a conversation with my designated aides.

I step through the Portal, only to be greeted by Saimon and Braxton. Like most Portal and teleportation locations, I've been dumped into a carefully reinforced security room, one that has numerous safeguards and security weaponry in place. I stride off the platform and grin at the pair.

"Did you get my list?" I say.

"We did. The Chief wants to know what is going on. It might behoove you to actually talk to him," Lord Braxton says. "Just because we can, doesn't make it right, for us to take these units. Especially when withdrawing them from a variety of armies."

"A variety?" Ali asks.

"We thought it better that we not draw down any single force." Saimon explains. "It makes it more polite. Also, it doesn't allow them to accuse us of favoritism."

"But we have enough, right?" I don't really care about the politics, not yet at least. I'm more concerned that we have what we need.

"Six teams, ten members each, as per your specifications," says Lord Braxton. "In addition, they all have their designated assault shuttles and destroyers, ready for your use."

It's not a large force the way an Empire counts things. Not even when you account for the Levels I asked for. Still, all of the team members are close to Master Class, and some already are. It means that they've got more punching power than the raw numbers would indicate. The teams' smaller sizes is why Brerdain's only making noises about wanting me to talk to him, rather than demanding I do so.

"And the logistic basis and the necessary permits?"

"All done. They'll go public in a day," says Saimon. "We also have the permit for your friend who has arrived. He'll be here tomorrow."

That last sentence makes me grin. It's been a long time since I've seen Dornalor—not since he quite resolutely turned down the production of his ship in Erethra. I'm really curious to see what he's done with his share of the earnings.

"Well, that was fast. We could've done all this by email," I say, lips twisting in a grin. When the pair of them don't react to my amusement, I sigh and throw my hands in the air. "Galactic language packs really don't do humor well, do they?"

"No. You're just not funny, boy-o."

I ignore the damn Spirit, confirm what Society's Web tells me about the pair, sign a few more documents, then I open up a Portal. I can't wait to meet my initiates after their break. I'm sure they're just dying to know what stage two is all about.

Chapter 16

The wind kicks up, blasting against my face, throwing up dirt and debris as the ship lands. It's a gorgeous ship, long and sharp-nosed to keep the vessel streamlined. Silver paint with just a touch of gold and blue lining on the edges. Bulbous equipment slots carry missiles, and gun turrets sit on the wings, carefully reshaped by projected force fields for atmospheric flying. Even from here, I can see how the weapons can pivot, shift, and retarget in full 360-degree angles. Multiple jets are arrayed along the wings, helping guide the ship and hurl it forward, aided by the main engines at the back.

Just before it lands, the ship's main engines switch off, engines in the wings altering direction and angle to do a vertical landing. Landing struts emerge from the ship itself, and it lands with the gentlest of thumps. I eye the bird, data about the ship scrolls past my eyes.

Nothing's Heartbreak II (Customized Cyrus Fast Destroyer v 172.5)

Core: Cyrus Fast Destroyer v 172.5

Speed: 12.8 Doms

Processing Unit & Software: Class A Xylik Core

Armor Rating (Space): Tier I

Stealth Rating (Space): Tier I*

Hard Points: 14 (9 Used)

Soft Points: 21 (14 Used)

Crew: 1 (+4 Maintenance Drones)

Crew Capacity: 7

Weaponry: 4 x Ares 8.2 Miu Beam Turrets, 6 x OneLir Missile Turrets

Defense: 4 x qBitum Point-Defense Force Shields, 1 x Repulsive Blurza Field, 24 x Point Defense Lasers

Core Durability: 100% (more…)

As the data streams in, I'm amused that I still have vice-captain privileges. After I lost him his vessel, I was sure Dornalor was going to bitch me out before letting me in. Once the engines die, the personnel doors open and Dornalor walks out, shading his head with one hand.

"I see you've planned for me," I can't help but tease the pirate. Beyond being a general upgrade over the first *Heartbreak*, the second *Heartbreak* also has a much higher number of redundant systems. Nearly half of the hard points and a quarter of the soft points in the ship are used for redundant systems.

"Oh, trust me. I'm adding it to your bill," Dornalor replies, crossing his arms in distaste.

I grunt, walking up to greet the man even as the rest of the team makes their presence known. Mikito, on the ground, uncrosses her legs as she finishes her meditation. Bolo flicks his fingers, dismissing the TV show he was watching with Ali, offering the pirate a grin. And Harry hurries over, tucking in his pants, a smear of lipstick still on his lips.

As I greet the ghatotkaca, I sigh mentally. Everyone I've been meeting recently is bigger than me. Like Bolo, Dornalor's nine feet tall, but unlike the Dragon Lord, he's entirely hairless, with a head shaped like a pot and a weird, dandelion-yellow skin.

Dornalor Xyrralei, Journeyman Trader (Master Merchant Captain Level 3) (M)
HP: 420/420
MP: 5490/5490

Conditions: Shortened Trade Routes, Shipboard Awareness, Hyperspace Fold, In His Place, Mana Drip

"Level 3 Master Class?" I splutter when I notice his Status. Even if it's mostly a lie, his Skill isn't good enough to hide his base Class tier. "Weren't you just Level 1 when I left? What the hell did you guys do?" I shoot an accusatory glare at Mikito and Bolo.

"Nothing. Nothing happened," Bolo waves his hands. "Isn't that right, Dornalor? Nothing that the Redeemer needs to know." He fixes the grinning Pirate Captain with a look and pulses his Dragon Fear, just once.

Dornalor's grin only fades a little since he's still standing on his ship's gangplank.

"Bolo…" I mutter. I stare at Dornalor since I know the Dragon Lord isn't going to tell me.

Dornalor hums, that pot-head rocking from side to side. It's weird, especially since he doesn't have ears, but in the end, the grin widens as I growl impatiently. "Nah, it's more fun watching you twitch. I won't tell."

I glare at the pair before I look at Mikito.

"It's settled. Relax," Mikito says, patting the air as if she's patting my shoulder. Or head. "Or don't. We could use that anger." With those words, she strolls up the gangplank, muttering appreciations to Dornalor as she regards the ship.

"Gah!"

"I could buy the information…"

"Don't bother. If it was really important, they'd tell me." I say, only allowing a small smile to break out when they're inside. I turn around, staring at the empty fields behind.

"She did say she wouldn't see you off."

"I know. Wasn't what I was looking for."

"Uh huh."

I snort out loud and ascend the ship. I know, in other fields, the rest of the initiates are doing the same. Soon enough, I have to brief them. Just before I slap the blast doors closed, I look back at the empty fields.

Once more into the breach.

Or something like that.

***

It takes a bit of time before we're up in space, but once we are, I open comms to everyone. Six displays, one for each of the remaining Paladin initiates, hover beside me. In a smaller window, identical ships are displayed—the vessels that the initiates will be in command of. I know I said that we can't really rely on the Erethran Armed Forces for support, but needs must. Anyway, with the data we had, we filtered out the untrustworthy.

Exactly how well we did, we'll find out. But among the requirements they had for this portion of their training was deciding who and what their team would look like. What I won't tell them is if I have time, I'm going to take a gander at all of their choices later on with Society's Web. It's not a foolproof method, but it might raise some interesting and unspoken alliances.

Each of the ships they're in, the *Randolf III* model, is in general classification, similar to the *Nothing's Heartbreak*. That means they're midsize military scout ships, armed to the teeth, but more focused on speed and stealth than being able to slug it out. Unlike Dornolar's, which has a few specific spots to allow people like Bolo and myself to make use of our Skills, the military vessels are geared toward tech solutions to the firepower question. On the other hand, their ships are also much higher-rated for speed. They're also configured to use a higher variety of disposable stealth drones, unlike Dornalor's.

"Welcome to phase two, ladies and gentlemen," I say, and the group shifts slightly, staring at me in impatience. "One of the things you're going to have to learn is that actions have consequences. And that our job isn't just swooping in, killing a bunch of people, and moving on. If you want to do your job properly, as a Paladin, you have to make sure that the unintended consequences of your actions, and the intended ones, all play out the way you need them to."

Memory rises, of a conversation with another. We're seated at home, a blasted, shattered remnant of a cave holed out from the mountain by a missed attack. Cracks from overheated stone abound in the ceilings and walls. The ground is the only thing that doesn't move, and that's because she's taken the time to use a spell to fix it up. In fact, most of the furniture is reshaped earth, easy to use, easy to discard.

Over cups of fermented mucus and vegetable matter, we rest. It's been another long, exhausting day of fighting on the walls. Technically speaking, having both of us off the walls is not necessarily a good idea. But with Blink Step and Portal, getting where we need to be isn't too difficult. And at a certain point, we all need a break.

"Why am I here? Unintended consequences. And obligations." Suhargur laughs bitterly, waving the dented mug around. It's not even a real mug, but a torn and reshaped plate of armor with a hand etched onto it in a slipshod manner. Not that she gives a damn, since it holds alcohol just as well. "I screwed up. Should never have killed them. Should have stayed behind, waited another month, another year. But I was impatient. There was always something else to do. I thought it was fine, that we—I—had fixed the problem. There was other work, other quests to finish. And I was so alone then. But I was wrong. And they slipped from normal to Restricted to Forbidden. All because I killed them."

I try to protest, to point out that she couldn't have known this would happen.

"Doesn't matter. Learn from me. Learn from this. Always finish the job. The real job. Protect the Empire, not the system."

Memory fades, and I find everyone still looking at me. Waiting. This time, luckily, it was only a few seconds. It just seems like a very long pause.

"The planet we just saved needs immigrants. Problem is, the only people who would immigrate to a Restricted Planet are undesirables. People who are born in Forbidden Zones, rim planets where the Empire has yet to complete rebuilding. Those who have no hope of a better life where they are. Failures, rejects, even deserters and draft dodgers."

Magine, Kino, and Gheisnan react at the last group. Interesting to note, but not surprising to some ways.

"Currently, they're being blocked from immigrating." A hand waves, a map appears. "Conventional immigration routes, the routes our targets need to use, mostly flow through Lord Ucald's holdings. Most are turned back, delayed. Others are thrown into jail, forced to work in mines and other undesirable locations because they can be targeted." I shake my head. "Lord Ucald has been informed to stop that bullshit. He's refused. Your job is to show him the error of his ways."

Silence lingers until Anayton speaks up. "And how are we supposed to do that?"

"With violence, of course," Freif says.

"What kind?" Anayton replies bitingly.

"First test. You tell me," I say, crossing my arms. I have ideas, but it will be interesting to see what they have to say.

250

"Kill him," Magine says.

Freif nods immediately.

Gheisnan, the little Pooskeen who has to hover in the air just so that he can reach the console, objects. "No. Even more unintended consequences. We'd have to deal with the succession."

"And if we let him get away with ignoring the Paladin—us—we create even more trouble in the future," Magine says, shaking his head. "Better to kill him now and make it clear the kind of Paladins we are."

"We could hit his holdings. Take them all out," Ropo offers. "Ulcer-refuse nobles all hate losing their stuff. If we take them away, he'd get the point. And it'd make a much stronger point than just killing him."

"Death is a very strong point," Freif says.

"Slow. Attacks on his holdings are slow. And we don't have the expertise to take away any illiquid assets," Kino says. "The immigrants are being targeted now. We need to fix that immediately."

Gheisnan's eyes go unfocused, his lips moving wordlessly. I stare at them for a second before realizing he's muttering in Pooskeen. Which I've picked up a few words of here and there, but not enough to lipread. Anayton has caught sight of the little Pooskeen triggering his Skills and shushes the group. She fails, as Magine, Ropo, and Kino continue to argue their points.

As for me, I stand there, hands behind my back as the ships head out of the local gravity wells. We could open up hyperspace jumps close in, but it's a significant toll on the engines. Easier and better to do it outside the local gravity wells, when Skills and tech don't have to strain as much.

We're in no rush.

After five minutes of increasingly angry conversations between the initiates, Gheisnan looks up. Watching them argue is interesting, since it's all very professional but heated. Well, except for Ropo, but constant, inventive cursing is his way of speaking.

When the Pooskeen first starts talking, no one listens. He has to let out a piercing, deep-in-the-back-of-the-throat shriek to shut them all up. It makes ears hurt, though the Erethrans seem more affected than the others.

"Checked the paths of the pack. Killing by Magine is bad. He dies. Killing by Freif works. Till he is killed later. Other paths are slow, uncertain of results. I smell blood, a lot of blood on all paths," Gheisnan says, ears turning down. "There are no paths where success is guaranteed and quick."

"No, there aren't," I say. "You're going up against an entire position. A powerful noble house. And they'll be bringing in more help from outside."

"Then let's negotiate," Ropo says. Magine and Freif nod reluctantly. "I might not like the moon-cratered, pustulant corpses, but they've likely got a good reason. Over and above their slime-infested Credit accounts. Reducing manpower on civilized planets for a Restricted Planet is a poor trade-off anyway."

"Not your decision," Kino rumbles, crossing his arms. "They have chosen. We have the right to choose."

"Goblin shit. The immigrants just don't know better. Better for us to send them where they won't die in a few months," Magine says. "I don't think we should let him defy us, but Lord Ucald has a point in stopping them. Restricted zones aren't for the under-Leveled. They'll be happy when they understand what we're doing for them."

"Not your decision," Kino rumbles again, even more angrily.

"Enough. You guys can argue about politics. Right now, we have our marching orders." Anayton draws a deep breath. "What if we did it all?"

"All?" Magine asks

"Everything that's been suggested," Anayton says.

Gheisnan is already going cross-eyed, running his Skills.

I interrupt, figuring I should clarify before things get out of hand. "No killing the noble immediately."

"But it's still on the table?" says Freif.

"Nothing is ever off the table." I give the initiates a wolfish grin. No need to get them too excited about the idea of killing though, not unless we really have to.

"Understood," Gheisnan says before he falls silent. I watch as he runs the math, using his skills to look at the future.

I know of transcendent strategists who can take plans and do the same, analysts who look for the most likely scenarios. I'm curious to see what he comes up with, what his Skills tell him. The problem with Skills like his is that they all look at an uncertain future, one that is constantly altered as others activate their own Skills. As mortals, giving into whims, alter their choices. And all of it under the shadow of beings who might as well be gods.

"Better. Less blood. There were fewer trails leading off, but still. Danger, enemies all around," Gheisnan finally speaks up. "Too many ending in his death. Lord Ucald."

"That sounds about right," I say. "So you've got your marching orders. And a failing grade. Most you guys really need to start thinking outside of a single-point solution. I know you're used to taking orders, having a clear objective. But as Paladins, you're going to be struggling with multiple objectives, unclear final results, and solutions that might not be perfect. Iterative fixes rather than a single solution will be your future. Remember that. Otherwise you're just going to be back at the start, making the same damn mistakes all the time."

It reminds me a lot of building websites for companies, throwing something, anything, up to fix the client's needs. As good as you can, but only eighty percent rather than a hundred of what they asked for. Then you move on.

Because the budget is out, your time limit is over. And in the end, they'll come back, asking for another change, another alteration. Because their business has changed, the environment has changed, or they just thought of something new, and that last twenty percent doesn't matter anymore. Iterative changes on an ongoing basis. It certainly kept the company in business, and me, bored.

"Were you always going to have us do this?" Freif says.

"Yup. Unless you guys came up with something brilliant," I admit quite readily. "Your marching orders should be downloaded into your ship's computers. We're splitting you guys up, taking his assets, freeing up some of those already taken, and dealing with this interdiction." I stare at the more confident group, watching as they look happier with a clearer set of marching orders. "Just because violence is the easiest option here doesn't mean you have to keep reaching for it. A lot of the time, you should be able to talk your way to a better solution.

"I recommend you do so." I fall silent for a time, waiting to see what they have to say. If they have anything else to say.

They do. Mostly to deal with the details of the orders. One thing that gets clarified is that they'll be swapping out regularly. Won't be much of a test if they all don't get a chance to experience the different aspects.

Once the initiates ships jump out, I turn around to see my team standing by, looking highly amused. "What?"

"Just funny, seeing you be responsible. Recommending they talk rather than beat people up," Harry explains.

"I can hope they can be better than me, no?" I offer them a half-smile, thinking of the poor initiates. My trainees. Is this what it's like to have kids?

If so, they're doomed. For we paint our children with the colors of our failures, then somehow expect them to be better than us.

"And us?" Bolo says.

"Doing what they can't."

That's the problem with sending a bunch of Advanced Classers to do this. The targets they've been given, they're just about manageable for their Level and team. But we're facing an entire solar system and a bit of trouble. There are targets the initiates can't touch, not alone.

Good thing I've got a team of my own.

***

We jump in just above the battleship. The thing is huge, a floating rectangular structure. Impulse occurs from numerous engines placed throughout the structure, allowing it to shift direction in ways that no atmospheric craft is ever engineered to do. Of course, considering its size, re-entry into a planet would cause problems. It's a couple of kilometers across one edge, more reminiscent of a Borg cube than anything I'd expect to see. Which makes "above" a rather loose concept.

We blip in, and immediately, Dornalor maneuvers for the closest entrance dock. Once we're close enough that momentum will slingshot us in, he uses the equivalent of a railgun system to launch us.

"Target locks everywhere," Harry calls out moments later.

Beams of criss-crossing energy target the *Heartbreak*—or where the ship should be. But Skills, technology, and a little bit of subterfuge keep us safe for a few seconds as we fool the sensors, allowing the *Nothing's Heartbreak* to begin its jump protocols while white death enlivens the area a short hundred meters away.

If not for the auto-generated overlays in my helmet, there'd be no way to spot the lasers criss-crossing space. Not until they struck. The railguns and mass drivers, on the other hand, are much clearer to see—for variations of clear for things moving at thousands of kilometers a second. Point-defense is mostly lasers though, since by the time most missiles activate, the attacks or the enemies would be gone.

I turn my attention to my own problems, even as chatter from Harry playing copilot fills the channels. Dornalor replies with grunts, focused on flying the ship and keeping it hidden. My problems in this case are the second layer of defenses—close-in mines. These things aren't even that powerful, they're just numerous, locked into place by a Mana field. They're so dense, there's no way for anything larger than a cat to float through without trigger them. By the time I notice, consider action, and dismiss most options, I'm already touching the mines.

"That tickles!" Bolo laughs as he plows feet first through the explosions.

Mikito's much more stoic when she goes through, but the mines are just an early warning signal. The retargeting of nearby point-defense is the more important thing.

I watch as lasers wash over me, lighting up my Force Shields, ticking down their durability. But I've got an idea, so I reach out. Toward the fast-spreading energy from the explosions, toward the closest mines. And I tap into my affinity, my gift from Ali. It's not a Skill. It's not even really part of the System. Much like Spells or Mana, it's categorized and subsumed to some portion, but it's not part of the System itself. It's something older, more innate.

And it lets me adjust the level of energy, lower the resistances, and increase the sensitivity of materials around me. Mana Sense reaches out at the same time, almost unconsciously, and I find myself manipulating the

Mana-reinforced nature of the metal, the System-generated strength of the drones. I find myself tapping into the edges of the System, seeing the weird System-glyphs as I do so, the way they affect things. I don't try to adjust them, but the Mana around them.

Explosions begin, but my mind and sense are racing ahead, moving faster than light itself as I hop-scotch between mines. They go off, one after another, creating a daisy chain effect all across the side of the battleship at first, then crossing over to the other sides. My head pounds, but the defense system is over-loading, point-defense lasers targeting non-existent enemies before the AI shuts it down and begins recalibrating its decision tree.

My feet slam into the bulkhead, creating a minor crater. I trigger the Abyssal Chains, hooking myself down as magnetic boots fail to hold. I use the Chains to drag myself to the docking bay doors which Bolo and Mikito, more focused on their landing, are already tearing apart.

I do all this subconsciously, while my concentration focuses on spreading the explosions. Focuses on the new mines being ejected outward, tracing them back, and setting them off. Shutting down point-defense, creating problems as internal batteries light up.

Ali floats alongside me, his face strained. What I'm doing is being aided by the Spirit, his greater expertise and Affinity multiplying my results. The battleship rumbles and bucks slightly, contained explosions as ammunition stores deep within the ship go off under our manipulation. Contained, but still dangerous.

"*We're in!*" Mikito shouts across party chat, bringing my attention back fully.

I spot Bolo ducking in even as fire targets him. Mikito follows seconds later.

By the time I enter, the breach they created is half-closed by flowing liquid metal. I tear through with my powered armor, shedding melted metal on my Soul Shield as I fall in, artificial gravity twisting me in the air. A second later, I refresh my Soul Shield as I search for my enemies.

There's nothing left to do. The pair have torn apart the droids and sailors within. I feel a flash of guilt as I notice the floating corpses. A Yerrick floats, missing his lower half, intestines unraveling in space, frost and ice crystals floating away from him. The majority of the corpses are Erethran though, all of them dressed in orange-and-pale-indigo house uniforms.

They're dead because I couldn't think of a better way to do this. They were just doing their jobs...

Then I dismiss it. The guilt, the pain, it can all be dealt with later. For now, we have a job to do. Get to the command center and deal with the captain. No time for guilt, not with everything moving so fast. So I focus.

For I'm getting left behind.

I rush through wrecked corridors, defensive doors and installations rent apart. Occasional floors are smashed open as the pair take a faster and more direct way to our goal. They make good time, often not even bothering to deal fully with sailors and marines as they continue the assault.

"*Down three corridors. He's moving... teleport circle... on... We're... bzzttzz... jam him...*" Harry reports, his party chat flicking on and off as communication flickers in and out.

"*Payout better be good...*" Dornalor mutters.

I sense it when they jump in again, staying close to where I've destroyed some of the point-defense. A momentary pause, then the *Heartbreak* deploys jamming drones to stop our target from fleeing.

I catch up to my team when they get stymied. They're in an all-out brawl as they face off against a team of Advanced Classers and a Master Class bodyguard. Mikito's on the Master Classer, polearm cutting and blocking beams as the man opens fire. Four arms and another half dozen metallic tentacles are in play, each of them firing at Mikito as she struggles forward, deflecting beam after beam. What he doesn't see is the ghostly horse she conjures behind him, charging forward.

Bolo's busy fighting the team. Unlike other groups, they aren't trying to face him directly. Instead, they hit him with slowing spells, momentum-robbing Skills, and gluing grenades. Trying to stop him from moving. They take away his friction, quadruple his weight, debuff his Strength. When that fails, their tank blocks him off with conjured shields. The Dragon Lord's struggling to get to them as they dodge out of the way and kite him forward.

"Go! We have them," Mikito snaps when I slow down.

In answer, I cut downward with my Blade Strike, tear a hole into the floor, and drop, ignoring the blasts and spells that follow and ping off my resistances. They're powerful spells, but Hod's and my resistances to Skills and spells are incredibly high. As is Bolo's—but they've had a lot more time to debuff him.

"Goblin's nest!"

"The hag's hanging tits, he's getting away!"

I laugh softly to myself, barrel past the next group that gets in the way, and keep going. An elbow to the face of the only marine dumb enough to not move aside brings him down. Ali shoots ahead of me, turning the corner, and I watch beams and a couple of missiles impact the corner. Moments later, he lights up the waiting defensive point with lightning.

In the corner of my vision, I spot the moving purple dot reach its destination. I pour on the speed, using Haste, the Aura of Chivalry, and even Thousand Steps to clear the way and speed me along, Blink Stepping every time there's an open space and the spatial lock falls below my ability to breach it. Trading pain and health for speed.

The last corridor shows up soon enough, and I trigger Vanguard of the Apocalypse. Ali's ahead of me, already engaged in battle. He's bleeding light as the Mage and dimensional weaponry tear into his energy form, ripping him apart. No way to Blink Step closer, no way to Portal—they've tripled the Spatial Lock here. So I swing my sword, sending Blade Strikes down the way, and toss my knives, watching as they cut through armor and defense and pin the defenders to the bulkheads.

Unlike many of those we faced before, they're all armed and armored in full power armor. It glitters yellow and pale-blue, sleek and beautiful and meant for shipboard action. Faces covered in non-reflective helmets, personal force shields buzzing. All of them are dressed and ready to do war, anti-Master Class beam cannons and defensive shields emplaced before them.

It's not enough, even as the beams burn through the Hod's defensive shield. Not enough to slow me down. Not enough to stop me from closing in or destroying their defenses.

Vanguard of the Apocalypse is built for charges like this, for that last-minute clash just before you hit an enemy line. It boosts my speed, my recover, adds itself to all the momentum generated from my other spells and Skills. So when I hit the flickering vestiges of the force shields, I go through them like an arrow through a soap bubble.

The metal barriers formed from the floor are like wet tissue paper, and the people behind are impaled on the blades of my Thousand Blades Skill. Thrown aside, disoriented.

As for the actual doors? Those are a little more difficult to break through. I find myself bouncing off them, the accumulated momentum wasted as the doors warp. I snarl, spin, and cut, watching as my conjured blades tear into them.

My enemies don't stop, some of them grappling with the lightning tentacles Ali wields, others jumping in with daggers and shivs, trying to cut through Hod's armor. I trigger the next use of Abyssal Chains and lock them down, rather than fight, and kick at the door again. Penetration is my main Skill, my most powerful ability, and even a simple kick is enough to shatter the weakened doors.

I stride in, smoke curling up around my armor, warning klaxons going off all around me. An underhand toss of a Mana Dispersal grenade disrupts the building teleport, shutting it down for a brief moment.

"*Paladin*! You cannot do this," the target screams, bald face sweaty, eyeliner running slightly, her admiral's uniform wrinkled and torn, smoking slightly as the teleporter sparks, sending energy surging through her body and failing as the grenade eats away at the Mana.

Next to her, weapons drawn in heavy hands, the rest of her staff stand.

I flick my hand sideways, sending the Toothy Daggers into the teleporter and saving up on Mana. The teleporter blows up, the Mana dispersal grenade and the added damage enough to override whatever safeties it might have.

"Watch me."

***

Clean up, after I capture the enemy Admiral, takes a little longer. Bolo and Mikito have to make their way to the power cores before the crew eventually decides they can't afford to piss us off further. We have to fight off a couple of Advanced teams each and two more Master Classers. Still, we're lucky. I don't think anyone expected us to take this kind of action.

Once we're secure, we kick off every single crew member but the Admiral and select staff. Mostly high-Level Advanced Classers and the couple of Masters Classers who survived. The rest of the crew are released into space.

In escape shuttles and capsules. We're not monsters.

Dornalor is laughing his ass off as he slaves the giant battleship to his own and hyperjumps us in unison, seconds ahead of the retaliation. We jump three times, losing our tails as Dornalor does his magic. Then we're back in Erethran Empire-controlled space, floating above the capital planet.

Of course, Ayuri shouts at me for a bit. The Queen sniffs at me in a very brief conversation. But they take possession of the ship and the men, as per my orders.

And then we turn around. To do it all over again.

Chapter 17

"Six battleships, including his flagship, the *Titan of the Seven Nebulas*. Two space stations, half a dozen mining locations, two prison complexes, and one fortified palace in one month," Empress Hasbata glowers at me over the communicator, projected larger than life into the cockpit of the *Heartbreak* as we float in the dead space between the stars. And somehow, her projection is still smaller than her presence, the pressure she's emitting.

In the corner of my eyes, just below in the pilot and copilot's seats, Dornalor and Harry are white-knuckling their chairs. They can barely breathe, her presence a physical weight upon our chests. Bolo's lounging out of sight, looking blasé about the whole situation. Except for the strain in his eyes, the way he cracks his neck every once in a while. Mikito's smarter, hiding in the engine room, taking care of the ship.

"Seems low," I say, doing my best to keep my face neutral. "Doesn't it sound low?" I turn to Ali, who is giving me wide-eyed looks of horror.

"Those are just your personal team's numbers!" the Empress snaps. "Are you *trying* to weaken my Empire?"

"Most of them are in one piece," I say. "We'll be able to return them once this is over. And the damage the initiates are doing, that can't be helped. Doesn't really matter anyway. They just have secondary locations."

"Doesn't matter?" Her nostrils flare, so small that they're almost imperceptible. She leans forward, growling out her next words. The Aura she bends on me increases even further. I should have had Dornalor jump us outside the Empire for this talk. That way her Aura would be less severe. "Are you trying to have me order your death? That's millions of Credits and hundreds of lives! Advanced and Basic Classers we have built up over years."

"And the immigrants, the refugees, and travelers he had taken?" I reply irately. "There were two Master Classers we found chained to their desks in those prisons. A dozen more Advanced Classers at the highest Levels. All trapped, forced to work for him. For... trespassing." I spit the word, shaking my head.

Of course the legal terms he'd used were more complex. Entry without permits. Fines for non-payment of the permits. Problems with their transportation that resulted in more fines. Lack of permits for Skills or spells, for transportation. All of it just so that they could capture those who traveled through.

And, of course, it worked. Because anyone traveling by mundane means or via short-hop teleportation is doing so because they can't afford the more expensive, long-range teleportation.

"Duke Ucald grew their Skills—"

"By selling their work. And then buying more materials and making them work on it again and again," I snap, pressing down with my legs against the bulkhead floor to burn off some energy. "He's been doing this for two decades, and you did nothing about it. So yeah, I have to break a few eggs. But he had it coming."

Memory comes back, recollection of the blood-soaked month. Thirty-five days, as per their calendar. Our first attacks went well, then his reinforcements poured in, teleportations of his best people. Things had gotten hairy for a bit as we fought his guard, his eldest son—who I'd been forced to kill—and the reinforcements from other nobles and a couple of mercenary guilds.

They'd even managed to track Dornalor down once. If not for the fact that the pirate is professionally paranoid, we'd have been caught. As it was, the close-in fission mines we'd set up had nearly torn the *Heartbreak* apart when they went off. Only the use of our combined Skills and me linking everything together, including Disengaging Safeties, had left us alive and limping out.

"Your actions have more consequences than just your problem with the Duke!" the Empress says. The chain around her neck trembles, swinging back and forth as she leans forward, glittering gold and emerald. "You are hardening their stance against you and your Paladins."

"The Empire's Paladins," I correct. "And so be it. We aren't going to stop until he stands down."

The Queen tenses for a second then calms down, leaning back almost languidly. My danger sense pings, and I tense a little. "And if I ordered you to end this?"

"Then I'd say you've got the wrong person for the job," I say. "Because I'm finishing what I started."

She nods, her eyes tracking upward to my Status above my head. When her eyes move back down, they are cold as her words. An arctic wind, blowing across a lake when it's -40 below. "Then end it. Soon."

I don't get to reply, as she kills the connection. The pair before me let out exhalations of relief in conjunction, while even Bolo relaxes further. As for me, I wipe my forehead, finding it slightly damp. Damn, but that woman can pressure.

"Well," Ali says, floating back down through the ceiling from where he's been hiding, "I guess we're done."

I purse my lips, hating to be pushed. But... she's not wrong. It's time to finish this.

"Call them back."

***

It takes the initiates the better part of a day to arrive. The last ship to flash in is Ropo's, and it does so in a dramatic fashion. The moment it materializes, alerts resound all across our notification windows. It's leaking fuel and radiation, large rents torn across the starboard aft of the ship. It's lost all of its cloaking abilities. Even the shadow skills of the Captain have been blasted away. Two-thirds of its weaponry is down, its main engines barely spluttering along. Repair drones deploy immediately, from ours and other ships nearby, burning fission materials as they near the damaged ship.

Ropo comes online seconds later, his bearded face half shorn of hair, burnt off in his latest scuffle. The bridge itself doesn't look much better, nearly half of the consoles wrecked, sparking electricity and releasing wafts of smoke. Good thing that for most ships, the physical controls are only built as a secondary failsafe. System-enabled controls are faster and more efficient. They're also more difficult to destroy. Though sometimes its easier to block. Thus, secondaries.

I draw a deep breath and dismiss the slight hint of funk that comes from not using a Cleanse spell for a full day and the remnants of chocolate bars on my breath. This time around, it was dark chocolate, the hard bitterness of the bar still present in my mouth, the slight hints of the strawberry and nougat lingering. I want another, but this isn't time.

Whether it was because I was pulling the initiates out or because the universe has a strange sense of humor, the Duke launched his payback today. Because of that, the team had been struggling to disengage.

Ropo's ship was the least worrisome. At least he made it. We lost Kino's signal in the middle of the day, and even Harry's access to the Shop cannot provide us details. They've locked it all down under multiple Skills. There's no way to know whether anyone survived without finding out ourselves.

Some of the other ships have come out fine. Magine had finished his attack, leaving him free to scuttle off before they launched theirs. Gheisnan never planned to do an attack today. I can't help but wonder how much of that was because he foresaw the attack. The rest were a mixed bag in between Ropo and Magine.

"Welcome back. I think that's all of us, no?" I nod to Ropo and gesture, reading the various communiques from the others.

The initiates have nothing to do with running the ships, so there's no reason to delay our discussion. They all look a little harried, just a little stressed. Even if we have access to the Shop and have adequate inventory and supplies to keep us going, a month of hit-and-run tactics, ostensibly against allies, can make people grumpy and stressed.

"Any word about Kino?" Magine asks.

I'm a little surprised the Dueling addict has paid enough attention to even realize the Risen isn't here. Then again, maybe that's just me projecting my own biases.

"Nothing," Harry answers for me, a frown etching his dark skin, deepening lines that are normally quite well hidden. "Not even an announcement of his victory."

Surprising that. Our attacks have been local news, news that has grown more and more harried over the month as the attacks from "unknown sources" have escalated. The Duke has a bit of a PR problem, with the truth of our face-off kept from the public. Still, we've done enough damage that they can't afford to say nothing.

"Did you know about the attacks?" Anayton is glaring at me, obviously having an answer to that question in her mind.

"Nope." I shake my head, letting my gaze flick over the blue screens filled with the initiates' Statuses.

At the same time, I get a glimpse of our own cockpit displayed from the camera feed of the ship. Myself above in the vice-captain's chair with full access to the system, Bolo at weapons and security console, and Mikito seated in the passenger chair behind. The new cockpit is big enough to fit all five of us, which is kind of nice.

"I had a call." When my pronouncement doesn't elicit a reaction, I continue. "From the Empress."

That gets a reaction. More than one of the initiates hiss, and Freif mutters, "I knew it." They all have the look of someone waiting for the other shoe to drop. Or a System notification to update, as the Galactics would say.

"She wants us to finish this. Now."

There are a lot of firm nods, straightening of spines. No surprise there.

Most of them have been doing well. Picking their targets with care, exploiting holes in defenses, using fake-outs and overwhelming force as necessary. Just as importantly, they've also come into close contact with the policies of Duke Ucald. And even the most blasé, the most supportive—like Magine—have begun to see the problems.

It's one thing to espouse intellectually sound policies, to weigh the lives of the masses against the needs of the few, to do what is right for the many at the expense of the minority. It's another thing to look in the face of those few and tell them they aren't worth it. To drag them out from their kennels, to unchain them from tables that have locked them in production forever. To stare at the children who ask you where their parents are. And know that you have no good answer.

Stage two was never really about training or Skill development. Stage two was all about reinforcing the only thing that's truly important to a Paladin. We serve the Empire. And the Empire isn't some corporate monolith or the nobles or some abstract series of rules and regulations that dictate the order of our lives. It's not even the social structure that holds it all together.

The Empire, society, is about the people.

Maybe it doesn't matter. Maybe some of them can look at the choices the Duke made for his own good, for the good of his domain, and call it fair and fine. Maybe all I'm doing is screaming into the dark. Maybe that's okay too. Because we're only a few, even with all the power we have. And if I've learnt one thing from the apocalypse and the library in my head, it's that there's no single solution. Maybe conflicting beliefs might be able to right wrongs in all kinds of places.

"What's the plan?" Gheisnan asks, ears curling down around his head.

"Duke Ucald has doubled down, refusing to change. We can't make him. So no more going around, no more playing nice. You have—" I stare at the estimates and dismiss them. It'll take too long for Ropo to fix his ship. I compose other orders to have him join another initiate. "An hour to get yourselves ready. Jump to the nearest Shop if you need it. But then, we're going."

All their faces go flat, game faces slipping on. Only Gheisnan has a slight smile on his face, as if he's seen this all. As if this is the best option. I hope it is.

I draw a deep breath, closing all the windows, and pull out the Duke's palace blueprints. A gesture brings over the rest of the team, and we pour over the details. Going over the plan one last time, making adjustments now that we're certain we've only got five.

And I can't help but wonder if I'm going to lose anyone else.

***

The center of Duke Ucald's domain is the Infinite Keeps. Are?

There's a different name for it in Erethran, one less flowery and more practical, but Ali translated it for me as Infinite Keeps. And I can see why.

It's a weird, highly defensive structure. The external structure is reminiscent of a stumpy fortress, something built in the fifteenth century, when we were still transitioning between guns and bows. It has multiple towers, sprawling crenellated walls that reach up and up into the sky. The walls themselves aren't just defensive structures, but residences too, apartment complexes for the unworthy.

There's technically a central keep, a location for defenders to fall back to. The obsidian walls shroud the inner courtyard in perpetual twilight, no matter how many lights they install. The Infinite Keeps were built for three reasons, and they do them well.

Firstly, the Infinite Keeps are where the Duke and his extended family reside. Because of the folded space design of the keeps, each location is embedded within the next, growing larger as one passes through the layers. Those individuals who are most in disfavor at the present moment are left on the outer rings, with the larger, more expansive grounds inside reserved for those in favor or within the direct line of descent.

The punishment of being forced to live in noble squalor, having only a few thousand square feet of space to oneself, was enough to drive the various branches of his family to compete.

Secondly, the smaller and more portable nature of the outer keep meant that the Duke could use it as his mobile fortress. Using its defenses, the Duke and his retainers could unleash their strength upon problematical locations throughout the solar systems. Whether it was a monster population that needed culling or an invading fleet, the keep could deploy forces directly.

It helped as well that as a mobile residence, the Duke could enjoy the various festivals and entertainment opportunities his planets offered.

Thirdly, and the reason why we're launching our attack, is the System Settlement Sphere. The Erethran noble Title system is a strange little thing. Not to say that other Galactics haven't taken it up, but it isn't extremely common. To reduce the burden on the System and to allow their nobles to anchor their Skills over a wide plane, the Erethrans created these Settlements Spheres.

Each sphere is like a pin in a staked-out handkerchief, warping the local area around it. By tying the noble Title to it, the Empire could rule over large swaths of space with lower System requirements and populations. In that way, pound for pound, a designated noble from Erethra had more powerful Skills than another of the same Level. On the other hand, it also left them more vulnerable.

A vulnerability we intend to exploit.

I take a deep breath, staring again at blueprints. Like an inverse Russian matryoshka doll, each keep we defeat will lead to another of greater size. Inversely, that also means that the concentration of fire and personnel will grow smaller. That doesn't mean less danger though. After all, Classes and Levels as much as politics dictate who stays within. The deeper we delve, the more dangerous it will get. For that reason, I sent the initiates in first.

"In three," Dornalor calls.

I give my head a quick shake and focus on what's happening. Exactly on time, the ships with the initiates drop out of hyperspace. All five of them deploy drones and fire missiles at specified locations. These are custom-designed missiles meant to punch holes in settlement shields rather than destroy them. They work, however briefly, before the shields regenerate.

It took a little bit of wrangling to get those missles from Brerdain. He hadn't wanted to let them go, especially because of how expensive they are to make. Each of them had components from Master Class Artisans, but they were the only way I could see to punch through in short order.

Ahead of me, leaning forward over his console and guiding the ship using his fingers, Dornalor controls the *Nothing's Heartbreak* as we fly along behind Gheisnan's craft. We drop down toward the keep as well, but so much more quietly. Whereas the initiates are here to make noise and deal with the main defenses in the front lines, we're supposed to cut through and take out the main target.

I eye the surroundings, taking in where we are as Dornalor flies us in. Beside me, Ali is focused turning aside lasers and electric beams with equal prejudice.

When we dropped out of hyperspace, we were just outside the shields. With the settlement shield down, the apartment walls have opened up almost immediately with attacks, firing upon us as we swoop in. Dornalor weaves us between fire, letting the lead ships soak up the attacks as we pass through where the shields should be.

The moment we cross the threshold, artificial gravity takes hold, enforcing its arbitrary concept of down. The hunk of land that makes the keep look like a floating castle in space is what we target, the open ground unrestricted—unlike the already cluttered space above the keep. Cluttered with lasers, missiles, drones, and rail-gun-driven masses of metal and enchanted rock. We get in low while the rest of the ships land, disgorging their occupants around the keep.

The initiates throw themselves out, rushing the wall-cum-towering-apartment-buildings, using tactical movement and cover fire to get close. They combine force shields, distracting robots and drones and moveable defenses to keep themselves moving. All the while, they return fire, using the ship's on-board weaponry and their own Skills to tear at the walls and defensive weaponry.

I can't help but wonder who else we're killing, who else might be injured by their indiscriminate attacks.

"Watch out, drones incoming," Harry barks. The War Reporter is in the copilot seat, doing his best to help without participating directly.

Luckily, passing information only mildly affects his status of non-combatant. It only really restricts his use of Skills, but in this case, his main Skill, Just a Bystander, is actually useful. It makes those targeting us, technologically or mentally, ignore him—and thus the ship itself. It doesn't stop stray shots from striking us, but by hovering off the ground and not firing anything, we're avoiding drawing attention for now.

"I see them. Now, stop bothering me," Dornalor snaps at Harry. He is focused, staring at the monitors, eyes flicking sideways at times to take in other images that only he can see.

The *Hearbreak* is jerking and weaving between drones, laser fire, and the occasional impelled mass as it attempts to keep us in the air, avoid the welcome party, and wait for our turn. Dornalor uses both fingers and mental commands, weaving the entire thing into a ballet of metal and gravitic impellers.

Bolo, seated in the gunner's seat, sniffs audibly. He has nothing to do right now, because any attack he could launch would break Harry's Skill. If Harry's Skill breaks, if we break it, the War Reporter would face a tremendous backlash. And while Harry's mostly not a huge factor in our fights, Dornalor can always use a second pair of eyes.

"Your initiates are breaching the main walls. Entrance in... two minutes for the earliest group," Bolo reports, having judged their progress. "The Pooskeen's at seven."

I grunt in acknowledgement. Gheisnan is running behind compared to the other initiates. His people are hunkered behind multiple layers of shield walls and projections, shifting forward in a turtle formation. They pop up to attack once in a while, taking out artillery weapons or concentrated groups of attackers. It's smart and safe, but slow.

Everyone else will breach in, at most, four minutes, but the Pooskeen is holding back. I'm not sure if it's because he has less firepower—his lack of personal offensive Skills is clear—or if he's doing this on purpose. Those lagging behind are more likely to survive, after all.

"Get us to Freif. I want us behind the sniper's team."

Dornalor acknowledges my order and hits the burners, risking revealing the ship to make it across the compound in time.

In the meantime, I sweep my gaze over the landed shuttles and their disgorged passengers.

Magine, the Duelist, is far ahead of everyone else. He's the first to breach, and even as I watch, he's leading his team into the gaping hole of a second-story apartment building. Soul Shield on, he jumps in, his tiny swords flashing as he cuts apart the gathered men. Seconds later, an explosion rips out from the wall as they detonate mines.

I watch Magine's health drop like a rock and stops about a quarter up. Briefly. Then it rises as Health potions, regeneration, and a Soul Shield trigger. Luckily, the explosion was sufficient to keep his attackers off for the precious few seconds his team needs to catch up. Shield walls slam down around his body while healing spells are cast, fast raising his health.

Unlike the vast majority of his team, Magine hasn't changed his style much. If anything, they've just doubled down on his Skill and preference. The team uses him as the spear-point, focusing on support, providing health to the damage dealer and keeping him alive while the rest of the team brace and hold the ground taken.

In contrast, Ropo's and Anayton's teams are more balanced. They move fast, using chained Thousand Steps to give the entire team the equivalent of a Haste Skill—without the need to cast the spell individually on the group. Chained Two are One's keep their tanks alive when damage exceeds the Soul Shields layered on those drawing fire. Ropo's focus on the defensive side shines through here, unlike Anayton, who has a noticeable dent in her Mana. At the same time, they use concentrated fire from soulbound gun-wielding members to either take out troublesome attackers or provide covering fire.

Still, the two initiates have their own individual style in this fight. Ropo uses his new stealth Skills, leaving his team to take the brunt of the damage. They're geared up to do so, while the little Grimsar is making his way to the base of the walls. Occasionally, he reveals himself to launch a series of poison gas cannisters at the wall, cloaking the attackers before he fades away again.

Once Ropo makes his way to the wall, he stops and switches out for his axe, charging up his new Skill. Combined with Army of One, he waits for a full two minutes, until his team is nearly with him, before he launches the attack. The energy from the attack is sufficient to tear a hole directly through the base of the wall and create a scar a third of the way up.

Unlike the upper portions, the base of the wall is thickened and reinforced to provide the foundational supports for the towering skyscrapers within. Even so, the sickly green light from Ropo's attack spreads, reaching outward and infecting the building material. Which makes no sense, but that's the System for you.

Anayton, on the other hand, is working with her team, commanding them and their actions. It's a surprising turn of events from her earlier solo work. Here, she leads, but not with her face like Magine or Kino.

In fact, she's switched out her soulbound chain and sword for an assault rifle. Unlike the others, she actually has two soulbound weapons—a gift from her Title of the Everlasting Light. That both weapons are as powerful as one another can be attributed to Mana Fount. The viewing of the particular boondoggle that got her both Titles and forced her to purchase the Skills to balance her new weapons was rather entertaining.

Let's just say that you should never let yourself get dropped into the middle of a combat zone without checking your comms. The fact that she managed to drag half her team across a hostile planet was the main reason she's on the roll for Paladin.

It probably also explains why she's babying her people, even against her personal inclinations.

"Get moving to the exits, John. I'm not hanging around," Dornalor calls, snapping me out of my review of the battlefield.

I stand and follow Bolo, hurrying down to the emergency exit chutes, where we strap in. They're the same exit chutes we've used before, geared to shoot us right out from the bottom. I'm wondering how Dornalor intends to get us in, because from what I've seen, Freif is already inside.

Information keeps feeding to me from the gaping hole in the fourth floor. I see glimpses of light, flashes of beam weaponry as they open up. The constant sizzling crack of lasers and driven masses, with Freif's figure shrouded in smoke and the glint off his Soul Shield. His team is right next to the man, small dots on my minimap as they bulldoze through the opposition.

Ever since we gave the man his mass combat Skills, Freif's taken to the calling of upfront damage dealer with a vengeance. Combined with his team, who have a preponderance of damage-dealing Skills, he's taken to heart the idea that victory can be achieved by having the biggest DPS.

My stomach lurches suddenly as the *Heartbreak* twists, angling itself in midair. Beneath my feet, the end of the escape chute opens, offering a brief view of the breach.

Brief, because the escape chute triggers, sending me shooting toward the opening. I accelerate at hundreds of kilometers per second, the G forces enough to slam my mouth shut, catching the tip of my tongue and filling it with the copper and salt taste of blood. Just as quickly, the damage is gone as the System heals me.

I careen past the startled members of Freif's team, clipping one of Freif's hovering guns before my feet impact undamaged internal walls. They tear asunder as I bleed velocity and Soul Shield defenses. It takes multiple walls before I finally come to a stop. My Soul Shield flickers, detailing damage taken, even as the crash harness detaches and ignominiously drops me to the floor.

"What happened to subtle?" I shout over the party chat.

Mikito drops down next to me, scanning the empty storage room, bits and pieces of reinforced metal cladding still raining down around us. Seeing no threats, the samurai strolls over and taps her arm. "Tick-tock."

I start, wondering where that polite samurai has gone. Once, a long time ago, she'd done the entire strong silent type very well. Of course, part of that had been her lack of English language skills. But now, now she's gotten used to me. And is giving me shit, just like the rest of them.

Bolo interrupts my musings by jumping through and widening the hole we made. When I raise an eyebrow at his image in the party chat, the Dragon Lord grumbles. "Smashed into a supporting strut."

My grin widens as Ali catches up, floating through the walls, cackling all the while.

"So glad I recorded that. Now get moving, boy-o, before the guards arrive. Donalor got you into the third ring, but we're going to have to get moving to the keep itself."

Mikito's already moving, running as fast as she can toward the nearest exit. The insides of the wall are utilitarian, burnished steel-gray metal, littered by pale yellow light every twenty feet. Occasionally, graffiti can be seen, gang signs and the occasional drawing of local entertainment shows. Some of the art is startling, graphic in its violence, 3D paint giving it all-too-realistic lifelike properties if glimpsed out of the corner of your eye. Others are risqué, showing anatomically impossible scenes of athletic splendor with aliens of a wide variety.

Beneath our feet, the floors are worn, scuff marks showing in even System-regenerated pathways. It says something about the amount of wear when the System is unable to complete regeneration. It's quite possible there are even worse areas, places that have broken down further.

We race down corridors, led by Ali and Mikito's summoned horse. It's not a real animal, the spirit horse. Recent Level-ups have allowed her greater control, and now the creature rushes ahead, playing both scout and tank. Not that we need one. Not just yet.

"No guards," I say.

It's not a call for them to appear, or a raised flag, just an indicator of my concern. There should be guards. Should be personnel blocking us. And even if my minimap glows with dots, most of them are pale gray. Marked by Ali as non-combatants, probably via a quick surface scan of their Statuses.

Mikito grunts, slowing her headlong rush. I note the sudden drop in her Mana at the same time. "Barrier."

"How many?" Bolo asks as he moves up.

Rather than wait for Mikito to inform me, I borrow Ali's sight. Arrayed just before the exit from the wall is a good score of the missing guards. Led by a pair of elite members—Erethran nobles with Advanced Classes. One's a Trick Shooter, the other a Baronet. Beside them, the others of the group block the way, reinforcing the exit and creating a chokepoint. Almost as if a signal was given, additional dots appear, hemming us in.

Between the layers of force fields, the personnel, and the in place firepower, it'll take us a few moments to break through. I frown, glance at the map again to ascertain that this is the fastest way in. We could go through the walls, but these are reinforced. Especially the exterior wall.

"Bolo, Mikito, punch us through," I command them. "I'll be right along." Already, my hands are filling with toys to slow our pursuers.

My friends charge ahead, Mikito reconjuring her steed and jumping on it. She has to duck low so that she doesn't knock her head, but that's fine. She levels Hitoshi over the horse's ears, ready to use. Bolo just starts running, conjuring his hammer.

I'm not worried that they'll be stopped. I do, however, have concerns about the initiates. Even out here, drawing the majority of fire, they all have their own targets. Unfortunately, the moment we entered the wall, communication between us and them dropped. I can only pray they don't die.

Traps in place, the sounds of Bolo and Mikito meeting our enemies resounding through the corridors, I hurry after them. Not a moment too soon, for a cluster of dots cross the line of installed traps.

The Galactic equivalent of a bouncing betty goes off, releasing enchanted shrapnel into the air. To my surprise, I get experience notifications almost immediately. And while I've filled the corridors behind us with equipment, drones, mines, and automated machine guns, I'm still surprised.

Are these guys that weak?

My answer appears as I reach the exit, stepping over broken bodies and shattered pieces of equipment. Yes, they are. I'm once again grateful that my helmet filters out the smells of battle. I've fought without it before, or when it's been damaged, and the smell of cooked flesh and viscera from torn-apart bodies is haunting. It leaches into everything, coats your mouth and stains the food you eat for days on end.

Once out of the internal wall corridors, the grounds open before us. A vista of pale green and purple grass and shrubbery. Even as we run, Mikito and Bolo are swinging their weapons, projecting energy at the emplaced artillery and defensive grid that breaks up the peaceful view. Temporal enchantments in the ground slow us down. Increased gravity weighs every action, draining Stamina. None of the defenses or artillery last longer than a single swing, but they keep popping up. Even the weapons on the walls have swung around, aiming at us with the ships grounded.

Even through our defenses, our health continues to drop as we enter the kill zone.

My Soul Shield shatters, metal around Hod's outer layers boiling away. Rather than let it continue, I trigger the next skill in the armor. Mirror Shade lets me hide among my doppelgangers as we split off and run in different directions.

Bolo and Mikito use their own Skills and equipment to lighten the load, adding purchased automatic weaponry, a conjured summons, and moveable shielding to the mix. Ali floats above, hands held apart. A semi-transparent dome forms around our small team, curving beam attacks, breaking apart mass projectiles, and weakening the bonds between them.

And all the while, we run.

A rumble starts without warning, and the ground beneath Mikito's horse gives way. A trench nearly six feet wide and twenty feet deep appears, dropping her into its depths. Bolo falls in a few inches before he kicks off against the crumbling ground, driving himself forward with a flip to land on stable dirt on the other side. I just keep running, triggering the hover options built into Hod.

From within the depths, Mikito rides up the steep wall of the trench, flames chasing her, catching me as I run. Massive shields spring into existence, pushing Bolo back before he smashes them apart. And we keep running.

Only our Health is down to half and our Mana is still dropping. Previously destroyed defenses pop back into existence as the defenders spend Credits like water.

"Where are they?" I snarl, spinning around and tossing my knives at an emplacement. I slip Blade Strike into the daggers. Otherwise, the tiny weapons would do nothing to the emplaced weaponry. But their ability to penetrate shields, added to my own Penetration Skill, gives me the oomph needed.

There's no answer to my question. I growl again and eye our health. In the end, I give in and trigger the Evolved portion of my Penetration Skill. Penetration's Evolved ability flicks on, and I throw Blade Strikes with abandon, sliding more of them into my daggers as I cast them at oncoming shields without regard to effectiveness. It all piles on, making the Evolved Skill Shield form around me, bolstering its hit points.

"Let me be the vanguard!" I call to Bolo. At the same time, Vanguard of the Apocalypse and Eye of the Storm are used.

Bolo glances back, only for his eyes to widen as the majority of the attacks switch to target me. The storm of fire lights me up, such that it's impossible to see my form within. But the Penetration Shield holds. In the meantime, with Bolo stopping his attacks on the defenses, I get a chance to replenish as I rush ahead and start cutting.

"I need an Evolved Skill," Bolo mutters.

I don't have time to listen to him, knowing I can't keep all these Skills running forever.

A few last automated emplacements—too dumb to be affected by my Skill—target my friends, but for the most part, I am in the Eye of the Storm.

"What took you so long?" Bolo grumbles as his health slowly creeps up.

"Uhh… I don't like using things when we don't need to." And truth be told, I'd never really wanted to use it so soon. Or have a reason to remember to use it. It's not as if I've often needed this Skill.

The secondary effect of my Penetration Skill has a duration of eighty-five minutes, and the cooldown on it is variable. Unfortunately, it seems cooldown for the Skill is affected by several factors outside of my control, including System resources, ambient Mana levels, and—I think—my own Intelligence and Willpower. What that really means is that once used, I often can't reuse the Skill for at least a day or two. Which is why I don't use it very often.

And that means I forgot.

Thankfully, there's no way for Bolo to know any of that, or my forgetfulness. Instead, the Dragon Lord stays a step behind, focusing his attention on emplacements while I forge ahead, tossing my knives out whenever they return and taking down shields. Even so, three quarters of the way in, we slow to a crawl as the sheer number of automated defenses and shielding systems block our way.

When I hesitate, Bolo snaps, "You want me to take it down?"

"No." I shake my head, glancing at the plethora of hostiles showing on my map.

Ali's shrunk down the size of his shield, the strain taking its toll on the Spirit. Mikito's dismounted, using her steed and her weapon to play rearguard. Even as we gather, our enemies are tightening their encirclement.

If things don't change soon, we're going to end up as just so much carrion. Bolo knows this, so my refusal makes his hands tighten on his hammer. But...

It's time for the kids to show us they have what it takes.

"Now or never, children," I mutter into the open comms, hoping they can hear me.

Silence greets my words as the air sizzles, the ground melts, and the acrid tang of ozone filters into my breathing.

Silence.

Chapter 18

"Redeemer!" Bolo's voice is growing frantic.

As more time passes, the greater the resistance grows against my taunt Skill, allowing more and more targets to switch over to my friends. Add the fact that a good portion of the defenses are automated and Bolo's health is dropping again. Mikito's not doing much better—in fact, her health is even worse.

"All right, on my mark," I snarl. Can't wait any longer then. I throw a returned dagger straight ahead, watch it plunge into the shield and pop it, only for another to spring into place. That's the problem with cutting our way through right now. Each time we take down a shield, another one forms in its place. Yet not all of them are active, so we can't destroy them all at once. "I'll strike after you."

"On three," Bolo snaps. "One. Two. Thr—"

Rather than move, the Dragon Lord freezes, because the shields we were staring at have disappeared. We look around quickly, trying to spot additional trouble, but in short order a quarter, then half of the emplaced weaponry stops firing. As we run again, the automatic fire grows even more sporadic while the few living guards look confused.

"About time," Bolo snaps in exasperation.

Hefting his hammer, he rushes forward, smashing aside the remaining guards. Without the majority of their defenses and artillery, the guards aren't as eager to do battle with us. They pull back, leaving us an open route to the keep's gates. Some of them aren't even bothering to fire their weapons, instead conserving Mana and health.

"Slow," Mikito complains as she rides past me, grabbing hold of my arm and pulling me along.

"Well, they're still learning," I say.

I can't help but agree though. The initiates took way longer than I thought they should have to complete their objectives. And, eyeing the shutdown weaponry, it looks as though they went for the smash-and-bash approach rather than taking them over. It'd make our lives easier, but I can settle for good enough.

Pushing aside the thought, I return my attention to our headlong charge. Through the main gates, into the main keep itself. The keep itself is a trick, in a way. The Portal to the next level stands within the main hall, right after we enter, rather than deep within. So all we have to do is run in, trigger the Portal with the password we bought, and fight our way through another two dozen levels.

The good news is that so long as we control the external keep, the keep isn't going anywhere. Not easily. Not without sacrificing decades of work. And I'm betting they aren't willing to do that.

Not yet at least.

***

A forest spreads out before us. We're two levels in, the first being a miniaturized town of double-story buildings connected to one another by walkways and narrow streets. We tore through them by the simple expedient of destroying the walls between, unleashing one after another of our ultimate Skills. Then we'd stepped through the entrance to the next teleportation circle and slid into the next zone.

We run through the transplanted forest where kept monsters are reared for training, for sport. I grab the Earth Troll that forms out of the ground and rip its head off with a yank of enhanced muscles. The wet tearing sound fills the air, blood falling in a rain around me.

The head thrashes, trying to bite me, its body already attempting to repair the damage, to fill in the rest of its mass. Earth rolls toward it, and flesh forms around the ragged mess of its neck. I drop the head and a plasma grenade at the same time, riding the explosion as I run.

I'm the vanguard still, my Evolved Skill Shield taking damage from the persistent acid in the atmosphere and the monsters and vegetation that try to stop us. Again and again, I unleash Blade Strikes and toss my knives, rotating through my attacks with abandon. I target everything, from vegetation to monsters, just to add damage notations to the shield. The ground doesn't count—much—since it's the transfer of Mana that is the true reason for my Skill to activate. So tearing up the earth doesn't do much, which is why Beacons of the Angels isn't on rotation.

Unless, of course, there's a clump of monsters.

I feel my Mana pulled from me, my Skill triggered, and watch as Ali holds up his hands, shrouded in a halo of slowly growing light, a runic circle right above his head. He's cackling with glee as he calls down the equivalent of artillery fire on the monsters in our way. That he's invisible to most eyes makes the entire act even more disturbing.

"How are they making even the jackalopes attack us?" Mikito mutters as she idly cuts one of the bouncing, horned rabbits apart.

"Forest Keeper, Druid, or maybe a Game Master?" Bolo says. "This isn't a true forest, so it might even be a Park Ranger. If they extended their domain over this entire area…"

"Stupid Skills," I grumble.

But we keep running, because we're on a timer. Not just for how long the initiates can stay alive, but for how long my Penetration Skill can last. Because once it's down, one of our major advantages disappears.

We run. And hope we can make it in time.

***

"Who lives in a damn maze?" I snarl, punching the wall. It cracks but doesn't give way, which is saying something when you consider my Penetration power is in play.

I shake my head, letting my anger bleed out while waiting for Ali to report back. Between him and Mikito's conjured horse and the half dozen drones we've deployed, we're mapping out the maze as fast as we can. Problem is, the walls keeps moving and the drones keep getting shot down. The walls are breakable, but every time we do that, the maze goes into overdrive. Considering they could be changing where the damn teleport pad is located with each second, each creak and twist as the floor rotates, as walls disappear or rise, we're taking a more subtle approach.

"They're running out the clock," Bolo states, eyeing the wall ahead of us again. I glare at him and the Dragon Lord shrugs.

"Ali will get us through," I say. But, truth be told, we're waiting on someone else. Someone a little more reliable.

"*Head left, straight through two crossroads. Take the crossing at two o'clock, then go up three levels,*" Harry mutters, his voice appearing on our party chat.

A moment later, we're moving, following his orders. Even if they change the maze, Harry has learnt they can only alter it so often. The cost of shifting the walls and the center is quite high, and—luckily—they'll eventually have to decide between draining the main Mana batteries for the keep or letting us through. Already, their attempt at keeping us out of the first Level has cost them.

I'm hoping they make the mistake and drain the main batteries. It'll mean access afterward will be easier. I'll take annoyance now to unknown traps later. But in either case, they'll run out of tricks on this Level soon enough.

It doesn't help that every time we find a Mana gathering point, I drop one of my Mana Dispersal grenades, letting it destroy the effectiveness of the environmental recharge levels. It'll speed up the rate that we get through the maze. It's a little wasteful, but between my Altered Storage space and a near unlimited budget, I can afford to be.

In the meantime, as beam fire and smoke wafts in from the corridor we approach, we'll continue to cut down their men. At the very least, it's experience.

"Thanks," I send as I catch a chain on my arm, let it wrap around my shield, then yank, pulling the surprised Erethran into my fist.

It's always good to have a ringer on the outside.

***

Idyllic clouds floating through an artificial sky, blocking out the trio of captured, shrunken suns, while forest-covered mountains in the distance are blanketed with white, powdery goodness. I almost wish for a set of skis and a few hours alone to carve some trails. It reminds me of another mountain range, one where a dragon whose child might have been born lives. I certainly feel a flash of homesickness pulling at me. A reminder of what I left behind, the people I cared for. It clenches my stomach, tightens my throat before I push it all aside.

Damn library. Dragging my thoughts here and there.

There's one additional feature here that isn't part of the Yukon, or at least hadn't been when I left. The giant floating platforms, like the ones under our feet as we hover in space. Wide, expansive gaps between them all. And no ways across, beyond jumping.

"What exactly is the point of this?" I don't feel the cold, though a small reading in the corner of my eyes tells me that it's -63.3 C. Frost rims our armor, coating Bolo's horns and the head of his hammer. Not that it seems to bother the Dragon Lord.

"Point?" There's a big grin on Bolo's face as he regards the platforms, the gaps, and the numerous guns and other defensive emplacements that make it all the more challenging. "Fun, of course. Don't you have obstacle courses in your world?"

"Ours don't include lethal weaponry."

"Actually—" Ali begins.

"Japanese game shows don't count," I snap.

With her free hand, Mikito smacks me over the back of my head. "Are we doing this?"

"Do we have a choice?" I shake my head, amused that the defensive emplacements haven't shot at us yet. I guess, being a sport, firing upon nonparticipants is a foul. I figure a man who actually knows what the hell is going on should be ahead in this case, so I say to Bolo, "Do you want to lead?"

"I haven't done this in four decades." Bolo's grin widens. "Don't break the rules."

He crouches then launches himself at the nearest platform. He lands with a thump, shaking off gathered snow before he continues sprinting, jumping over laser barriers, pivoting around a cannonball the size of a Mini before jumping for the next platform. The moment he leaves the original platform, it shifts, changing configurations.

"What rules?" I shout after the Dragon Lord in exasperation.

Mikito shrugs. Then she's off, chasing the Dragon Lord. For a moment, I have a flash of déjà vu. Is this what it's like to be chasing after me all the time? When I don't tell people what the hell I'm doing, keeping all my plans to myself?

If it is, I don't like it.

"We going, boy-o?" Ali taunts. *"Tick-tock, you know."*

I exhale a tired breath and run. Hopefully we don't break any rules. Whatever they may be.

***

Fire burns above us, magma flows beneath our feet. Obsidian rock juts out from the hellish landscape where little black-winged imps, their skin highlighted with red, sit in glowing cracks. They form balls of plasma between their legs and thrust them at us. Each attack makes the temperature around us spike, and we're already taking environmental damage from the heat.

The Hod is whining, its Mana levels and durability dropping as it struggles to cleanse the air, feed cool liquid to my body, and repair surface damage. My Penetration Shield ticks down constantly, even as heat bleeds through to the armor beneath and is trapped. It's an interesting failure point, if it wasn't potentially going to kill me.

I'm grateful that the armor continues to provide clean, fresh air at least. Even if it is drawing from reserve tanks. I get the feeling that the outside air is less than savory. Idly, I conjure my sword and bat aside an incoming fireball before tossing my blade at the imp. The attack causes the imp to explode, taking out another two of its brethren. Heat rolls out from the exploded imp, making the temperature rise again.

"Stop doing that!" Bolo snaps. "Some of us aren't in expensive, heat-resistant armor."

I eye the Dragon Lord, noting how his health fluctuates as his regeneration fights against the heat. Unlike myself, he's taking damage at a significant rate. Only he's healing it back via his System-aided regeneration. That is, it'll continue working to a certain point until the System stops regenerating him, considering the constant yo-yo a matter of torture.

"This new provision by your Galactic Council will impact our information-gathering abilities. You have to vote against it." The speaker is a tentacled, squid-like being with an aborted body that just kind of stops. All mouth and tentacles, without many other parts. I know, from the library, that the remainder of its body is semi-displaced, in another portion of the universe.

"You will have to learn to live without it. The Council has learned of your tests. Some of the members strongly disapprove. You know they don't want you to do this. And then you had to take the boy's nephew." The speaker glares at Tentacles.

Information flows, reminding me who they are. A Questor, an old Corrupt Questor, now dead at the hands of an incensed Heroic.

And a Legendary. A member of the Council. One who still lives. He has a lot of names, a lot of Titles. But is best known as the Weaver. Short, thin, all angular bodies once upon a time. Now, his bloated body is pushing the edges of his robes. Seven eyes spin constantly, watching the world from the corners of his face, while a pair of eyes on individual tentacles rise from his forehead, fixing on the Questor.

"I didn't know."

"That's not good enough," The Weaver stares at the trembling creature before he flicks his hand sideways. Tentacles flinches, but nothing happens, and it relaxes. Only to tense again when the Weaver speaks. "Do not fail me again. This lesson should be sufficient."

The memory ends, but further information streams in. Details about the Weaver, his abilities, his Skills. And what happened to the Corrupt Questor.

It wasn't him that the Weaver killed, but his family. All of them. Two hundred thirty-eight members. With the barest twitch of his hand and a single Skill.

The action was actually counterproductive, driving Tentacles mad. He'd stopped researching, trying to Level, trying to find a way to beat the Weaver. He failed when a vengeful Heroic found him. And along with his death, new data, new information had flowed into the Questor's library.

Scarily enough, I get the feeling that the Weaver is actually on my side. He wants to know what the System is about. Wants it so badly, he'll do anything, kill anyone, destroy anything to find out.

I shudder, coming back to find myself still floating down the lava river. I don't even understand the point of this particular keep, the creation of a hellscape like this. It's not even for fun. It's just pain and annoyances.

"Can you ride the Dragon, Redeemer?"

"I'm fine." I reply to Bolo, pushing aside the problem of the quest for now. Instead, I return to an earlier issue. "Maybe if we were all on board about what the rules are, we'd all know what not to do."

"Are you still upset about that?" Bolo says. "Everyone knows not to have two contenders on the same platform."

"Obviously not everyone," I snap.

Mikito, at the back of the raft, guiding the cobbled-together vessel with her polearm, lets out an audible snort. "Enough. You two can bicker later. Let's get out of here fast."

The river of lava might be flowing at a decent rate, but at this speed, I'll be well out of my Skill use by the time we're done with all these keeps.

"Fine." I flip over backward, landing in the lava. A few short kicks gets me to the back edge of the raft, then I push. Flutter kicks, added with the Hod's own internal thrusters, move us at speed. My Shield starts dropping, but I don't need to regenerate it anymore. It's going to die off soon anyway. Might as well make full use of it.

As if our new emphasis on speed has pissed off the imps, they act out, throwing more fireballs. With Ali playing lookout and guide, Bolo and Mikito take over defense.

And me? I play human motor in a river of lava.

***

Infinite Keeps is a bit of a misnomer. There aren't an infinite number of levels or infinite number of structures we have to break through. But they do fold their defenses within one another, again and again. Each level, each keep, is larger than the other. Surprisingly, after a certain point, the resistances taper off. Automated defenses keep at it, but we stop seeing Erethran guards.

Doesn't mean that the fight on top is getting any less intense. In fact, a glance at the notes Ali has sent has filled me with grief. We'd lost, more than I care for. More than I wanted, more than I estimated. But, loss or not, we can only keep going.

It's only when we emerge into the very last keep, an idyllic city in the distance, that we discover why.

We appear on the outskirts of the city, towering skyscrapers before us, floating cars and wind turbines surrounding us. After everything we've gone through, I'd expected a castle with a forlorn princess within rather than a city. Small, as these things go, by Galactic standards. But a city nonetheless.

And right before us are the combined guards and defenses of the last few keeps. I'm a little intimidated, looking at the sheer number. Ali helpfully provides Status data, showing that the vast majority of those facing us, all one hundred forty-three, are Advanced Classers. There are another fourteen Master Classers in the group, but only two are Combat Classers. The others are there to provide buffs and deploy their manufactured equipment.

There's a momentary pause when we appear. A brief second when everyone takes in their surroundings, the environment, and the situation. When their brains ask "Are we really going to do this?" They answer, dumbly, yes.

And chaos and carnage begins.

Mines go off, a rainbow assemblage of beam weapons and lasers target us while sonic and mass disruptors thrum. Even mental and magical weapons are used, all to end our progress. The bubble and hiss, the sharp cough of weaponry is only dampened a little by my helmet. Gases, toxic and distorted, boil up from the ground even as it softens.

Bolo steps forward, twisting his hand sideways. A shape forms around him, a watercolor sketch of a dragon. Legs explode from the crouch, hammer in hand as the dragon roars, screaming its defiance. We charge behind, Mikito on her ghostly companion equine, myself skimming across the soupy ground in my personal armor.

We have just a few minutes before the dragon conjuration Bolo is using runs out of energy. Without a linked dragon of his own, the Skill is much less powerful than it could be. On the other hand, when it does end, it'll explode. That'll save us time, but we still need to get to the settlement room.

"Ali? Are we ready yet?"

"Nearly there," the Spirit says. His face is scrunched up, his body invisible to most. He's flying beside me, staying out of sight because most is not all. And he's got more important things to do than dodge Mana missiles.

I watch, in the lee of the roaring, ripping energy dragon, as the guards are thrown aside, their wall torn apart. The two Master Classers are attempting to stop Bolo, but the dragon fights alongside him, stymying their efforts.

It's only when the dragon turns a deep, dark purple, that Ali shouts, "Go."

So I go. Blink Stepping, leapfrogging, my way out of the encirclement. Into the city itself.

Behind me, Mikito triggers a last-minute Skill, covering herself and Bolo in a protective bubble as the dragon explodes. The energy contained within Bolo's Skill, absorbed from attacks, tosses apart earth and bodies, shattering equipment and force shields. I just hope they can hold out long enough for me to do what I need to do.

I keep Blink Stepping, heading deep within, dodging any attacks that chase me, thankful that Ali managed to figure out a workaround the Spatial Locks. Given enough time and effort, any lock can be broken. If you're willing to take the pain, pay the cost.

***

I expected Master Class defenders in mass numbers. Maybe even a couple of golems or a mecha ready to stop me as I Blink Stepped past the outer walls of the final settlement structure onto its main grounds. Located in a tetrahedron of a building, I Blink toward the front door, past open ground, ready to punch my way in. I expected resistance.

Instead, there's Bob.

"This way, sir." The protocol droid bows, its rotund black-and-white body guiding me through the front doors and down the corridor to the settlement sphere.

I look around warily, concerned that this is a trap. But nothing in my map—and nothing that Ali can find, even darting through walls and ceilings—shows that there is anything else. "Where is everyone?"

"Greeting the other guests, sir," the protocol droid chirps happily.

We come to the main doors and they slide open without a problem. I glance at them, eyeing their thickness, their density, their enchantments. And mentally wince. Would've taken me at least a couple of minutes to break through. Unless I trigger something like Army of One.

"And Lord Ucald?"

"The Lord has left. A rather hasty departure," Bob informs me, spinning its head all the way around.

Seeing no danger, I walk into the room, still expecting to be assaulted. Nothing. Carefully, I place my hand on the settlement sphere, beginning the countdown for takeover. I eye the entrance, wondering if they'll appear now.

Instead, I get a call.

"Baka. They stopped," Mikito's voice is a little incredulous.

"Who stopped? Stopped what?" I reply.

"Attacking us. They are pulling back. All of them."

I blink, then call up their information. Linked to her own armor and Bolo's, I can see the truth for myself. I also note that they're both a little bruised and worn, their health and Mana only now recovering from the quarter level. "Why?"

"I don't know, but I'll take it," Bolo says, breathing a little heavily. "This was more of a workout than I expected. Those Master Classers were pretty decent."

I grunt, then turn my attention to the only thing that might have an answer.

"Lord Ucald left orders that if you were to reach the inner keep, to allow you to take the sphere. According to him, he did not want his city destroyed." Bob pauses, flickers, then a recording appears, video and audio of Krenmock Ucald.

"So. You have made it. I hope you didn't destroy too much of my keeps. If you did, I'll have to take it off your head," Krenmock says. I snort while the man glares at me. "Do not think this is over, Paladin. You and your worthless impostors are a thing of the past. A useless, defunct past that has no place in Erethra's future. We will have your head. Yours and your initiates."

"Blah, blah, blah," Ali mutters, making himself fully visible. He waves at Bob, who shuts down the recording.

"Hey, I was listening to that!" I protest.

"Really?" Ali raises an eyebrow.

"There might have been something useful in there..." I say. After all, people who felt the need to monologue might give away something.

"Whatever. We can listen later. For now, maybe you should take the settlement?" Ali says, pointing out that I've got a waiting notification.

I sigh, then mentally acknowledge the prompt.

And just like that, I take away his seat of power.

And create a whole new set of problems.

Chapter 19

Once I got back, after dumping the Lordship onto poor Saimon to deal with, I'd been literally jumped by the young lady. We'd had quite a vigorous welcoming party, so common after death and lost.

Dark green hair leans against my chest, a fingernail tracing down my body. A glittering ring of dark gold with a small inset ruby gleams on it. I eye the ring and the individual the finger and hair belongs to. She's shifting slightly to get the corals around her head to settle better.

We're both naked, and I feel the pleasant warmth of her body pressed against me as we lie in post-coital happiness.

"And you never found him?" Catrin says sleepily.

Our conversation has been lazy, filled with small intimate details at first, before moving on to my recent foray into the universe.

"No. We tried to track him down, but he'd taken enough Portals and teleportation that locating him was too difficult. He's got a Skill running so that even the Shop's information dump shows him in one of three locations," I say, shaking my head. It's a pretty neat Skill, to be able to split information like that within the Shop.

Of course, we could still break it if we threw more money at it. But all three of those locations had significant political implications if we went in. So for now at least, we're going to let him stay. I might not care that much about politics, but starting a new war or restarting two cold wars is a bit much. Even for me. Anyway, it's better to let Lord Braxton and Saimon try the diplomatic option first.

And if that fails, when I do kick in the door and drag him out, it'll cause a lot less problems.

"You sound disappointed," Catrin says softly.

"I am." I try to shrug, realize I have her on me, and just kiss the top of her head. "We killed a lot of people and still didn't get the guy on the top." I chuckle softly. "Was easier when we were just bounty hunters."

Catrin shifts, sliding along my body to put her chin on my chest and look back up at me with those slitted cat-eyes. "You don't like leaving things undone, do you?"

"No, I don't." I smile, meeting her gaze. "And you? What do you think of what I've done?"

Catrin laughs, hair spilling across her eyes as she shakes. "What does an Administrator know of these matters?"

"Mmmm… we used to call secretaries the gatekeepers to those in power, so I'd say… a lot," I say, tapping her on the nose.

She opens her mouth to object, then, seeing how serious I am, rolls off me and sits up, pulling the blanket with her. "You're a strange one. Asking the thoughts of one like me." But when I wait, she brushes her hair out of her face. "I think what you did was right. The nobles have taken to running their fiefs like their personal empires. The Empress—May the System Guard Her—is too busy holding the borders to divert our legions to deal with them. If she could…"

I raise an eyebrow, and she offers me a wry smile. "The nobles produce the weapons and the equipment our armies rely on. If a General was to act against a single noble, he'd find himself cut off." She shrugs. "And even with the Shop and the System, the shipping delays, the additional cost, it would harm them. No General, not even Brerdain, would upset the nobles for such a minor matter."

"Tens of thousands of immigrants, lives enslaved for decades… that's a minor matter?" I say with some heat.

"To them who fight on the borders and lose as many soldiers in a year?" Catrin asks rhetorically.

I clamp my mouth shut, once again remembering how big the Empire really is. It'd be unwieldly without the System. Or maybe it is unwieldly even with the System.

"Not a fan of the wars?" I cock my head, having heard something in her voice.

She turns her head to the side, and I watch the lines of Society's Web pulse and flash, watch as she considers what to say. How to say it. Picking at truth and lies, or truth and partial truths.

"I understand the need. I understand why we do it." Catrin falls silent, then shakes her head. "But I grew up on the border. Near the Forbidden Zones. I knew we would one day be swallowed. We had monsters spawning all the time. And we could have used the armies there, fighting them. Instead, we had to rely on... on Adventurers." The last word she says with some distaste. "The Guilds and the nobles who ran them, they were our best hopes. Because any guard, any individual who had any talent, was snatched up."

"We?"

"My family." When I make a noise, she shakes her head. "Nothing to worry about. I have no older brother looking to protect my chastity. No family left to worry about me."

I frown, then sit up and wrap my arms around her. She might make it sound light, but I hear the pain in her voice. The loss. It's an old loss, much like some of mine. But that kind of pain doesn't really go away—it's just forgotten. Until you remember it again, and it hits you like a truck.

I hold her in silence until she pushes away. "Are you going to continue then?"

"Continue?"

"Cleaning up the nobles, sorting out their… their mistakes."

I pause, then shake my head. I catch the flash of disappointment in her eyes, the slight turning down of her lips. It's gone in a blink, but still remembered. "Nah. I got to get the kids going onto the next stage. And sort out the funerals."

She sucks in a slight breath as I remind her why I'd been so passionate only a short while ago. Death and loss is a good reminder that life is worth living.

A lesson the apocalypse taught me.

One of many.

***

The funeral is held in space. We stand in the docking bay of a space station not far from Pauhiri's primary sun, staring at the baleful glare of the star and protected by the energy shields of the station. Solar collectors spread from the wings in a thin halo of monomolecular sails, absorbing energy to power the station, to be collected in batteries and beamed off to feed other stations.

Within the docking bay, we stand in lines, facing the pair of caskets. The remnants of the initiates I'd led to battle, or what we could find of them. On one side of the caskets, we stand, my team and me and the remaining initiates. On the other side, we have their families. I see tears, blood and hair torn asunder, the ravages of grief.

And my stomach clenches tightly. Bile rises in my mouth as I realize I have to say something, the Erethran equivalent of a chaplain slowly droning to an end. I have to say something, and I don't know what. Because of all the funerals I've been to, all the loss I've faced… it's rare that I had to speak. And even rarer have I been a direct cause of the loss.

They fought on my orders, for a cause I chose for them. Not like on Earth, where we fought for our lives, for our own planet. These people, these deaths… they might have walked away. Might have refused if they had a choice. But I never gave them one.

And now, they'll never have a chance to choose again.

Maybe my understanding, my feelings on this isn't exactly logical. Loss. Grief. Guilt never is.

If I'm also mourning the lives of the guards I killed, the people I murdered who were just doing their jobs, no one else needs to know.

"… and to the System and the flame, we consign the bodies."

"To the System and flame," echoes the voices of those in the building. Bolo and Harry do so without a problem, while Mikito and I are left stunned, catching up a second after everyone.

At the chaplain's and everyone else's regard, I smooth out my grimace and take the place the chaplain has vacated. I let my gaze travel along the initiates for a second, stopping on Kino. We found him locked away in a cell, unharmed if annoyed.

Then I turn to look at the families as I speak. "Ropo Dhagmath and Gheisnan of the Two Palms were… good soldiers. Brave Grimsar and Pooskeen. They fell finishing the tasks that I set out for them."

Out of the corner of my eyes, I see Bolo grimace, even as the Grimsar family of Ropo straighten. He's got a big clan, multiple children and their grandkids. All of them paid to be Portaled over. There aren't many tears there—maybe because Ropo was that old. Even so, some beards look a little more bare, their roots torn off.

303

On the Pooskeen side, there's a lot more wailing and gnashing of teeth, fur torn out and long bloody scratches left on their skin. While I wanted his whole clan here, when I realized it literally numbered hundreds, I cut it down to immediate family only. Even then, they're double the size of Ropo's group. My gaze is drawn to the small clutch of grandchildren who stare around mutely, eyes full of unshed tears as they're caught up in the emotions without truly understanding the cause.

"*John…*"

I shake my head slightly, dismissing the message from Ali. "They were great soldiers and would have made great Paladins." A lie. I was about to fail Gheisnan. He didn't have what it took to survive, not with his Skills. Not really. I should have failed him before. That was my mistake. "I would have been proud to fight alongside them." Truth. "I know that they fell doing what Paladins do. Fighting for the Empire.

"For everyone in the Empire." My gaze falls on the families, shifting from adult to adult. "Not just those who have the luck, the fortune to be born in the right place, at the right time, to the right parents. But for those who are crushed under the wheel of progress, who just want a chance for something better."

I draw a deep breath, seeing the echo of understanding in their eyes. Because, and I know it's true, they understand. They've seen it. Experienced it.

"And they succeeded."

I turn slightly and gesture to the ceiling. Notification windows appear, visible for all to see. Videos of Ropo and Gheisnan. Taken from news feeds, from their suit cameras, or from above, via the drones they used. So many videos, so many scenes. A prison cell thrown open, Ropo standing in the door as the individuals within shrink away in fear, then approach in wonder as he calls to them. Another of him standing on top of the smoking form of a mecha tank, enslaved miners staring at him with wide eyes, some falling to their knees. Grubby, emaciated, broken individuals seeing a glimmer of hope.

Gheisnan gets much the same reaction in the half dozen windows showcasing his own victories. Ushering the captured out of the "merchant" ship, receiving thanks from a transport vessel's Captain. A more savage video as, fangs bared, he tears out the throat of the medical scientist while the research subjects cheered.

Freedom, hope, justice. Vengeance and punishment.

They deliver it, as Paladins were meant to do. And I let their families view their successes. What they managed to do. I let them stare, to remember, and if there are a few more tears, there are also straighter backs. Grim smiles.

"They died doing what a Paladin should do. And for that, they have my gratitude. And that of a thousand others." I pause. "They have my gratitude and my promise—I will have Lord Ucald's head."

My last words bring forth a baying from the Pooskeen clan and a heavy thump of fist to chest from the Grimsar. I get approving nods. And then I'm done and I step back, letting others speak. Letting old friends, the other initiates, their old commanding officers talk.

I let them speak, and I try not to think about what I didn't say. About my own failures. And my own regrets.

***

In the distance, the coffins float to the sun in a slow and stately progression. Not really that slow in actual velocity terms, but slow when viewed on the projection of the solar system that is being shown at the wake. Part of the ritual is the watch as friends and family mingle, waiting for the coffins to be drawn into the sun. Depending on how much time there is, the thrust set upon the coffins vary, making some wakes take days and others, mere minutes. Ours is a little more reasonable, a couple of hours long.

We're hosting it in one of the viewing galleries at the top of the station, the stars displayed in clear glass windows. Of course, much of the sight is dominated by the sun taking up a large portion of the starscape, but there are sufficient windows to glimpse other, non-gaseous views.

Floating between the attendees are droids, plying both station personnel and funeral attendees with the Galactic equivalents of alcohol. There's a wide variety of drugs and poisons on hand, all of which will bypass System regeneration. It helps that the entire viewing gallery is blanketed by a debuff, lowering poison and toxin resistances of those within by 50%.

From the second floor of the gallery, hiding in the shadows, I watch the group below as I nurse my drink. I did my duty, spoke with others for the first hour, shaking hands and offering words of consolation. But now, I glower at them all, wondering if I should have overruled Bolo's recommendation of a few hours and gotten this over with.

"Not much for parties, are you?" Anayton asks as she walks over and leans against the railing beside me.

She's got a glass in hand, the drink reminding me of a lava lamp more than something I'd consume. I could try to figure it out, but I'm not that curious. I do note though that rather than needing to drink it, the grip in the center allows the liquid to slowly absorb through her skin itself.

"This isn't a party." I say.

"True." Anayton pauses. "Your speech wasn't horrible."

"Not good either."

The initiate shrugs in reply.

"So are you here to tell me you're out?"

That catches the woman by surprise, making her look at me head-on. "Why would you ask that?"

"I can't think of another reason to speak to me. Debriefing is later, after all."

Anayton lets out a huff, her nostrils expanding. I hear the exhalation, smell the hint of myrrh on her breath. "You really aren't very good at this social thing, are you?"

I shrug.

"I came by to check on you."

My eyes narrow, then I chuckle. "Drew the short straw?"

There's a moment of puzzlement before she nods. "Yes, I got the lowest Mana clip. We all noticed your... distraction."

"Smooth," I say at her choice of words. "But I'm fine. I've lost others before."

"To your orders?"

"Yes," I say. And that too is true. Just not in the way she thinks.

"They chose, you know, just like we all did. Just like Smo'kana did. To try to be Paladins. And it's not our first excursion. We've fought, we've killed for worse reasons," Anayton says. "This. This opportunity you offer? It's perhaps the first time we'll have a chance to do what we think is right."

I shake my head in negation of her words. Their choice, my orders.

"Our lives for our honor?" Anayton shakes her head, something dark passing through her eyes. "A victory at twice the price."

I consider the young lady for a moment, then glance at the attendees below. I watch them walk around, cluster and break apart, chat and laugh, with that tinge of despair and grief that rises and fades around the edges. They're a militaristic society. They're used to loss, so there are no giant outbursts of anger or raging. But the grief is still there. Because loss is loss.

In the end, I pluck a memory of her from her reports and speak. "The Diyamant attack."

Anayton flinches.

"That's your reason, isn't it? For becoming a Paladin."

Anayton looks away, refusing to meet my eyes. But her hands clench and she shrinks a little into herself. I can be patient, so I stay silent. Waiting. Eventually, my patience is rewarded.

"We were seconded to the Lord Sockuya. It was supposed to be a regular assignment. Guard him, make sure he survived his trip, come back. We didn't know where he was going. We didn't know what he would do when he got there. And when they came for him, braying for his head..." Anayton shudders. She tries to say more, to explain. She tries and fails.

I put a hand on her shoulder, squeezing it. I know the rest of the story. The things she didn't say. He massacred the town—not because of anything important, but because his ex-lover's family had come from it. He couldn't touch her, not anymore. Not since she got together with his sister, received her protection. But he could destroy his lover's village. When the others came for him, he let the Honor Guard do their job, follow their orders. Made them choose between orders and what was right.

They chose their orders. Because that's how they're taught.

It's what soldiers do.

"It's not what Paladins do," I say out loud. Finishing my own thoughts.

As if she managed to follow along, Anayton nods. And then she walks away as if she can't stand to be near me anymore. Maybe it's herself she can't stand to be near. Self-loathing is a pernicious poison. Hard to get rid of, no matter how hard you scrub, no matter how much you drink.

In the silence of the second floor, as the hubbub of those below caresses my senses, as I sip on the drink in my hand and grip the lava lamp Anayton left behind, a figure emerges from the shadows. I don't jump. I don't even startle. Hard to miss someone when you've got a big glowing thread leading right to them.

"I didn't want to bother you," Catrin says as she sways over. She leans against the railing, brushing her shoulder against my chest as she does so, putting a little weight into my body and passing on the heat of her body. "It looked serious."

"It... was," I say, shaking my head. I breathe in, catching the hints of nutmeg and flowers that is all hers, and find myself taking a deeper breath. "Just a talk of loss. And pain."

"Ah. That kind of talk." Catrin lowers her gaze.

I reach out, pulling her closer. "You know it?"

"I've lost others. Friends. Family," Catrin murmurs.

"Work?"

"Mmmm... and life. I grew up—well. You know. It wasn't easy."

"Yes." I look down. "What do you think of them? The initiates?"

"They seem good. Strong. Dedicated." She nods to the group below.

I absently note how they've gathered again, talking amongst themselves. Already, I see the way the lines are drawing between them and everyone else. Even if members of their teams are here, there's a line. Between those who eventually have to make the calls and everyone else.

"They trust you. To lead them."

"More fool them. And you?" I say. "Do you trust me?"

There's a slight hesitation, one that makes me reluctantly turn to meet her waiting eyes. There's a light smile on her lips, amusement at my question. She makes me wait, makes me regret asking such a stupid question.

"Yes." When I open my mouth, she places a finger on it. "If you say I'm foolish, I'll throw you off this balcony." I clamp my mouth shut. "They're no fools. Nor am I, Redeemer. They're exactly what you wanted, aren't they?"

I cock my head to the side but eventually nod. They very much are. I find myself drawing a deep breath and exhaling as I realize what it means.

"You're leaving again, aren't you?" Catrin says softly.

"Soon. Debriefing and then… well. The next step."

Catrin makes a face.

I pull her close with one arm and give her a squeeze. "Make my excuses for me?"

When she wrinkles her nose at my request, I chuckle and plant a kiss on her lips. It's time. For the quest. For setting up their next step.

***

We meet in the pale yellow room of the Shop. The meeting rooms are often rented out, the time dilation affect one of the few time-related effects that are viable. I'm not entirely sure if it's an aspect of the teleportation to the location or if the entire Shop is affected by a time dilation bubble. In either case, time seems to move at a much slower rate within the Shop, compared to everywhere else.

I've done some research into Classes that mess with time, in the very limited ways that the System allowed, and with the library in my head, I've learnt the hell a lot about it. Time, movement within it, and all the resulting research takes up a large chunk of the information in my brain. Even now, there are research projects in play.

So far, time dilation is the extent of the System's effects on the timeline. We can look into the future by guessing what will happen, but it's all estimation. Sometimes eerily accurate guesses, but still guesses. You can look into the past by using various Skills to shift light, to draw on spiritual energies, to read the vibration of quantum entanglements. But you can't go back in time or forward into the future.

That doesn't stop us from trying.

Magic, unconstrained by the limitations of the System, is the go-to option. Numerous mages have attempted to manipulate Mana, trying to pierce the veil of time itself. The most successful of those spells rebounded, damaging their casters. The greatest failures had a tendency to create horrors.

Monsters that grew too fast, that aged and died in the blink of an eye. Sapient creatures whose very life force was sucked out to power the spell. Even the mass replication of the spell using an entire city's lifeforce was insufficient to make a dent. The veil was more like a diamond wall than diaphanous cloth. You could slow time down, dilute it. But you couldn't move through it.

"Cider?" the dark elf asks, holding out the clear glass of alcoholic apple juice.

When I take it, he shifts his hand slightly, making sure I touch his fingers. I have to admit, his touch still sends a thrill through me. Even when a portion of my mind records the ongoing Charm effects I resist. Roxley has a full suite of Skills and tech to make him alluring. I would almost accuse him of vanity, except I knew he'd just bask in the accusation.

It's due to his past. Being a competitive dancer in Truinnar society meant he had to look good. No, better than good. While the winners were generally easy to pick out, the sponsorship of the contenders was another thing entirely. You couldn't just win; you had to win with style.

And that meant looking good.

And smelling good.

And yes, feeling good.

"We could adjourn somewhere else," Roxley drawls. His dark skin frames the now purple-and-yellow hair, highlighting those sharp ears and that wide smile. He leans against the table, pushing his hips out as he does so, and stretches.

The ass.

"No. Not getting distracted." I step back and sip on the drink to buy time. Immediately, I get notifications that I'm resisting a variety of drugs, over and above the normal alcohol content. "What the hell?"

"Third Sol apple cider," Roxley says. He makes the bottle appear, and I look at the very long list of warnings. "Quite in demand. The orchard is a dungeon, the loot drops the apples. Only way to make the drink is via, well, questing. It's even more in demand than Apocalypse Ale."

I can't help but chuckle and take another sip of the drink. I should've guessed. Even in our world, apple trees have mutated. "Tastes pretty good. But this isn't a social call."

"I assumed so." Roxley grows serious as he puts aside the flirting. It's like flipping a switch, and I kind of envy him that ability. I'm still letting my gaze linger on his biceps. "I've heard about you and your latest... fling."

"Jealous?"

Roxley doesn't answer, instead wandering over to a seat. When he's facing me again, he just cocks an eyebrow.

"Yeah, I figured." I sit down across from him. One of the advantages of our relationship, if you could call it a relationship, is the lack of strings. Roxley understands, something Lana never could. "You still taking care of the Duchess's place?"

"Of course."

"Good. And you've got contacts with the rest of the council." I say.

That's a new thing, as they've formalized the power structure within the planet. The major players in each faction have divided the seats into a semi-permanent ruling Council. Rob's still the World Leader, but the Council has chipped away at his strength, forcing him to play politics. Or lose his seat. It's still shaky foundations, with a lot of maneuvering. But they've managed to keep the planet united so far.

In fact, from what I hear, a number of Dungeon Worlds have made moves to unite their own worlds. The advantages we've managed to acquire by locking down the entire planet have made it apparent that they've been leaving a lot of Credits on the table. Now that they've got a working example, old rivalries that kept them apart have driven Galactic groups together. Still, there's a weight of history behind a lot of the fractious enmities on other Dungeon Worlds. And so while plans might be in play, nothing has actually happened. Yet.

Roxley nods, confirming my understanding.

"Good. Because I have got a business proposition for all of you."

The Truinnar cocks an eyebrow, and I can't help but smile back. Just because I've left doesn't make me any less a child of Earth. And I still need to have the initiates pass their quest.

Chapter 20

"This is a blatant abuse of power!" Magine complains.

I grin at the Movanna, then turn my gaze on the surviving Paladins. Only four of them are left: two Erethrans, Kino, and Magine. I'm surprised Freif hasn't broken. I'm surprised Magine hasn't flamed out. A lot of surprises, including Kino's survival. But considering I started with seven, having four left is a pretty decent number, I figure.

If only I could have gotten to this stage by kicking them out. And not losing them.

"Yes, it very much is." I grin.

We're in a briefing room, back on palace grounds, where we've been training for the last week. There's a little more polishing left to do for the initiates to learn how to work with their team, to fix problems we focused on in the debrief.

They weren't happy after that meeting, not at all. Between Bolo, Mikito, myself, and three guest lecturers from the armed forces we'd invited, we spent the better part of the day tearing apart every single mistake they did. Everything they could have done better. Everything they could have done so that their friends hadn't died.

We go through the recordings, sparse as they are. We pull out the video of the main fights, and when the cameras are destroyed, we go through the reams of reports they and their people provide. Lines and lines of data, of people explaining where they were, why they went there, why they were separated. More than enough, for all of us to dig in.

Because that was the underlying point. If they had pulled enough aggro, done enough damage, freed up enough of the weaponry, turned off the safeties on the mobile drones, or taken over the first level fast enough, then maybe instead of four, maybe five or six members would be here.

We drove the point home, again and again.

We traced how Freif, at the controls of the shielding station, destroyed it rather than hacking it. Not because he didn't have the personnel who could, but because he got a little too gun happy.

We showed how Gheisnan was swarmed, forces turning on him, hemming him in. Till he was stuck in a corner, unable to break out, his Skills no longer as useful. He and his team had fought, back to back—till the sensor grid went down and we lost the ability to see his end.

The grid had gone down late because Anayton had been too slow, too careless in dealing with the personnel in her own target. They'd refused to listen, refused to hand over the work, and when she finally acted to kill them and release the controls, it was too late.

Magine, focused on taking out the AI controlling the wall, had torn his way through two different command centers, searching for the right person. Never taking the time to actually locate the main control personnel, relying instead on speed and violence. And failing.

Over and over, we went over their actions, what they could have done better. Should have done better. We didn't even spare the mistakes made by the dead. Because there's a lesson there. We drill in their mistakes, their failures, the tragedy of their actions.

And the initiates don't break.

Irritated, hurt, maybe a little ashamed. But not broken. Maybe it's their old training, maybe some of the steel we've managed to bury in their backs. But even after everything, they're still willing to bitch me out. In public. Just less colorfully.

"We do have a facility there," Freif says, frowning. "The training you want us to do, it won't be that much different—"

"Not training. Your Quest."

"You're finally ready to give it to us?" Anayton says, distrust deep in her voice.

"Yes. You're ready. Or as ready as I can get you." I shake my head. "You know all the dangers now, have an idea of what you need to fight for. The rest, you'll figure out yourself. Or not. That's the only other lesson I have to impart."

"We've got to figure it out ourselves?" Magine says derisively. "That's worse than an unClassed fortuneteller's five-Credit pronouncement."

"I'd have gone with fortune cookie, but you do you."

Of course, the Galactics all looked puzzled. I doubt System downloads on Earth culture contained fortune cookies. I don't think I've even seen one since the end of the apocalypse. At least, not one that wasn't pre-System. Though the cookies all taste the same, even years later.

"The test?" Kino rumbles.

I stop teasing the easy target that is Magine and flick my hand. I don't really need to do that, but a little drama is useful once in a while. The group falls silent as they read over the System notification.

System Master Class Quest: Paladin of Erethra

You have been granted the opportunity to become a Paladin of Erethra. To do so, you must complete a Master Class Quest of sufficient difficulty at the behest of your Paladin of Erethra mentor (John Lee).

Do you accept?

[Y\N]

"*Are you sure of this, boy-o?*" Ali sends to me. There's a tinge of concern coming through the mental pathways that the System carves for us.

"*Yes.*"

Truth is, I'm not. But I do know that holding off any longer is a bad idea. In the last fight, I managed to eke out another Level, between the deaths and the System updates from the library. I'm trending up, and up, and there's only so long before the Queen gets impatient.

As for my doubts about what happened? The niggling concern that the two pureblood Erethrans are still here and my losses have all been non-Erethrans? Those I keep to myself. It could be coincidence. It could be something else. I could research it, dig into what really happened. Even through the Skill-shrouded Keeps' defenses, even if there are locks in place that stop me from buying it directly from the Shop.

I have my doubts. But in the end, we need more Paladins. Or at least, the Erethrans do.

System Master Class Quest: Paladin of Erethra

Your Paladin of Erethra mentor (John Lee) has designated the following requirements for your Master Class Quest:

- *Defeat 5 Master Class Monsters (Level 150 or more) in the designated locale (Earth) without aid beyond your bonded team.*

"What the hell is a bonded team?" Magine calls.

"Whatever you decide to make it." I lean over the table, dropping my voice to help make this clear. "But make sure it's a nice, tight bond. Because otherwise, the System won't count it. Make it a Serf contract, make it an Oath or a Gaea's. Or a Feudal Bond." I incline my head toward Mikito, who smiles slightly. "But these people are people you'll trust with your life. For now. And for the rest of your time as Paladins."

"So like your group," Kino accuses.

I glance back at Harry and Bolo, then turn back to the group and shake my head. "Not exactly. Those guys are more hangers-on."

I admit, I cheat. I use the security cameras installed in the meeting room to watch Harry's and Bolo's reaction to my dismissal of their loyalty. Bolo glares at the back of my head, as if he could bore through with just his gaze. Harry's steadier, shrugging as if what I said was true. I know Dornalor would agree. It's not as if he's ever made any bones about his loyalties. It's a good thing that I've got the Credits.

And he's one of those rare, rare pirates. He stays bought.

"But you guys aren't me. You've got friends, comrades, brothers in arms. People you've fought with that you can draw upon. Your job, what you're going to do, is quite well-defined. At least in societal terms. They know what they're getting into." I lean forward, looming over them, the feel of the hard light table cool against my touch. "And if you don't have anyone, I suggest you start thinking really hard about what you've done to achieve that in your life."

"After all, even this mutilated corpse of a human has one person who'd follow him into the depths of hell," Ali helpfully adds.

Mikito coughs into her hand, trying to hide the laughter that bubbles out. Bolo and Harry don't even bother, guffawing behind me. The initiates are a little more wary, but they do all crack a smile.

"Five Master Class monsters. That's quite a number." Anayton shakes her head before regarding me fully. "Do you really expect us to survive doing this?"

"I do. And so does the System." I pause, then admit, "At least, some of you."

"And you did this? You beat five Master Class monsters?" Magine says, eying me up and down. There's a glint of the competitive Duelist there. And something more.

I raise a hand and waggle it side to side. When they frown, I explain. "Probably. The Quest was the same. Mostly. But I was in the Forbidden Zone, so Levels were a little weird. I mostly just killed the biggest, baddest city-stompers I could find and hoped that it was enough. We couldn't even check that often."

"You and your team?" Kino says.

The other initiates are already shaking their heads, remembering details, but I answer him anyway. "No. No team. The Champion tossed me in alone."

Those words bring a long, long silence.

Kino shifts, little rocks trembling across his body, ground dust falling. Magine continues to eye me, and I wonder if maybe I shouldn't have reminded him. He only gave Mikito that look—as if she was worthy, unlike me—until now.

The other two are silent, possibly reviewing their own chances. Truth be told, I'm not entirely sure how I survived. A hell of a lot of stubbornness and a good dose of luck. My affinity helped, that I know.

"But this is the System Quest. Kill, defeat, or otherwise deal with five Master Classers while you're in Advanced Class. I adjusted it a little for the Dungeon World, but the goal is the same. Do more than you think you can," I say those last words, facing each of the four initiates in turn, meeting their gaze and weighing them. "You have a week to get ready. Build your teams, bond them however you wish. Pass the information to me. We meet in a week. And we'll Portal you straight in."

I don't tell them I've already decided where they'll each go. It doesn't really matter. It's a big world and there are a lot of monsters. Dividing them up across Earth will keep them busy and out of each other's way. And give my allies a few more favors to call in in the future.

Seeing that I'm done speaking, the group troops out. Ali's already deposited the basic information they need, but for the rest of it, they'll have to do their own research. No handholding this time.

As the last of them trundles out, leaving rock dust in his wake, I feel a weight leave my shoulders. I've done everything I can for them. Now…

It's time for me to deal with the rest of my obligations.

***

Ayuri finds me lounging on a deck chair beside the pool in my residence. I've had to reconfigure the building a little, replace the basement with the deck chair and diving pool. Finding pool water was an interesting experience. Especially when the building offered a million and one different variations. From seawater from different atolls and planets, to different kinds of spring water, specially curated and oxidized H_2O, and more. It was kind of annoying, especially when I realized that I had to add some chlorine anyway. Thankfully, Ali swept in and helped with the reconfiguration before I blasted a hole in the building itself in exasperation.

So.

I lounge beside my pool under an artificial sun conjured from the holographic projectors hanging overhead. Blue skies and rolling wisps of clouds float by, while the occasional caw of birds and insects blare from the speakers.

"This is where you are?" Ayuri says, glaring at me.

I smile at the tall champion and raise my glass at her. "Pina colada?"

Ayuri eyes the blended, pale-yellow slushy of a drink with vague interest before she shakes her head. "I'm here on business, Redeemer."

"Your loss."

"You gave the initiates their Master Class Quest." Ayuri says.

"You here to kill me now?" I reply, mostly in jest. After all, they still need my help for one other thing. Though rumors are that the Queen is doing pretty well. She might last another couple of decades before someone kills her.

"Obviously not. I do think you should be raising your Level instead of lounging." Ayuri crosses arms, glaring at me. "Or are you waiting for your indulgence?"

"Indulgence?"

Ayuri raises a single eyebrow, skepticism and suggestion written across her face in broad strokes.

I laugh, shaking my head. "I think Catrin would find being called an indulgence amusing. Don't you?"

I open up Society's Web and stare at the numerous lines radiating out from the Champion. There's a very thin line that touches upon my current flame. Nothing like the thread Ayuri has to Saimon. A lot of old feelings there, between her and the Seeker.

"Are you using that Skill on me?" Ayuri says, anger flaring. She steps toward me, fist clenching. "Don't you know that's rude?"

"Actually, pretty sure it isn't." I sip on the pina colada, ignoring her show of temper. This isn't the time or the place for a fight. Nor is she gonna commit. "So what are you doing here? If not getting drunk?"

Ayuri stares at me for a second more, then snorts and flops down. Seconds before she hits the ground, a floating, cloudy chair forms, catching her in its pillowy goodness. She twists her hands, making a drink from the sidetable float over before she pours herself a glass. Only when she's suitably seated does she speak. "The cover is blown. Add your acts against the nobles and… well. You're in danger."

"Heck. As if they weren't pushing it already," I say, chuckling a little.

Mana mourns, I've had to fete the two major contenders. Then there are the half dozen other wannabes who have made their way over, watching our training, offering suggestions, Credits, and other less subtle bribes.

Spuryan has been much more subtle, sending members of his congregation to meet me, to talk to us quietly whenever they have a chance. Just small ways, messengers and other documentation, to show that his people, his way can work too.

I'm not looking forward to the hard press. But I need to speak with them all more. See the other options, learn a little more of their world. I've only seen a half dozen worlds so far, after all. There's more to learn, more to fight.

"You need that level." Ayuri says rather firmly. "On top of that, Unilo has something to talk to you about too."

"About time she asked for her favor." I wonder what she needs from a poor benighted soul like me. "Anything I should know?"

"You know, she is my teammate," Ayuri says.

"That a no?"

I watch as Ayuri fights herself. Loyalty to the Empire warring with loyalty to her friend. In the end, the Empire wins out. It always will with someone named the Champion. "She's a noble, as you know. But the family has been in disgrace for years. What she might ask will benefit her family more than herself."

"No hints on that?" I continued to prod.

"No." There's a little doubt, a little concern in Ayuri's voice. I wonder if she even knows. She tilts her glass back, draining it, then pours herself another. "What is this astringent taste? And why is it so enticing?"

"Pineapple." I go into the building menu. A second later, a pineapple pops into existence, teleported here by the System. I wince at the extravagant cost. I catch it and hand the whole fruit to her. "This one's unmutated. Which, by the way, makes it a premium product these days."

Ayuri dubiously eyes the spiked, bright pale-yellow fruit. Eventually, she puts it into her inventory. And then, she downs another glass.

"Let her know I'll see her tomorrow. And get Mayaya to come so that he can port me over directly." I stand, leaving my glass behind. As I walk over to the water, I add, "You know, your pet Paladins might not be what you think they are."

There's only silence from behind me as I approach the edge of the pool.

I stare at the pale blue waters, rippling from the artificial breeze I have blowing through the room. "But that's the thing about people, isn't it? They can always surprise you."

I don't let her answer before I dive in. Letting the cold wrap me. Letting the fear of the water clutch at me as old wounds, old memories rise up. But this is a fear I've learnt to deal with. I've learned to live with. It clutches at my chest, stutters my heart, and makes it beat faster. It consumes my mind.

As for all my other worries, of the Empire and the games being played? Those get driven out, at least for a time.

Chapter 21

We step out of the Portal together, dubiously eyeing the small island we've arrived on. Already, Ali, who had gone ahead, is updating my minimap, giving me location data and information about the surroundings. He's blocked off from a lot of information and restricted in his flight paths, but basic geography and the Galactic equivalent of GPS is fine. All of that tells me we're on another planet, though I could have told you that from the shift in gravities. Three times Earth normal, which means little when your Strength is in the hundreds. But annoying anyway.

"Paladin. Thank you for coming," Unilo says, greeting me when I walk forward. The Erethran is clad not in her military uniform but something more relaxed. It's a mixture of a corset, floofy dress arms, and ultra-tight pants, all in dark pink and lined with white fur.

That's the other thing. The crisp, freezing air tugs at my exposed skin, leaving ice crystals. The temperature is just above -40 Celsius, not including windchill. Sadly, I have to admit, it reminds me of Whitehorse.

Not that I'm a native. I still think of Vancouver as home more than Whitehorse. But that city—really, a town—is still central to who I became. And so my memories of it dominate. Including the damn cold. On top of that, the white snow that layers itself over the landscape, the snow glare the makes my pupils shrink, is another reminder.

"Unilo. Good to see you." I give her one of the Erethran salutes, sloppily done because, well, no one ever told me how to do it properly. Also, I must admit, I never bothered to find out. "Your invitation was… expected."

Unilo sniffs and turns, popping open a Portal. She steps in, and Ali and I follow. Harry is the only other member of my party who decided to join, raring at the chance to see another planet. One that isn't trying to eat his face.

Dornalor decided to spend the week running another job, wanting to test out his ship on a more routine assignment. Those were exactly his words. I really didn't want to ask.

Given the choice between lounging around and joining Dornalor, my friends ran off. Even Mikito. I feel insulted, but I'm not a fan of politics either.

To my surprise, rather than leading me to a board room, Unilo brings me to the entry courtyard of her residence. Then she keeps walking, past servants and a doorway to a living room. The entire place is tastefully done, luminescent pale blue and white, shades of a dark purple accent highlighting the wallpaper. The couches have a light brown accent with yellow trim and are placed in a rectangular circle with one end open and sitting tables alongside each couch.

Unilo takes a seat on one of the chaises, and I take a more traditional couch diagonally opposite hers. Harry, on the other hand, is taken by the arm and guided out by a waiting servant, to be shown around the estate.

The moment he walks out, both spatial locks and privacy locks appear. Surprisingly, there are three in place. One for the room, one for the residence, and one for the planet. Powerful enough to stop me from jumping out if I need to and to keep the vast majority of our conversation hidden.

"So what is this about?"

"One second. We're waiting for one more person," says Unilo.

She turns her head, and a man saunters in. He's older, lines on his face, his neck, and his hands. He has tattoos all across his face, branching swirls reaching from his neck and up to his face, highlighting the coral on his ears. And his hair is shorn short, unlike the common flowing locks I've seen sported by most Erethran nobles.

He's also sporting an assortment of Mana enchantments. Multiple rings, bracers, anklets, something around his chest region, more attached to his belt. And they're not low-level enchantments either. At least three are Master Class level.

"John Lee, Paladin of Erethra. I present to you my older brother, Kilgave d'Cha, Warden of the Thrilsala System," Unilo says.

Kilgave bows to me, while I offer him a half-hearted wave from my seat. Ali slips around, coming to hold a position just slightly behind the man as he stops next to Unilo's seat. Ali's out of their direct line of sight though. Only I can see him directly. This gives him an opportunity to stick out his tongue and waggle his fingers in suggestive ways.

Kilgave d'Cha, Warden of the Thrilsala System, Champion of the 631st, 632nd and 648th Mithril Man Competition, Monster Bane, Slayer of Goblins, Hakarta, Movanna,... (Level 33 Sundered Champion) him (M)

HP: 8480/8480

MP: 5230/5230

Conditions: Warden's Reach, Broken End, Aura of the Sundered Champion, Mana Warden

"*Sundered Champion?*" I send to Ali.

"*Disgraced? Might be better. It's not exactly right. There are a lot of cultural connotations involved. I think disgraced is a little too much.*" Ali shrugs. "*It'd take a bit to explain. But he's the ex-Empire Champion. Class got changed.*"

"*I thought there was only one.*"

"*There can only be one.*" And because he's Ali, he plays an all-too-familiar riff. I snort, but he doesn't take too long, considering the two of them are blathering at me with the usual pleasantries of our meeting. *"He had the job before Ayuri. Before his fall."*

"Oh boy."

I tune back into the conversation, something about the drink and snacks that have arrived. A part of me has been busy chatting with them, grunting and making tasteful, social noises. And stuffing my face with the little lemon bar snacks they've put out. Of course, they're not really lemon bars, but a close enough Galactic equivalent.

As they talk more, going into detail about the recipe, I trigger Society's Web. It takes minutes before I gain an understanding, watching the way the many, many threads fly out from Kilgave and touch others. The only people I've ever seen with more threads are the Queen and Ayuri herself.

I guess that's part and parcel of being a Champion.

I'm almost tempted to ask about his Skills. A surge from the library has me almost choking on a bite as I struggle to pin down the incoming information. I don't need another download right this second.

After swallowing the bite, tasting the astringent sourness and sweetness, and washing it down with a gulp of flavored water, I gesture at the pair. "All right. Enough already. What is it that you guys want?"

Unilo almost makes a face at my abrupt change of topic. She looks exasperated, but the former Champion laughs.

"I was beginning to wonder if the stories were true. I'm glad they are," Kilgave says. "It's simple. My niece tells me that you owe her a favor. We are here to collect."

"I'm not going to kick Ayuri out of her place," I say. "I don't even think I'm allowed to."

"I would never do that to my beam sister," Unilo says, looking scandalized. She's so angry that the cup she was holding cracks before dropping to the floor and shattering.

We're all distracted for a second, before the cleaning bots sweep and tidy it away.

By that point, Unilo's got her temper back in control. "We want you to do something else."

"Yeah, I don't really have daddy issues. At least, not like that," I say.

Ali, over and behind him, is flipping in circles, choking on laughter. It's a nice contrast to the two who just looked very puzzled.

"Stop talking nonsense, Redeemer," Unilo snaps. "We want you to give my brother the Paladin Master Quest."

"Huh." I lean back, sinking into the chair as I regard the pair. I could say it was a surprise, but really, when she brought him in, there weren't that many other options. Well, other than me being dragged into a random, erratic quest for justice. "Why?"

"It doesn't matter. You owe me," Unilo snaps.

"It does." I cross my arms, fixing the pair of them with a firm gaze. "Talk, or I won't do it."

"You'll break your word!" Unilo says, raising her voice for the first time.

"Yep."

Before Unilo can dig herself any deeper, the man puts a hand on her shoulder. She subsides almost immediately. There's no doubt who's in charge of this little conversation.

"It's very simple, Redeemer. I might be old, and my honor might be questionable to some. But I still serve the Empire," Kilgave says. "This, this opportunity is the best that I can find."

"So why me? Why not go to the Forbidden Zone yourself?"

He hesitates before he answers. "I did. Your mentor turned me down."

I snort, staring into space. More correctly, at the line that leads to my mentor. There's a lot packed in there—both duty and obligations, and something personal. In fact, that personal bit wraps itself around the thread that holds them together. It balloons and sizzles in every interaction, tainting every responsibility and duty they might have.

"Why?"

"We disagreed. About what she was supposed to do, what I was supposed to do. We disagreed about the King and her duties, and by the time I realized she was right, it was too late." Regret flashes across Kilgave's face and I start piecing together their history.

"You were the Champion for the mad King," I state.

"He wasn't mad. He was just..." Kilgave seems to try to find a word. In the end, he shrugs. "Selfish. In need of control. Narcissistic. But not mad."

I snort at him cutting such a fine line. But it's past history, not one I'm interested in digging up. I fall silent, regarding him. Prodding at the System in my head even as data, at the slightest loosening of my will, floats in. Information about his Skills, his abilities, what he can do, what he lost, and what he gained. A lot of information, but a fallen Champion is something the Questors would be very interested in.

I come back to myself, the pair still staring at me patiently. I can't help but shake my head, wondering if they thought I was considering the offer. Or accessing information about them. I wish Harry was here, but even the party chat is blocked right now. Communication seems to be off the tables.

"You're a Master Class. With quite a few Levels. How are you going to take mine?"

"I'll give this one up. I'll take the penalty. If you're willing to give me the opportunity," Kilgave replies, his voice firm and without any trace of hesitation.

"Again? You've already lost quite a few Levels, changing Classes once."

"It is what it is. For the Empire, losing a few Levels is nothing," Kilgave says fervently.

I stare into his eyes as he speaks, trying to judge how true he is. Not just because he's not using a Skill, but how true it is in his soul. And I'm not surprised to see, to believe, that he's telling the truth. He would give it all up. For an Empire that threw him aside once before.

"And the Queen?" I turn to Unilo, fixing her with my stare. "What does she think of this?"

"She doesn't know," Unilo replies, her voice dropping as she stares at the retreating cleaning robots now that they've done their job. Now that they've removed any speck of the liquid or glass she had broken. Leaving us in beautiful, serene, blue cleanliness.

"And if she did?"

"She would be less than pleased," Unilo replies, the words seemingly dragged out of her.

"Does Ayuri know?"

"She... guesses."

I sit back, idly picking up one of the lemon bars and biting it. This one is more raspberry than lemon, but it's tart and sweet and something to do with my mouth while I think. Plus points—it'd annoy the Queen. Negative points—it'd annoy the Queen.

On the other hand, Ayuri knowing what is about to happen means that while it might anger the Queen, it probably is good for the Empire itself. That's one of the constraints about her Class. Though I'm not entirely certain how constrained she is. Even that giant library in my head doesn't have specifics—mostly because they haven't done in-depth research into the Champion's Class directly.

Class restrictions are a known issue, but while it was useful for knowledge's sake, it didn't seem to help the System Quest. So that branch of research was dropped by the Questors. At least, in general. Others have continued to do research, of course, and it's from those studies that I know more of Class restrictions. Which, as with most things in the System, can be as loose or as constrained as the System deems it. The trade-offs in power are significant though, which is why many continue to explore the intricacies.

"Why do you want to be a Paladin?" I say. It's almost a rhetorical question now, because I think I know. There are only a few kinds of people who become Champions.

"To serve the Empire. The real Empire," Kilgave says. When my silent and steady gaze demands more, he sighs. "I failed. The first time. Thinking I served the Empire, but what I served was a man. Now… now I want to make it right."

"You know, I put the initiates through a lot of training…"

"Which I do not need," Kilgave says, sounding almost affronted. I can't help but chuckle, seeing the spark of arrogance in his eyes. "I have fought more and harder monsters than those you sent them for. And I learnt my lessons, the lessons you tried to impart, decades ago. At greater cost than I would wish on anyone."

"One last question then. Tell me the story."

"What story?" Unilo says.

But Kilgave knows and squeezes that hand on her shoulder. She looks at him and he offers her a pained half-smile.

"It is not an easy thing, to tell of your failures…" Kilgave begins, before he launches into the tale. It's one of mistakes, of indecisions. Of lives taken and lost. And in the end, of a man who chose to stand aside when it was necessary. To fail his own Class to save an Empire.

When that somber tale is over, I ask, "And what? You've been chilling at the family estates since then?"

"I've been doing what I can to aid the Empire. Even a fallen Champion is a powerful force," Kilgave says. "But I'm limited in what I can do internally. By those who believe what I did was wrong. By my former position. By my present Class." He gestures upward. "I cannot affect the change I need…"

"Yeah, yeah, I get it." I wave, shutting him up. I see the flash of anger, the pride that he bites down on while I run pell-mell over his need to monologue. At his peak, he was nearly a Heroic. Then he lost it all and has had to claw his way back. "Don't care. You want the Quest? Let's see what the System has to say about it."

I feel for the System. It's kind of like reaching behind your back, except not with your hands but with the tail that you never realized you had. And then punching a bunch of buttons, still sight unseen, with that same tail to make it dance to your commands.

It's weird.

And, sadly, with the way the System has increased my Intelligence, with the way the library has downloaded so much information, all too doable. I find the portion of my Class that lets me designate new Paladin initiates, that allows me to offer them the Quest.

It balks at first, because he's a Master Class. And when I press, overriding the initial resistance, I feel the mental fuzz it throws at my will, the shock of its cold jaws clamping down on my desire. It strains and bucks at my commands, refusing to let me do it.

That's the worst thing the System could have done. Because suddenly, I want it.

Not because of Kilgave and his idiotic need to serve an Empire that doesn't give a damn about him. That might even hate him. I want it because the System doesn't.

I grunt out loud and ignore the pair before me as my head throbs, as my vision goes red. Will against System, I bring all the tools I have to play with—Mana Sense, affinity, knowledge from the library, and will—to bear.

It buckles and finally gives in. Because while it might not want to, the Quest is still a possibility. Like stabbing a fork into a clogged up, dirty electric outlet to free it up till you could slot your computer in. It's not smart and you might get shocked a little, but it'll work.

Eventually, I stare at the Quest notification.

System Master Class Quest: Paladin of Erethra

Your Paladin of Erethra mentor (John Lee) has designated the following requirements for your Master Class Quest:

- *Reset and lose Master Class Levels (XP will be refunded and banked at a reduced rate)*
- *Defeat 11 Master Class Monsters (Level 150 or more) in the designated locale (~Error!~) without aid beyond your bonded team.*

Huh. I blink, prodding at the Quest with my mind and will. But that last error keeps throwing itself up, firmly deciding not to resolve itself. I get a feeling it won't, not till it's given.

"Redeemer?" Unilo calls.

"So… this might be interesting." A push of will and I make the blue notification screen show up.

Unilo's face scrunches up and she leans forward, trying to assess what the hell it says.

Kilgave's reaction is much more dramatic. His knees give way and he flops down onto the chaise, missing it by inches and being saved from an ungainly spill by the chaise itself moving to catch him. His jaw is working while the couch moves itself and its occupant back into place.

"Can't have the furniture at the wrong angles," Ali says, sounding amused.

"You know, being shocked over a simple Quest doesn't engender a lot of faith in your ability to complete it," I say, drawling.

"That… you… the location. Why…?"

"The Error? Not my fault." I lean forward, pouring myself more of the fruity drink, then glug it down, trying to wash away the slight headache conjuring that damn Quest notification had produced.

"What error?" Kilgave says, sounding confused. "I'm talking of sending me to Bohmer."

The name sends a shiver through me. I know that name, though I rarely use it. Because that name brings too many bad memories. Too many horrors from the four years I spent there. And so, instead of facing the fear, I wall it away, pushing it down and focusing on something else. Something a little more incongruous.

"Why there?" Unilo mouths my question.

"I…" I shake my head. The System… sometimes. I wonder about it. Some of its decisions, some of the things that happen, it makes no sense— unless it's alive. As circles get completed, as narrative and karmic ends… fit. For Bohmer is more than just another Forbidden Planet and the center of my own slew of nightmares.

It's also the ex-capital of Erethra. And where their ex-King fell.

Where Kilgave chose to stand aside.

And where Suhargur refuses to leave, fighting her never-ending battle to save those citizens who refused to go. Or, in many cases, have nowhere left to go, on pain of death.

So many circles completing. And staring at the Quest, I laugh softly. And do as the System wants. Because I can think of nothing more fitting. I offer him the Quest and all that it entails. The danger, the despair, and the return to his failure.

And maybe his salvation.

While Kilgave stares at the Quest notification, his brash certainty gone, I stand. My motion does nothing to distract the pair, so I walk out, leaving Unilo and the ex-Champion to their considerations.

Though not before snagging the plate of snacks.

Chapter 22

They came for me when I was Leveling. Gaining access to the city dungeons was simple enough, just a matter of showing up. I'd gone alone, leaving my friends behind. Not wanting to be burdened by their XP debuff, not wanting to be slowed down by Harry. And, most importantly, because they'd found better things to do.

Like indulging himself in the city for Bolo, and fighting in the arena for Mikito. Dornalor left almost immediately after his mission, to run another trip. From what the trio said, the "routine" mission had turned out to be just that—a pure pick up and deliver event. When asked, Dornalor had pointed out that most missions didn't involve violence.

Harry was enjoying himself on the planet, bouncing from city to city. Restricted as he was in the palace, he'd found a niche doing touring documentaries all through the planet. It wasn't his preference, but he was still waiting on additional approval to get to the frontlines.

Which left me to myself. Alone and vulnerable.

The dungeon itself was nothing special, other than the fact that it wasn't a fantasy rip-off. Instead, we had robots in all kinds of configurations that you could think of—swarming across walls like spiders, flying through the air as hordes of mini drones, even a few humanoid terminators.

Most interesting of all were the bipedal robots wielding gun arms, firing upon me as they twisted all around their torso. They were mini-bosses, roaming sentinels. They popped up every time I was between zone transition in levels, before I hit next level boss.

The city dungeon itself is twelve levels deep, and I'm down in level nine when they come.

I'd started at the top, working my way down in quick order before slowing down at the last couple of levels. Partly to keep my Mana levels high, partly because things are beginning to get interesting.

I skip along the pale gray walls, armored feet tearing into the metal as I run along it, mass impacts ringing throughout the rectangular room we're fighting in. For the creativity shown in building out the robots, in developing the variety of androids, the actual environment is a letdown. Other than the occasional blockade of metal, most of the rooms and corridors are smooth surfaces, leaving open lines of sight and few places to hide. Good thing I'd recently been fighting in a space station with almost the exact same problem.

An exertion of will and the spell finishes, the formula for the Mana escaping my mind as I release it, creating a small hill on the floor. Not a large hill, but more than adequate to throw off the aim of the sentinels as they fire. The small hill grows, metal warping and bulging, and the sentinels stagger, trying to right their balance.

I'm grinning, ready to destroy the staggering sentinels, when a pair of two-foot-long blades fly through the air. These attackers are new, and definitely not a dungeon feature as they make their presence known.

The first two blades sink into my back, punching right through my active Soul Shield and Hod's Armor before digging into muscle and bone. I fall off the wall, the weapons embedded in my back as I tumble to the ground. Notifications flash, too fast to keep track of all, but I get glimpses.

Successful Dual Backstab!
+1787 Damage Inflicted

You have been Poisoned! (54% Resisted)
+214 Damage per second

Additional Effects: You are Disoriented!

Duration: 6.3 seconds

The blades fly out seconds later as my emergency Shield Ring kicks in, throwing the weapons away from me. Hod's secondary defensive shields turn on as well with a quick exertion of will. I roll on the ground, coming to my feet, but the others are already attacking.

Mana, that I hadn't noticed building up, is unleashed. No fancy elements here, no special projection, just raw, harnessed Mana slamming into the shields. I tumble through white light, trying to balance out the damage the moment it pierces my shielding. It doesn't do much, especially when I bounce off the floor.

Instinctively, I reach for the Mana with my Elemental Affinity, hoping to see it off a little. And, of course, fail. Mana has no electromagnetic force, no physical aspect for my ability to grasp. Whatever it is, it's not one of the fundamental physical aspects of the universe.

A second after the raw Mana flames die off, as I regain my sense of balance, I'm slammed into by another figure. The Ram's Rush throws me into the wall again, bouncing me off it, the ceiling, then the floor. My armor is smoking, damage notifications flaring everywhere and reminding me that I'm in a dire situation. Surprise assassinations are a nasty, nasty business.

As I roll onto my knees, I spot the rushing, eleven-foot, stone-like creature—one of the Risen—on his way to finish the job. I feel Mana rising as the Mage continues his casting, readying another powerful spell. All of this in microseconds…

More than enough information gathered. That's when I act.

"Standard formation," I send to Ali.

Abyssal Chains, rising from the ground, wrap around the tank and the mage, restricting their motions. I wish I could get the rogue, but he's gone, a ghost in the System.

That's fine, because I keep moving, throwing my daggers at the tank, layering another Soul Shield onto my defense. Hod's force shield flickers back on after a second, regeneration kicking in as the Mana Engine goes to work. If the rogue wants to backstab, he'll have to get into position, and I'm not looking to make it easy.

Even so, uncertain if there might be more waiting, I keep angling around the tank as he breaks free. A second team perhaps, waiting for me to waste my Mana on these guys. So rather than do that, I use my knives, the inbuilt beam weaponry on Hod's Armor, and my blades to trim down the Risen.

Risen Tank (Erethran Vanguard Level 47) (A)

HP: 2138/4840

MP: 983/1780

Conditions: Structural Integrity, Wrath of the Masses, The Sacrifice of One, Earthen Density, Lightfoot, Greater Health Regeneration, Greater Mana Regeneration

A quick stutter in his health, when it drops after an attack and starts rising, makes me grit my teeth. The poison coursing through my blood is painful, fogging my thoughts, eating at my nerves and slowing down my reactions. That's why it took me so long to realize it.

An exertion of will, and threads appear. I dismiss the minor ones, then I dismiss those that lead to family, to those he loves. His crazed obsession with the Champion and another Legendary Artiste. Within seconds, the details of their team are all too apparent. I feel someone slide into my mind, share my senses for a second, then Ali pops out.

"Three o'clock, three feet behind that crushed mass."

I can only grunt my reply as I block the swings of the Risen. He sends me skittering seven feet in the wrong direction. I wince, my hands throbbing, my blades all scattered by the sheer force of his attack. The Risen winds up again, getting ready to throw another gauntleted punch with a Power Punch combined.

But I'm already murmuring, both hands up, my sword dropped to the ground. Power floods into my hands as the spell ignites. I can't help but grin as I mutter, "Fastball special, coming right up."

Electricity, lightning drawn from the very air around us, erupts from my hands. I reach out with my Elemental Affinity even as I note how Ali swoops down to join the stream. He's adding his gifts, but seeing the battered, shattered remnants of the monsters we've been fighting has given me another idea.

I reach for the energy sources of these creatures, touch upon the Mana batteries. I can't control Mana, but the engines, the converters, are using enough electricity for me to manipulate. I make them go into overdrive, using a combination of Mana and Elemental Affinity. It's easier than it ever has been—partly because of the library, I think.

The ground before me erupts as lightning, flowing from my hands into the tank, strikes the ground and the shattered corpses of the robots, going into overdrive and jumping right out with even more of a charge. It skips, low to the ground, into the air, directed by Ali and me. Creating a chain of destruction through the entire dungeon floor.

My eyes squint and water even as Hod filters out the light. The smell of ozone permeates the air, sinking in through the armor, its environmental seals cracked under the onslaught it had faced. I pick out, over the crackle of lightning and the muted screams of the tank, the screams of the mage and hidden healer as they're caught in the web of electricity.

"That's right, eat lightning!" Ali cackles, his invisibility faded as he directs the flow like a conductor at a symphony.

I bring lightning to the world and I don't stop channeling Mana into my attack until the robots' batteries are drained, until the corpses are smoking husks. I stare at the crispy figures of what used to be sapient creatures. Their bodies, their equipment are so damaged, it's impossible to tell what most of them once were. Only the Risen is still vaguely recognizable, a melted slag of rock and metal.

And all I can really think of is that I'm rather disappointed. I was expecting more of a challenge.

"Four..." I shake my head.

A normal team would be five strong. The thread I noticed showed a fifth, but it was frayed, broken. This was a team, there's no doubt, but recently restructured. A team of four Advanced Classers sent to assassinate me.

The plan was good, but I guess they hadn't thought of my Elemental Affinity—and what I could do with it here.

Then again, it's hard to blame them. I hadn't thought about it until just now.

"*Looks like you ranked up again on your Affinity, boy-o.*" Ali's eyeing me slightly dubiously, having flown back after collecting the corpses.

"*What?*"

"*Never seen someone get so used to playing with Mana and their Affinity so fast before,*" Ali says.

I open my mouth to counter the Spirit, then pause. I remember my struggles, the way I fought to learn even a basic Spell modification in space. How hard it was.

And this... this was simple. Just a matter of creative thought, focus, and desire. And poof, I was suddenly generating multiple nexus points of energy, drawing from Mana batteries and transforming it. It was...

"*Weird.*"

"*No shit.*"

"*Any idea why?*" I say as I wait for the Hod to begin its healing process and for my Mana and Health to recover. Thankfully, the poison had timed out at some point in my little bout of madness. Which leaves me a lot clearer-headed.

"*Only thing that changed was you being poisoned. And the you know what,*" Ali says flatly.

I freeze, and for a second, I feel my heart speeding up. I draw a breath, inhaling and exhaling to steady myself. And I wonder, once more—what exactly did Feh'ral do to me?

***

Finding Saimon was a matter of a few calls. Finding him and a secure location where we could have the necessary discussion was a little harder. Not that there aren't secure locations scattered throughout the city, but finding one that's secure for our purposes was little more complicated. Which is why we end up in a private room of the Galactic equivalent of a strip club.

You have to give it to sapient creatures, privacy when you've got weird kinks—and Erethran kinks are really weird considering how open they are about sexuality in general—is a common theme. Considering how powerful certain Skills are, and the need for this level of privacy, the highest quality clubs are highly guarded.

Which, amusingly, sets up almost a sideline of non-sexual meetings. After all, getting caught arriving at such a location can be a lot less embarrassing. Safer too, than being suspected of plotting treason or the sale of state secrets. It's still not agreeable, but it's better than nothing. And so, when I make the request from them for a private room, one with a large enough area and a sterile environment, they don't even blink.

"Those really aren't the kinds of bodies I want to look at when I come to a place like this," Bolo complains.

The Dragon Lord is why I located this place on such short notice. He's also invited himself along. Mikito's still stuck fighting her tournament but has promised to arrive soon.

"Not asking," I reply to Bolo once more.

What is it with a certain type of person who feels the need to tell you all about his exploits? I don't want to know, I don't care, so please stop talking.

"I have to agree with the Dragon Lord," Saimon replies. He's staring at the corpses laid out, floating in midair due to the room's gravity checks. They're all shrink-wrapped, or the Galactic equivalent of it, so that they don't smell or otherwise stink. Considering how they died, that's something we all find comforting, I'm sure.

"Very funny, you two." I point at the bodies. "These were military personnel. Their Classes are a clear indication of that, along with the information I managed to pick out. Now, there's an obvious culprit. But Harry and Ali have already begun to hit a lot off cut-outs. So the obvious culprit might be just a red herring."

"Is that a human saying?" Saimon asks.

"Yes," I reply. "You've got the resources, so I'm leaving this to you."

Harry looks up from where he and Ali are seated on one of those plush red couches with a lot of space in front of them and glares at me. I give him a shrug. I doubt he has the ability or the Credits to find out who sent assassins. These guys, they've been playing these games for decades, centuries even. And while Harry might be good at his job, he's still learning the new landscape of the System. Given enough time, he might be able to track down the people who ordered these assassinations.

But time isn't what I have.

"Perhaps we should look at this from another point of view," Saimon says, even as he makes the bodies disappear into his storage.

"What view?"

"Who would want you dead?"

Bolo laughs as Ali snorts. He's focused on trying to crack the trail of payments. Either that or he's given up and is watching another Earth TV show. Sometimes, I can't tell.

"The Redeemer is very hateable," Bolo helpfully adds. "And all three of the major contenders have reasons to end him."

"Yes, but why now?" Saimon says. "They've existed with him, without such overt action, for this long. What triggered the attack?"

I narrow my eyes, thinking about it. The obvious answer is the release of the initiates. The other one is the inclusion of the ex-Champion as an initiate. Both could be a tipping point for contenders. When I mention it, Saimon nods.

"That could certainly drive some to action." When I raise my eyebrow, prompting him to go further, Saimon continues. "The Viscountess might take objection to the inclusion of a man who stood aside when the royalty died. She is, distantly, related."

"There's also the concern that your Paladins are in the majority all Erethran natives." Harry looks up. "I could see the Prophet being concerned about their introduction. Magine is known for his support of the nobility."

"Anyone have a reason why the General might want me dead?" I ask, just to check. I can't think of one, but I'm not perfect.

Saimon shakes his head, as do Bolo and Harry. Ali's the only silent member, and he spins himself in circles.

"So… I might have one," Ali says. "Boy-o here is sleeping with one of his women."

I snort, and the others just shakes their heads, discarding Ali's suggestion. It's pretty clear Brerdain doesn't give a damn about Catrin.

"So we can assume that he's out," I say. "What do we do?"

My question brings a long long silence. The way I see it, there isn't much we can do. Take the usual precautions, start looking into who might want me dead. And that's it.

"Great. Pleasure talking to you all. If that's the case, I'm going back to training," I say, throwing my hands in the air. If there's nothing else better to do, I might as well get back to grinding during the day and meeting with the contenders—and wannabe contenders—in the evening.

"I'll double your protection force, shall I?" Saimon calls after me as I stalk out.

I ignore him, knowing that any team can be suborned or bypassed.

"I'm gonna stay here for an hour." Ali calls, his voice much louder and deeper.

I glance back, realizing that he's increased in size, and I wince. Sometimes, I really don't understand the Spirit. Then again, sometimes, I don't think I want to.

***

The last three Levels of the dungeon have been a pain to handle. Not just because monsters have cropped up from Level 100+ to Level 150+, but also because they kept coming in swarms and launching themselves at me. I've got to keep my Mana and health at at least 50% at all times. Add the fact that while I wait for the Hod to fix itself, I'm borrowing a suit from the Erethrans, and my combat effectiveness and speed are just down.

It's not even as if the suit is bad. It's the kind of thing they give to the Honor Guard to use. It's biggest bonuses are to my strength and agility, with some increases to my defenses and resistances. However, it doesn't have any useful Skills, just a short range Blink and a trio of movable force shields. None of them are that powerful, but because they're built-in layers, they're useful against certain types of attacks.

For all of that, my experience bar creeps up ever so slowly. At this rate, I'll be grinding for the next couple of weeks or so to hit another Level. Even with the high-Level monsters involved, the experience requirements I have are just getting ridiculous.

But that's for tomorrow. Right now, Ali and I have something much larger to handle.

Maydi Duz Dungeon Boss (Level 176 Final Boss)

HP: 17,613/17613

MP: 283/283

Conditions: Coalesced, Movable Parts, All for One, the Dungeon's Gift

What I see before me is a towering mass of droids, robots, and other mechanical servants. It's a hive mind kind of thing, except not. Each of the droids is a portion of its body, each individually run, but also beings managed by a central processing unit somewhere deep within the creature's body. I've learnt of numerous ways of beating this creature, from slowly wearing away at the robot pieces and other appendages to shattering off portions and dropping them away into different dimensions so they can't reattach. Acid baths melt the creature into a puddle of liquid metal.

There are other, more subtle approaches. Cyber hackers send in tracers, burrowing their way through communication links, destroying network accesses, corrupting files, and making the entire thing come apart before they destroy the CPU directly.

Mages who pull power drain the Mana from the environment and the creature itself, until such time as it's no longer able to move, making it easy pickings. Oracles who are able to pinpoint the exact location of the CPU in the flowing mass of robots are able to direct their team to destroy the boss in one single combined blow. Necromancers, conjuring phantom facsimiles of ghosts, send them spinning into the center of mass to pull and extract bits and pieces.

There are a million ways of getting this done. But I'm a simple man. I take the simple approach to things.

Grinning, I conjure my swords and rush the boss. Daggers go out first, followed by Blade Strikes, each impacting a different location.

Missiles, fast-driven masses fired from railguns, lasers, and other beam weaponry, explode around me. Electricity arcs through the ground, sweeping at my feet, while gravitic mines turn on, trying to pull my balance off, to crush me or tear me apart in their competing spheres of influence.

The world goes insane, and for a time, I forget my problems and get lost in the fight. The minutes of peace when there's nothing to do but struggle and survive.

***

A circle of light and alien glyphs form around me, punctuated by the temporary presence of additional, conjured soulbound swords. There are fifteen blades around me now, each glowing with compressed power. A single swing of the original weapon in my hand is copied fifteen-fold, sending a compressed Blade Strike at the torn and tattered Boss.

The Dungeon Boss is smaller, significantly smaller, than before. I've attacked it multiple times, destroying robot spiders, humanoid fighters, robotic sentinels, and the various liquid-metal externalities it's used to attack me. I've littered the floor with pieces, shattered remnants of the monsters that appeared from the multiple hallways in their vain attempt to form up, to heal their master.

It's why, through the fight, I've worked to control the environment. Lava rivers flow from one section of the hall to the other, blocking off easy access for respawns. Metal and earth walls clog up spawning entrances, making the creatures work to exit, while gravitic mines of my own sweep aside falling figurines, shifting their trajectories. Some land in traps, others on the spiked piles of other, older corpses. I have temporary wards set up in one section of the Boss Chamber, blocking off a swarm of tiny hornets, none of whom individually can shatter the wards.

And more.

The only thing I don't have are my automated drones and weaponry. The wreck of an artillery drone, hacked and turned against me, lies discarded in a corner. A failure of imagination on my part.

I've fought the Boss for an hour, tearing him down until he's half his original size. Just about big enough to be covered by my final attack.

Army of One's manifestation is a screaming mass of bound Blade Strikes, spiraling in a formation of criss-crossing crescent energy to impact against the Maydi Duz. The Boss doesn't take it lying down, reforming its mass to create a temporary shield of adamantium and electronics. I hear the tortured screams of drones and metal as they face my ultimate attack Skill. As it tears them apart like a six-year-old's dreams of getting a pony.

One attack.

And the glowing green-and-red sphere of the monster's core is exposed briefly. Before a chunk of it is torn aside, damaged but not dead. It managed to scoot aside just enough to avoid a quick death. Sadly, it never notices Ali floating down from above, a giant cartoonish hammer of formed energy in hand.

He swings with all his might, all the while sporting bunny ears and crowing, "Gotcha, doc!"

"Oy!" I shout at Ali. "No playing around."

Ali sniffs, but the energy hammer he formed from the remnant energy expended by Army of One and the sizzling corpses is more than sufficient to end the Boss. I fly down, kicking off with hoverboots until I land next to the monster. I'm too late, as Ali loots the corpse and stares at our earnings.

Grumbling, I check my notifications.

Maydi Duz Dungeon Boss (Level 170 Final Boss) Defeated!
+98,484 XP

I grunt, waving away the rest of the information. While Ali blathers on about the loot, I walk toward the exit. Tomorrow—later today—I'll hit the next City Dungeon, and the one after that. And then I'll Portal to the next one and keep doing it. Grinding, till I hit my experience cap. I still have to find time for my interviews with the various members of the Erethran society, but I'm in a rush now. To hit my Levels before it's time to let the Queen know. To protect myself from what might be a nasty confrontation.

Because I've got an idea of what I'll do. Who I'll choose.

And I know the Queen won't like it.

But for now, rest.

***

"I got to admit, I'm a little disappointed," I say softly.

My words startle the figure hovering over my bed, not with a knife or dagger or even an explosive, but with a bottle and dropper. It jerks, glancing at me then at the form lying there, finally spotting the differences. The way the hardlight projection shimmers just a little, at rates that would be impossible to see with naked, non-System eyes. The way its breathing is too regular.

My poisoner—which is what I assume the bottle is—doesn't hesitate to flee, heading straight for the wall and the opening it had created. A neat trick that, making the nanite-created walls open up. It made no sound at all when it changed, and a simple force shield kept the wind and exterior temperature and pressure at bay.

My throwing dagger takes it in the thigh, sending the figure stumbling. I watch the overly generous curves go bouncing, a lock of colored, rainbow hair escaping its mask. The figure rolls and comes up to its knees, reaching for the dagger, only for it to disappear and return to me.

There's a low hiss before it darts for the exit again—only to bounce off the elemental shielding Ali has formed. No touch of Mana there, just an adjustment between the air molecules. Making the loose air molecules harder than titanium.

"You can stop now," I say.

I don't throw my other knife, though I'm ready to. There's something disturbing about the figure, something off about it. The way it lacks any threads leading to others is paramount among them.

Nothing—no one—can go through life without attachments. Without debts and obligations tying them down. Even a simple transaction of purchasing coffee sets up a reciprocal thread between you and the server. Those who think they are islands are just blind to the ground that connects them to the continents of humanity.

"You will fall." The voice is high, pitchy. Feminine.

Before I can reply, the figure dissolves, the shadows that held it together coming apart. I reach out with my senses, Mana and Affinity, hearing and smell, and note that it's gone. Completely. No hint of its scent, no trace of the Mana that bound it. I don't bother checking my minimap, since it never showed up. Or the building's security—for it had shown up, but as a friendly. And I sigh.

"Interesting. Doppelgangers don't get threads," I mutter. I recall how my own doppelgangers from Hod never gained any. They're not real, just temporary constructs with no soul. Like a broom. Or a golem. No obligations, no duties, no threads. And thus, no way to track them. "Smart."

"Yes, it is." Ali floats in, already commanding the System to fix our bedroom. "So, basement?"

"Basement." I open a Portal and sigh. "That's two."

"Mmmhmmmm…"

Chapter 23

"Kino," I say to the Risen, "I met one of your relatives recently."

"My fissure-sire is no longer of this earth. Was it a grotto mate?" Kino says, rumbling over the table in the Shop.

Around the conference room, the other Paladin initiates are seated, some of them taking the few minutes in the Shop to look around, quite impressed by the surroundings. Others look more blasé, like Magine.

"Risen, not a close relative. He was quite insistent on meeting me. Had a very rough way of talking," I say.

"He tried to kill you," Freif replies, not all amused.

"Mmm, yes. And I only made one knock-knock joke," I say.

Even Ali doesn't get my joke, the Spirit in his full form.

So I give the jokes a rest. "All right, boys and girls. It's been two weeks. Brief me. How's it going on Earth?"

The group looks a bit awkward, most of them looking surprised that I want to talk to them.

Eventually, it's Anayton who breaks the silence. "Were we not meant to do this quest... well, alone?"

"Oh, you mean, throw you guys into the middle of nowhere, watch you flounder and die?" When the group acknowledges my words in their own ways, I snort. "Yeah, that's the way the Paladins used to do it. Kind of dumb, really."

Freif reacts hard to that, leaning forward and almost snarling. Anayton isn't far behind in her reaction, mouth opening. Magine is the most interesting of the group, the way he just stills.

"Don't you dare—" Freif starts.

"What? Tell the truth?" I cut him off. "You're going to be Paladins, if you survive. About time to take the blinders off. The way they used to do things? It was broken." When Freif continues to try to speak, I twitch a finger and mute him, letting the sound distorters neutralize his words. "Sure, they kept you guys running. But there were barely two dozen Paladins at the best of times, and the vast majority of times, we're talking about seven or eight."

"Standards were high," Freif says.

"Standards were idiotic," I say. "Five Master Class monsters while you're an Advanced Class? Do you know what the survival rate on the Master Quest was?"

There's a long pause as the group looks from one to the other.

It's Anayton who answers. "Seven percent. We checked."

"Exactly. The best and brightest of you guys, and not even one in ten survived," I say. "And so, you bled people. Again and again. And the ones who survived, they weren't even the best people who could uphold what it was to be a Paladin, just the best killers."

"Yes. That's what Paladins are. The best of the best," Magine says. "Well, with one obvious exception."

"Bullshit." I turn to Kino who stirred at Magine's answer. "You have something to say?"

"Paladins are the pillars of justice, the levers of equality. They fix what must be fixed, when no one else will do so," Kino says. "They were never, they should never, be just killers."

"Exactly," I say, pointing at the rockman. Freif is almost shouting now, or maybe he is. But he's struggling and I realize I've still got him muted. I wave a hand, killing the mute and letting him free to speak again. "You have something to say?"

"They might not have been perfect, but neither are you."

"All too true, as my friend will tell you," I say and point at the Spirit.

Ali, in his corner, has a plateful of snacks rising from the table, which he's hoarding over on his side. A twitch of my fingers drags one plate of yellow lemon bars and chocolates over, along with a glass of Apocalypse Ale. The group starts making orders for their food, and for a time, there's silence.

Anayton, rolling a rainbow slime across her fingers and letting her skin absorb the poison, says softly, "So they were not perfect. And you think you can change that?"

"I intend to start." I tap the table. "The rest, that's up to you. We're going to start by pushing the limits of the rules." I see them stir, and I wave at them. "Relax. I checked. It's fine." I don't tell them how I checked, or about the pounding headache created by reaching backward and prodding at the Quest. "We can talk. Offer suggestions. Recommendations. Training. But you can't fight in teams with one another. Just as the Quest says."

There are a few relieved looks, Freif seeming to stabilize a little. Magine is still eyeing me in that too-still manner he has. He's got the smallest pile of snacks before him, as if he's unhappy with the selection. Or uninterested in such talk.

"The rest of it? I'm just an interloper. Making do with what I can. But if you don't want your Empire to be stuck in this same situation in a few thousand, a few hundred years, I'd start thinking, and thinking hard, about what needs to change."

***

The actual process of the debrief was routine. The initiates informed me of their various activities, the monsters they'd met—and killed—the Earth-based teams they'd worked with or avoided. More of the last than the first, though Kino seemed to have integrated better than the others. In short order, I berate them, pointing to Kino's continued success at integrating and developing his contacts, including finding out about the monster he needed to attack.

"The Guilds might not be as prominent in Erethra, but they've grown very important on a Dungeon World like Earth," I say. "You need to make friends, work with them. Just because you're supposed to fight the final boss alone doesn't mean you can't simplify your way there. Most of them live in treacherous, dangerous locations. Use the resources available, use the environment available. That's the only way you're going to win."

"Is that how you did it?" Freif asks.

"For the most part. I sometimes ran away, sometimes got the monsters to fight one another. Other times, I trapped them, injured them, slowly bled them out. Piled on damage inches at a time until they couldn't handle it any further." I shake my head, remembering. "Sometimes, rarely, I did what you guys were going to do. I faced them straight-on without concern for my life. I fought them to a standstill and I won. In other words, I was an idiot."

That last sentence brings a round of laughter, but I continue. "Sometimes, being an idiot is all the choice you have. Sometimes there isn't a better option. But let's at least try for something more than the depths of idiocy, shall we?"

I work with them, helping them figure out some initial plans, some goals of what they can and should do. And then we set up the next meeting. They disperse soon afterward, chatting among themselves, a slowly developing team. As I stand up after they've left, Anayton pops her head back in.

"I do have a message for you," Anayton says. "From a Lana?"

I gesture her in, frowning at the question mark in her statement. "What's with the hesitation?"

"A woman's intuition. That you might not want to hear it," Anayton says.

I glare at the initiate before gesturing for her to hurry up and speak. When she's done, I find myself shaking my head. It's nice of Lana to send the message, to let me know of how things are going. It's kind and thoughtful, just like the woman. I sigh, loudly and deeply.

"That bad?"

"No. Not really." I consider for a second, then flick my hand sideways. Pictures, a slew of them. Little children—Lana's own eldest and a slew of older kids, nieces and nephews, all playing with a triplicate of babies. "Just a reminder of what could have been."

"Oh…" Anayton looks at the pictures, letting her gaze roam over the laughing children. There's a bit of longing in her voice, squashed soon after. "They're quite cute. Strong. Though this red hair. Is it a mutation? It seems to be a quite prevalent one. Over half of these children have it. "

"You could say that. Harmless, for the most part," I say. "And you? Do you have any regrets?"

Anayton looks surprised. She hesitates a second and glances at the photos again. In the end, she shrugs. "I've had opportunities. But nothing ever felt right. Being in the Honor Guard, being a Paladin, that's what I want to do. Serving the Empire, doing the best I can. And children…"

"Children get in the way," I say.

She nods, looking a little uncomfortable with that though. "I should get going. The others are already browsing the Shop. You said we didn't have that long?"

"Forty-five more minutes. That's what I've bought for you," I say.

The guest passes will run out soon, though Foxy might decide later to extend a permanent invitation. If they survive. After all, Paladin Master

Classes are rather rare. I watch as she scurries out, ready to go shopping, curious to see kind of things there might be.

Leaving me alone. With pictures of redheaded children and memories of what could have been.

***

"You're quiet tonight," Catrin says, leaning against the table.

We're at another restaurant, another mildly expensive indulgence. Now that I'm grinding Levels again, I've decided to put most of these meals on my personal tab. All things considered, the cost is insignificant. Not when compared to the amounts I'm earning from the dungeons every day. One of the advantages of the Altered Space Skill is being able to drag along expensive corpses when they're left behind. And, at worst, extra loot.

This restaurant is a variation on a deep sea vessel, one used to explore the world beneath the oceans. Sloping ceilings, braced metal plating, projected imagines of creatures in the deep approaching our "windows." They swim from the inky blackness, highlighted by floodlights, to stare at us as we eat before they swim away again. Occasionally, the entire room shakes as a particularly large and enthusiastic projection prods the "ship." It's highly thematic and immersive, going well with the seafood menu.

The food itself is delivered to us on polished coral, seashells, and giant mollusk platings. The restaurant has even gone so far as to hire semi-aquatic waiters, who move toward us with gills and flippers flaring as they serve.

"The meal not to your liking?" Catrin mouths the words, not wanting to start rumors. Considerate of the restaurant.

She enjoys coming to these restaurants, letting her presence be known. It's a chance to see old friends, to glad-hand nobles and businessmen, establish connections. And potential relationships, later. For her, it's work and enjoyment.

I admit, her running commentary on those we see has added to my understanding of Erethran society, of how it works. And those who control it at the highest levels.

"Nothing like that. Just thinking." I shake my head, then fix her with a gaze. "Past regrets. You know the kind, don't you?"

"Dresses not bought, shoes not purchased, a limited line of grenades passed by?" Catrin chuckles lightly. "Oh yes, I have many."

"I was thinking more paths not taken. Choices not made. Because we couldn't, we wouldn't, let things go. The things we gave up in pursuit of duty. Or our dreams."

Catrin grows serious, eyeing me. She sees how I speak, what I've revealed, and she matches my somber mood. The truth I've alluded to. "Yes. To all that. Too many dreams given up in pursuit of duty, of what has to be done. Rather than what I would want."

"You could change. Make a new path. You're still young," I offer, seeing the regret in her eyes.

She laughs, but this one is not filled with mirth but a tinge of bitterness. "Sometimes the choices we make, they are permanent. Because others won't let you change. Sometimes we find what we're good at, and it might not be what we'd want to do, to be. But it is what is necessary."

I stare at her, seeing the truths in her eyes. The strong sense of duty, the refusal to bend, even when she probably should. And once more, I turn on Society's Web. I see the threads that lead between her and those she's known, between her and those she serves. And for once, I see how the thread wraps her close, holds her tightly in her place. Sometimes the threads we bind ourselves with are all the stronger because they were our choice.

I see the hidden pain, the way she struggles, in her own way. And I squeeze her hand. Because I don't have an answer.

We eat, and there's a more somber silence for a while.

We finish another two dishes before she places her utensils down. "I'm done. Shall we just go?"

I acknowledge her request and lead her out. It's only a minor effort to send a notification and payment to the waiter, making sure they know it's nothing to do with them.

When we are outside, waiting for the shuttle car, she speaks again. "You know, you could change too. Pick a new path."

I laugh and pull her close as the air shuttle drops, blasting air around it, catching at her skirts. It throws her hair around, bringing a whiff of her perfume, of that hint of nutmeg that is hers, and the burnt ozone smell of electric use. I hold her tightly till the doors slide open and I usher her in.

Memory, too much memory, pulls at me. Threatening to sweep me away, threatening to drown me in a whirlpool of regret and sacrifice. My memories of a red-headed man, fallen and lying bleeding, his sister holding him tight in dark caves, illuminated by the glow of steady, yellow Mana lights. Another of a woman with sun-kissed skin, a friend, a sword driven through her body on white-steel decks. A failure, when I should have acted. When I could have...

And memories not my own. Of experiments. Of screaming men, women, and Yerrick. Mana stripping the very flesh and bones as Classes are removed. Of a Heroic, the Hakarta's limbs removed, trying to grow them back and failing. His body, his System, failing as the ship records his destruction as it leaves System space. Until, eventually, the Mana levels fall too far and the recordings stop. Decades later.

Atrocities and losses. Questions answered.

And still, one question left.

I get in, never answering her. Because some paths, some questions need an answer, an ending. Or all else that came before would be wasted.

***

They come for me again when I Portal in the next day. Not in single numbers. Not even in small groups. But as a horde. I almost conjure my weapon, staring at the group awaiting my arrival. And I can't help but curse, because the law forces me to use only specific locations. Unless there's a need. I could have broken the law, done what I wanted. But I was trying to be polite. Must be the old Canadian in me.

"I'm sorry, Paladin, they were insistent on waiting for you." The captain of the guard is, at least, brave enough to speak with me directly.

I step off the teleportation platform, getting out of the way. Staring at the hungry masses of servants and minor nobles, all of them bearing invitations. Some, I'm sure, are just here to curry favor. Others want to progress the campaign of their chosen leader.

It seems, along with the attack by the assassins, other social norms, including the quiet dismissal of my presence, have faded away. Now, they're all bent on making their cases. All bent on making sure I know what is best, truly best, for the Empire.

"Saimon." I make the call, bugging the man directly.

Saimon answers my call almost immediately, making me smile. I do like competent minions. "Lord Braxton is on his way, Paladin. Just wait a few minutes. He will handle this."

A couple minutes later, Lord Braxton appears, fading in next to me from the teleportation platform. He takes one look at the group, grunts, and turns to the people he brought along. "You may begin."

To the increasingly frazzled Captain of the Guard's relief, Lord Braxton puts the minor horde of functionaries into order within minutes, each of them providing business cards, contact information, and details. A brief conversation with Braxton confirms that I'll have to meet with them, but for now, I can grind in peace.

He only asks that I inform him when I intend to exit the Dungeon. I admit, I hesitate at that, realizing how much of a potential opening that might offer. But then, staring at the crowd, I realize I'm much more of target as I am. Some changes to my routine will have to be made.

Chapter 24

"Paladin! I'm sorry for the late introduction. No one told me you were coming!" The manager hurries up to me, wringing his hands.

I stare at him, then dismiss him from notice. Instead, I turn back to the factory floor beneath my feet, where the Artisans are hard at work. Lines and lines of them, each of them at their own workstation, attaching, building, creating drones. Putting together the expendable equipment for war that drives the Erethrans onward.

Dirty gray-steel robots move between stations, picking up finished drones, marking them off, and moving to the next, delivering the finished work for inspection. A few inspectors check over the work, scanning the Status of each item before they're packed away in appropriate bins.

In the meantime, the Artisans work unceasingly. Garnering small amounts of XP as they grind away at their job. Small amounts—for the lack of innovation, the lack of development—means that most Classes get nearly nothing from this process. Just Credits, paid by the factory owners.

It's why there's such uniformity between Levels for those below. Why so many peak and hold steady, whether they're twenty-year-olds or seventy-year-old Artisans. The only real continuity among those below is the diversity of races and the lack of Levels. Even clothing—or lack of it—is different except for the lack of enchanted material. There's no need for uniforms, and dress styles are wide and varied. Fashion—on a Galactic scale—is so varied, and yet, can often be local.

"Paladin?" the manager calls again, hesitantly. "Is there anything I can do for you?"

"Tell me about the factory," I say.

This is the fourth such location I've visited in the last three days, popping in in between my grinds, when it's unexpected or when I'm done.

Unsurprisingly, these factories work all hours. Churning out drones, ammunition, even repurposing monster parts.

"Ah, well, we make the d'Ius line of sentry drones here. They range from the Mark IV to Mark VII prototypes. Once made, we classify the results"— a wave of his hand encompasses the QA trio—"pack, and ship them. All those below are independent contractors. They purchase the rights to use the respective blueprints, then manufacture them to the best of their ability. Completed works are then paid to them, direct via the System."

"Interesting system," I say non-commitally.

"It certainly is. Ever since we've instituted the commission rate system, we've seen a tripling of our output," the Manager says proudly.

I grunt, staring down below. What he doesn't say, what Harry found out when Spuryan's people sent us the note, was they'd also managed to keep their payroll cost from ballooning by reducing payouts. The people below are producing more, for less pay. Unfortunately, Credit loans for the purchase of the blueprints lock the workers in, forcing them to work themselves to the bone. Worse, when someone does manage to Level up and thus increase their production levels, they're often convinced to try their hand at another blueprint in another factory. Of course, there's more chance of Leveling with a new blueprint, but it also means they're locked in again.

It's a vicious little circle, and one of the ongoing trends in industrial production among the Erethran capitalists. The Generals don't complain— they get cheaper equipment to use. The Adventurers are happy, because their loot drops sell for more. And the merchants and nobles, they laugh at their Credit balances.

It's just the Artisans, caught in the middle and exploited, who have issues. And no one, at least not yet, is talking for them.

"How many d'Ius factories are there?"

"In this sector?" The manager appears to mentally count. "Eleven of this size. Another two larger. And another forty subsidiaries."

"And you've implemented this in all the factories?"

"Yes, Paladin."

I don't bother asking further questions, opening a Portal and walking through it. This one takes me to the nearest planetary teleportation point. I'm done with the dungeon on this world. So it's time to move on.

***

"Paladin, thank you. If you hadn't arrived…"

"No thanks needed. It was the right thing to do." I offer a smile to General d'HaBarn, letting my gaze flick across to the battle plot next to him. "I'm surprised though, that you got caught out like that."

"It's rare that planetary invasions are done before the space battles are complete," the General admits, shaking his head. "I never expected the Uswain to be so bold. Or that they'd let their Lesasson come."

I grunt. That had been a painful beating. If I hadn't been able to get Mikito and Bolo to come with me, fighting off the equivalent of a mini-Heroic Champion of the Uswain Confederacy would have been… impossible. It'd taken all three of us, pounding away at him, and the four Master Classers on the planet to make him run. If we hadn't managed to displace the majority of the fight out of the city and over what used to be the local newbie hunting ground, the damage would have been a lot more extensive.

"Why did they?" I say, frowning. "Harry tells me that they've never let him leave his Empire before."

"Ah... well, what can one say? The Uswain are difficult to understand," d'HaBarn says, waving in dismissal.

"I'd think you'd want to understand your enemy," I say, letting my voice cool.

"Bah. Crezar are too animalistic to really understand," d'HaBarn sniffs.

"Really." My voice grows flatter as I stare at the General. Information from Ali, from Harry scrolls up at a thought. I'd set the reporter on it the moment we learnt of the attack. And what he managed to dig up—from tapping into non-Erethran news sources—was enlightening. "So you really have no idea why the Lesasson might show up?"

"I don't try to understand the thoughts of such enemies," d'HaBarn repeats.

"Fair enough. I'll be sure to let Brerdain know," I say.

"Let him know what?" d'HaBarn's voice goes higher.

I smile grimly. "About your lack of imagination. Understanding that attacking the Crezar Creche and 'accidentally' killing a generation of their pups seems like a simple conclusion to draw. Even for a non-military man like me." I lean forward, glaring at d'HaBarn. "I expect the Chief will have his own words on the matter."

To my surprise, d'HaBarn relaxes a little. My eyes narrow, and a quick query to Ali brings up the information. And the respective family trees. A quick check with Society's Web confirms my feeling and I internally debate the matter.

Throw him out of the airlock and leave the fleet without a commanding officer? Weakening this sector of space? Or let him pull the strings he thinks he can pull to keep his position? I'm reminded, once more, that the army he controls holds loyalty to him, not Brerdain or the Queen.

"We all have much to do, Paladin. In lodging our respective reports," d'HaBarn says, his voice cool too. "If you don't mind…"

"Yeah, I get it." I walk to the exit of the command deck. Already, I'm composing a message to Brerdain and the Minister of War.

Let's see how they handle this. And if not… well. I can always space d'HaBarn later.

Or let one of the other Paladins do it.

***

My fist hammers into the prison, and it cracks. Seconds later, the prison reforms. I growl, kicking at the prison again, watching it reform and feeling a little of the shock from my attack rebound. I can feel the prison of light and Mana they used moving, the assassins taking me to another location.

Smart. They couldn't kill me, not here. Not in the middle of the city. But move me to a different location? Maybe torture, mind-smash me into submission while getting their person in play? That's doable. Especially since a half dozen Mages are forming this ritual prison.

I could try breaking it with Army of One. But the secondary rebound effect on the prison would kill me if I failed to break through. I can't help but wonder if the cracks I see are there on purpose, to make me overconfident.

"Ah hell. Let's try this…" I mutter and pull out a grenade.

Not a Chaos Grenade. I'm not that desperate yet. Just a Ghostlight Mana Dispersal grenade. Four dropped at my feet, and three minutes later, it's sufficient to make the poor prison falter, the Mages who've been holding it aloft drained and unable to continue feeding the prison Mana.

Cleanup after that is simple. I even leave most of it to the local police force—after beating the Mages to the ground and locking away their escape methods. Idiot Mage team seemed to have forgotten to bring non-Mana based backup.

Afterward, while I watch them get carted away, Lord Braxton makes an appearance. The Houndmaster is looking a little harried, and that's no surprise. This is, like, the tenth or eleventh attack I've had to deal with. Not counting whatever my guard personnel have stopped.

"Paladin, you need to tell us where you're going beforehand!" Braxton complains. "At the least we can alert local constablury."

"And let my enemies know what I plan to do?" I shake my head. "No thanks."

"Do you think what you're doing is working?" Braxton gestures around. "You're only heading off the least prepared. A good Path Analysis later, they know where you're going."

"So why aren't you doing that?" I say, cocking an eyebrow at Braxton.

"We are!" Braxton snaps. "But we're on your side. There's no reason for us to be wasting Credits and time, guessing at what you're going to do."

I pause, considering if I should point out that this is more an Empire problem than mine. "Oh come on, this is at least giving the new staff a good workout, right?"

I nod toward the group of Administrators, Public Interfaces, and Investigators who are talking to the local police force. There's even a growing argument between the Investigators and the force on the disposition of the prisoners.

"Any idea who hired these guys?" I ask my now routine question.

To my surprise, Braxton has an actual answer this time. "We do. We lucked out this time. The second-last cut-out was someone already under investigation, so we had a tap on him. Your Title came up under a routine search when you called it in." Braxton shakes his head. "We're still refining the automatic AI searches on the data. It doesn't help that you've got so many Titles."

I snort, but can sort of understand it. When there are a million ways to describe me, setting up an automatic search on general data trawled through the million and one information sources they have must be a pain. "So?"

"So what?"

"Who is it?"

"Oh, Lord d'Frami. Minor house noble. He's the second cousin of Lord—"

"K'was." I sigh. "And they still think that idiot has a chance?"

"Not with you talking about it publicly," Braxton growls.

I shrug unrepentantly. "I wouldn't trust him to find the throne with a GPS, a seeing eye dog, a Boy Scout, Delta Force Rangers, and the System all aiding him. Never mind rule anything more complicated than a Lego playhouse."

Braxton shakes his head. "If you're trying to confuse me, you can stop. Your Spirit introduced me to a proper culture pack download. I now even know of *M.A.S.H.*"

I shoot a look over to where Ali is busy watching the growing argument between our men and the police force, a bucket of popcorn in hand. The Spirit's sense of humor can get arcane at times. *M.A.S.H.* is a little before my time, but I decide not to pop Braxton's bubble.

"So. You got a good scent for d'Frami?" I say. "Able to track him down?"

"We'll catch him, don't worry about that," Braxton says, shaking his head. "I just hope you Level soon. This is getting…"

"Interesting." I grin, waving goodbye to Braxton as I open up the Portal.

My surprise visit to the nearest healing shop, where Spuryan had fed me some more information, is scuppered. So I move on to plan I.

Or is it J?

***

The gas giant beneath me reminds me of Jupiter, both in coloration and size. Giant, swirling brown clouds pass beneath my feet as the ship continues its routine patrol. I'm crouched next to the nervous recruit, hooked onto the open strut and feeling the barest tug of increasing velocity as the ship continues to gain thrust.

"So this is routine maintenance?" I say.

"Yes, Paladin," the recruit says, nervousness evident in every word. He's got a welding torch in one hand, a fistful of crafted metal-horn hybrid wire in the other. I see the overlaid glyphs his helmet is displaying on the strut, where he's carefully attaching the wire in exacting detail. "We have to replace the glyphs every month. But with the size of the *K'trum*, Paladin, it's—"

"I get it. Neverending work. And not enough of you guys, right? There's always more than enough people with guns, but people with actual skills..."

The private looks up and shyly offers me a nod. It's a shared smile, as if I get it. And I do, in a sense.

Random Recruit Whose Name You've Already Forgotten (Erethran Space Cadet Level 17) (B)
HP: *130/130*
MP: *210/210*
Conditions: Mana Sense

"Seriously, Ali?"

"You're telling me you remembered it?"

"That's not the point!"

"So they put you through special training for this, right?" I say, gesturing below.

"Yes, Paladin." The recruit offers me a proud smile. "We get trained in the basics now, if we have the aptitude. Start specializing with some of our Skill choices. Then as an Advanced Class, we can further specialize. I'm going for Erethran Spatial MagiMechanic."

I nod. "And until then, you grind this? Get experience for it?"

"Yes, sir. Cadets get experience for following orders and combat, Paladin."

"Very good. Well, I won't bother you. I'm sure your Sargent will be on you if you don't get this done." I grin and wave goodbye to the kid before opening a Portal to send me back into the hull itself.

There are a few others I want to chat with, to get a feel of their navy. Overall, in contrast to the weirdness of the Generals, the navy is almost entirely of one mind and loyalty. I guess it helps that the navy and their ships get paid for by the Queen. Add in a constant rotation of membership, and while there's intense loyalty to their immediate Captains, there's less of the insubordination I noted with the Generals.

As I snap shut the Portal behind me, I muse about their social structure. About the challenges Brerdain and Julierudi face in keeping their people contained, in gaining loyalty otherwise. And, worse, of the deeper corrupt currents at play. Too many damn people have their fingers in too many pies, all of them refusing to extract them.

And somehow, they think a few Paladins can fix it.

I'm not sure whether to be flattered or appalled. But I make sure to compose another cautionary note for my friends on Earth to watch out for my initiates.

***

A few days later, Harry is finally back. I'm still mostly running around by myself, my friends busy with their own activities. Mikito occasionally swings by. More often than not, an attack materializes soon after. It's an uncanny ability, one that she's loath to explain beyond saying that it's just a feeling she gets.

I get a feeling too, that it's both her Skill and Harry's quiet influence. Surprisingly, Bolo rarely shows up, busy with his own activities. I'm almost annoyed by his abandonment. But the vast majority of the attacks are less than effective. The only few times it matters, he makes an appearance.

It's hard for assassins to surprise someone when said person spent his formative years in an apocalypse, and then most recently spent the same amount of time doing the same job as the attackers.

It also helps that the majority of the true threats—teams of Master Classers, Heroic level bounty hunters, and the like—are kept at bay by the presence of the Erethran military. Few bounty hunters or assassins are willing to risk angering an entire kingdom.

Finding Harry waiting for me in the dining room is a bit of a surprise. What's not so surprising is the array of fish and chips before him. I join him, eyeing the multiple plates, each of them with a slightly different golden coloring to the batter and each "fish" piece in different sizes and shapes. Each set of chips is formatted in a different way. All of them are within easy reaching distance, except for a plate of chips that's been shoved far away. The thinly sliced potato serving isn't exactly what I'd call chips anyway.

"Harry, what exactly are you doing?" I say.

"New job. I'm being paid by the local culinary circle in the capital to rate their attempts at my national dish," Harry says, the last words dripping with contempt.

I'm slightly amused a second later as the dark-skinned man spears another crispy golden fish flake and shoves it into his mouth. He chews slowly, eyes narrowing, then writes a note on the pad.

"Huh. I wonder why no one's asked me to do that for poutine," I say. Seems like an easy money day, and I get to try a lot of food. Then I spot certain irregularities among the dishes. What should be tender, flaky, and moist white fish flesh is, at times, different. There's a myriad of colors, a variety of unusual shapes and consistencies hidden beneath the batter. In fact, one of those... "Is that Krishna meat?"

"Yes," Harry says, sounding annoyed. "It's not enough that they try to recreate the dish. No, they've decided to add a Galactic twist to it."

I can't help but chuckle a little at the disgust in Harry's tone. I take a seat beside him and conjure a set of dining utensils. After all, I can't let him suffer by himself.

"I do blame you for this, John." At my raised eyebrow, he points with his fork. "You've been dining out, with your lady friend, so much that you started a trend. Of making the human Paladin satisfied."

A little thoughtful hmmm at his words while I pin down a chip and raise it to my lips. Spicy. Why would you make chips spicy? "Anything else I should know?"

"Assassinations, minor border skirmishes, random poisonings. Any of that sparking any brain cells?" Harry says.

"Yes. I do get the reports from the guards and my security detail. And, of course, from the nobles with Brerdain and Julierudi when they're trying to get their digs in at one another. But I get the feeling you've seen something?"

Henry snorts and flicks his fork at me. Luckily, there's no food on it, which means all I have to worry about is the flood of notifications he sends. News articles, his analysis, additional details that don't make it to the reports. I get to reading while we gorge on the dishes. He occasionally interrupts me, asking for my feedback.

We pass plates back and forth, along with silent notes on the events. And there are lot of notes. Fish and chips should not be made with vegetables. Firstly, System vegetables are mutated and have a tendency to poison or otherwise drug eaters. Secondly, incidents like the accidental delivery of a container of Master Class monster parts are sparking up border skirmishes between nobles and other smaller planets. Thirdly, fish. It's in the name.

When we're done, I can't help but sigh. "Any luck on finding my attackers?"

"Nothing. And I don't think we will. Even if there are more attacks, they know what they're doing," Harry says. We're obviously talking of the major players, the ones who have placed, and keep increasing, the price on my head. "These other incidents, they might offer more information, if you're willing to look into them."

I shake my head. Even if I could step in and investigate the other assassinations, put a stop to some of these trade—and shooting—wars, it'd only slow down the incidents. It wouldn't solve the underlying problem. Worst, there's a danger of overreach, of overplaying my hand. My job isn't just saving the empire from itself; it's choosing an Empress Apparent who can fix the increasingly volatile cracks.

Stopping the attacks, stopping the individual players from going too far might be the worst choice I could make. Knowing where each person—Brerdain, Julierudi, Spuryan, or one of the other half dozen contenders—will draw their line in their quest for power is important. Necessary information.

Maybe I'm wrong. Maybe I'm just naïve, thinking there should be limits. Maybe I'm too human, too basic. After all, I'm just an ex-programmer.

"Keep tracking. Let me know what you find. On all our candidates," I say to Harry.

"For how long?" Harry asks, fixing my gaze with his own.

I know what he's asking. The longer we delay, the longer we take, the more deaths there will be. But I don't dare be wrong either.

"Until I'm sure."

***

Ayuri finds me in the middle of a dungeon. We're on a different planet, one I can't even remember the name of. I've spent weeks bouncing around, clearing dungeons, monster swarms, and threats. All in the race to increase my Levels. It's only the Champion, who can cover the cost and the jumps, who can find me out here. Well, her and a few of the more insane assassins.

We fight together, in silence, for a time. You'd think it'd be a disaster. After all, two Master classes, neither of which have really fought together much, unleashing Skills that tear apart the tiny swarm creatures and dark shadow monsters that prey upon us. It should have been a disaster, by any rational viewpoint. Except both of us are trained combatants, used to fighting with others. And even if I'm not a real Erethran Paladin, many of my tactics, my skills came about from watching and learning from them. So we fit together easier than I would have expected.

It helps that we're both specced to a higher level of Intelligence. That System addition allows us to anticipate, understand, and grasp the motions of our counterpart. It's not *really* futuretelling, just anticipation. Very, very good anticipation.

We tear apart the swarm, the tiny biting insects, each of them barely Level ten. But when they're the size of your hand and there are literally millions of them, flying in swarms and carnivorous, it can be a problem. The shadow monsters are nearly as bad a problem, since they hide within the shadows of the swarm, attacking when our backs are turned. Thankfully, the System generally designates swarms as a single mass creature and so provide experience for the designated threat Level of the swarm, not individual amounts. Or else this entire dungeon would be a waste of time.

Of course, you also then have to destroy the entire swarm to get the experience. But that's what area control and area effect spells, along with chained attacks, are useful for. We lob all of those around, everything from gravity mines, which hold and crush monsters to one another, to chain lightning that jumps from monster to monster for miles. And of course, I've got the Beacon of the Angels and Ayuri has Ire of the Champion.

When we're done and the drones are released to chew up the last of the stragglers, Ayuri speaks. "The Queen is getting impatient."

"I'm trying to gain Levels here. I would think that you'd understand how long that takes."

"Isn't raising your Level at an outstanding rate part of your package?" Ayuri says.

I find myself grinning, because she's right. I do need significantly lower amounts of experience than most Master Classes. Skipping the entire Basic Class gives me that benefit.

"It's not just about the Levels," I admit eventually. I look around, reaching out with my senses, checking.

Ayuri senses my caution and raises an eyebrow. "Do you want to talk? In private?"

"Ah, Champion, you're cute, but I'm seeing someone…"

"Not that, you idiot."

"Well, if you insist…" I waggle my eyebrows at the Champion.

She snorts and gestures, triggering her Skill and enveloping us.

When we pop out, minutes later, she's glowering at me.

"Look, it's a thing. Performance issues. But don't worry, I don't hold it against you," I say blithely.

She unleashes a punch, energy wrapped in compressed air.

I skip aside with ease. "Sorry."

Ayuri turns her head from side to side as if she's looking for the unseen watchers, even though we both know that if people are watching, we'd never spot them. Not if they were really serious. Buying direct from the System is nothing we can block.

"Will you do it?" I've already asked and confirmed once. While we were within the cannibal sphere. There are a lot of things I asked, least among them being information and control over the numerous security feeds to the throne room. But it's a lot to ask of the Champion.

"I will. But…" Ayuri falls silent, realizing no more can be said. Not out here. "You better be certain."

"One hundred and ten percent," I reassure her.

Ayuri nods. A second later, Mayaya has a Portal open, which Ayuri walks toward. I'm assuming they're using a party chat system similar to ours. Just more advanced.

Before she leaves, she turns back and asks, "You think I'm cute?"

Chapter 25

"Thirty-four."

"Thirty-eight."

"Thirty-four. Intercepted attacks don't count," Bolo says.

"Ninety-seven," Harry insists. "They do count, but we're also including the ones intercepted by regular security personnel."

"Doesn't count. It never reached John." Mikito crosses arms, shaking her head. "Only those attacks that are a serious threat, and that reached the internal security perimeter, should count."

"Thirty-four. Only the ones he thwarted himself count," Bolo snaps. "That's what we said."

"No, we didn't," Harry and Mikito chorus together.

"John!" Harry and Mikito call, at the same time as Bolo says, "Redeemer!"

I groan, glaring at the team. As I turn, I note the pale gray walls, the floating vid projections of past, glorious battles that display on each wall, just below the hanging banners and crests of defeated armies and kingdoms. The waiting room has a few chairs, though most just pop into existence when needed. They're not the most comfortable of chairs though, since those same projectors are used as secondary shield defenses.

"I'm not getting involved," I state. "Also, betting on how many times someone was going to try to kill me was in rather bad taste."

"Bah!" Bolo says. "If we bet that you'd die, that would be bad taste. This, this was just a way to pass the time."

"The constant attacks weren't enough for you? Especially that Master Class team?" I find myself rubbing my hip gingerly. Master Class worms are just unfair. It was like Frank Herbert had grabbed his idea of giant worms from the Mana-diffused air of pre-System Earth. Except he missed the fact that they had Classes and Levels. And had a tendency to take on unwinnable bounties. That's just wrong.

"That was amusing. It was a good team," Bolo says musingly. "If you hadn't climbed down your attacker's stomach, we probably wouldn't have gotten to you in time."

I can't help but shudder, remembering. The pulsing flesh, the slosh of acid that ate at my shields. The remains of its previous meals and the hard rock. Nightmare inducing.

Ali looks interested, mostly because he was banished at the onset of the attack. Leaving me to deal with three Master Classes. Not a fun place to be, not at all.

"We still haven't found them?" I say to Harry.

We managed to kill the worm. Seems like having me inside, blocking any teleportation, had seriously messed with its Statsis Block Penetration Skills. The three worms hadn't even realized it was a problem till Bolo, Mikito, and Ayuri made it to me and the battle started to turn.

Unfortunately, the other two worms escaped. And considering I only got a portion of the worm's experience, and from what we've learned of his Class and race, his "death" was somewhat truncated. It hurt my head—literally—to think about it.

"No. Ayuri assures me they're out of the Empire though," Harry says. "I verified they turned in the bounty as a failure, so I'd agree with her assessment. They've even got a counter bounty placed on them by the Empire. Though… it's not a lot."

I shake my head again, deciding not to touch that last comment with a ten-foot pole. More politics. We've been stuck in the waiting room for the last hour, waiting for the Queen to find time to see us. You'd think, after nearly four months of grinding, attacks, and repeated questioning, she'd be excited to see me. Especially since I finally reported I was ready.

*John Lee, Monster's Bane, Redeemer of the Dead, Duelist, Explorer, Apprentice Questor, Galactic Silver Bounty Hunter,... **(Paladin of Erethra level 41)***

HP: 4870/4870

MP: 4380/4380

Of course, that's a lie. My actual Level at this time is 45, but they don't need to know that. And altering that single line in my Status via the ring is easier and safer than playing with everything else. I wanted to gain more Levels, but time and tide waits for no Paladin.

Still, the new Levels are great. It made surviving those attacks a lot easier. But, just as much, I'm kind of proud of my new Skills. I spent nearly everything I had, since I now publicly have access to the final tier of the Paladin Skill tree.

Figuring out what I wanted to add was interesting. On the last tier, I'd had four options. Judgment of All, Immovable Object/Unstoppable Force, Shackles of Eternity, and Domain. I couldn't get Domain without purchasing Shackles, but since I had to get Shackles for the Erethrans, it'd been a possible option to focus upon.

Truth be told, I would never have picked up the Shackles of Eternity if I wasn't forced to. Just by its name, I didn't really like it. Then again, I've never been into the entire slave thing. Kill someone when you need to. But leaving them enslaved? It's... wrong.

Shackles of Eternity (Level 1)

A Paladin's job is not just to see, but it is to judge and enforce the judgment. The Shackles of Eternity provide a Paladin another method of enforcing his judgments. Once used, the Shackles bind an individual, forcing them to abide by the Paladin's decree. Activation of the Shackles will leave a brand, a visible Mark, and will deal punishment immediately and on an ongoing basis when the decree is violated. All law enforcement personnel, of whatever Class or society, will be able to see broken Shackles on an individual.

Effect: Shackles of Eternity are gaeas that an individual must follow. The restriction will warn an individual when they're close to breaching, and upon breach, will layer a number of effects upon them.

Effect 1: A permanent, and highly visible, nark will appear to all law enforcement individuals, whether by Title, Class, or System designation. They will be able to access data at no cost on the broken Shackles, including breakage reason and the original Shackles' use. This can lead to a loss of Reputation and other effects.

Effect 2: Shackle breakers will receive a (Skill level multiplied by half Mana costs) amount of damage upon breach of decree. This is Mana damage and may only be mitigated by Mana resistance.

Effect 3: Broken Shackles deal ongoing (Skill level multiplied by 1/10th Mana cost) damage per minute to the Shackle breaker. This damage is Mana damage and may only be mitigated by Mana resistance.

Cost: Variable depending on Shackle requirements (channeled)

The Shackles of Eternity is a very strange skill. I wish I could've played with it more, but other than using it on a few semi-sapient monsters, I've left the testing alone. For one thing, there's no way to dismiss a Shackle. Using it on an intelligent creature for that reason is a no-go. Not without a very, very good reason.

In addition, unlike most Skills, this one requires a significant amount of startup time. Depending on what I'm trying to do, I have to hit a certain minimum threshold of channeled Mana before the Skill will trigger. Only after I add that minimum amount can I release the Skill. Before that, it locks me in place, leaving me intensely vulnerable. Furthermore, even the lowest level use of the Shackles requires a thousand points of Mana. Higher, more elaborate conditions, require even more.

All that means that it isn't the kind of Skill you use in battle. Digging into the Paladins' archives made me realize it isn't even a Skill that was taken by most Paladins. Especially in the later periods, when dealing with the enemies in the more immediate, violent manner was favored. When required, they'd just dragged people before a Paladin that had specced the Skill and left them to it.

I do understand why the Queen wants me to have it though. Or, more correctly, I have a pretty damn good idea. Especially after reading their histories.

All that said, it'd left me with three other Skills to choose from. Judgment of All was the simplest. Like Army of One, it was a pure combat Skill. It was, in a way, similar to the Champion's skill, using the combined strength of many to power the attack. It could be extremely strong but had one major weakness. It required you to be part of a strong, unified community.

The reliance on that Skill was also part of the downfall of the Paladins in the last fight. After all, they lost the faith of many, so the Skill they'd come to rely upon had decreased in effectiveness. Even so, a single planet's worth of trust can be quite damaging. As my mentor had showcased.

On the other hand, Immovable Object/Unstoppable Force was a weird dual-use Skill. Upon activation, the Paladin had to select between the two.

The choice would provide a boost to himself and to anyone within his aura range.

Immovable Object increased Constitution, health, and passive damage resistance by a significant number. It also negated all knockback effects on the Paladin. Basically, it made him the ultimate tank. Unstoppable Force, on the other hand, increased movement speed, Agility, calculated momentum, and damage done by the same percentage. Unfortunately, it had a major negative in that the moment the Paladin stopped moving, the Unstoppable Force buff would automatically turn off. On the other hand, it also gave a smaller buff to everyone within aura range.

As for Domain? That one was kind of messy. Domain allowed the Paladin to alter reality within the range of his aura. Enemies entering his Domain would receive a debuff to all attribute and Mana cost and a damage-over-time effect. Allies received a heal-over-time effect and a buff to all attributes and Mana cost. At the same time, the Paladin received a minor boost to health, Mana regeneration, resistances, and speed, while reducing damage done to them that passed through the domain. It was an all-encompassing Skill, but each of its individual effects were lower than any of the individual Skills it drew upon.

For that reason, and others, I'd had the hardest time allocating my remaining Skill points. It wasn't as if I could get another evolved Skill, so for my choice, I had to decide which of the three would suit my fighting style best.

My musings over whether I'd chosen right was interrupted by the entrance of the major domo. He looked at my group with a sneer before he waved us in. I idly considered using Shackles on him to stop him from sneering ever again, then kicked myself.

Really. Ultimate power can so easily make one evil...

***

The throne room is similar to before, but this time around, it's filled with courtiers. One group is streaming out, their leaders having a hangdog expression. But the subtle smirk on another's face, as he trudges beside and behind the group, indicates not all of them are as unhappy as you'd think. There's probably something in all that byplay, considering the entire group is supposed to be together. I can see how having a Paladin with Society's Web stationed here could pick up a number of interesting missions.

For that matter, I wonder what kind of Skills the Queen has, her and her personnel. Society's Web might be somewhat different in how it displays information, but it isn't a unique Skill at its base. I vaguely recall that Catrin has a Skill that allows her to process social information in an entirely different manner. Not as useful for meeting random strangers, but more robust and detailed in the information provided in a known social setting.

My team troops in, taking our place in front of the Queen as she finishes speaking with one of her retinue. Subtle cues send out various courtiers and others stream in, joining the group behind me. The man the Queen is talking to steps back, offering her a nod, and I'm only slightly surprised to see that it's Saimon. He is, after all, the Exchequer of her Purse. Or something like that.

More surprisingly, what I don't see is the Champion or any of her team. There are, of course, a few Honor Guards around, standing at the sides of the throne room and keeping watch. Even more are hovering midair, near the walls. Today, the room itself is muted, the moving images and projected banners reduced so that everything, all our attention, is focused on the woman seated on her throne. And even without the help of her Aura, she definitely has everyone's attention.

"Tell me, Paladin, how are my initiates?" the Queen asks once we are done with the formal greetings.

I idly watch as Harry scurries to the side, moving to join the group of reporters near the base of her throne. He's gotten special permission—after some insistence on my end—to record what's happening today.

"Well enough. No one has died, but they're a bit slow," I say.

Four months in, and they're all only two monsters in at most. There have been some close calls, especially when Magine decided to charge in and be an idiot to showcase how tough he is. On the other hand, his example drew the team even closer together as they seriously got into sharing information. The fact that he lost half of his team members in that attack just to save his ass had been sobering.

"And when do you expect that I will receive my new Paladins?"

"That, I believe, is up to them. But at this rate, probably another six months." I meet her disapproving gaze, knowing she wanted them out faster. Especially since my life has been put in danger recently and even the initiates have had a few close calls.

The assassins going after the initiates were less worrisome, mostly because they were lower Level. Those few who did try were often in for a rude awakening as Rob's many, many safeguards against random assassinations had been extended to the initiates. After Earth's own experience, there'd been a significant investment—completely out of proportion to our GDP—in anti-assassin measures.

Harry and Saimon have struggled to find additional information on our attackers. Even with the System, there's a certain level of expense required to cut through things. You can't just ask the System "give me the attacker's employers." You have to know the right questions to ask, which could mean multiple questions, each costing Credits.

Worse, my Society's Web can only connect direct relationships when I'm watching the person. When you've got suspects who are highly connected, just because of their roles or their places in society, finding the correct thread to pull upon is difficult. Even if we managed to capture the attackers, the threads often led to dead drops, cut-outs who had no clue why they were doing what they were doing, and other System subterfuge.

Could I find the people behind all of our attacks? Probably. Given enough time, given enough motivation, I could track each thread, each individual. Override the Credit requirements, pay it all out from our budget. Problem is, we don't have time. And so while the investigators are hard at work, I've kept Leveling.

"Very well." The Queen stares at me, then frowns. "Only a single Skill Level? Is that sufficient?"

I grimace, wondering how she knew. And what else she can see. But then, I flash her a smile. "That depends on what you think I need it for."

"I might have given the impression of being a kind and forgiving ruler, but I would not test my patience, Paladin." The Queen leans forward, fixing me with a glare. Portions of her aura leak out, making Harry and the reporters stagger, and even Mikito winces.

"*Stop talking back at the angry woman,*" Harry sends over the party chat.

I straighten a little, push against her aura, and feel it ripple backward. "It's not enough. Not for what we need. *If you want me to shackle the other competitors, I'm going to need more.* I need access to the Crown's Purse to increase this Skill. It seems my budget is still blocked." I look to the side, fixing on Saimon, who just shrugs.

The Queen doesn't even blink when I think the middle sentence rather than say it. Instead, she gestures, and Saimon steps forward. He focuses on me, and a second later, an access window blooms. Surprisingly, it's a direct access to the Shop. I take a deep breath, place my hands by my sides and clench them, and purchase the Shackles of Eternity Skill twice more. That should be enough. Especially considering how much I expect the basic use will cost in terms of Mana. When I'm done, as information stops flowing into my brain, as the Skill finishes its download, a light sweat has broken out. I look at the Queen and give her a single nod.

"Then let us finish this. Bring them," she says.

The words create a ripple through the courtiers as they stir with excitement. Gratitude that they've been allowed to see something so momentous. As I get ready to do what I was brought all the way here for, I can't help but smile grimly.

Time to make a choice.

***

I'm not surprised that they managed to find Brerdain and Julierudi. They both have quite public jobs. The same can be said for the half dozen other, minor contenders who are led out. At one point or another, I've met with them all, spoken with them, pressed the flesh and been left with an impression. None of those impressions have been particularly vivid though. There's a reason they're considered minor contenders.

I'm surprised to see Spuryan here, as well as some other, less reputable individuals. Some are known for their opposition to the government or to specific policies of the government. Others are crime lords, semi-independent Guild leaders or corporate Managers, individuals who exist on the gray edges of Erethran society and law.

Guess the Queen has decided that everyone and anyone needs the Shackles. Which, come to think about it, makes sense.

"*Huh. She's got all seven of the Polygon here,*" Bolo comments on the party chat.

I blink, surprised. Not about the Polygon, which is the Erethran equivalent of the most powerful crime lords, but that Bolo knows what they look like. I eye the Dragon Lord again and he flashes me a smile. His time in the kingdom has, obviously, been a little more interesting than mine. I guess, for a Dragon Lord who hung around Spaks for decades, I shouldn't expect him to be an upstanding citizen. I do wonder what he's been up to when he isn't saving my ass though.

At the tail end of the group comes Ayuri and her team, backed up by another dozen or so Honor Guards. I quickly note that no other military personnel are here. At least, no army personnel, no space navy. Just Honor Guards. Those directly sworn to the Empress.

"*Defcon 1, children,*" I send over the party chat.

There's no external reaction among my friends, but I know they've gone further on alert.

"Thank you, all of you, for coming." The low-level murmuring by those brought in silences as the Queen's words echo through the room. It's like a teacher smacking a ruler on a table among a group of unruly children. "We're here today to see an end to certain… irregularities… in activities. And to set aside, once and for all, the question of who shall rule after me."

There are a few gasps, but mostly, the group takes her pronouncement with equanimity. Brerdain is looking confident, and there's not a shift or twitch in his threads. If anything, the number of threads flowing to him increases, deepens in connections as loyalties shift or harden.

Julierudi sniffs, covering her face for a second, then blows her nose with a handkerchief she makes appear. She sets her hand down a moment later, but I see the change, the way some threads fray away and others deepen in color. My stomach clenches as information continues to flow.

Spuryan looks vaguely hopeful, which is a bit confusing. His threads don't change at all. He doesn't even seem particularly surprised. Though I'm surprised to see some of the connections he has in the room. Especially among the Polygon.

"Paladin. Are you ready to take on this task?" the Queen's voice rings out, interrupting my musings.

I step forward and open my mouth to speak, only to find it dry. I clear my throat a little, then speak up. "Yes. I'll make the choice of the one most suitable to rule the Empire."

The moment I finish speaking, I receive a surprise notification.

Empire Quest: Erethran Empire (M)

Designate an individual to become the Presumptive Emperor of Erethra
Reward: +4,353,593 XP

"If they'd told me I'd get that Quest, I wouldn't have bitched as much," I send to Ali.

"You know, they can still hear you."

"Oh, I know."

The Queen waves, encompassing the throne room and all those within, the moment I take the Quest. "Very well, Paladin. I believe the field is yours."

I turn on the balls of my feet, staring at the group, and find myself meeting the gazes of a group of apprehensive faces. A part of me hates what I'm going to do. This Skill is wrong. Evil in a way. But I weigh my choices. Leave them to fight it out? Allow an entire Empire to fall because I'm scared to get my hands a little dirty?

Perhaps someone else might choose otherwise, someone with stronger morals. But I lived through an apocalypse. And doing what needs to be done is something I learnt a long time ago.

I grin at the group, hiding my doubts with joyful sadism and a trace of rage. "Don't worry, boys and girls, no one has to die today."

***

The Honor Guards help me line them up by order of status. Amusingly, this means they start out with people who have the lowest levels, but not potentially the least amount of political or financial strength. Sometimes, Levels matter. Especially when the insane little human monkey is about to test his new Skill on you.

My first victim is sweating bullets, licking his lips continuously as he's brought to me. A quick check of his Status gives me his name.

Aditter Fullaway, Scion of the West, Profligate Creditor, Slayer of Goblins (Level 32 Industrialist Heir) (A)
HP: 470/470
MP: 1730/1730
Conditions: System Tip, Industrial Efficiency, Mana Drip

I grin and slap my hand down on his shoulder. "Don't worry, this won't hurt a bit."

"Really?" There's a flash of relief on his face, and I feel his shoulders relax.

"Definitely. It's going to hurt a lot."

When he's busy trying to back off, to escape from my grip, I tighten it and trigger my Skill.

Shackles of Eternity is weird to use, mentally. First is the usual plethora of Mana formulae that form and flash away, bundles of data that the System uses in a preprogramed fashion that allow me to cast at a fraction of the time I'd need normally.

Then comes the movable parts of the Skill. I have to adjust the portions, the parts of the Shackles I lay on him. I could do this in silence, leaving the poor bastard to wonder, to figure out the Shackles himself, but that doesn't serve our purpose today.

Also, that increases my Mana cost significantly.

"Adirter Fullaway, I, as a Paladin of Erethra, now Shackle you. From this day to eternity and a day, so long as the System holds, so long as the Mana flows. You will bear faithful allegiance, provide unconditional loyalty, and sincerely serve, in all manners and form, the Empress and the Empress Apparent of Erethra."

A ritual circle blooms around my feet and my victim's as I speak. Mana is drawn from the environment, converging on the circle, helping to power it. The Mana flow grows so dense within the circle that wisps of power can be seen by the unaided eye. More Mana—from the System, from my body—floods out, joining and taking hold of the ambient Mana, even as the Skill formula flows around the ritual circle. More and more glyphs of the unknowable, unspeakable System controls appear.

At first, my victim looks puzzled. There is no pain, no effect. He stops struggling, which is a mistake. Not that it'd help. A moment later, chains erupt from the circle. They pierce his body, digging into his flesh. The black chains are covered with spikes at irregular intervals, and they slide through his twitching body, tearing through flesh and muscle, wrapping around his bones. His health drops, but not by much, for these chains are more immaterial than they are physical.

No, the damage it's doing, that will come later, if he breaks the Shackles. If he defies the warning. That's when he'll suffer. For now though, it's only the pain of the attack he feels.

More and more Mana flows as I pour it in, waiting for when the System deems it sufficient. My eyes widen, realizing that I'm fast reaching the bottom of my Mana pool, and I grit my teeth. We hit the three thousand Mana region and keep climbing, no end in sight. When I finally hit four thousand spent Mana, only then does it finally peter off.

When we're done, the ritual circle disappears and I release my grip. Adriter staggers away, his clothes bloody and torn, his flesh unmarked. His eyes are wide—he's fearful of me—and his aides come rushing over, dragging him away before he can say or do something foolish.

I'm ignoring him as I wait for my Mana to regenerate. That took a lot more Mana than I expected. And he's a low Advanced Level. I expect I'll pay even more for those with higher Levels. Thankfully, due to the speed of my Mana Regeneration and how slow the actual ritual is—comparatively speaking—I can handle it for the moment. Later on... well. We'll work it out then.

"I told you he was never a real contender," Brerdain says to Julierudi. Almost crowing about it.

"Nor are you," Julierudi says, tilting her head downward to meet the portly man's eyes.

"Har. We'll find out very soon." He turns to me, raises an eyebrow. "Unless you want to inform us now."

I ignore the byplay, instead conferring with the Honor Guards. A short time later, more guards appear, forming a circle around me.

"Did you not have enough guards already?" Julierudi says. "Are you that afraid of us?"

I snort. "Neither. These are channelers. They're going to feed me Mana during the ritual. Unfortunately, I'm just not cut out for this."

My answer settles them because they both can tell how far my Mana dropped. Seeing that requires a cheap Skill and I'm not trying to use my ring to hide the drop.

We stand in silence while my Mana recovers, the crowd slowly relaxing as time ticks on. The Queen, high above, gets back to running the Empire. Talking with her retinue. Holding vid conferences for those she needs to speak with. None of us can hear a damn thing.

Time crawls as, one by one, I drag the courtiers before me and place the Shackles on them all. Some try to leave, try to bargain their way out. They fail. No one tries to fight—not with the Champion, the Queen, and myself right here.

One after another, the Shackles are laid on all the courtiers present. Most don't look happy about it, about the "honor" of being allowed to watch anymore. I don't care. I keep at it. A day passes, as we take breaks for my Mana to recuperate, for the pain in my head from using the same Skill and bottoming out my Mana again and again to fade.

I push through as the courtiers slowly get on with their lives. Answering limited calls. Making others. Running their businesses, their noble houses. Their armies and fleets and cults. And news of what is happening leaks out.

In time, the reporters are allowed to broadcast, the information going wide. There are social disturbances, a few hot-headed fools deciding it's time to raise the banner of revolution or to try to force. But for the most part, it's pretty quiet. After all, the point of dragging everyone here was to keep it contained.

Eventually, there's no one else. No one but Spuryan, Julierudi, and Brerdain. The top three contenders. They look at one another, weighing the options. Trying to determine who I'll take next.

"Spuryan," I call.

The Prophet's eyes widen then narrow. One of the guards moves to push him forward, but he starts walking before the hand can more than twitch.

I place a hand on his shoulder, calling up the Skill. There's no argument, no discussion. I cast the Skill, and it slams through him. Once more, the guards channel Mana into me, flooding me with Mana over and over again. It's a sweet agony, pushing my control to the brink.

When we're done, Spuryan staggers back to his position, looking wan, but I still sense he's somewhat satisfied. I note how Julierudi has her fingers pressed together in a birdlike shape, while Brerdain has his arm up by his ear. Both of them are staring at me as I breathe deeply and center myself. As I slowly enter a meditative trance to discard the pain.

When my eyes open, a second ring of Honor Guards have appeared. Channelers, all of them. I watch as the pair of final contenders look between them and me. Waiting for my pronouncement. To see who has won.

"Ayuri." A single word, a single request.

She appears behind the pair of new guards. Before they can move, she triggers her Skill, wrapping all of us in the Sphere of Gramus. Within her Skill, blocked off from reality, only the channelers, the contenders, Mikito, Bolo, Ayuri, and I will know what is said.

And done.

Chapter 26

When we emerge, neither of the two contenders are happy. At least Julierudi is on her feet, while Brerdain is slumped over, held up by a pair of the Honor Guards. Our reappearance raises a bit of a ruckus, as some of the smaller contenders—individuals in power who'd backed Brerdain—try to make a fuss. Some quick use of the backs of hands and the butts of rifles quiets the group down.

"He's alive," I tell them all. "He just had a bad reaction to the Shackles."

I don't think most of them believe me, but I don't really care. Some of the other audience members are shooting Julierudi inquisitive looks, as if they think she'd warn them. But she's not meeting anyone's eyes, her gaze fixed on the floor.

"*Dornalor, bring her in.*" I send a message to the pirate captain over the party chat.

We debated for hours beforehand on whether to have the team with him or if he should go alone. In the end, I just have to rely on him, on what he can do. Well, him and some friends.

Dornalor and the initiates come marching through the doors, pushing aside the individuals ahead of them. Making sure the way is clear. In the front is Kino, followed by Freif just behind. Freif's main gun and the numerous floating duplicates float alongside him, on full display.

That creates a reaction among the Honor Guard, even if they were warned. They grow more alert, a few filtering down to stand just underneath the throne. I feel multiple Honor Guards slap Two are One on the Empress. She only looks up briefly before she turns back to conferring with her advisors.

Behind the pair comes Dornalor, walking beside a cloaked figure. And, right behind, are Anayton and Magine, bringing up the back of the troop.

The initiates are wary, entirely on guard. Their presence is a surprise to many, and even Queen Karlelo is frowning when she realizes something and looks back down.

The Queen's voice rises, crossing the room, followed by a wave of power. It shakes feet, makes knees weak, and men sway as she expresses her displeasure. "Paladin, what are you doing?"

"My job."

I stride over to the group, ignoring Ayuri, who's moving toward me, conjuring her weapon as she does. Everything will happen quickly now. Julierudi and Brerdain are still frozen from what we did inside the sphere, but their supporters are realizing that their person isn't in line to win. Some of them, the most impetuous, move to head off the woman in the cloak. Guns, swords, even spells appear as they grasp at the last few moments of opportunity.

Because not all of them were shackled. I wasn't about to waste Mana and time on a non-contender, on a bodyguard. More so, even the ones who are shackled are bound to protect the Empress Apparent. But I haven't declared her yet, and until I do, she's vulnerable.

Skills trigger, washing over the cloaked figure and burning them even as Honor Guards act. They clamp down on the Mana in the throne room, pushing against the attacks, reducing their effectiveness. Healing spells fly, as well as some people reaching out with Two are One. Other Honor Guards are more direct, weapons targeting, cutting and firing at the attackers.

The Queen is the slowest to make a move, though hers is the last major action. Her aura flares and hammers the attackers. Whether or not she agrees, attacks in her throne room are an insult to her.

Some—the smarter ones—realize their mistake. Too late. Those who were Shackled are torn apart, the chains erupting from their bodies, criss-crossing and squeezing. Blood and viscera spray as they're ripped apart. Those who weren't shackled find themselves crushed by her aura, taking damage from the sheer pressure she exerts. Attacks fail to form, defenses crumble. And then the Honor Guard finishes the job.

Meanwhile, Dornalor has moved aside from the attacked figure, leaving it to burn. Some of those Skills used against it were damage-over-time ones. Others were one-off uses. None of it was particularly useful as the melted figure sags and burns before finally disappearing. The Doppleganger Skill turns off, Dornalor releasing the cast. Even from where I am, I can see the wide smirk on the Pirate's face.

"Baka!" Mikito mutters, staring at the mess made by the courtiers.

So many of them, acting without thinking, torn apart. Cleaning robots appear to deal with the corpses.

I shake my head, having reached Dornalor, and clap him on the shoulder. He steps back, muttering something about payment, before I stride past the smoking portion of floor where the doppelganger used to be. I stop next to Anayton.

"Are you ready?"

Hasbata doesn't object, not any longer. Ayuri's a short distance away, weapon in hand, but eying the surroundings, not me. They're not stopping me because they maybe, just maybe, trust me. To do what is right. To do what a Paladin always has to do.

Put the Empire first.

***

The entire problem with this has always been, and would always be, finding an Emperor or Empress who could survive the job and who could improve the Empire. What's a new challenge is the state of the Empire.

The Erethran Empire has endured over a century of neglect by the lack of Paladins, by the nobles, and by the Generals wearing away the direct power of the Empress. Corruption is rife. Attacks on each other continue. They're more concerned about expanding their personal fiefdoms than the Empire. And the Empress has to push, pull, balance out their needs and keep everything held together.

The Generals keep expanding, forcing her, the ruler, to focus her attention on the military. Leaving the domestic to run riot.

And that isn't enough. Not anymore. No matter what I thought, no matter what was said, the Reluctant Survivors aren't crazy pacifists. Their recommendations—while somewhat over-the-top or unrealistic in places— have a grounding in reality. The Empire has grown too large. Too unwieldy.

Like Rome, it will eventually fall, as the barbarians at the gates press against the ever-widening borders. Or something like that. I never claimed to be a historian. I just played *Total War: Rome*.

So we need someone the military trusts, who can see the problems among the domestic world, and who isn't entrenched in the corruption.

That, by definition, ruled out all three contenders almost immediately. Not that I intended to tell them that, but it was true. My concern was that anyone I chose outside of the contenders wouldn't be able to do the job of an Empress. They wouldn't have the personal strength to fight multiple attacks. Nor would they have the Skills required to bolster the already thinly stretched Armed Forces. More concerning was that any major disruption could set the enemies of the Empire rushing in to finish the job.

The first glimmer of a potential solution appeared when initiates were introduced to me.

But now, here we are in the throne room. And before anything can be done, I need to resolve one last issue.

I walk past Anayton, catching a whiff of a familiar nutmeg scent. I note the tension, the slight nervous sweat on all the initiates' faces. Then I turn to the initiate next to the woman.

"We spoke to Brerdain," I say softly. "He didn't really want to give you up, but we didn't give him a lot of choice. He's loyal, I'll give him that."

Magine stills. I wait, before he steps back quickly, sword hilts appearing in his hands. He's glaring at me.

"I don't really care if he had one of you suborned. If any of you were suborned," I raise my voice, letting it ring out to encompass all the initiates. "I figured multiple corrupt individuals would balance each other out eventually. I couldn't, wouldn't, keep looking.

"But you killed Ropo and Gheisnan. And that I won't accept."

Magine falls into a combat stance, one sword raised and pointed at my face. The other, held low and covering his chest, the lower line of attack. He could stab me from here, but between my Soul Shield and my emergency shielding ring, he can't kill me. Not in a single attack. So I ignore the blades.

"Why?" I say. "It wasn't even in your orders."

That fact, we had confirmed. It was the reason Kremnock was alive, the reason we hadn't just killed him.

"They didn't deserve it," Magine sneers. "That old Grimsar, he never made anything of his life. And then he thought he could be a Paladin? While I've worked all my life, struggled, to be something, only to fail because I was born too late." The Movanna turns his head to the side and spits, even as he continues. "The Pooskeen? I would never serve beside one of those creatures. Disgusting monsters, daring to think they're equal to me."

I see his incandescent fury, the burning rage in his eyes, from being overlooked again and again. His towering pride and the blame he set upon everyone else for his failures. For the fact that he never amounted to more than what he thought he was. And in doing so, he turned that anger on others.

His friends, his fellow initiates, back away, giving him and me room. We stare at one another over the edge of his blade. I see the light shimmer of energy that marks the creation of the monofilament edge. Around us, the other guards, the Queen, the Champion, and the courtiers are but bystanders to this little drama.

"Will you fight me? Or will you shoot me down like the honorless creature you are? You pitiful, fortune-favored, stumbling fool. You disgrace every Paladin, every true Erethran who has ever born that title," Magine spits his words like knives. Hoping to score a blow, to cripple my self-control, to force me to fight him. To win back some honor at this late stage in the game.

It's a good choice in most cases. Anger, anger has always driven me. But this time, he misses. Because I have no pride, no investment in being a Paladin. The Title is a tool, one that I've used and used again, to survive. To drag those with me who survived into the light.

When he fails to make me act, Magine chooses to do so himself. He lunges, his sword aimed straight at my eye. I watch as the blade nears, growing larger with each fraction of a second. Only for it to be deflected by a familiar, burning polearm. A short Samurai steps in front of me.

"Your opponent is me," Mikito says.

I can't help but stare at Mikito's back in amazement. It takes long moments before I can speak. "You actually said that."

I see just a little bit of her profile, enough to see that she blushes. Magine, for all his talk of honor, takes her blush as a distraction that he can exploit and he lashes out with his small swords.

Unfortunately for him, Mikito's ready, and she blocks it and the follow-up thrust from his other sword. I back off, and in short order, we create an open space. Shields form, trapping the pair within, allowing them to duel without interference. Even the Queen stops her work to watch. I guess in a society like this, a high-level duel between two arena champions is considered high entertainment.

Weapons clash, Mikito doing her best to keep the fast-moving ex-initiate away, using the extra reach of her weapon and its greater weight to beat him around. He, in turn, uses multiple quick shedding blocks, cutting at the edges of her polearm as she swings, driving it farther off Mikito's center line by inches each time. Each move, each block, each attack is designed to open a gap between strikes so that he can slip in.

Intermixed among the mundane skills are their Skills. Blade Strikes, Power Blows, Cleave, Haste, they all trigger, giving them surprise attacks, explosions of energy, or even unblockable attacks that slip past blades. Blood blooms, staining both of them, as shields fail, armor gets pierced, and blood rolls to the floor.

A quick flicker of the small swords, barely a foot of movement, and the paired Blade Strikes push Mikito back, forcing her to block them with Hitoshi. The polearm swirls in a quick form, breaking apart the attacks. Seconds later, the ground around Mikito explodes in flames. A preset Skill trap, or potentially a spell, engulfs the Samurai. The damage is significant but not fatal. More dangerous is the fact that the flames block her vision, allowing Magine to trigger a new Skill.

By the time she's out, three figures, all looking exactly the same, are charging her. You would think that they're just illusions, and you would be wrong.

The Skill Magine uses actually creates, temporarily, three duplicates. All of them are reduced in strength and health, but not in speed. He can't use any other active Skills while the duplicates are in use, but that's not his fighting style. A lot of passives, a lot of damage bonuses to attacks, that's his way.

Magine rushes Mikito, pouring out quick, blurring attacks that are coordinated between all three duplicates. Against anyone else, that might have been dangerous. It might have been a fight-ender.

But Mikito out Levels him. And she's finally done playing. She triggers her Skill, and Haste, Blitzed, it all combines. Her movements become a blur, much, much faster than the still-locked Advanced Classer can keep up with.

She tears through one of the figures with a simple rising cut from her front leg, spins the naginata blade around to block a pair of cuts and a lunge, reverses and strikes with the butt of the polearm, then cuts again with the blade. A figure drops, bleeding, missing a limb.

Together, the injured mirror images continue to attack. She cuts and cuts again, bringing an overhand sweep down with such speed and force, it throws a duplicate into a shield, cracking it. Long seconds, then the blurred forms within the shields freeze.

Hitoshi is buried in the chest of Magine's final body, one hand raised, the held blade trying to push away the polearm. The second sword is deep in Mikito's thigh. Blood dribbles from both their wounds even as the mirror images disperse, the corpses becoming no more than motes of light.

"You cheated. You used... a Master Class... Skill," Magine complains as he slowly slides off Mikito's weapon to land on his bum. He releases the weapons in his hands, letting them clatter to the floor, glaring at Mikito and the unfairness of life. That she dare cheat him.

The Samurai stares at the dying elf, poison and flame burning from the wounds Hitoshi layered on him. His chest rises and falls, fueling the unnatural flame. Mikito waits. She will not explain how her view of honor, of loyalty, works. Not to him. Not to a dying man. Not to a traitor.

He coughs one last time, then falls over. She doesn't move, keeping a wary eye on the corpse, until one of the Honor Guards comes along and lops off his head. Just to be sure. Only then does she limp over to me, her body glowing with the repeated healing spells the guards are casting.

"Satisfied?" I ask her.

Mikito gives me a short nod.

I can only reply with one simple and appropriate word. "Baka."

Chapter 27

It doesn't take the attendants and robots long to clean up from the duel. Even the scarred flooring, damaged by the passage of the fighters, is healed and perfect within minutes. Throughout all this, the courtiers and other guards are watching my initiates, studying them.

"Well, Paladin. If you are done with the theatrics, shall we finish this?" the Queen says.

"Got to agree, boy-o. This is getting quite tiring," Ali sends as well.

I stride forward, and the team moves out, the initiates and my people coming to stop before the Queen. No more attacks, no other actions are taken. Ayuri only hesitates for a second before letting us approach the Queen, then Blink Stepping to the Queen's side.

"My apologies, Your Majesty." I feel a grin pull at my lips. "I have a tendency to be a little bit dramatic at times."

"At times," Bolo says incredulously.

It'd be wrong, kicking him.

I turn back to the initiates, to the crowd of courtiers who have approached. Brerdain has recovered and is staring around, somewhat paler but with his regained confidence. I hadn't blamed him, hadn't killed him, for his part of putting Magine among my initiates. Truth be told, Julierudi and Spuryan had tried as well. They just weren't as effective. Or more.

Julierudi is looking a little more confident, a little more certain of herself. My little trick with the doppelgänger, to draw out the idiots, to lure those who would act without thinking had thrown her at first. But now, with no obvious candidate left, she must consider herself in the lead. Even if she's Shackled, the wording lets her function – after all, you can't betray yourself. Especially since I've dismissed Spuryan. The Prophet is the only one who looks at peace. I guess losing once and for all can settle you down quite well.

"So, thank you for waiting," I say. I step toward my initiates. "I'm sure you'd all like to meet your Empress Apparent."

I turn around and walk back, stopping in front of Anayton. I idly watch as Bolo shifts, glaring at a noble who looks as if they might do something foolish. Mikito is behind the initiates, as is Dornalor. Harry's the only one who's moved ahead, facing perpendicular to all of us, just a short distance from the rest of the reporters so that he can capture both the Queen's reaction and me.

"*Do you trust me?*" I send, touching upon the comm channel. It's a tight beam, but it's not fully secure. It doesn't have to be.

I stop before Anayton, waiting for my answer. It's a strange question, especially after they've been dragged so far, pulled all the way here to watch.

Silence draws out, and I feel the pressure of their gazes, of their expectation. I can smell her scent, the blend of nutmeg and musk that is all hers. I feel her, see the threads flowing out from her. To touch upon the Queen, to the Lord of the Hounds, to the Guard, and to so, so many of the nobles, the power players behind us.

"*Yes.*"

"Then let me present her to you." I raise my hand.

Anayton's eyes track my hand, watch as it comes down. Not onto her shoulder. Missing it by inches.

To land on empty air.

Only for a short moment, for Dornalor's and Ali's twin Skills finally fail.

"Lords and ladies, Generals, Admirals, and soldiers, your new Empress Apparent."

The susurration of scandal, of shock has already started. Bolo shifts, crackling with power to bring the involuntary steps toward us to a stop. Mikito levels her naginata at Brerdain, who's looking shocked.

And on the throne... Ali shows me the Queen, her mouth open as she tries to order me to stop. Surprised in her own place of power, surprised at having her Skills locked out. Ayuri's eyes are wide, realization striking her regarding why I asked for control of the room's security apparatus. Why I'd asked for it. There's no ultimate Skill, nothing that can't be blocked or hidden, given enough information, time, and Credits.

"Catrin Dufoff."

Congratulations! Empire Quest: Erethran Empire (M) Completed!

Designate an individual to become the Presumptive Emperor of Erethra

Rewarded: +4,353,593 XP

Mana floods into me, as does experience. I shudder, multiple Level Ups appearing and disappearing in a cascade. Another larger notification appears, one that I shelve to the side as chaos erupts around me.

"Redeemer! What is the meaning of this?" Hasbata snarls, leaning forward in her chair.

Her aura snaps out, smashing down on all of us. People stagger. Anyone who isn't a Master Class sinks to their knees or, worse, drop directly to the floor. Even those with Master Classes stagger, some unable to keep their feet.

My team does, but it's a struggle, because her anger, her displeasure is directed at us. The only person who looks unfazed is Catrin. If the Mana vortex that formed around me as I gained experience from the System Quest was large, the one that flows around the new Empress Apparent makes mine look like a dust devil next to a Class III tornado.

Catrin's changing with each strand of power, each tendril of the System as it takes effect on her. She's discarding her old Class, gaining a new one,

409

receiving the approval and approbation of the Empire, and gaining a series of Titles to mark her new place in society.

Memories of prior tests, prior Class changes pull at me. A desire, a need, to stare and record the change, to compare it to past studies rises up. It almost disrupts my concentration, pulling my focus from the irate Queen before me. I've never felt this before, this need from the Library. If not for the immediate pressure exerted by the Empress's Aura, I might have even given in. To the library and my own curiosity.

Attention, pulled back, when Ayuri appears, Blink Stepping right up to me. Her friends are behind her, squaring off against Bolo and Mikito, but Ayuri only has eyes for me. And the Empress Apparent. Our only threats here are the Honor Guards, the Champion, and the Empress herself. Everyone else is either too weak or Shackled.

"She asked you a question, Redeemer," Ayuri snaps. Anger at being betrayed, at being tricked pulses from her. She's just out of easy reach, though with our conjured weapons, it'd be a simple matter to hurt one another. But we're not there yet.

Not yet.

"Exactly what you asked me to do, Champion." I nod to the Empress, trying for nonchalance. Failing, mostly. "Empress."

"She was not the candidate you mentioned," Ayuri replies.

"No. But she is what you guys need."

"You will fix this, Paladin," the Empress says from her position above. She's leaning forward, focusing the aura on me.

My knees buckle again, and I have to force them up. Warnings flash as I start taking damage, my body compressed and crushed by a pressure that swallows me up, makes it impossible to move. "And if I refuse?"

"Then we have other candidates. We can wait," the Empress snarls.

I watch a finger of hers twitch, and I realize she might act against the still-transforming Empress.

The simplest, easiest way to resolve this situation would be to kill Catrin. But they haven't. Which means as much as they're opposing my words, they're still hesitant. Because this is my choice as a Paladin. Webs of social expectations, of engrained duty, of what we imagine our own honor and beliefs are, they can bind our actions. Bind us motionless in threads stronger than titanium.

Especially when you've got a reporter feeding this all directly to the world and the Empire at large.

Gainsaying me, in full public view, would be dangerous. Sneaking Harry's report around the throne's security system was annoying, but worth it. He's still getting significant pushback, but his Skills are letting him do it. His Skills and those of fellow Reporters, Galaxy-wide and in this Empire. Building friends, building resources. The Empress could shut it down, but at this point, the information is out.

"Here, let me make it easy for you." I step back to draw their attention to me again and lessen the threat to Catrin.

Then I spin around, stumbling a little under the pressure exerted by the aura. I can't help but chuckle at the blood that comes from my mouth as I inadvertently bite my lip. I focus, pushing back against the aura. Triggering my own to help alleviate the pressure. It helps. A little.

I meet the gazes of the four initiates, including Anayton's disappointed gaze, and see concern in all their eyes. I see it all, then ignore it.

I reach for the library. For the knowledge I have within me, my understanding of the System. I remember how I did it before, then reach sideways and back, touching upon the Quest I gave them. Feeling for the Levels of success they each had.

Then I reach for the Quest I just completed. The one only a Paladin could have received.

And I push.

It's like trying to move a car in snow. As you put your shoulder to it, as your feet slip and slide, as wheels spin, offering no traction. And you strain, putting everything you have into the push, knowing that if you wait just a little too long, if you fail, the wind, the dropping temperature at night will get you. Have you ever felt metal so cold that to place your skin against it would glue it together?

Ever had to put your hands on the car anyway? And push? Because there's no one else, no other choice but to do the work. You push, against cold, against the slick ground with booted feet, as you sink deeper and deeper into the snowbank. You push as wheels spin. To live.

If you've ever done that, then you know what it's like, in small part. Maybe a thousandth of what it is to pitch myself against the System.

There's no additional willpower attribute increase, no System-aided benefit to this kind of work. It's all human stubbornness against cold, unfeeling glyphs and an unspeakable language. Throwing myself into torrents of information with nothing more than the tether of my will and spirit to hold me aloft.

All so that I can demand the System do what I tell it to do. And it's only because there's a groove, an option within the Class Quest System at all, that I can make it work. That I can bump the initiates from one portion of their completed Quest to another Quest, to the completed Empire Quest, and let them finish that too.

I make them Paladins because they helped me bring the Empress Apparent here. They safeguarded her, through threats, external and internal.

And because it's an Empire Quest, because they're Paladin initiates, the System yields.

Not without taking a payment from me.

Because everything has a cost. Even if you aren't the one paying it.

I scream into the void as the payment consumes my fragile soul, as the System extracts its price from me. I scream, and all I can do is wrap myself up in my most trusted of protections before I fall unconscious.

***

When I come to, Sanctum is still up. Ayuri, her people, the Empress Apparent, my team sans Harry, and the initiates are all captured within the bubble. Everyone else is kept outside.

My body feels as if every bone in it was shattered and put back together. Ali, hovering beside me, is muttering imprecations, fingers dancing as he manipulates the System, data streams and notifications that I barely glimpse. Too much, too much data, too much information. Though I see more and more boxes set aside for my later perusal.

But he's not the most important figure among those here. What he's doing for me is, as always, left unsaid and unappreciated by most. For there's bigger drama. The Paladins—the former initiates—are standing in a semi-circle around the still-transforming Empress Apparent. The Empress Apparent's last line of defense.

My team, on the other hand, is looking worse for the wear, as are Ayuri and her people. Bolo's facing off against Ayuri, his hammer out, glowing. His scalemail is chipped, one entire shoulder pauldron shattered, portions of it embedded within his body. Ayuri's nursing a broken hand, one that is slowly healing, while Mayaya glares at Dornalor, who's smirking. The Pirate

Captain hates to look as if he's not in control, but he's lucky we're stuck in this Sphere. Mayaya's severely curtailed, locked out of reality as she is here. On the other hand, Mikito is the least injured, her naginata blade resting on Unilo's neck.

"Owww!" I complain.

My word draws attention, making everyone look at me. I push myself to my feet, careful to keep an eye on the Champion. My health is still glowing red, slowly ticking upward but at a slower-than-normal rate in this benighted hellhole of a Sphere. But I'm alive.

"Damn good thing, boy-o, that you didn't take your Class up. You definitely wouldn't have survived if you'd done that," Ali sends.

I grunt, acknowledging his words. Acknowledging how close I got. If I'd raised my Class, the System would have yanked me down again. Forced me out of it. And that kind of damage added to everything else...

Pushing against the System like that isn't something you should do. Or, hell, something I thought I could do. "What exactly did you do?" Ayuri says. She's glaring at the Paladins, adjusting her grip on her weapon.

"I gave you what you wanted," I tell her. "I gave you your Paladins."

"They had a Quest. They hadn't finished it," Unilo says. She clamps her mouth shut when the talking brings blood to the blade.

I wave at Mikito, who frowns but removes the polearm, to Unilo's relief. I grin, feeling my body slowly heal. The System may not have liked my actions, but it isn't holding back its usual processes either. My body fixes itself, putting me back in fighting condition, the longer we talk. "I fixed that."

"How?" Anayton asks.

I look back, seeing the puzzled looks on all the Paladins' faces. I can't help but grin. "Questor secret."

Funny thing is, that's not even a lie. If not for the library, emplaced within my mind, there would be no way that I'd know how, or even if, such an action was possible.

Before the others can ask for details, Sanctum falls, revealing us to the crowd. I'm a little surprised to see the ring of Honor Guards surrounding us, the addition of artillery weapons that have been deployed all around the throne room. The Empress is still seated on her throne, though a beefed-up protection squad surrounds her. Nearby, Lord Braxton is watching, wary but cordoned off by another group of guards.

As for the rest of the watchers, the old contenders and the nobles, the other courtiers, they've been pushed out of the line of fire. Unable to do anything, their bodies and souls Shackled, they're just an audience for our little drama.

Surprisingly, Harry's been left alone. I wonder if it's his Skill or his status as a non-combatant. But he's still standing, recording. As are the other reporters.

"Champion, what has happened?" Hasaba asks.

"It seems we have three new Paladins," Ayuri says. "The Redeemer is no longer necessary."

I grin, all teeth and challenge as I bow to the Empress. "As requested, as promised. Your Paladins. Now we can stop acting as if what I did was a damn travesty and finish this. You can accept my choice. Or kill me."

Gasps and hisses arise from more than a few guards, from the audience, from Bolo. Mikito doesn't seem at all surprised, while Donarlor is eyeing the exit, plotting the best way to escape and not looking at all happy that there isn't one. I kind of feel bad for the Pirate Captain.

"You..." The Queen quickly takes hold of herself as rage burns in her eyes at my open defiance. I can see her mind spinning, working out implications even as the Mana swirl around Catrin slowly dies.

"My Empress, before you act," Anayton speaks up. She steps away from Catrin, coming up to my shoulder, then passing it. She stops between myself and the Queen and Champion. She spares only a glance at Ayuri before she continues. "Paladin Lee might be loud, confrontational, and overly melodramatic in his actions, but he's a Paladin."

"And what do you mean by that?" The Queen's voice drops, almost hissing.

Freif walks over, his feet somewhat unsteady, his face pale. He's clenching his fist again and again, as if he wishes he was holding something. A bottle, perhaps. "His choice is our choice."

Kino, the last to speak, rumbles from his position next to Catrin, "If you kill him, you'll need to find new Paladins. For we will guard him and the Empress Apparent."

The Queen doesn't answer us directly, instead turning her Aura on us. Except this time, there's something else added to it. I'm not entirely certain what, but it's sharper, deadlier. None of us manage to hold our feet except the Empress Apparent. Not this time. We crash almost in unison to the floor.

Even Ali is squished, his body made of energy beginning to disperse. I feel newly healed bones and organs crack, split, and bleed. For a second, I regret my actions. Not because of where it's led me but for those I've dragged along. I hadn't expected the initiates to stand up for me. Hoped, maybe. But not expected.

I hear a commotion from behind. Those who have been Shackled are finding themselves caught in an impossible situation. The Shackles require them to protect the Empress Apparent—who is now under attack from the Empress herself.

If they do something, they die. Do nothing and they die.

Already, Shackles are ripping out of bodies, tightening across flesh and bone, threatening to tear them apart. I assume that's part of the reason why Hasbata's been slow to act. To lose so many of her people would weaken the Queen, the Empire greatly.

But I pushed her too far, too hard, perhaps. This time, there's no let up as her Aura does nothing but crush us, tear at our bodies and souls. As my life slips away, I hear the screams from the Generals, the heads of industry, the nobles rise.

I gambled. Once too often.

And failed. For the last time.

And then, suddenly, blessed relief.

The Aura's pushed back, the pressure lessened. It's not all gone, but most of it fades. Like a tide broken by tide-breaking rocks. I stagger to my feet out of sheer stubbornness rather than any sense, driven by anger. My head pounds, blood drips from my nose, eyes, ears, and fingertips themselves. I'm seeing double, triple at times.

But I force myself to stand. Shame at being crushed that easily turns to anger. I stand.

Only to see Catrin before all of us. Pushing back against the Empress with her own Aura. I blink, even as my Mana Sense triggers, showing me the almost unseen struggle. I see the waves of pressure as Auras fight one another. I'm surprised that Catrin's able to do this, to push back this far.

And, as I think this, the System answers.

Title: The Empress Apparent of Erethra

As the Empress Apparent of Erethra, the titleholder gains certain benefits, reputation changes, and the collected regard of the Empire to wield. In return, certain Class Skills effects by Title Holder will apply to the populace of the Empire.

Effect 1: Gain a lesser version of the Aura of the Empire affect

Effect 2: Major reputation changes among Galactic society

Effect 3: Selected Class Skills affect citizens of the Empire

"Thousand Hells, that's a Title!" I blurt.

Ali, having pulled himself together, literally, floats over. He joins me in staring at the Empress Apparent before his voice enters my mind. "Yup. How she's holding the Queen's aura back to this degree, I don't know. Must be a combination of her own Skills."

I shake my head, not interested in the answer. Not right now at least. Instead, I walk forward, joining Catrin. The Empress and the Empress Apparent have their gazes locked upon one another, while everyone else is disregarded.

The very air between them warps, as the System, as the Auras press upon one another. It's clear that Catrin's the weaker. That's why a lesser effect of the pressing, cutting Aura of the Empress is still upon us. But people aren't actively dying. Not by much at least. Not from the Aura. But there's a price— I note the nosebleed on Catrin's face as she strains.

I glance over, spotting Ayuri. She's standing, her weapon held by her side. But not attacking. I'm grateful that she hasn't. And I wonder, for once, if she can. As Champion, can she? I don't know. But I'm grateful, either way. For we are more than our Classes.

"If you were men, I'd say put the... Mana sticks away and stop measuring. Because if you don't, you're going to be down a lot of citizens." I turn, pointing backward to where many of those I Shackled writhe on the floor.

A few of the weaker, more Administrative side of society aren't moving anymore. My chains, my shackles, with their spiked obligations continue to dig in, grinding away at the health of those bound.

There's a long pause as the Queen considers. Then she finally relaxes her aura, sitting back. Mental commands follow, and the Honor Guard casts spells, fixing the audience. Others are chivied out, pulled away.

I watch, wondering what would happen if she managed to kill the Empress Apparent out of sight. Would the Shackled still die? I've bet a lot on the Empress's sensibility, her desire to keep her Empire strong. I wish I knew better how the Shackles worked, how it might affect them. It was probably explored and discussed in the Paladins' histories. I just never got to it.

In tense silence, we wait, as the Paladins behind me, as my friends, recover. Only when we're alone but for the guards and the Queen's attendants, but for my allies, does the Queen speak.

"Why her?"

"Ask Lord Braxton," I reply.

The poor man looks startled to be drawn forward like this. But he eventually sighs and prowls forward, some of his earlier subservience fading away, his back straightening. "How long have you know?"

"Since the first night," I say.

I turn to Catrin, stepping close to her, and take her hand. She looks slightly amused—until I raise it and turn over the hand to showcase the dark gold ring she always wears.

"When you didn't ever take this off, when the thread between you and Lord Braxton was so intensely woven. When the Houndmaster and his Hounds made their presence known, helping me. I knew."

"She's one of yours?" the Queen says. Now, she's less angry, more intrigued.

"Yes, Your Empress. One of my internal security members," Lord Braxton says. Houndmaster, but there are no hounds. Not physically at least. Just figuratively. The Houndmaster chases down those who would be the enemies of the state by loosing his Hounds on them.

"Even so, a spy is not a General. And we need a General," Hasbata says. But now she's more argumentative than angry.

"No, you don't. Your contenders, Brerdain, Julierudi, with the Shackles in place, they can be used to the fullest extent to hold your borders, especially since you've got three new Paladins," I say. "Catrin's also only mid-Level Advanced Class, so rising in experience, gaining the Skills to aid the entirety of your Empire as your heir Apparent, should be simple. She can grow, given time."

"So is…" The Queen hesitates, her glance flicking to Anayton. Then realizing that the gig is up, she says it. "Anayton. She who you told us would be your choice. She would have been a good Queen. Honor Guard, loyalty guaranteed, a fighter who could have been a Paladin."

"Yes. A good Queen." I look at Anayton, whose face is carefully blank, though I see the confusion within her eyes. The tinge of regret. "But she'll make a great Paladin."

When the group looks doubtful, I sigh. "Catrin, your heir Apparent, can play the game, your political game, better than anyone else. She knows what your world needs because she's been both swanning around among the top of your Society and crawled up from the bottom.

"Working for Lord Braxton, she knows where the bodies are kept, how to clean it all up, who has to be cleaned up. And she can do it, now that you have your Paladins back. And once we let the world know what she did, what she really was, they'll be a lot less doubtful about her suitability from the military. Especially since her first targets will be the nobles."

I shake my head and wave. "I've also Shackled the major players. So you've got time. Time to let her train, to gain in Levels. Maybe not a lot, before the others take over, before the Generals we've Shackled are replaced. But enough. If you let her."

Hasbata continues to frown, obviously not entirely convinced.

Then, before I can keep pitching the woman, Catrin puts a hand on my arm. I shut up as she steps around me, approaching the throne. Ayuri moves to block the way but stills at a glance from the Queen.

Hasbata's retracted her Aura, making it easier for all of us to breathe, to continue healing. As Catrin strides forward, glancing between Ayuri, Lord Braxton, the other attendants, and the Honor Guards before her, I can only hope I was right. Silence stretches out before us as the click-clack of her heels on the floor resounds, the only noise within the expansive throne room. As she leaves, the hint of her scent, that nutmeg and musk, fades. We wait. The room waits.

Catrin finally comes to a stop at the foot of the stairs leading to the throne. She looks up, meeting the Empress's gaze, and speaks.

"We should talk. Privately."

Chapter 28

Not with a bang but with a whimper.

That's how things get resolved in the end. They kicked us out, my team and me. We're put on watch, even if the new Paladins are ushered out to be debriefed and checked over. They go without much complaint—for now.

Once the check is done, they're released to do their thing, Leveling and searching down Quests to complete. Annoyingly, it seems that the Empress has been withholding a number of Empire Quests from me. Quite a number that are Paladin only have stacked up, giving the new Paladins a lot to choose from. It keeps the Paladins and their teams busy, Leveling and righting wrongs.

The Empress and the Empress Apparent speak for hours on the first day, before the announcement is made. Not that Harry's transmissions hadn't spread. But the official broadcasts reaffirm and ensure that Catrin's place is officially backed. There will be no midnight assassination, no random body turning up, skewered by the Champion.

Our captors let us get news and messages from outside the cells they hold us in. Carefully monitored, but they let me read the news. Which is nice. I'm sure they'll let us out eventually. Or so I hope.

The first to find me is Anayton. The Paladin finds me in my gray, drab, utilitarian cell with its single tiny window. She finds me staring at the ceiling, running over the experiences, teasing at the memories and information that the library expelled. That told me of what was to come when what I'd done to the Paladin initiates was spread around.

And staring at the single notification I've refused to dismiss.

System Quest Completion Rate: 89%

"Redeemer," Anayton greets me softly.

I swing my legs from the bunk so that I can sit up and stare at her. "Not Paladin anymore?"

"Not between equals." She takes a seat across from me, the nanites forming a chair for her.

"I'm surprised they let you see me."

"I've… been given some additional privileges. Informally. Because of what they heard," Anayton says, glancing toward the door she came in from, where the guards await.

"Ah, right." My lips twist. "And you wanted to talk about that."

"Yes."

I pause, considering. "I'm sorry. For using your name. I needed—"

"A distraction," Anayton replies. "I understand. Why me though?"

"Because you and the Empress Apparent are similar in many ways. Your sense of duty, your understanding of war and what it truly means," I say. "Life on the frontier or the Restricted Zones."

"You used me to test the waters with the Queen." When I nod, she adds, with a little more heat in her voice, "Then why not just choose me?"

"Did you want it? Do you want it?" I say.

"Of course I don't!" Anayton says. "To be trapped by politics and compromises, to weigh the needs of each person, each army with every single decision I make? Or refuse to make? Who'd want that?"

"Who would, I wonder?" another voice, this one softer, interrupts Anayton's rant.

I twist my head to the side, raising an eyebrow. "How'd you get in here?"

"Why can't I?" Catrin says as she sways over. There's a little less sex kitten in her movements, more confident businesswoman—and damn is it hot. She smiles, as if knowing what I think, even as her new bodyguards behind her glare at me. "I am the Empress Apparent."

"Your Grace." Anayton bows and salutes, a blush creeping up on her face. "I-I meant no disrespect."

"None taken. I wasn't offered much choice either," Catrin says, stopping before me.

She keeps smiling, even as she hauls back and slaps me into the nearby wall. I peel myself off the shattered cell wall, spitting out blood and a couple of cracked teeth.

"Owwww. And how?" I say. That was a powerful attack, but there's no way it should have done that much damage.

"Empress advantage. Your resistances don't work on me," Catrin says lightly. She turns her head to the still-bowing Anayton. "And get up. You're a Paladin. You shouldn't be cowering. Look at John here. He didn't cower when he made decisions on mine and your lives. Without asking."

I wince again, this time the dig being a little more pointed. When Catrin beckons, I walk over warily.

"Yes, Your Grace. But it seems you two have much to speak of…" Anayton slowly edges out of the room.

"Are you done then? Content with your place?" Catrin asks while I stop nearby, nursing my aching jaw. The worse part of losing teeth is feeling the System replace them in real time.

"I am, Your Grace. I was… unhappy with being used. But I understand the Redeemer's choices. Even if I might not agree with them." Anayton shoots me another glare.

"Very well. We look forward to seeing how you progress, Paladin Nichortin."

Anayton scurries out, leaving me alone with Catrin. The Empress Apparent turns to regard me, her eyes trailing from my eyes to rest at my swollen jaw. At a mental command, the cell doors close at her bidding, blocking off the guards and bodyguards. I hear muttered imprecations from outside, but I ignore them.

I can't help but marvel at the changes. She's shed the false front, removed the ring that hid her true Class, dropped the dual Classes she had to take to help hide her Status. The things she needed as a Hound. And with it gone, her true Levels, her true experience shines through.

Empress Apparent Catrin Dufoff of the Erethran Empire, Empire Top Companion, The Hidden Blade, Class 2 Human Resource, Slayer of Goblins, Wexlix, Crilik, (more)... (Erethran Empress Apparent Level 2) (M)

HP: 2410/2410

MP: 3480/3480

Conditions: Aura of the Empire (retracted), Trust of the Empire, Never too Late, Pheromones, A Good Impression

She steps closer, and I tense as she brings her hand up, turning my red and bruised face from side to side, before she leans in and kisses me. Rather hard.

"Owwww…" I complain when I get my lips back.

"You idiot." She steps back again, dropping her hand. "Why did you do that? Did you think I was some Artisan you had to save?"

I mentally wince, doing my best to hide my reaction. I doubt it works, but I have to try. There's truth to her accusation, at least partly. Playing the white knight might have factored—did factor—into this. Saving others, helping them, it has become habit. Even if they felt they didn't need it. But I know better than to say of that.

"Well?" Catrin arches an eyebrow.

"Need! The Empire doesn't need another General or noble or damn cultist. Could you imagine them? They all have their agendas, and none of those agendas give a damn about those beneath them—or the realities of the System. And it's not as if I know that many others. Most who could, who would have worked, would turn it down. You..." I shrug. "I knew you wouldn't. You're already enmeshed in the political system and the power players, without actually being beholden to anyone but the Queen. You're smart enough to know what needs to be done, and your background..."

"My background?"

"Your background means you're likely to sympathize," I say. "With those who are always crushed under. A monarchy isn't the best option at times, but with the right person... it might work."

"And my Levels? The fact that I can't boost the army?"

"You were always going to need to grind to get the best Skills in your Class. But if you think your Skills don't help the army, then you're just as blind as the rest of them."

"My Skills..." Catrin's eyes go distant as she stares at the Skills that the System decided was relevant to pass on to the rest of us.

In turn, I pull up the information on my side.

Empathic Bond (Empress Apparent Title Effect) (A)

Understanding a target is paramount to extracting information from them. Empathic Bond allows you to sense and reflect the feelings of your target with greater accuracy.

Effect: +16.3% in empathic connection, emotional and body language recognition and reflection.

Data Analysis (Empress Apparent Title Effect) (B)

Data is just knowledge, unsorted. Data Analysis allows user to analyze and acquire information at an increased rate, increasing learning speed, and knowledge acquisition. Effect: +11.4% in data analysis.

Never Too Late (Empress Apparent Title Effect) (A)

A socialite is never too late. They might be late, but they are never too late. This Skill gives a socialite a dual effect Skill, first in event timing and the second in movement speed.

Effect: +13.4% in event timing intuition. +47.2% movement speed when required

The first Skill was an Advanced Class Skill. I knew on her side, it actually had a much larger effect—one that allowed her to almost intuitively grasp what people all around her were thinking. In fact, at higher Levels like she had, it combined with the minimap option and offered almost a sixth sense, as the System fed in emotional readouts from even normally hidden attackers. It allowed a Skill holder to take the temperature of a room or read killing intent just as easily.

As for the second Skill, it's a Basic Skill from her base Class. It's a non-combat Skill, but its uses extend to training and duels, to practice and tactical analysis. As a base Administrative Class Skill, it's the basis of a lot of their work and the ability to handle and deal with solar system levels of information.

The last Skill is the one that amuses me the most. It's the Skill that might just be better than the Admiral's, since it might get people to where they need to be, when they need to be there. I'm still not sure if it'll play out that way, but there's only one way to find out. I hadn't expected that Skill to turn up, though I'd hoped.

All three Skills are more subtle in their effects, less in-your-face than a General's XP increase, or a damage upgrade from a Sargent. It's not as powerful, by far, as the Admiral's if she had taken over. Her domain Skill would have made some clear changes to merchants, to interstellar commerce. But, I believe—I have to believe—that these Skills will have a wider effect. Because everyone, anyone, will have access, will use these Skills every single day.

"Empathy, knowledge, and social grace?" Catrin smiles at me. "And you gambled the Empire on these soft skills?"

"Hey, I'm a West Coast kid. We're all crystals, granola bars, and sunshine." I don't stop to let Catrin answer, because I know she can't understand the reference. Or is unlikely to, at least. "And I didn't know, not for certain, but I had a guess. The rest of it, you can grind up. You'll have to."

"Yes." Catrin touches my face again, the bruise on my jaw already faded. My skin is unmarred again, smooth and perfect. "I will. The Queen has given me a year to Level. To prove myself, to prove that your choice was not a complete mistake. To convince everyone else."

I pause, then nod slowly. It makes sense. A stay of execution for my non-combat-based choice. "When do you leave?"

"Today."

I open my mouth to ask where, then clomp my teeth together. Best not to ask, best not to know. She'll be safer that way.

"I came to ask. And to say goodbye. To cut ties."

I step back, putting space between us. Offering her a half-smile. "I know."

I knew. The moment I made my choice.

I bow low, sweeping a hand behind my back, bending my knee. "Empress Apparent, Catrin Dufoff. Rule well. Rule long."

Catrin steps back too, offering me the barest inclination of her head. Accepting my words, my offer. And if there's regret there, of what could have been. Only the two of us will ever know.

"Live well, Paladin."

***

When she's gone, I close my eyes and breathe. I let the emotions exist for a time. Let them rest within my mind, let my breathing go heavy and tired. And then, like everything else, I sweep it up and bottle it away. Put it in that box where I store away all the pain, all the loss, all the anger of an apocalypse. It's hard, harder than before. Because this time, I can't blame the System, can't blame a cruel and uncaring world. Or fate, forcing me apart.

It's hard this time. Because I chose this ending.

I draw a deep breath and let it out, and with my mind clear, my path cleansed, for the first time in days, I turn to my notifications.

Level Up!

You have reached Level 50 as a Paladin of Erethra. Stat Points automatically distributed. You have 14 Free Attribute Points and 14 Class Skills to distribute.

That had arrived when I finished the Empire Quest. I shouldn't have gained five Levels from a single Quest like that, even if it was a Heroic Level Empire Quest. But my cheaty experience requirements meant I jumped up fast. Of course, I wasn't the only one who cheated. Mikito gained some experience from her Skill too.

Just as important is the next notification.

Heroic Class Possible!

Would you like to challenge your Heroic Class Quests? Available Quests include:

— Grand Paladin of Erethra

— The Lord of Light

— Shield of Rage

— more...

Unfortunately, my little stunt with the System had seen that taken away from me. My choices, my options. In a bitch slap that robbed me of some of my experience from the Quest, that robbed me of some of the benefits of my Level Up, the System had also enforced a new Class. One that I only dared to look at now, when I'm alone and certain of my safety.

I turn my gaze to the small window and look at the twinkling night lights of the city in the distance. The cell, the corridor outside, the prison, they echo with an emptiness that seem to wrap me up, remind me of how alien this world is.

And then I stare at my new Status Screen.

Status Screen			
Name	John Lee	Class	Junior System Admin (Grand Paladin)

Race	Human (Male)	Level	1	

Titles				
Monster's Bane, Redeemer of the Dead, Duelist, Explorer, Apprentice Questor, Galactic Silver Bounty Hunter, Corrupt Questor, (Living Repository), (Class Lock)				

Health	5170	Stamina	5170
Mana	4660	Mana Regeneration	429 (+5) / minute

Attributes			
Strength	368	Agility	446
Constitution	517	Perception	300
Intelligence	466	Willpower	529
Charisma	220	Luck	121

Class Skills			
Mana Imbue	5*	Blade Strike*	5
Thousand Steps	1	Altered Space	2
Two are One	1	The Body's Resolve	3
Greater Detection	1	A Thousand Blades*	4
Soul Shield	4	Blink Step	2
Portal*	5	Army of One	4
Sanctum	2	Penetration	9c
Aura of Chivalry	1	Eyes of Insight	2

Beacon of the Angels	2	Eye of the Storm	1
Vanguard of the Apocalypse	2	Society's Web	1
Shackles of Eternity*	4	System Edit	1
(Grand Cross)	(1)		
External Class Skills			
Instantaneous Inventory	1	Frenzy	1
Cleave	2	Tech Link	2
Elemental Strike	1 (Ice)	Shrunken Footsteps	1
Analyze	2	Harden	2
Quantum Lock	3	Elastic Skin	3
Disengage Safeties	2	Temporary Forced Link	1
Hyperspace Nitro Boost	1	On the Edge	1
Fates Thread	2	Peasant's Fury	1
Combat Spells			
Improved Minor Healing (IV)		Greater Regeneration (II)	
Greater Healing (II)		Mana Drip (II)	
Improved Mana Missile (IV)		Enhanced Lightning Strike (III)	
Firestorm		Polar Zone	

Freezing Blade	Improved Inferno Strike (II)
Elemental Walls (Fire, Ice, Earth, etc.)	Ice Blast
Icestorm	Improved Invisibility
Improved Mana Cage	Improved Flight
Haste	Enhanced Particle Ray
Variable Gravitic Sphere	Zone of Denial

There are quite a few changes in play. All that Leveling meant I never had a chance to make use of the free attribute points and the free Class Skill points. I still have forty-two free attributes and two Class Skill points from the Erethran Paladin Class. And another ten attribute points from my Class upgrade.

I stare at my Class and bring up the entirely unhelpful explanation. Strangely enough, the explanation—in its entirety—is in English. Not Galactic that has been translated by Ali into English, but English to begin with.

Class: Junior System Administrator (H)

A Junior System Administrator has a minor role in overseeing the smooth operation of the System. They have access to the basic code of the System and may make minor changes to ensure the continued, smooth functioning of the System and the achievement of its primary goal.

+4 in Strength and Agility per Level. +5 in Constitution per Level. +8 in Intelligence per Level. +10 in Luck and Free Attributes points per Level.

External Mental Manipulation and Information Access is Barred.

All other Resistances increased by 20% (stackable).

Damage received reduced by 25%

Access to Level 3 installations and code

+1 Class Skill per every two Levels

If I hadn't known something strange was going on, the new Title—which is hidden from all but Ali's gaze—would have told me.

Title Achieved: Class Unlock

You have a limited, secret Class. As per Galactic Order 4.1, all such System Administrative Classes and Titles are hidden. You have access to equivalent Classes and Skills as per Galactic Order 4.1.1.

Effect: Your Class shows as—Grand Paladin of Erethra. You may access the equivalent number of Class Skills (1) of the Grand Paladin Class (1—locked to Grand Cross).

I never even got a chance to choose my Skills. Never got a chance to look them over, decide if this was the right one. And unlike so many other Skills, the singular Skill offered to me by the Administrator Class is incredibly simplistic in its description.

System Edit

A core Skill for System Administrators.

Effect: Make trivial to minor amendments to System processes

Cost: Variable (HP & MP)

I stare at the information once more and reach out, touching the tendrils of the System, the way it overlays and encompasses the Mana it marks. The way it presses upon my skin, twists itself into me and the very air we breathe. It's everywhere, a part of everything. Making it all work.

And I can change it.

The memories that lie within unlock finally. They tell me what I have stumbled upon, what I forced on the Paladins, and then myself. They tell me how it was all logged.

And that there will be consequences.

Epilogue

Six Pauhiri months. As the world spins, as Empire Quests and dungeons spawn are defeated. I stick around, studying my mind, making full use of the Empress Apparent's bonuses for Data Analysis, doing my best to understand what the Corrupt Questors have learnt.

What I've stumbled upon.

As good as her word, Catrin is gone. Spirited off for training, for developing her Skills. The first time she placed a point in her Skills, we all noticed. And again, a few months later, as she Leveled up enough to get another point. She's grinding, under the protection of the Honor Guards. Protected by the promises I drew from the others with the Shackles. Though rumblings of discontent, of Brerdain and Julierudi losing standing even as Spuryan and his people grow in numbers, rise every single day.

The Paladins take to their jobs with a vengeance. Freif travels to the frontlines, bringing his brand of destruction and violence to hot spots across the Empire. He and Ayuri are out there constantly, making it clear that the Empire is not any weaker with the choice I made.

Kino's taken a different tack, going after the nobles and the corruption. The big Risen has connections with others of his kind, with the disposed. Aided by Gheisnan's packmates and Spuryan, Kino's tearing a whole new swath through the corrupt practices that have flourished in the absence of the Paladins. Amusingly enough, Kino's the lowest Level of the three since he's often stuck babysitting a multitude of Auditors, Investigators, and the like. There's only so much the Eyes of Insight can do.

As for Anayton? She's the busiest of the group. Though she concentrates a lot of her time in Restricted Zones, she also hops over to help Kino or Freif as needed. She's absorbed a large number of the surviving team members of the deceased initiates. To my surprise, Smo'kana is added to her team. He's back on track to potentially become a Paladin under Anayton's tutelage. I disagree with her choice, but that's the thing—variety is the spice of life.

In the end, they don't need me. Even when we locate Krenmock—ex-Duke of the Inifinite Keeps—the fight is over long before it starts. Without the aid of his most powerful allies—who are all Shackled to not betray the Empress—he's cornered on the floating asteroid he calls his base. The only reason it was a challenge was because we decided to play nice and go in instead of bringing a fleet to blow it to bits at a distance.

I'm left alone, and that leaves me more than enough time to grind and, very carefully, test my new Skill. I explore the System, the way it changes lairs to dungeons, the unClassed to Classed. I watch as people complete new Quests and accept new Classes, when Settlement Orbs flicker and die and when Mana overpowers technology. I eye Skills as they trigger, as the System takes over the heavy lifting.

And I understand more than ever.

But my System Quest doesn't tick up, no matter what I learn of how the System works. I'm stuck at the 89% mark. I'm missing something, and I can only believe that it's in my head somewhere. And so, I study. I suffer through the headaches and the pain, the bloody noses and the brain bleeds that are fixed by the System in my trawling through the library.

Searching. And failing.

Six months, and finally, the other shoe drops.

Because choices have consequences. And consequences have babies.

The call comes as I ready to open a Portal to another dungeon. I step off the teleportation platform, allowing others to take my place. Mikito frowns, drawing her naginata—to the chagrin of the guards. But she ignores them, watching Ali and me.

"John?"

"Katherine." I frown, staring at Earth's Ambassador to the Galactic Council. All these years and she's managed to hold the position. She's grown into it, from the brief conversations we've had. But there's a haunted look in the woman's eyes today, her hair in disarray, a smudge of something dark and black on her cheek. "What's wrong?"

"They destroyed the Embassy," she says, her voice shaking with each word. "Killed half of my staff, those who didn't have enough health. We need you to come."

"To Irvina?"

Her head bobs like a marionette's. She drops her voice, whispering the next words and sending a chill through me. "They killed Peter. They'll kill us all if you don't come."

"Who?" My fingers ache, my fists clenched so tightly they hurt. "Who's threatening you?"

She startles, looks over her shoulder at a noise only she can hear. "They're coming. I have to go."

"Who's coming?"

A pair of last words, before the connection cuts off, before my head hurts as the System shuts down the jagged call.

"The Council."

The End

Thus Ends Book 9 of the System Apocalypse.

John will be back in Broken Council (Book 10 of the System Apocalypse)

Author's Note

Stars Asunder is the end of the Galactic arc for the System Apocalypse series. This arc was always meant to showcase John's journey through the System universe, showcasing to him the effects of the System on planets not his own and also, providing him further clues to the ultimate question – *What is the System?*

The next book, Broken Council will start the final arc of the System Apocalypse series. Having drawn the ire of the Galactic Council, he'll be forced to make difficult choices, and do his very best to survive the coming storm.

As always, I'm grateful for everyone who has followed me on this long journey. I've received more support in this little story in my head than I could ever expect and hope that you've enjoyed the journey thus far.

If you enjoyed reading the book, please do leave a review and rating. Reviews are the lifeblood of authors and help others choose to continue with the series or not.

In addition, please check out my other series, Adventures on Brad (a more traditional young adult LitRPG fantasy), Hidden Wishes (an urban fantasy GameLit series), and A Thousand Li (a cultivation series inspired by Chinese xianxia novels).

To support me directly, please go to my Patreon account: https://www.patreon.com/taowong

For more great information about LitRPG series, check out the Facebook groups:

- GameLit Society

https://www.facebook.com/groups/LitRPGsociety/

- LitRPG Books

https://www.facebook.com/groups/LitRPG.books/

About the Author

Tao Wong is an avid fantasy and sci-fi reader who spends his time working and writing in the North of Canada. He's spent way too many years doing martial arts of many forms, and having broken himself too often, he now spends his time writing about fantasy worlds.

For updates on the series and other books written by Tao Wong (and special one-shot stories), please visit the author's website: http://www.mylifemytao.com

Subscribers to Tao's mailing list will receive exclusive access to short stories in the Thousand Li and System Apocalypse universes.

Or visit his Facebook Page: https://www.facebook.com/taowongauthor/

About the Publisher

Starlit Publishing is wholly owned and operated by Tao Wong. It is a science fiction and fantasy publisher focused on the LitRPG & cultivation genres. Their focus is on promoting new, upcoming authors in the genre whose writing challenges the existing stereotypes while giving a rip-roaring good read.

For more information on Starlit Publishing, visit their website: https://www.starlitpublishing.com/

You can also join Starlit Publishing's mailing list to learn of new, exciting authors and book releases.

Glossary

Erethran Honor Guard Skill Tree

John's Erethran Honor Guard Skills

Mana Imbue (Level 5)

Soulbound weapon now permanently imbued with Mana to deal more damage on each hit. +30 Base Damage (Mana). Will ignore armor and resistances. Mana regeneration reduced by 25 Mana per minute permanently.

Blade Strike (Level 5)

By projecting additional Mana and stamina into a strike, the Erethran Honor Guard's Soulbound weapon may project a strike up to 50 feet away. Cost: 50 Stamina + 50 Mana

Thousand Steps (Level 1)

Movement speed for the Honor Guard and allies are increased by 5% while skill is active. This ability is stackable with other movement-related skills. Cost: 20 Stamina + 20 Mana per minute

Altered Space (Level 2)

The Honor Guard now has access to an extra-dimensional storage location of 30 cubic meters. Items stored must be touched to be willed in and may not include living creatures or items currently affected by auras that are not the Honor Guard's. Mana regeneration reduced by 10 Mana per minute permanently.

Two are One (Level 1)

Effect: Transfer 10% of all damage from Target to Self

Cost: 5 Mana per second

The Body's Resolve (Level 3)

Effect: Increase natural health regeneration by 35%. Ongoing health status effects reduced by 33%. Honor Guard may now regenerate lost limbs. Mana regeneration reduced by 15 Mana per minute permanently.

Greater Detection (Level 1)

Effect: User may now detect System creatures up to 1 kilometer away. General information about strength level is provided on detection. Stealth skills, Class skills, and ambient Mana density will influence the effectiveness of this skill. Mana regeneration reduced by 5 Mana per minute permanently.

A Thousand Blades (Level 4)

Creates five duplicate copies of the user's designated weapon. Duplicate copies deal base damage of copied items. May be combined with Mana Imbue and Shield Transference. Mana Cost: 3 Mana per second

Soul Shield (Level 4)

Effect: Creates a manipulable shield to cover the caster's or target's body. Shield has 1,500 Hit Points.

Cost: 250 Mana

Blink Step (Level 2)

Effect: Instantaneous teleportation via line-of-sight. May include Spirit's line of sight. Maximum range—500 meters.

Cost: 100 Mana

Portal (Level 5)

Effect: Creates a 5-meter by 5-meter portal which can connect to a previously traveled location by user. May be used by others. Maximum distance range of portals is 10,000 kilometers.

Cost: 250 Mana + 100 Mana per minute (minimum cost 350 Mana)

Army of One (Level 4)

The Honor Guard's feared penultimate combat ability, Army of One builds upon previous Skills, allowing the user to unleash an awe-inspiring attack to deal with their enemies. Attack may now be guided around minor obstacles.

Effect: Army of One allows the projection of (Number of Thousand Blades conjured weapons * 3) Blade Strike attacks up to 500 meters away from user. Each attack deals 5 * Blade Strike Level damage (inclusive of Mana Imbue and Soulbound weapon bonus)

Cost: 750 Mana

Sanctum (Level 2)

An Erethran Honor Guard's ultimate trump card in safeguarding their target, Sanctum creates a flexible shield that blocks all incoming attacks, hostile teleportations and Skills. At this Level of Skill, the user must specify dimensions of the Sanctum upon use of the Skill. The Sanctum cannot be moved while the Skill is activated.

Dimensions: Maximum 15 cubic meters.

Cost: 1,000 Mana

Duration: 2 minute and 7 seconds

Paladin of Erethra Skill Tree

John's Paladin of Erethra Skills

Penetration (Level 9—Evolved)

Few can face the judgment of a Paladin in direct combat, their ability to bypass even the toughest of defenses a frightening prospect. Reduces Mana Regeneration by 45 permanently.

Effect: Ignore all armor and defensive Skills and spells by 90%. Increases damage done to shields and structural supports by 175%.

Secondary Effect: Damage that is resisted by spells, armor, Skills and Resistances is transferred to an Evolved Skill shield at a ratio of 1 to 1.

Duration: 85 minutes

Aura of Chivalry (Level 1)

A Paladin's very presence can quail weak-hearted enemies and bolster the confidence of allies, whether on the battlefield or in court. The Aura of Chivalry is a double-edged sword however, focusing attention on the Paladin—potentially to their detriment. Increases success rate of Perception checks against Paladin by 10% and reduces stealth and related skills by 10% while active. Reduces Mana Regeneration by 5 Permanently.

Effect: All enemies must make a Willpower check against intimidation against user's Charisma. Failure to pass the check will cow enemies. All allies gain a 50% boost in morale for all Willpower checks and a 10% boost in confidence and probability of succeeding in relevant actions.

Note: Aura may be activated or left-off at will.

Beacon of the Angels (Level 2)

User calls down an atmospheric strike from the heavens, dealing damage over a wide area to all enemies within the beacon. The attack takes time to form, but once activated need not be concentrated upon for completion.

Effect: 1000 Mana Damage done to all enemies, structures and vehicles within the maximum 25 meter column of attack

Mana Cost: 500 Mana

Eyes of Insight (Level 1)

Under the eyes of a Paladin, all untruth and deceptions fall away. Only when the Paladin can see with clarity may he be able to judge effectively. Reduces Mana Regeneration by 5.

Effect: All Skills, Spells and abilities of a lower grade that obfuscate, hinder or deceive the Paladin are reduced in effectiveness. Level of reduction proportionate to degree of difference in grade and Skill Level.

Eye of the Storm (Level 1)

In the middle of the battlefield, the Paladin stands, seeking justice and offering judgment on all enemies. The winds of war will seek to draw both enemies and allies to you, their cruel flurries robbing enemies of their lives and bolstering the health and Mana of allies.

Effect: Eye of the Storm is an area effect buff and taunt. Psychic winds taunt enemies, forcing a Mental Resistance check to avoid attacking user. Enemies also receive 5 points of damage per second while within the influence of the Skill, with damage decreasing from the epicenter of the Skill. Allies receive a 5% increase in Mana and Health regeneration, decrease in effectiveness from Skill center. Eye of the Storm affects an area of 50 meters around the user.

Cost: 500 Mana + 20 Mana per second

Vanguard of the Apocalypse (Level 2)

Where others flee, the Paladin strides forward. Where the brave dare not advance, the Paladin charges. While the world burns, the Paladin still fights. The Paladin with this Skill is the vanguard of any fight, leading the charge against all of Erethra's enemies.

Effect: +45 to all Physical attributes, increases speed by 55% and recovery rates by 35%. This Skill is stackable on top of other attribute and speed boosting Skills or spells.

Cost: 500 Mana + 10 Stamina per second

Society's Web (Level 1)

Where the Eye of Insight provides the Paladin an understanding of the lies and mistruths told, Society's Web shows the Paladin the intricate webs that tie individuals to one another. No alliance, no betrayal, no tangled web of lies will be hidden as each interaction weaves one another closer. While the Skill provides no detailed information, a skilled Paladin can infer much from the Web.

Effect: Upon activation, the Paladin will see all threads that tie each individual to one another and automatically understand the details of each thread when focused upon.

Cost: 400 Mana + 200 Mana per minute

Shackles of Eternity (Level 4)

A Paladin's job is not just to see, but it is to judge and enforce the judgment. The Shackles of Eternity provide a Paladin another method of enforcing his judgments. Once used, the Shackles bind an individual, forcing them to abide by the Paladin's decree. Activation of the Shackles will leave a brand, a visible Mark, and will deal punishment immediately and on an ongoing basis when the decree is violated. All law enforcement personnel, of whatever Class or society, will be able to see broken Shackles on an individual.

Effect: Shackles of Eternity are gaeas that an individual must follow. The restriction will warn an individual when they're close to breaching, and upon breach, will layer a number of effects upon them.

Effect 1: A permanent, and highly visible, nark will appear to all law enforcement individuals, whether by Title, Class, or System designation. They will be able to access data at no cost on the broken Shackles, including breakage reason and the original Shackles' use. This can lead to a loss of Reputation and other effects.

Effect 2: Shackle breakers will receive a (Skill level multiplied by half Mana costs) amount of damage upon breach of decree. This is Mana damage and may only be mitigated by Mana resistance.

Effect 3: Broken Shackles deal ongoing (Skill level multiplied by $1/10^{th}$ Mana cost) damage per minute to the Shackle breaker. This damage is Mana damage and may only be mitigated by Mana resistance.

Cost: Variable depending on Shackle requirements (channeled)

Grand Paladin Skills

Grand Cross (Level 1)

Details not revealed as yet.

Junior Administrator Skills

System Edit

A core Skill for System Administrators.

Effect: Make trivial to minor amendments to System processes

Cost: Variable (HP & MP)

Other Class Skills

Frenzy (Level 1)

Effect: When activated, pain is reduced by 80%, damage increased by 30%, stamina regeneration rate increased by 20%. Mana regeneration rate decreased by 10%

Frenzy will not deactivate until all enemies have been slain. User may not retreat while Frenzy is active.

Cleave (Level 2)

Effect: Physical attacks deal 60% more base damage. Effect may be combined with other Class Skills.

Cost: 25 Mana

Elemental Strike (Level 1—Ice)

Effect: Used to imbue a weapon with freezing damage. Adds +5 Base Damage to attacks and a 10% chance of reducing speed by 5% upon contact. Lasts for 30 seconds.

Cost: 50 Mana

Instantaneous Inventory (Maxed)

Allows user to place or remove any System-recognized item from Inventory if space allows. Includes the automatic arrangement of space in the inventory. User must be touching item.

Cost: 5 Mana per item

Shrunken Footsteps (Level 1)

Reduces System presence of user, increasing the chance of the user evading detection of System-assisted sensing Skills and equipment. Also increases cost of information purchased about user. Reduces Mana Regeneration by 5 permanently.

Tech Link (Level 2)

Effect: Tech Link allows user to increase their skill level in using a technological item, increasing input and versatility in usage of said items. Effects vary depending on item. General increase in efficiency of 10%. Mana regeneration rate decreased by 10%

Designated Technological Items: Neural Link, Hodo's Triple Forged Armor

Analyze (Level 2)

Allows user to scan individuals, monsters, and System-registered objects to gather information registered with the System. Detail and level of accuracy of information is dependent on Level and any Skills or Spells in conflict with the ability. Reduces Mana regeneration by 10 permanently.

Harden (Level 2)

This Skill reinforces targeted defenses and actively weakens incoming attacks to reduce their penetrating power. A staple Skill of the Turtle Knights of Kiumma, the Harden Skill has frustrated opponents for millennia.

Effect: Reduces penetrative effects of attacks by 30% on targeted defense.

Cost: 3 Mana per second

Quantum Lock (Level 3)

A staple Skill of the M453-X Mecani-assistants, Quantum Lock blocks stealth attacks and decreases the tactical options of their enemies. While active, the Quantum Lock of the Mecani-assistants excites quantum strings in the affected area for all individuals and Skills.

Effect: All teleportation, portal, and dimensional Skills and Spells are disrupted while Quantum Lock is in effect. Forceable use of Skills and Spells while Skill is in effect will result in (Used Skill Mana Cost * 4) health in damage. Users may pay a variable amount of additional Mana when activating the Skill to decrease effect of Quantum Lock and decrease damage taken.

Requirements: 200 Willpower, 200 Intelligence

Area of Effect: 100 meter radius around user

Cost: 250 + 50 Mana per Minute

Elastic Skin (Level 3)

Elastic Skin is a permanent alteration, allowing the user to receive and absorb a small portion of damage. Damage taken reduced by 7% with 7% of damage absorbed converted to Mana. Mana Regeneration reduced by 15 permanently.

Peasant's Fury (Level 1)

No one knows loss more than the powerless. The Downtrodden Peasant has taken the fury of the powerless and made it his own, gifting them the strength to go on so long as they manage to make others feel the same loss that they did. -5 Mana Regeneration per Second

Effect: User receives a 0.1% regeneration effect of damage dealt for each 1% of health loss.

Disengage Safeties (Level 2)

All technological weapons have safeties built in. Users of this Skill recklessly disregard the mandatory safeties, deciding that they know better than the crafters, engineers, and government personnel who built and regulate the production of these technological pieces.

Effects: Increase power output from 2.5-25% depending on the weapon and its level of sophistication. Increase durability losses from use by 25-250%.

Cost: 200 Mana + 25 Mana per minute

Temporary Forced Link (Level 1)

Most Class Skills can't be linked with another's. The instability formed between the mixing of the aura from multiple Mana sources often results in spectacular—and explosive—scenarios. For the 02m8 Symbiotes though, the need to survive within their host bodies and use their Skills has resulted in this unique Skill, allowing the Symbiote to lend their Mana and Skills. (For more persistent effects, see Mana Graft)

Effect: Skill and Skill effects are forcibly combined. Final effect results will vary depending on level of compatibility of Skills.

Cost: 250 Mana + 10 Mana per minute (plus original Skill cost)

Hyperspace Nitro Boost (Level 1)

When you've got to win the race, there's nothing like a hyperspace boost. This Skill links the user with his craft's hyperspace engine, providing a direct boost to its efficiency. Unlike normal speed increases for hyperspace engines, the Nitro Boost is a variable boost and runs a risk of damaging the engine.

Effect: 15% increase in hyperspace engine efficiency + variable % increase in efficiency at 1% per surplus Mana. Each additional 1% over base raises chance of catastrophic engine failure by 0.01%

Cost: 250 Mana + (surplus variable amount; minimum 200 Mana increments) per minute

On the Edge (Level 1)

Shuttle racers live their lives on the edge, cutting corners by feet and dodging monsters by inches. There's only one way to drive a ship with that level of precision, and no matter what those military Pilots tell you, it's with On the Edge.

Effect: +10% boost in ship handling and maneuverability. +10% passive increase in all piloting skills. +1% increase per increment of surplus Mana

Cost: 100 Mana per level + (surplus variable amount; minimum 100 Mana increments) per minute

Fate's Thread (Level 2)

The Akashi'so believe that we are all but weavings in the great thread of life. Connected to one another by the great Weaver, there is not one but multiple threads between us all, woven from our interactions and histories. Fate's Thread is but a Skill expression of this belief. This Skill cannot be dodged but may be blocked. After all, all things are bound together.

Effect: Fate Thread allows the user to bind individuals together by making what is already there apparent. Thread is made physical and may be used to pull, tie and bind.

Duration: 2 minutes

Cost: 60 Mana

Spells

Improved Minor Healing (IV)

Effect: Heals 40 Health per casting. Target must be in contact during healing. Cooldown 60 seconds.

Cost: 20 Mana

Improved Mana Missile (IV)

Effect: Creates four missiles out of pure Mana, which can be directed to damage a target. Each dart does 30 damage. Cooldown 10 seconds

Cost: 35 Mana

Enhanced Lightning Strike

Effect: Call forth the power of the gods, casting lightning. Lightning strike may affect additional targets depending on proximity, charge and other conductive materials on-hand. Does 100 points of electrical damage.

Lightning Strike may be continuously channeled to increase damage for 10 additional damage per second.

Cost: 75 Mana.

Continuous cast cost: 5 Mana / second

Lightning Strike may be enhanced by using the Elemental Affinity of Electromagnetic Force. Damage increased by 20% per level of affinity

Greater Regeneration (II)

Effect: Increases natural health regeneration of target by 6%. Only single use of spell effective on a target at a time.

Duration: 10 minutes

Cost: 100 Mana

Firestorm

Effect: Create a firestorm with a radius of 5 meters. Deals 250 points of fire damage to those caught within. Cooldown 60 seconds.

Cost: 200 Mana

Polar Zone

Effect: Create a thirty meter diameter blizzard that freezes all targets within one. Does 10 points of freezing damage per minute plus reduces effected individuals speed by 5%. Cooldown 60 seconds.

Cost: 200 Mana

Greater Healing (II)

Effect: Heals 100 Health per casting. Target does not require contact during healing. Cooldown 60 seconds per target.

Cost: 75 Mana

Mana Drip (II)

Effect: Increases natural health regeneration of target by 6%. Only single use of spell effective on a target at a time.

Duration: 10 minutes

Cost: 100 Mana

Freezing Blade

Effect: Enchants weapon with a slowing effect. A 5% slowing effect is applied on a successful strike. This effect is cumulative and lasts for 1 minute. Cooldown 3 minutes

Spell Duration: 1 minute.

Cost: 150 Mana

Improved Inferno Strike (II)
A beam of heat raised to the levels of an inferno, able to melt steel and earth on contact! The perfect spell for those looking to do a lot of damage in a short period of time.
Effect: Does 200 Points of Heat Damage
Cost: 150 Mana

Mud Walls
Unlike its more common counterpart Earthen Walls, Mud Walls focus is more on dealing slow, suffocating damage and restricting movement on the battlefield.
Effect: Does 20 Points of Suffocating Damage. -30% Movement Speed
Duration: 2 Minutes
Cost: 75 Mana

Create Water
Pulls water from the elemental plane of water. Water is pure and the highest form of water available. Conjures 1 liter of water. Cooldown: 1 minute
Cost: 50 Mana

Scry
Allows caster to view a location up to 1.7 kilometers away. Range may be extended through use of additional Mana. Caster will be stationary during this period. It is recommended caster focuses on the scry unless caster has a high level of Intelligence and Perception so as to avoid accidents. Scry may be blocked by equivalent or higher tier spells and Skills. Individuals

with high perception in region of Scry may be alerted that the Skill is in use. Cooldown: 1 hour.

Cost: 25 Mana per minute.

Scrying Ward

Blocks scrying spells and their equivalent within 5 meters of caster. Higher level spells may not be blocked, but caster may be alerted about scrying attempts. Cooldown: 10 minutes

Cost: 50 Mana per minute

Improved Invisibility

Hides target's System information, aura, scent, and visual appearance. Effectiveness of spell is dependent upon Intelligence of caster and any Skills or Spells in conflict with the target.

Cost: 100 + 50 Mana per minute

Improved Mana Cage

While physically weaker than other elemental-based capture spells, Mana Cage has the advantage of being able to restrict all creatures, including semi-solid Spirits, conjured elementals, shadow beasts, and Skill users. Cooldown: 1 minute

Cost: 200 Mana + 75 Mana per minute

Improved Flight

(Fly birdie, fly!—Ali) This spell allows the user to defy gravity, using controlled bursts of Mana to combat gravity and allow the user to fly in even the most challenging of situations. The improved version of this spell allows flight even in zero gravity situations and a higher level of maneuverability. Cooldown: 1 minute

Cost: 250 Mana + 100 Mana per minute

Equipment

Hod's Triple Fused Armor

The product of multiple workings by the Master Blacksmith and Crafter Hodiliphious 'Hod' Yalding, the Triple Fused Armor was hand-forged from rare, System-generated material, hand refined and reworked trice over with multiple patented and rare alloys and materials. The final product is considered barely passable by Hod—though it would make a lesser craftsman cry.

Core: Class I Hallow Physics Mana Engine

CPU: Class B Wote Core CPU

Armor Rating: Tier I (Enhanced)

Hard Points: 9 (6 Used—Jungian Flight System, Talpidae Abyssal Horns, Luione Hard Light Projectors, Diarus Poison Stingers, Ares Type I Shield Generator, Greater Troll Cell Injectors)

Soft Points 4 (3 Used—Neural Link, Ynir HUD Imaging, Airmed Body Monitor)

Battery Capacity: 380/380

Active Skills: Abyssal Chains, Mirror Shade, Poison Grip

Attribute Bonuses: +93 Strength, +78 Agility, +51 Constitution, +44 Perception, +287 Stamina and Health Regeneration per minute

Note: Hod's Triple Fused Armor is currently under limited warranty. Armor may be teleported to Hod's workshop for repairs once a week. All cost of repairs will be deducted from user's account.

Skills in Hod's Armor:

Abyssal Chains

Calling upon the material connection to the shadow plane, chains from the abyss erupt, binding a target in place.

Effect: Target is bound by shadow chains. Chains deal 10 points of damage per second. To break free, target must win a contested Strength test. Abyssal Chains have a Strength of 120.

Uses: 2/3

Recharge rate: 1 per hour

Mirror Shade

Mirror Shade creates a semi-solid doppelganger using hard light technology and Mana.

Effect: Mirror Shade create a semi-solid doppelganger of the user for a period of ten minutes. Maximum range of doppelganger from user is fifty meters. Doppelganger has 18% physical fidelity.

Use: 0/1

Recharge Rate: 1 per 4 hours

Silversmith Jeupa VII Anti-Personnel Cannon (Modified & Upgraded)

This quad-barrelled anti-personnel weapon has been handcrafted by Advanced Weaponsmiths to provide the highest integration possible for an energy weapon. This particular weapon has been modified to include additional range-finding and sighting options and upgraded to increase short-term damage output at the cost of long-term durability. Barrels may be fired individually or linked.

Base Damage: 787 per barrel

Battery Capacity: 4 per barrel (16 total)

Recharge Rate: 0.25 per hour per GMU

Ares Platinum Class Tier II Armored Jumpsuit

Ares's signature Platinum Class line of armored daily wear combines the company's latest technological advancement in nanotech fiber design and the pinnacle work of an Advanced Craftsman's Skill to provide unrivalled protection for the discerning Adventurer.

Effect: +218 Defense, +14% Resistance to Kinetic and Energy Attacks. +19% Resistance against Temperature changes. Self-Cleanse, Self-Mend, Autofit Enchantments also included.

Silversmith Mark VIII Beam Pistol (Upgradeable)

Base Damage: 88

Battery Capacity: 13/13

Recharge Rate: 3 per hour per GMU

Tier IV Neural Link

Neural link may support up to 5 connections.

Current connections: Hod's Triple Fused Armor

Software Installed: Rich'lki Firewall Class IV, Omnitron III Class IV Controller

Ferlix Type I Twinned-Beam Rifle (Modified)

Base Damage: 39

Battery Capacity: 41/41

Recharge rate: 1 per hour per GMU

Tier II Sword (Soulbound Personal Weapon of an Erethran Honor Guard)

Base Damage: 397

Durability: N/A (Personal Weapon)

Special Abilities: +20 Mana Damage, Blade Strike

Kryl Ring of Regeneration

Often used as betrothal bands, Kyrl rings are highly sought after and must be ordered months in advance.

Health Regeneration: +30

Stamina Regeneration: +15

Mana Regeneration: +5

Tier III Bracer of Mana Storage

A custom work by an unknown maker, this bracer acts a storage battery for personal Mana. Useful for Mages and other Classes that rely on Mana. Mana storage ratio is 50 to 1.

Mana Capacity: 350/350

Fey-steel Dagger

Fey-steel is not actual steel but an unknown alloy. Normally reserved only for the Sidhe nobility, a small—by Galactic standards—amount of Fey-steel is released for sale each year. Fey-steel takes enchantments extremely well.

Base Damage: 28

Durability: 110/100

Special Abilities: None

Enchanted, Reinforced Toothy Throwing Knives (5)

First handcrafted from the rare drop of a Level 140 Awakened Beast by the Redeemer of the Dead, John Lee, these knives have been further processed by the Master Craftsmen I-24-988L and reinforced with orichalcum and fey-steel. The final blades have been further enchanted with Mana and piercing damage as well as a return enchantment.

Base Damage: 238

Enchantments: Return, Mana Blade (+28 Damage), Pierce (-7% defense)

Brumwell Necklace of Shadow Intent

The Brumwell necklace of shadow intent is the hallmark item of the Brumwell Clan. Enchanted by a Master Crafter, this necklace layers shadowy intents over your actions, ensuring that information about your actions are more difficult to ascertain. Ownership of such an item is both a necessity and a mark of prestige among settlement owners and other individuals of power.

Effect: Persistent effect of Shadow Intent (Level 4) results in significantly increased cost of purchasing information from the System about wearer. Effect is persistent for all actions taken while necklace is worn.

Ring of Greater Shielding

Creates a greater shield that will absorb approximately 1000 points of damage. This shield will ignore all damage that does not exceed its threshold amount of 50 points of damage while still functioning.

Max Duration: 7 Minutes

Charges: 1

Simalax Hover Boots (Tier II)

A combination of hand-crafted materials and mass produced components, the Simalax Hover Boots are the journeyman work of Magi-Technician Lok of Irvina. Enchantments and technology mesh together in the Simalax Hover Boots, offering its wearer the ability to tread on air briefly and defy gravity and sense.

Effects: User reduces gravitational effects by 0.218 SIG. User may, on activation, hover and skate during normal and mildly turbulent atmospheric conditions. User may also use the Simalax Hover Boots to triple jump in the air, engaging the anti-gravity and hover aspects at the same time.

Duration: 1.98 SI Hours.

F'Merc Nanoswarm Mana Grenades (Tier II)

The F'Merc Nanoswarm Grenades are guaranteed to disrupt the collection of Mana in a battlefield, reducing Mana Regeneration rates for those caught in the swarm. Recommended by the I'um military, the Torra Special Forces and the No.1 Most Popular Mana Grenade as voted by the public on Boom, Boom, Boom! Magazine.

Effect: Reduces Mana Regeneration rates and spell formation in affected area by 37% ((higher effects in enclosed areas)

Radius: 10m x 10m

Daghtree's Legendary Ring of Deception (Tier I)

A musician, poet and artist, Daghtree's fame rose not from his sub-standard works of 'art' but his array of seduction Skills from his Heartthrob Artist Class. Due to his increasing infamy, Daghtree commissioned this Legendary ring to change his appearance and continue Leveling. In the end, it is rumored that his indiscretions caught up with the infamous artist and he disappeared from Galactic sources in GCD 9,275

Effect: Creates a powerful disguise that covers the wearer. The ring comes with six pre-loaded disguises and additional disguises may be added through expansion of charges

Duration: 1 day per charge

Charges: 3

Recharge via ambient Mana: 1 charge per Galactic Standard Unit per week

F'Merc Ghostlight Mana Dispersal Grenades (Tier I)

The F'Merc Ghostlight Mana Dispersal Grenades not only disperse Mana in the battlefield, the Ghostlight Dispersal Grenades degrade all Mana Skills and spells within its field of effectiveness. Used by Krolash the Destroyer, the Erethran Champion Isma (prior version) and Anblanca Special Forces. Five times Winner of the Most Annoying Utility Item on the Battlefield.

Effect: Reduces Mana Regeneration rates, Skill and spell formation use in affected area by 67% ((higher effects in enclosed areas)

Radius: $15m^3$

Evernight Darkness Orbs

When the world goes light, the Evernight Darkness Orbs will bring back blessed darkness. If you need darkness, you need Evernight!

Effect: Removes al visible light and mute infrared and ultraviolet wavelengths by 30%

Radius: 50m³

Seven Heavenly Spire Wards

Quick to set-up, the Seven Heavenly Spire Wards were crafted by the Thrice Loved Bachelor's Temple of the Sinking Domain as their main export. Using the total prayer and faith of the temple, they produce a set of wards every month.

Effect: Set's up a 30' by 30' defensive ward; protects against both magical and technological attacks and entry

Fumikara Mobile Teleport Circles

These one-off use mobile teleport circles allow connection to existing and open teleport networks.

Effect: Connect to open teleport networks within a 5,000 kim radius of the teleport circles. Allows teleportation of individuals to the networked teleport centers

PoenJoe Goleminised-Mana Generator Mark 18

The latest Mana Generator by the infamous PoenJoe, the Mark 18 is guaranteed* to not blow up on you in optimal conditions. This partially sentient Mana Generator can extract up to 98% of a Mana Crystal's saved energy in 0.003 seconds. Currently loaded in an Adult Kirin Mana Core.

Effect: It's a Power Generator. Guaranteed to provide up to 98 x 10*99 Standard Galactic Mana Units

*Not actually guaranteed. In fact, we're 100% certain that containment failure will occur.

Payload (Level 2) (Embeded in Anklet of Dispersed Damage)

Sometimes, you need to get your Skills inside a location. Payload allows you to imbue an individual or item with a Skill at a reduced strength.

Effect: 71% effectiveness of Skill imbued.

Secondary Effect: Skill may be now triggered on a timed basis (max 2:07 minutes)

Uses: 22

Recharge: 10.7 charges per day in SGE

Made in the USA
Monee, IL
31 March 2022

93906996R00277